BECKETT'S DESIRE (SPECIAL FORCES: OPERATION ALPHA)

TACTICAL OPERATIONS
BOOK THREE

ANNA BLAKELY

PUBLISHER: ACES PRESS

COVER BY: LORI JACKSON

Editing by: Tracy Roelle
Proofreading by: Beverly Findlay, Shirley Kilgore, Suzie Waggoner

Dear Readers,

Welcome to the Special Forces: Operation Alpha Fan-Fiction world!

If you are new to this amazing world, in a nutshell the author wrote a story using one or more of my characters in it. Sometimes that character has a major role in the story, and other times they are only mentioned briefly. This is perfectly legal and allowable because they are going through Aces Press to publish the story.

This book is entirely the work of the author who wrote it. While I might have assisted with brainstorming and other ideas about which of my characters to use, I didn't have any part in the process or writing or editing the story.

I'm proud and excited that so many authors loved my characters enough that they wanted to write them into their own story. Thank you for supporting them, and me!

READ ON!
    Xoxo
    Susan Stoker

For my family. Thank you for always supporting me, even when I drive you nuts with long nights and rushed deadlines. I love you all with everything that I am.

PROLOGUE

Four days ago...

"I WANT MY MOTHER."

Evie Mitchell turned to the terrified little girl sitting to her right. Nine-year-old Armineh Shah was sitting with her butt in the dirt with her back leaning against the rough rock wall behind them. Tears welled in the young girl's terrified eyes as they searched Evie's in a desperate, silent plea for help.

"You'll be with both your parents again very soon," Evie reassured her young student.

"P-promise?"

A forced smile lifted the corners of her dry, chapped lips as she held Armineh's fearful gaze. "I promise," she whispered softly.

God forgive me if I'm lying.

In her heart, Evie believed her words to be true. Their kidnappers had to release them soon. They *had* to.

The alternative was too horrifying to accept.

"It is an impossible thing, what you say." The muttered comment came from the girl at Evie's left. "You do not know if we will be freed. None of us do."

Of the four Afghan students Evie had been assigned to teach,

1

Benesh Sayyid was the youngest. A few months from turning nine, the tiny bit of a thing was wise beyond her years and sharp as a tack.

"You're wrong, Benesh," she countered. "It's *not* impossible. You heard what the men who took us said. As soon as the ransom demands are met, we will be released and reunited with our families."

It was clear by the look on the girl's saddened face that she wasn't convinced.

"We have already been here four days." Benesh's accent was thick, like the others', but her English was spoken with clarity. "They have stopped bringing us food...we are barely allowed any water...and the bathroom smells disgusting."

Despite the truth in Benesh's words, Evie felt her lips lift into a more genuine smile. With a friendly, gentle nudge, she told the frustrated girl, "You're right. The bathroom *does* smell disgusting."

Even calling it a "bathroom" was such a massive stretch. The space they took them to do their business was little more than a hole carved into one of the walls inside the mountainous cave serving as their prison.

Inside were two small but deep holes she and the girls were forced to use as latrines.

"That is because boys use it," Sadia Rahman used a matter-of-fact tone. "Girl bathrooms are clean and smell like flowers and perfume."

"Sadia is right." Malalai Alam, the fourth and final girl in Evie's care, kicked the dry dirt with her heel with a pout. "If my brother were with us, he would say this one smells like shi—"

"Malalai!" Evie scolded as she leaned forward to meet her student's dark gaze.

She didn't let her students see the hidden smile tugging at her dry, cracked lips.

"My apologies, Miss Evie." The young girl lowered her head in shame. "My father would surely give me a lashing if I said such a word in his presence." A single tear drew a shimmering

2

line through the dirt on Benesh's adorable cheek. "Even so, I wish he were here."

"I know you do, honey," Evie took the frightened child's hand in hers and gave it a squeeze. "We're all scared and frustrated by the situation, but we can't give up hope. The second we do that, those men out there win. And we don't want the bad guys to win…do we?"

They can't win. They just can't!

"No, Miss Evie." Malalai tightened her hold, giving a jerky shake of her head.

At nearly the exact same time, Armineh, Sadia, and Benesh each offered a united, "No."

Though their situation was still as dire as ever, her students' strength in the present sent a renewed sense of hope flourishing up from somewhere deep inside. Evie understood the terror they must be feeling because she was absolutely scared out of her wits.

Father warned you something like this could happen. He warned you, and you didn't listen.

The truth was she hadn't been concerned about her personal safety, or that of her students, because of their tender age.

Current Taliban laws stated girls over the age of twelve weren't allowed to attend school or receive any sort of formal education. Because the girls she'd been charged with teaching were below the cutoff, Evie hadn't considered themselves targets.

She also hadn't considered the possibility that a group of militant extremists who believed *all* females—despite their ages —should be denied the right to learn would kidnap them and hold them against their will.

He tried to tell you.

Of its own accord, her scattered mind began replaying the last conversation Evie had shared with her father. The day had been sunny and bright. So perfect, in fact, she couldn't recall even a single cloud hovering above her in the brilliant blue sky.

Of course, the multi-million-dollar view from her family's estate in the Hamptons had always taken her breath away.

Between the vast, open skies, white, sandy beach, and sparkling blue water for as far as the eye could see, there wasn't a single thing she didn't love.

But then, as she always eventually did, Evie had forced herself to turn away from the water to face the monstrosity that was a so-called home. Even now, with her butt numb from having sat in the same position for far too long, she could almost feel the heavy, gut-tightening sense of dread that always came with stepping foot inside her family's estate.

It hadn't come as a surprise when her father had expressed his disapproval of her plan to travel to Afghanistan. In fact, he'd flat-out forbidden it.

I've looked the other way for the last time. You do this, consider yourself out.

It was the last thing the man had said to her that day before turning and leaving the room.

"Do you think your father will pay for your safe return?"

Evie spun her gaze toward Sadia. The wary expression directly contradicted the child's usual happy-go-lucky attitude. But even someone as blissful and positive as Sadia had their limits, and from the skeptical expression on the little girl's dirt-smudged face, Evie knew her optimistic young student was on the brink of reaching hers.

"Of course, he will." Evie sounded far more convinced than she actually felt.

There was more than enough money in the bank. Of that, she was certain. Paying the combined ransom amounts—hers plus the four girls'—would be the equivalent of Evie spending the loose change buried deep within her couch cushions.

So, no. Her father wouldn't let her rot in this place with monsters who called themselves men. She'd make the call; he'd pay the money. And soon, she and the girls would be on their way back home.

You willing to bet your life on that? Because that's pretty much what you're doing.

No, it was *exactly* what she was doing. Evie was betting not only her life but also the four precious, innocent souls she'd been charged with keeping safe.

She was betting it *all* on the hope that her father would find some sliver of compassion in his money-hungry heart and arrange for their immediate release. Unfortunately, all they could do now was wait.

And wait is what they did.

For the next several hours, she and the girls passed the time by telling stories. They of their favorite memories to date, and Evie of the times she'd been most mischievous as a child.

In the back of her mind, she wondered if perhaps she shouldn't be telling her students about the few harmless stunts she'd pulled as a teenager. But it was never anything truly bad.

Mostly, Evie told them about the times she'd snuck out of the house in the middle of the night to sit by the pool and read beneath the stars. Or when she'd spy on the help or her father and his colleagues, eavesdropping on their hushed—and hopelessly boring—conversations.

Her imaginative side had always hoped for some massive revelation. Like discovering that their cook was actually in the CIA or that the gardener was some international assassin who worked for the good guys.

The silly stories made the girls smile and—on the rarest of occasions—even laugh. So, to Evie, that alone was worth any potentially bad influence she may or may not have bestowed.

"I do not think I have ever been this hungry," Armineh complained.

She couldn't blame the poor girl. They were all so very, *very* hungry.

Evie opened her mouth with the intent of appeasing her student again when the rugged, wood-slat door pushed open, and one of the kidnappers stormed inside.

"You!" He marched straight over to where she sat. "Come with me."

Before she could even think of protesting, the man reached down, grabbed hold of her upper arm, and yanked her roughly to her feet.

ANNA BLAKELY

"Hey! That hurts!" Evie instinctively tried pulling herself free. "Where are you taking me?"

Hauling her unceremoniously toward the room's exit, the man growled back, "Move! No talk!"

"Miss Evie!" One of the girls cried out in her defense.

Another one begged the man, "Please don't hurt her!"

She could hear the girls' whimpers and sniffles as she stumbled, nearly falling to the dirt floor below when the jerk shoved her roughly through the open doorway. For the sake of her students, Evie did her best to put on a brave front.

"I'll go where you want," she informed her escort. "You don't have to push."

"I said, no talk!" He yanked her down one of the cave's crude tunnels.

What looked to be dug by hand, the labyrinth of hallways and rooms must have taken ages to complete. And given that she and the girls had each had their heads covered with black hoods for the ride here, Evie guessed very few people were privy to the hideout's location.

A fact that didn't exactly bode well with her hope of being found.

The smell of the makeshift bathroom filled her nostrils well before they passed it. Evie wanted to ask more questions. To demand this man tell her where he was taking her. But she bit back her inquiry, fearing she'd only anger him further.

They continued following the shadowed path. Positioned in wide, even intervals at the base of the walls, Evie noted several small, battery-operated lamps dimly lighting their way. A rough, painful pull of her upper arm swiftly brought her wandering thoughts back into focus.

Several more rooms were passed as she was forcefully guided down a second corridor on their left. Some, presumably used as sleeping quarters, held blankets, pillows, lamps, and books.

Evie was led past another carved-out room. A modest wooden desk and chair faced her from its place near the back wall. As they passed, she caught sight of a handful of manila folders stacked neatly on the desk's rugged surface.

The man slowed his steps as they approached the next room on the right.

This one had a crude, wooden-slat door blocking their path. Her jerk of a guard kept his tight hold on her upper arm as he used his free hand to slide the door out of their way. With the path now clear, the man shoved her unceremoniously inside.

The first thing Evie noticed was the slivers of moonlight cutting through the dusty, dank air. A small, glassless window positioned high in the center of the room's exterior wall allowed for the natural night light, and after having spent days in what amounted to a dark prison cell wondering if she'd ever be set free, it was a welcomed sight to behold.

Soak it in, Evie. This just might be the last time you ever see it.

"Inside."

Other than herself and the jerk who accompanied her, the space was empty. Unable to keep quiet a second longer, Evie turned to face the coldhearted man glaring back at her.

"Why am I here?"

He took a menacing step toward her as spit flew from between his yellow, crooked teeth. "Because you are a liar," he spat angrily.

Her stomach dropped, and her mind raced, despite already knowing she'd done no such thing. "I-I don't know what you're talking about. I haven't lied about anything! Y-you know my name, where I'm from...I gave you my father's information and told you how to contact him for the ranso—"

The man's meaty fist slammed into the side of her face. The unexpected blow sent Evie's entire body flying backward. Pain exploded, and tears immediately filled her eyes as she landed on the dirt floor with a loud thud.

A metallic taste crossed over her tastebuds, and it took her a moment to realize the warm, wet liquid dripping from her nose and one corner of her mouth was blood. Bringing a trembling hand to her throbbing face, Evie used her palm to carefully wipe it away.

"The number you gave to us was a fake." The asshole squatted down beside her.

"W-what num…*ah!*"

A flash of pain ignited along her scalp as the man filled his fist with her hair. Giving the thick strands a hard pull, the bastard yanked her head back, forcing her to look him in the eyes.

"The phone number," he growled. The hold he had on her left no escape from his hot, rancid breath. "We called. The man who answered said he had no children."

What?

Evie's stomach churned with dread. No. That couldn't be right. Sure, her father had made it clear she'd disappointed him with her life choices, but he'd never go so far as to denounce her to the point of allowing her to be *killed.*

Would he?

"There's been a terrible…m-mistake." She cried out again when the pressure at the back of her head increased. "I swear! I don't know what happened. Maybe…m-maybe the person dialed the wrong…number."

"*I* am the one who made the call." His grip tightened. "I dialed the numbers I was given."

A small whimper escaped the base of Evie's throat, but she refrained from moving even an inch for fear the jerk would actually pull her hair from its roots. The man shoved a scrap of paper in her face. "You wrote this yourself, no?"

Through her tears, she studied the inked digits scribbled across the paper's white surface. The handwriting was a bit off, but that wasn't surprising given how utterly terrified she'd felt while being forced to write it.

"Th-that's the right number," she confirmed softly. "I…I didn't lie. My father…he has *more* than enough money to cover the ransom. For me and the girls."

She'd added that last part because there was no way she'd ever consider leaving her young students behind with these monsters.

"The man who answered said—"

"Maybe he thought it was a scam," Evie blurted. It was the only thing that made sense. "I get calls like that all the time, you know? Every day, in fact. People claiming to be one thing, when really they're just trying to scam me out of my money. Please," she begged, her lip starting to swell. "Please, just try the number again."

"It is a waste of my time."

"No!" She started to shake her head, but the fire in her scalp forced her to stop. "Please. Just...let me talk to him. If he hears my voice, he'll know this is for real, and you'll get your money."

Considering this, her captor released her hair with a rough shove before grabbing Evie's upper arm and forcing her back to her feet as he stood. Without a word, he reached behind his back, and for a brief but terrifying moment, she was sure he was about to shoot her.

Instead, the coldhearted terrorist revealed a satellite phone he'd apparently had clipped to his belt. The jerk shoved it toward her.

"Call your father," he ordered brusquely. "The cost of your freedom is ten million U.S. dollars. Two million for each."

For a man like her father, that amount was a drop in the bucket.

"Ten million." Evie took the phone with a jerky nod. "Got it."

Ignoring the trembling in her hands, she studied the keypad. "Do I just dial like normal, or..."

The man nodded but said nothing.

Okay, then.

She swallowed against the dryness in her throat as she began to dial. Very few people were privy to her father's personal cell number. Evie, her father's business partner, and the family attorney.

Given her father's social status and the numerous business-related calls he received throughout the day, she couldn't blame the man for needing control over at least one aspect of his personal life.

Evie prayed with all she had that her father would answer the call. Then, she started to put the device to her ear.

"Window." The man gestured to the opening in the room's outer wall before pulling her in that direction. "No signal. Must talk near window." Positioned next to the open hole in the wall, he gave her another order.

"Speaker."

The simple demand was understood, and after pressing the button to do as he'd asked, she held the phone between them so he could hear. Evie's nerve endings fired on all cylinders as she waited for the ringing to begin. When it did, she held her breath and prayed.

Please let him pick up.

Several rings passed before the call was answered. The voice on the other line was the very one she'd been so desperate to hear.

"I don't know who this is or how you got this number, but—"

"Dad, it's me," she cut him off, reverting back to what she'd called him as a young child. "I-It's Evie." When she was met with nothing but silence, she feared the phone's signal was still too weak. Tilting the thick antenna to face the night sky, she added, "I-I've been k-kidnapped."

The stark silence that followed did little to ease her nerves. Knowing this was most likely her only shot at survival, Evie continued speaking.

"These men are holding me and my students hostage," she explained. "Four innocent, precious little girls who desperately want to get home to their families. These men...they're demanding you pay two million dollars for each of us. They said they'll release us as soon as they have the money."

The man presented her with another scrap of paper. This one with more digits.

"Bank account," he explained what he wanted in broken English. "Transfer."

"He just gave me the account information," Evie told her father. "Do you have something to write on, or—"

"There's no need," her father finally spoke up again.

When he didn't add anything further, Evie asked, "Are you sure? There are a lot of numbers, so it might be hard to remember them all."

She certainly couldn't memorize a set of numbers that long. Not without some practice, anyway.

"I'm afraid you misunderstand." Her father's tone sounded almost rigid. "There is no need for me to write anything down because there will be no transfer of funds to that or any other account."

Her stomach dropped, and her eyes flew to her captor's hardened gaze.

"This is for real, okay?" She tried desperately to get through to him. "These guys…they aren't playing around. Please, you have to transfer the money," she begged. "It's the only way they'll let me and the girls go free."

It's the only way they'll let us live.

"As I told the man who called before, I have no daughter. Please don't call this number again."

The line went dead, and Evie was left standing there, wondering what the hell had just happened.

A rush of tears formed as real panic began to set in. Her father—the one man on the planet who should have been willing to lay down his own life for hers—had just severed the only life-line she had left.

Oh, God!

She bent over at the waist, her hands slapping against her knees for support as Evie fought the urge to vomit. She couldn't breathe. Why couldn't she freaking *breathe?*

Because your very own father is willingly going to let these monsters kill you.

The voice filling her head was right. There was no way out of this. Not for her or the girls.

Evie had told her father about the men who'd taken her captive. That she and the girls would *die* if he didn't pay their ransom. And rather than having done everything in his power to ensure their safe return, what had he done?

He hung up on me.

A fresh onslaught of tears filled Evie's frantic gaze, but she ignored them as they poured down over her dirty cheeks. Disbelief unlike any she'd ever known threatened to crush her very soul. What the hell was going on? Did he *want* her to die at the hands of these terrorist extremists?

You do this, consider yourself out.

Her father's ominous words from their last day together returned with a vengeance. At the time, she'd been saddened and deeply hurt that he'd even speak of disowning her the way he had.

Evie had convinced herself he hadn't meant them. Now, however...after hearing the callous man act as if she didn't even *exist* in his world...

It was almost enough to break her.

And from the look on her captor's face as she handed him back the phone, Evie knew her father—her very own flesh and blood—had just sentenced her to die.

CHAPTER ONE

"Sorry, guys. Looks like this is gonna be a solo act, after all."

Beckett "Bones" Stone adjusted the tiny mic in his ear. "Uh… Shadow? Can you please repeat that? My comms must've glitched because it *sounded* like you just said we're on our own with this one. Which is—"

"Exactly what I said, Bones," the brilliant woman's jovial voice filled his ear once more. "Owens just got word that the Delta Force team that was supposed to assist got diverted to a potential situation somewhere near the Iraqi border earlier this morning."

Rafe Owens was former British Intelligence and the brain-child behind Tactical Operations. Known as Tac-Ops for short, the private hostage rescue team consisted of Beckett—or *Bones* as his teammates called him—and three other hostage rescue specialists.

Like Beckett, his teammates were all former special forces who'd decided to use their military experience and training to continue fighting the good fight for private citizens who found themselves in dangerous situations.

Sometimes the people Beckett and his team rescued were clients of Travel Assurance Corporation—the privately owned travel protection insurance agency also owned by Owens—and sometimes Tac-Ops was sent around the globe by none other than Uncle Sam himself.

Every job the team had been tasked with, so far, had been nothing short of mission success. But Beckett and the others knew it didn't take much to fuck up an op, and there wasn't a single man on the team looking to fail.

"And we're just now hearing about this change of plans because..." The trailing question came from Digger, their team leader.

As a former Navy SEAL, Digger—whose real name was Slade Garrison—should be used to rolling with the punches by now. But Beckett had worked with the stoic man long enough to know the guy hated surprises. Especially when those unexpected moments threatened the success of their mission.

And even more so when innocent lives—especially *children's* lives—were involved.

"Hey, now, don't shoot the messenger." Shadow went with her go-to response. "Besides, this is the U.S. government we're talking about. Nothing ever goes as quickly as it should, and it rarely happens as planned. But you don't need me to tell you that, do you, Dig?"

Pushing aside his own frustration at the unexpected turn of events, Beckett felt his lips twitching with the urge to smile. Shadow wasn't just the team's sassy tech goddess, she also served as their overwatch.

Despite never having met the woman, every man on the team trusted her. Not only with their lives, but also those they'd been charged with saving.

Hell, they didn't even know Shadow's real name. Yet, the amazingly mysterious woman was as vital to their success as anyone else on the team.

Beckett included.

He looked to his right, where Digger was currently lying belly-flat in the dry and rocky dirt. Like Beckett and the rest of their elite hostage rescue team, the man was dressed in head-to-toe desert camo. The man's M110A1 automatic sniper rifle was resting steady against the weapon's bipod, and though Digger was actively involved in the conversation, his sights were locked on what he was seeing through the Geissele optic mount.

"The good news is, twelve members of the Taliban faction you're currently observing left the area about twenty minutes before your team arrived," Shadow spoke up again. "Not sure where they went or what's on their terrorist agenda for the day, but as long as they stay away, you should be golden."

"Copy that," Digger grumbled. "I've counted seven tangos moving in and around the target, but there's an unknown number inside, which means—"

"You could be gravely outnumbered," Shadow finished the sobering thought. "Trust me, I know. I've been watching things closely from here for the past several hours, and our current satellite footage supports the intel of no more than ten tangos currently on site."

"If only that satellite of yours could see through mountain walls," Falcon mused.

Positioned at an elevated spot several yards behind where Beckett and the rest of the team waited, the former Army Ranger was the best shot Beckett had ever seen.

"Look, guys," Shadow spoke up again. "I get that this isn't ideal, but it's our current reality. And the bottom line is, our marks are running out of time, and that means—"

"We need to quit our bitchin' and start making an alternate plan," Beckett wrapped up the woman's thought for her.

Because Shadow was right. It didn't matter that their backup team got pulled onto another op or that there was an unknown number of tangos inside the cave. The fact was, an American schoolteacher and four young Afghan girls had been taken hostage days ago, and it was up to him and his team to rescue them from hell.

We're here, darlin'. Just a little while longer and your world will be right as rain.

Okay, so perhaps that was a bit optimistic. Especially since they had no way of knowing what the woman or those poor little girls had been through. Beatings, rape, and humiliation were just a few of the horrific possibilities someone in their situation could possibly face.

Beckett just prayed this group of extremists were like most they'd dealt with in the recent past, and they'd merely kept their hostages locked up somewhere, bypassing the unnecessary abuse.

His gut tightened as a familiar image filled his mind. Big smile. Adorable dimples. Long, brown curls his fingers itched to touch.

Evelynn Mitchell.

That was the name of the thirty-one-year-old teacher currently being held against her will by a group of militants. Assholes who hid behind their so-called ideology that believed females shouldn't be afforded the same education as men.

If you asked him, it was a total bullshit excuse for them to act like misogynistic pigs, and Beckett and the others were looking forward to teaching those assholes their own kind of lesson very, *very* soon.

"Okay, so new plan." Digger's deep voice rumbled through the comms. "We wait until dark. Once the sun goes down, we'll make our approach. Falcon, you'll remain in position while Bones, Apollo, and I move in."

"Don't forget the drone," Shadow reminded them. "It won't do much after you breach the cave, but she can offer another set of eyes in the meantime."

Beckett had almost forgotten about the drone. Designed specifically for the team, Shadow had created the tiny flying machine to do exactly as the woman had just described. It didn't shoot bullets or launch explosives, but it could give them a bird's eye view of the enemy to ensure no tango went unnoticed.

"Once Falcon activates it, I'll take over the controls. That way, I can alert him of any threats he may not otherwise be able to see."

"Sounds like a plan to me," Falcon commented.

"Too bad it doesn't have X-ray vision," Apollo chimed in. "Don't know about the rest of you, but I'm not really looking forward to busting into a cave without knowing for sure what we're up against."

Like Slade, Apollo—A.K.A. Ethan McAllister—was a former SEAL. The guy's specialty was hand-to-hand combat, hence the nickname. At six-four and weighing in at roughly two-twenty-five, the man was a muscular beast. It didn't hurt that his reach was nearly eighty inches, giving him an even greater advantage over the average asshole.

"I know this isn't ideal," Shadow repeated the sentiment. "But all intel we've received so far on this thing has all been solid, so there's no reason to think the max head count of ten is inaccurate. Besides, you guys have worked with much less in the past, and you're all still here to talk about it, aren't you?"

Beckett grinned, knowing the brilliant woman's lighthearted comment was meant to calm the waters, so to speak.

"Let's just hope luck remains on our side," Apollo grumbled low.

"Luck has nothin' to do with it, my friend," Falcon told their disgruntled teammate. "Like Digger said. We'll wait until it's dark, sweep the place clean, and get you back home to that new wife of yours before she can even have time to miss you."

And there was the real reason behind Apollo's concern. During a recent op, the other man had been unexpectedly reunited with his high school crush. The two reconnected while Nicki was under the team's protection, and after the sweet artist was kidnapped and nearly killed, Apollo wasted no time in claiming her as his own.

The happy couple had been married a few weeks now, and though Beckett had never had the kind of soul-deep love his teammate was lucky enough to find, he understood his friend's desire to make it back to his bride in one piece.

Same went for Falcon whose sweet wife, Avery, was back home, no doubt waiting for the sharpshooter's safe return. The two met on a cruise ship, of all places, and according to his teammate, they had an instant and undeniable connection.

Ironically enough, both Avery and Falcon were taken hostage while on an excursion in the Dominican Republic. Thanks to their quick thinking and brave actions, the couple—along with the other hostages—had been rescued, and the militant group responsible had been effectively taken down.

Both men were lucky enough to find the kind of love that would stand the test of time, and Beckett couldn't help but wonder when, or even *if*, it would happen for him, too.

Of its own accord, the image of Evelynn Mitchell's smiling face flashed before him once again. Before he could remind himself how incredibly inappropriate it was to even be thinking about such things on an op—especially since he'd never met the woman—Apollo's voice rang through the comms once again.

"You'd better be right, Bones," the other man offered. "Something happens to me, Nicki will have all your asses."

"Same goes for Aves," Falcon added to Apollo's warning. "Trust me, I've seen that woman in action. She's a helluva lot tougher than she looks."

Beckett scoffed. "Tell us something we don't know. Hell, I'd rather take my chances with the pricks we're after now than be on Avery's or Nicki's bad side."

"I second that." Shadow's slightly raspy voice returned to the conversation, despite having never met them or the Tac-Ops wives.

Redirecting the conversation to their current situation, Digger took control once more. "Hey, I have an idea." The decidedly single man's tone oozed of sarcasm. "How 'bout we focus on why we're here and leave the lovesick bullshit back home, where it belongs."

Silence filled the comms for a handful of seconds before Apollo popped back with a drawled, "Says the man who's more afraid of a committed, long-term relationship than a room filled with C4."

"I'm not scared of jack shit, asshole. Now can we please keep our heads in the game?"

"A bit defensive, are we?" Beckett chimed back in. "Besides, our game has been delayed until sundown, remember? We've got nothin' but time to waste."

"This is an op, jackass. Not some chick-flick gab session. If it doesn't pertain to the mission, it doesn't need to be discussed."

"Damn, Dig," Falcon addressed their team leader directly. "Someone piss in your cornflakes this morning or something?"

"Cornflakes, Digger?" Shadow joined in the fun. "For some reason, I always pictured you as a Honey Nut Cheerios kind of guy."

Several snickers filled the small mic in Beckett's ear as his shoulders shook with a chuckle. But after a quick glance in Digger's direction, it became very clear the irritated man hadn't found the humor in Shadow's joke.

"Not gonna bite, huh?" Shadow asked rhetorically. "Okay, fine. I'll check in when it's closer to go-time. Until then, you know the drill."

"Heads down, eyes on the prize," Beckett answered for the group.

"Exactly. Talk soon." Shadow signed off, leaving the men of Tac-Ops to do little more than sit and wait.

They passed the time by fine-tuning their new plan of attack. When the time came, Falcon would remain in his current position. With the expert sniper watching their sixes, Beckett and the others would carefully make their way down the steep hill they were on.

Once they reached level ground, he and the others would quietly take out any tangos standing between them and the entrance to the faction's man-made cave. After that, they would go inside and get what they came for.

From the intel they'd studied on the plane ride here, there was a small labyrinth of tunnels and rooms the Taliban militants they were after had built. Living quarters, workspaces, places to store their weapons and ammo...

The crude system also provided the terrorist group with space for their food and water caches, as well as an area to keep their money and other stolen valuables safe.

Through the scope mounted on his M27 IAR—infantry automatic rifle—Beckett could see a cook station built around the base of a tree. The design allowed the smoke to dissipate throughout the limbs and leaves above, preventing detection from the air.

Clever bastards.

He brought the tango covering the cave's entrance to the center of his crosshairs. His gut tightened, and his trigger finger itched, but he drew in a deep breath and forced his muscles to relax.

As hard as the waiting could be, he understood full well the importance of patience when it came to an op, especially when five innocent lives were on the line. But by the time the sun was nearly set, Beckett and the others were more than ready to get the party started.

"You boys still with me?"

Shadow's return sparked the team back to life.

"We're in position and ready to move," Slade responded instantly.

"Excellent. Okay, so from what I'm seeing, nothing's changed, numbers-wise. There are five tangos moving around the cave's exterior on the east, where you're facing. I show one at the entrance, two standing guard on either side, a few yards away at the mountain's base, one where the road leading out of the valley begins, and one in a sniper's position located on the second ledge on the eastern portion of the mountain. Satellite shows two additional guards at the cave's west entrance, but we're hoping you can get in, secure the hostages, and get out before they even realize you've been there."

"Copy that," Digger acknowledged.

"Everything's a go on our end, so whenever you're ready, you've got the green light. Oh, and I'm sure it goes without saying, but watch for boobie traps. Groups like these tend to have a hard-on for that sort of thing."

The woman wasn't wrong. Beckett and the team had definitely had their fair share of experience in trip wires, hidden IEDs, and all sorts of other homemade traps set by the enemy.

Lucky for them, they'd all been well-trained in the art of detecting such devices. Even so, one could never be too careful when dealing with murderous assholes like the ones in their sights.

Letting Shadow know he'd heard the warning she'd given, Digger responded with a clear, "Hard copy on traps."

"The chopper will be waiting at the designated exfil location to retrieve your team and the hostages." The woman who'd served as the team's overwatch from its conception gave a brief pause before adding a slightly softer, "Our connection will be lost as soon as you enter the cave complex, so be very careful, gentlemen. I'll be here when you get out."

Beckett hated the idea of losing touch with Shadow for even a minute, but thanks to the mountain's impenetrable surface, they didn't have a choice. It wasn't the first time they'd entered the enemy's territory blind, and it wouldn't be their last.

"Okay, boys." Dig wasted no time pushing himself to his feet. "You heard the woman. Keep your eyes peeled and watch your step. We're no good to the hostages if we get our asses blown to bits."

As he and Apollo followed the man's lead and stood, Beckett's mind immediately turned to the beautiful schoolteacher being held captive somewhere inside that cave. He prayed they were all still alive and that they'd be able to walk out of their prison.

He had no way of knowing what shape Evelynn and the girls would be in when they located them, but it didn't matter. Beckett and his teammates were getting them the hell out of there, even if they had to carry them the entire way back to the chopper.

Even if it's the last thing I do.

To some, the fact that he and the others were willing to put their lives on the line for complete strangers probably seemed crazy. Certifiable, even.

But for the men of Tac-Ops, it wasn't about the risk to their own personal safety. It was about helping those unable to help themselves and making the world a safer place in the process.

One sadistic prick at a time.

"Copy that, Boss Man," Apollo acknowledged Digger's directive.

Beckett piggybacked with his own, "You lead, we'll follow."

Just as they did with every one of the team's lifesaving missions.

"We need to move fast on this one." Digger started to walk. "Shadow may have eyes on the west entrance, but without the additional team, there's no way for us to cover both sides of the bastards' hideout."

They also had no way of knowing for sure how many tangos were inside the cave, which meant this could turn out to be a very bad day for them all.

Come on, God. Give us another one. Evelynn and those girls deserve a chance at freedom.

With the silent prayer sent to the heavens above, Beckett and Apollo fell in line behind their leader.

The three men began marching down the side of the hill. The ground they covered was mostly dry dirt and rocks, with the occasional boulder or bush to help provide cover.

Like his teammates, Beckett kept his rifle up and at the ready. All three men had removed their field sunglasses and switched instead to their clear, Gatorz non-polarized shooting glasses.

With their eyes protected and their vision unobstructed, the team kept their targets in sight by using the L4G24 NVG—night vision goggles—attached to their Ops-Core Maritime helmets. The three men continued traversing the rugged terrain, and when they approached the point of no return, Digger held up a fist as the universal signal to stop.

Both Beckett and Apollo halted their movements, waiting silently for their team leader to give them further instructions.

"Falcon, what's your status?" Digger whispered into the comms.

"Ready when you are, brother. Say the word, and I'll start cleaning house."

Beckett's pulse spiked as a hefty dose of adrenaline was pumped into his system. This was it. There was no going back.

Once that first shot rang out, every man down there would know he and the others were here.

The goal was to take out the tangos watching the cave's exterior with enough speed and precision so they could avoid alerting those inside of their presence. But if they lost the element of surprise, the hostages' lives—as well as the team's—would be in immediate mortal danger.

Come on, Falcon. Do your thing.

He held his breath and waited, keeping his previously designated targets in his sights. Digger lifted his fist once more, silently counting down from three. When he reached one, he gave Falcon the green light the sniper had been waiting for.

"Go!"

Falcon's first shot was silent, thanks to the man's elevated position and the suppressor locked in place at the end of his gun. Though they couldn't see the target fall, their teammate confirmed his latest kill.

"Sniper down," Falcon informed them.

With his next breath, Beckett watched through his goggles as the men positioned near the cave dropped where they'd stood. First one and then the other.

It wasn't until the second man at the cave's entrance fell that the asshole watching the road even realized what was happening. By the time he spun around and raised his rifle in defense, it was too late.

Beckett had already taken aim.

Like the others, the man's body gave a slight jerk before falling lifeless to the ground.

"Let's move!" Digger spoke with authority.

The three men covered the distance remaining between them and the cave's dark entrance. Keeping Shadow's previous warning in mind, Beckett kept his head on a constant swivel to avoid making a rookie mistake and setting off a trap designed to kill them all.

Lucky for them, these guys hadn't bothered with boobie traps. Arrogant bastards probably thought they were too invincible to fall prey to an attack in the middle of nowhere.

Guess you thought wrong.

The three men passed by the bodies of the two guards as they entered the cave. Almost in unison, they slid their NVGs back up to their helmets with one hand while keeping their weapons steady with the other.

As planned, Digger took the lead while Apollo remained sandwiched between Digger and Beckett. As the tail of the trio, Beckett spun around to double-check that no surprises were heading their way through the cave's entrance.

Seeing the coast was clear, he turned back and fell in line behind Apollo. The air around them felt thick and smelled of rock and dank humidity as they made their way further into the enclosed space.

Several small lights had been placed along the cave's narrow path, aiding in their efforts to traverse the main corridor with speed and efficiency. Rooms had been cut out within the cave's interior walls, and it was obvious multiple people had, at one time or another, used the space for shelter.

Disappointment threatened to steal his focus. So far, there'd been no signs of the hostages, and other than the men they'd handled prior to entering the cave, they had yet to cross paths with any additional targets.

Come on, Evie. Where the hell are you?

The unplanned nickname just sort of came to him as they approached the end of the cave's main corridor. Forming a T, the rugged path split into two directions, and Beckett prayed Dig made the right choice.

Using only hand signals to communicate, the man in charge motioned to the right. As they walked in single-file, Beckett noted how much smaller the underground compound was compared to others they'd encountered in the past.

In theory, that should make locating the hostages a much easier task. But after clearing the five rooms positioned along the path they'd recently entered, his gut tightened with worry that they may not even be here.

Digger pointed to another turn up ahead. After confirming no immediate threat was present, Beckett and the others began their march in that direction. Every booted step they took carried with it another layer of dread as Beckett and the others were met with more of the same…

Empty rooms with no sign of life.

But as they approached yet another narrow pathway of rooms, Digger held up his fist, and all three men halted their steps immediately. The former SEAL motioned to something at the end of the shadowed hall, and it took Beckett and Apollo each a split second to realize what their leader had spotted.

A man was there, and he was standing guard outside a closed-off room.

Bingo.

Beckett's grip on his gun tightened. He readied his trigger finger and didn't dare take his eyes off the asshole. Digger gave the signal to begin their approach, but before the trio could take their first step, their target turned his head toward them.

The surprise in his eyes was clear to see, even from where Beckett stood. The man shouted something he didn't understand as he raised his rifle and aimed it in their direction.

Digger's bullet tore straight through the terrorist prick's head before the other man could even start to pull his trigger.

"There!" Beckett pointed to the crude wooden door where the deceased had been posted. "That has to be where the hostages are being held."

With their weapons held steady and their eyes laser-focused, the three members of Tac-Ops approached the door with caution.

"Watch my six," Digger ordered as he slung his rifle over his shoulder. Squatting down, he began inspecting the door for possible explosives.

After giving them a thumbs up to let them know they were in the clear, he stood and readied himself to make entry through the door. Beckett and Apollo got into position. Beckett stood to Digger's right, keeping his back against the rough rock wall adjacent to the door.

To Digger's left, Apollo stood with his back to the wall, his head moving from side to side to keep watch on the section of hallway from which they'd come.

Their team leader dipped his chin, letting them know he was ready to make entry. Mimicking the man's move, both Beckett and Apollo let the man know they were ready.

Please let them be okay.

Digger opened the door. The stench of sweat and fear filled Beckett's nostrils as he and the others kept their weapons up and at the ready.

Someone screamed. Another whimpered. And in the very next moment, Beckett realized...

It's them!

Terror filled the girls' faces as they remained huddled in one of the back corners of the room. Squished together for comfort, it was clear these were the four students from the file their boss had provided.

Their olive skin was ashen with dirt, and their hair matted and disheveled from days of neglect. Dark circles marred the skin beneath their innocent eyes as they stared up at him, but other than being dirty and weak—most likely from being dehydrated and malnourished—the girls thankfully appeared to be unharmed.

And right now, they were looking back at him, Apollo, and Digger as if they were public enemy number one.

With Digger watching the door for any threat that may arise, Beckett quickly lowered his weapon and put a hand in the air. Keeping his tone soft and his movements slow, he inched his way toward them.

"It's okay," he promised. "We're Americans, and we're here to take you home."

One of the young girls rose to her tiny bare feet. Her accent was thick, but he understood her perfectly when she asked him, "Are...are y-you really here to save us?"

"We are," Apollo backed the claim.

Beckett glanced around, his gut tightening when he realized the fifth hostage was nowhere to be seen.

"Your teacher," he prompted. "Where is she?"

"They took her," the little girl he recognized as Benesh spoke up next.

"Took her where?"

"We don't know." She shook her head. "The man who has been guarding us came and got her a little while ago, but we haven't seen Miss Evie since."

A string of curses flew through Beckett's mind. Had the bastard taken her somewhere else so he could question her? Beat her? Worse?

With no way of knowing for sure, they had to assume the worst. Which meant they needed to find Evelynn Mitchell fucking yesterday.

We're here now, darlin'. And we aren't leaving without you.

CHAPTER TWO

Evie spat out blood as she pushed herself up, her arms trembling with weakness and fear. The man who'd brought her here had taken his frustrations out on her by way of his meaty fists and booted feet. And after hitting and kicking her until Evie was certain she would die right here in this room, he'd left, taking any hopes of her survival right along with him.

Hers. The girls. And there wasn't a damn thing she could do to stop it.

I can't believe my father refused to pay the ransom.

Not only had the coldhearted man acted as if she didn't exist, but he'd also singlehandedly stolen any reason for their captors to keep them alive. They'd been taken for one reason, and one reason only—money. If these men didn't see a big fat payday in their near future, they'd no doubt rid themselves of the burden that was Evie and the girls.

She glanced over at the door. It had been several minutes since her guard had left, and she could only assume he'd gone to deliver the bad news to his terrorist friends.

How will they do it?

The macabre question was one she couldn't help but ponder. She'd read horror stories of Taliban prisoners being shot, stabbed, beheaded... That last one scared her more than the thought of enduring another beating.

At least it would be quick.

A humorless laugh bubbled up inside her chest, bringing with it a waterfall of tears. How had this become her life?

Evie had been born into privilege. She'd been raised in a mansion with enough bedrooms and bathrooms to accommodate a small country. Had attended the most elite private schools in East Hampton with kids whose parents were all mega-rich doctors, lawyers, famous actors, or politicians.

But no amount of designer labels or fancy schools had ever made her feel like she'd belonged. Not the way she did when she was in front of a classroom filled with students eager to learn.

Her first two months here with the girls had been every bit as rewarding. If not more so. But now...

Now they were going to be executed in this Godforsaken cave, and the rest of the world would probably never even know.

How could he do this to me? To us?

It was a question to which Evie knew she'd never get the answer to. Not when the man who'd left her here had promised her death upon his return.

More tears escaped, falling in unending streaks along her bruised and tender cheeks. Painful sobs tore through her as she remained on her hands and knees in the dirt. She was almost certain the bastard had cracked one of her ribs in his unprovoked attack, and it was all she could do not to cry out when she began the slow ascent back to her feet.

Another glance toward the door and more thoughts began to form. Rather than focusing on her impending death, Evie began to contemplate her odds.

She'd been down on the ground, crying and doing her best to breathe through the pain when he'd stormed out of the room. But even through her blurred vision, Evie had been able to see there was no other guard posted outside the room.

One could have been sent after the fact, she supposed. But something told her the arrogant jerk who'd left her here probably assumed she'd be in too much pain to even think about trying to escape.

People were always doing that. Her whole life, Evie had been underestimated. The kids she'd gone to school with. Her fellow teachers.

My father.

He was the worst offender, by far. Always lecturing, spending what little time he'd carved out of his busy schedule to be with her over the years to mansplain why every choice she'd ever seemed to make was wrong.

But they weren't wrong. They were just different than the ones he'd made for himself. Of course, going against her father in any manner was unacceptable. Lord forbid the only heir to the Mitchell fortune have a mind of her own.

I do have a mind of my own, damn it.

And right now, that mind was telling Evie to get herself and the girls the hell out of here now, before it was too late.

The sound of muffled male voices reached her ears, and her head automatically turned toward the source. Keeping a hand pressed against her injured side, Evie took slow, shallow breaths as she made her way across the room to the window.

Standing to the side, she kept her back plastered against the wall. Careful to keep her face from being seen, she risked looking out into the night.

Through the shadows, she could just make out two men standing near the cave's entrance. From the looks on their faces, they appeared to be almost bored. Not upset or angry, like the way the man who'd beat her had looked when he'd stormed out.

Maybe he hadn't yet passed along the news that they wouldn't be getting paid for their troubles. Or maybe they didn't care.

Guys willing to kidnap innocent young girls for money probably had other marks already picked out. Other unsuspecting souls going about business as usual, living their lives without the slightest inkling that they could be the next to be kidnapped and held for ransom.

Evie had been there, done that, and she had the bruises to prove it. And if she didn't find a way out of this mess soon, she and the girls would be little more than fleeting statistics.

She gave the window another quick glance to ensure the men

outside hadn't seen her. With their focus on the blackness of the night, she moved as quickly as she could across the dirt floor. Reaching up, she hesitated briefly, knowing if she got caught trying to escape, it would mean certain death.

You're going to die no matter what, Eves. At least this way, you'll go down fighting.

The encouraging voice in her head was right. She may not be a physical match against these guys, and this was almost assuredly a fool's errand, but Evie knew she had to at least try. For the girls, because damn it…they deserved a chance at a life.

A *real* life. One where females of all ages had the same rights as males. A life that promised a future filled with laughs and love and joy.

Regret seeped into her veins just then as Evie accepted the fact that she'd likely die without having experienced love herself. Oh, her mother had loved her, of course. There was never any doubt about that.

Unfortunately, her mom had died suddenly, and far, far too young. And for the remainder of Evie's childhood, she'd been forced to contend with being raised by a father who seemed to tolerate her—barely—and a nanny and staff who followed his strict instructions to the letter.

But true love, the kind between a man and a woman destined to be together until the end of time…that was something she'd never known. And unless a miracle happened, and she somehow managed to escape…

It's now or never, Eves.

Pulling in a breath as deep as her tender ribs would allow, Evie inched the door open as slowly and silently as humanly possible. The pounding in her head had nothing on that within her chest, but she pushed through the pain and fear enough to look out into the dimly lit pathway.

Relief nearly had her weakened legs crumbling beneath her when she found the corridor empty. New tears formed, but she blinked them away as best she could. There'd be time for tears later. At least, she *hoped* there'd be time. Now, though…

Now, it was time to act.

Act. Right. Which means you need to actually start moving.

The first step was the hardest, but with some mental encouragement—and the support of the wall beside her—Evie eventually made her way down the length of the empty path. As she moved, her thoughts bounced between the fight to ignore the incessant headache her guard's blows had created and trying her best to recall the turns she'd taken while being forced after leaving the room.

She reached the wall's end and was faced with a choice—go straight into a black abyss or turn right. Evie could recall at least one turn while being dragged away from the girls and into that room, so she rounded the corner and headed right.

Several yards later, she was coming up on another dark room when she heard a man shouting something in Pashto. Though she didn't understand the words being spoken, it was clear the man was angry.

Less than half-a-second later, she heard what she thought was a muffled gunshot. The man's words were silenced almost instantly.

Fear raced through Evie's veins. With her palm still pressed against the wall's cool, rough surface, she stopped and waited, listening intently for further signs of trouble.

The girls!

Though part of her wanted to hide, Evie knew that wasn't an option. If that *was* a gunshot, and she was pretty damn sure it was, then it couldn't have come from anyone good.

No one knew she and her students were here, so an unexpected rescue was most definitely out of the question. But who had just shot the gun and...why?

Maybe you're wrong, and it wasn't a gunshot after all.

Maybe. Unfortunately for Evie, there was only one way to find out. With the girls' safety at the forefront of her mind, she resumed her steps and continued through the shadows.

She couldn't remember a time when her heart had beat as hard and fast as it was right then. Her legs quivered beneath her, and her ribs and face hurt from the abuse she'd recently suffered. But she kept going.

Step after shuffled step, Evie carried herself closer to the place where she and the girls had been held. In her mind, she silently prayed with all she had that her young students were still locked safely away from any danger.

And how ridiculously ironic was *that*?

For days, she'd begged God for a miracle. Pleaded for Him to provide her and the girls a savior. Some sort of miraculous event that would ensure their return to safety.

Now here she was, throwing herself at His mercy with the hope that those sweet, precious girls were still in there. Still locked away in the very prison cell where they'd been forcefully kept.

Better there than in the hands of these monsters.

Evie was almost there. Just a few more rooms to pass before she'd be to the girls and—

Someone's there!

It was hard to make out, and for a minute, she thought maybe her throbbing mind had conjured up something that didn't actually exist. But even as she considered this—even in her frantic state—Evie was convinced she'd seen something move.

There it was again!

She crept a few feet closer, stopping just before the opening of the next to the last room on her right. Laser-focused, she honed her vision in on the spot where she'd seen the shadow move just seconds before.

The small lights along the narrow path weren't enough to make out any specific details, but even from here, she could tell the shadow belonged to a person. Beads of sweat formed on her forehead, and Evie's lungs worked faster as they filled themselves with several quick, shallow breaths.

A glimpse inside the room to her right yielded nothing more than the same crude rock walls and dirt floor as the others. With her focus bouncing back to where she'd seen the ominous shadow, Evie watched the area like a hawk.

Her heart thudded against her ribs with maddening fear as she prayed whoever the shadow belonged to would decide to go the other way. Rather than shrink in size, however, the shadow expanded, and the sound of muffled footfalls grew closer.

Evie wasn't as naïve as everyone always assumed, and she understood perfectly how dire her situation had become. If she were caught out here—caught trying to *escape*—she'd likely be shot on sight. Especially if these guys knew their anticipated windfall wouldn't be coming anytime soon.

Pain knifed through her broken heart, but she refused to let it steal her focus. Being systematically disowned by her only living parent had been a massive blow. Add to that the knowledge that her father had seemingly had no problem letting her die, and…

That was a realization from which she may never fully recover.

But right now, none of that mattered. Survival was the number one goal, and given her current situation, Evie knew her odds of making it out of this hellish cave alive were slim to freaking none.

I have to at least try.

She slipped quietly into the empty room. Rough edges scraped against her back as she made herself as invisible as possible, keeping her trembling form plastered to the wall just inside the unobstructed doorway.

Evie listened and waited, praying the room's unlit shadows were enough to conceal her presence from whoever was about to walk past. The room's state of emptiness provided hope that those she'd heard would simply walk on past. If they did that, she'd at least have a chance at getting to the last stretch of hallway, and to the room where she prayed the girls were still secured.

Approaching footfalls sounded, and Evie knew they were getting closer. She pressed her entire body back against the wall, making herself as small as humanly possible.

The air in her lungs ceased all movement as she refused to allow even the tiniest of breaths. Her injured ribs ached painfully from the pressure, the urge to reposition her arm as a makeshift brace tempting. But she didn't dare move a muscle.

Sore ribs she could live with. A bullet to the head, not so much.

Evie listened intently as she waited, hiding in the darkness. Within seconds, it was clear the person whose shadow she'd seen was coming her way.

Don't move, Eves. Don't move. Don't breathe. Don't—

A bright light appeared, its rays cutting through the room's center. She made herself impossibly smaller as the thick beam swept the space from left to right, and it took her a moment to realize the light's source was a long, terrifying-looking rifle.

Evie's lungs burned with a desperate need for air, but she refused to draw in even a partial breath. Seconds ticked by, and the pressure in her head and lungs increased ten-fold as the light made another pass, pausing dangerously close to the edge of her right foot.

Her toes curled inside her worn and dirty shoes as if that would somehow make her feet invisible should the light catch them. The aching in Evie's jaw worsened, not only from the blows she'd endured but also from clenching her teeth in terror.

She began to feel a bit lightheaded and feared she would pass out at any second. But then the beam—and the weapon it was mounted to—vanished, sending tears of relief rushing to the surface.

With several quick flutters, Evie blinked them away, finally releasing the air trapped in her lungs. She wanted to gasp like a fish out of water. To fill her lungs to their capacity again and again. But her fear of being heard overrode her body's instinct to suck in as much air as she could.

Instead, she carefully allowed some much-needed oxygen to enter her system through slow, silent breaths. At least, she hoped like hell they were silent. The man behind the intrusive light may have continued on his path, but that didn't necessarily mean she was safe.

Not even close.

Whoever he was, it appeared as though he was searching the rooms. For someone or something, she wasn't sure which.

Either way, she had no intention of still being in here when he returned.

Evie began counting the seconds silently in her head. When she reached one hundred, she decided it was time to try to move.

Going against her natural instincts to stay hidden, she slid her body to the edge of the doorway and risked a glimpse outside the room. Her shoulders sagged when the hallway appeared empty from both her left and her right.

After another glance in each direction, Evie decided the coast was clear and rushed from the room. She could only assume whoever it was had gone down one of the tunnel's other passages, so while he was busy sifting through the remaining rooms, she moved as fast as her quivering legs would take her.

Her pulse raced like never before, and the pain in her left side had worsened to the point it was nearly impossible to pull in a full breath. But she kept on. Pushing her tired and sore body to its limits, Evie was almost to the room where she and the girls had been held when something caught her attention from behind.

She started to spin around, her lips automatically parting in preparation of releasing her scream. But she never got the chance.

A gloved hand filled her vision half a heartbeat before it came crashing down over her gaping mouth. Evie flinched, doing her best to prepare for the pain she just knew would be coming. Though her attacker's hold was steady and firm, however, there was a gentleness there she had not been expecting.

"Evelynn Mitchell?" The man's hot breath struck her ear as he asked her name as if to confirm her identity.

Her spine straightened, and her muscles locked down all at once as a new set of fears took hold. The men who'd kidnapped her and the girls already knew her name. So why was this guy asking who she was?

He's not one of them.

Evie was pulled into the nearest room. With her back to the jerk's front, he moved lightning fast, spinning her fully around.

It took a moment for her to register the fact that her back was now pressed against the wall near the doorway...and his front was pressed against hers.

The irony in that she'd been in this exact position minutes before as she'd been hiding from, as it turns out, this very same man wasn't lost on her. The only difference was he hadn't been with her then.

Now, however...

Now I'm probably going to die.

No, screw that. If this asshole thought he could use her as bait to draw out the remaining Taliban terrorists—or as a human shield, those bastards wouldn't think twice about shooting to get to him—he was sorely mistaken.

She was going to die regardless, but that didn't mean she had to make it easy on the son of a bitch.

"My name is—"

The man started to speak. At the exact same time, Evie lifted her right knee straight up with as much force as she could muster.

The blow struck the man square in the crotch. He grunted as the hand that had been covering her mouth slipped free. And when his left knee started to buckle, Evie saw it as her one and only chance to escape.

She pushed against his vest-covered chest with all her might. Pushed. Shoved. Began kicking and slamming her fists against any and every part of the jerk's body she could reach.

If anyone had walked by at that very moment, they'd probably think she was some sort of psychotic banshee who'd completely lost her mind. And maybe she finally *had* gone crazy. But at least she wasn't rolling over and letting this asshole kill her—or use her as a pawn in whatever sick, terrorist game he was trying to play.

Her side burned with every movement she made, but unlike the other man, this one didn't hit her. Instead, he grabbed her wrists while twisting his lower body from side to side to avoid her incoming blows.

But he never once retaliated.

Though she'd fully expected his fist to come flying her way any second, this guy didn't so much as even *act* as though he were trying to hurt her. Not with his hands or the automatic rifle strapped to his chest.

He did, however, regain control over her by resuming their earlier position.

Evie wasn't even sure how he did it. One second, she truly thought she was gaining the upper hand, and the next—

"Damn it, Evelynn, stop!"

The hushed order came with her being pressed back against the room's rough wall. It was only then that she realized this man was keeping his body against hers, but he wasn't pushing himself against her.

If she didn't know better, she'd almost think he was trying his best *not* to put pressure on her injured core. He also didn't have an accent, which was also odd in this region. Well, he *did*, but it sounded almost like…

A southern drawl?

"Who…" She cleared the dryness from her throat. "W-who are you?"

"My name is Beckett Stone." The man took a step back, keeping his voice low enough for only her to hear. "I'm an American, and my team and I are here to take you home."

Confusion tore through her as she stared up at her newest captor. Because the room was so dark, it took her a moment to process what she was seeing…and what this man had just said.

He wasn't dressed like the others. Or like any of the local Afghan men she'd seen during her time here, for that matter. Instead, he had on a helmet, a camouflage shirt and pants, and a protective vest that held extra ammunition—among other things she couldn't even begin to guess.

In the center of that vest was a patch. Not just any patch, however. An American flag.

Evie's eyes flew back up to his. "Y-you're really American?"

Even in the shadows, she could see the man's scruff-covered lips curve into a small smile. "Born and raised."

Her own knees threatened to buckle as she threw herself into the stranger's arms. Having surprised him with the unexpected move, it took him two full seconds to react. But then—

"Hey," Beckett crooned, wrapping his arms around her in a warm and gentle embrace. "It's okay. We're here now, and you're safe."

After a few wonderful seconds, he pulled back. An assessing gaze fell over her tear-filled face, but then...

Beckett's expression turned lethal as he slowly lifted a hand toward her split and swollen lip. "You're hurt." The low growl a direct conflict with his soft, gentle touch.

"Just some bruises," she did her best to brush off his concern.

"Where else?"

"I'm okay. Really."

Okay was a bit of a stretch, and from the look on Beckett's face, he knew it. Countless questions whirled in Evie's overwhelmed mind, but for a moment, she reveled in the fact that help had finally arrived.

Tears of relief poured from the corners of her eyes because she knew—she *knew*—that this man was the answer to her prayers. But then she remembered...

"My students!" Evie blurted much too loudly. Lowering her voice, she rushed to tell him, "There are four young girls being held here, too. I'm their teacher, and I need to get to—"

"The girls are fine," Beckett promised. "They're with one of my teammates. All four are safe and already headed to the chopper."

"Oh, thank God!" More tears fell as the rest of what he'd said sank in. "Wait...you have a helicopter?"

That smile of his grew with a hint of a nod. "Yes, Ma'am. And trust me, Falcon will guard those girls with his life."

"Falcon?"

With every new detail Beckett shared came more questions.

"Falcon is my teammate who's taking care of the girls," he explained. Then, as if he'd read her most recent thoughts, he added, "Look, I know you probably have a ton of questions, but right now, we need to focus on getting you the hell out of here and back with your students. Sound good?"

Good? No, it didn't sound good. It sounded more like…

A miracle.

She'd prayed for one, and here he was…standing right before her like a camo-wearing warrior. There was always a chance he was lying, she supposed. But Evie didn't think so.

This man hadn't caused her harm in any way, despite having had multiple opportunities. In fact, Beckett had gone out of his way to make sure he *hadn't* hurt her. Or at least, that's how it had felt.

He was clearly an American, and since she was out of options, at this point, anyway, she decided to go with her gut and trust he was speaking the truth.

Evie wiped her face dry and straightened her spine. "Getting the hell out of here sounds freaking amazing. But—"

"But?" Beckett's dark brows rose beneath his helmet.

"I need to see the girls."

She needed to see with her own eyes that they truly were okay.

"And you will," he promised. "In fact, if we leave now, we can probably catch up to them."

"What about the others? The ones who took us hostage, I mean. What if they—"

"They've been handled," he answered vaguely. "But this place does have a lot of hiding places, plus a rear exit located on the other side of the mountain, which is why I'm keeping my voice down and my eyes peeled. Until we're in the clear, you need to do the same, okay?"

After posing the seemingly rhetorical question, Beckett pulled himself back a smidge and glanced down. Starting at her feet, his darkened gaze traveled all the way up the length of her body. The assessment wasn't sexual in nature but rather more cautionary. As if he was checking to make sure she was physically okay.

"I saw you holdin' your side earlier." A muscle in his chiseled jaw bulged beneath the strap holding his helmet in place. Studying what she assumed was the dried blood still present beneath her nose and at the corner of her mouth, he asked, "Are you hurt anywhere else, or are you okay to walk out of here on your own?"

"My ribs are sore, but I'll sprint out of this place if that's what it takes."

It would hurt, and she wouldn't be very fast, but she'd damn well do it all the same.

Beckett's lips lifted in a sideways smirk as he drawled out a low, "Not surprised, given the way you tried kickin' my ass just now."

"Sorry," Evie whispered back, feeling slightly chagrined. "I thought...I-I thought you were another group of militants wanting to take me captive, too." *Or worse.*

The man's smile fell, and even in the dark, she could tell his expression had once again grown hard. "No one else will lay a hand on you." His hard swallow was audible. "You have my word on that."

As Evie stared up into the darkness of his eyes, she found herself believing this man's word meant something to him, which was good because it meant everything to her.

"I just need to find the girls and make sure they're okay."

"Let's get you out of here, and then I'll contact my teammate so you can hear for yourself that they're just fine."

"Thank you, Beckett."

"No thanks needed, darlin'." He flashed a quick smile before detailing his plan to get them both out of the mountain safely. "You stay with me the entire time. No exceptions. If I tell you to do something, you do it without question. Shit goes sideways, and I go down, you take off in that sprint you teased about. And you don't stop until you find a safe place to hide. One of my men will find you and get you to safety."

"You want me to leave you if you get hurt?" Evie shook her head in earnest. "I'm sorry, but I can't do that. The rest of it, sure. But not that."

This man had come here to rescue her and the girls. She had

no idea how he even knew they were here, and that was a question she'd definitely be posing later. But regardless of the hows and whys, the fact was, he was here, risking his life for her and her students.

For now, that was all she needed to know.

"That's not up for discussion, Evelynn. You stick around, we could both end up dying, then all this was for nothin'."

Crap. The man had a point.

"Fine. If you go down, I'll...leave."

Maybe.

Probably not, though.

Evie kept her expression steady, hoping Beckett bought the fib. He must have because the next thing she knew, she was being carefully pulled behind his tall, muscular form.

He lifted his automatic rifle and held it out in front of him. Glancing back over his shoulder, he met her gaze before asking, "You ready?"

Boy was she.

"Oh, yeah." Evie nodded. "I'm ready."

With a quick lift of his lips, Beckett began to move. Almost as if on reflex, she reached up with one hand and held onto the belt loop at the small of his back.

When he looked back at her again, Evie asked quietly, "Is this okay?"

He smiled down at her with a wink and said, "It's perfect."

She followed him just like that the entire way. Where he stepped, she stepped. When he turned, she turned. But Evie's steps faltered when she spotted a man's body lying motionless on the ground up ahead.

"Don't look," Beckett ordered. "Just focus on my back and follow me."

Evie tried to obey his command. She really did. But at the last second, she glanced down as they passed the obviously dead terrorist.

"That's definitely one of them," she told the man serving as her guide out of hell. "He brought us food and water sometimes. But he always taunted me with lewd comments and threats."

The asshole was constantly reminding her how he could—and eventually would—"have his way with her" anytime he wanted. Thank God he never made good on the horrifying promise.

Without missing a beat, Beckett responded with, "In that case, I wish he was still alive just so I could shoot his ass again."

She didn't say anything to that because...what *was* the appropriate response to a comment like that? Deciding there really wasn't one, Evie remained quiet as she inched toward the room where she and the girls had been forced to stay.

"Evelynn?" he uttered her name softly. "You okay?"

She stared into what had been her and the girls' prison and shook her head. "That's where they kept us," she told him unnecessarily. "We were only allowed to leave to use the bathroom or when..." Her delicate throat worked with a wince-driven swallow. "Or when they took me away to question me."

Of course, he already knew that was the room they'd been held in. He and his team had already rescued the girls from there, after all.

"Look at me, darlin'," he whispered softly. When she did, Beckett solemnly vowed, "You'll never be in a place like that ever again."

Her heart gave a hard thump as it filled with the realization that he was right. She was being rescued—they were *all* being rescued. And right now, that was the only thing that mattered.

CHAPTER THREE

Beckett stole another glance at the woman walking behind him as he led her toward the cave's carved entrance. He was in awe at how well she'd handled herself so far. Sure, she'd fought him like mad when he'd pulled her into that room, but who could blame her?

At the time, there was no way Evie could've known who he was or be aware of his intentions. If anything, her reaction to being manhandled after days of captivity had impressed the hell out of him.

Rather than crumble into a weeping, hysterical mess, the woman had fought with everything she possessed. Granted, her blows were nowhere near strong enough to overpower him, but even in her weakened and bruised state, the pretty schoolteacher had made it clear she'd been prepared to break free...

Or die trying.

Fury he fought to contain raged within him as he thought about the bruises and dried blood marring the skin on her beautiful face. He'd seen those same types of markings countless times in the past.

On hostages. His teammates. Hell, he'd personally suffered enough black eyes and busted lips to know exactly how painful they could be. Not to mention whatever damage had been done to her ribs.

The grip on his M27 IAR tightened as he tried like hell not to envision the type of abuse the poor woman must have endured. God, he'd love the chance to blow a few more rounds into each and every one of the terrorist assholes.

At this point, however, it would just be a waste of perfectly good ammo. And guys like the ones they'd taken down…they damn sure weren't worth the bullets.

"Are they all dead?"

The soft question ripped Beckett back into the present. Belatedly, he realized Evie was referring to the men he and his team had taken out before breaching the cave.

"Yes."

He didn't insult her intelligence by trying to sugarcoat the situation as they stepped out into the night through the hell-hole's arched entrance. Nor did he attempt to shield her from the carnage, as she'd already proven earlier the strength she possessed when coming face-to-face with death.

"Your team did this?"

"We did."

There was a slight pause before he heard her sweet voice give a resounding, "Good."

Beckett couldn't help but smile as the two made their way past the slain terrorists. A few yards up ahead, he saw Digger and Apollo walking down the hill toward them.

"Falcon and the kids are secure and on the bird," his team leader announced.

Before Beckett could make introductions, Shadow's voice suddenly filled the comms.

"Nice work, Bones," the mysterious woman commented. "Though, I have to admit, you were inside a bit longer than I would've liked."

He put a hand to his ear to adjust the small mic still nestled there. "Sorry 'bout that. Ran into our fifth hostage and needed to make sure we were clear to exit." Looking back over his shoulder at Evie, he found her still following his directions to the letter. "You don't have to hold onto me anymore if you don't want to"—he veered from his current conversation and addressed her directly— "but if it makes you feel safer, you can hang onto me until we reach the helicopter."

Without a word, the newly freed woman released his belt loop and began walking at his side. The void from her touch created a sense of disappointment, which was confusing, to say the very least.

"I'm going to assume that's Evelynn Mitchell you're talking to," Shadow commented. "The others already filled me in on eliminating the single tango guarding the girls. Is she good to make it to the extraction point, or does she need a medical evac from your location?"

"She's good." He glanced down at her and smiled. "A little banged up and dehydrated, but she's...good."

His assessment of her condition might be a bit embellished, but they wouldn't know the extent of her injuries until they could get her to a hospital for a thorough check-up. He could, however, get a jump-start on the issue of dehydration.

As Shadow continued speaking, Beckett grabbed the military-grade water bottle each man carried with him in the field and handed it to her. "It's not cold, but it's wet. Just be sure to take small, slow sips so you don't get sick."

"Thank you." She took the bottle and immediately began to unscrew the top.

He watched her closely to ensure she didn't gulp down too much too quickly, but like all the other orders he'd given up to this point, Evie followed his instructions and took her time.

"That's great, Beck," Shadow responded to his assessment of Evie's condition. "Any additional casualties I should be aware of? And none of that plausible deniability BS you guys are always trying to pull."

"Ah, come on now. You know we're just lookin' out for our favorite techie."

"Well, as much as I appreciate the sentiment, it makes my job a hell of a lot easier when I have all the intel in my arsenal. I can't protect you if I don't have all the facts."

"You've got 'em all this time," he assured her. "Trust me, if there were more to share, I'd tell ya."

"Good. Now, how many tangos did you encounter inside?"

"Just the one guarding the room where they'd been holdin' Evie and the girls. Dig took him out shortly after breaching. He and Apollo stayed behind to watch the entrance while Falcon took the girls to the chopper, and I finished clearing the remaining rooms. That's when I found Evie. Other than her, the rest of the place was like a terrorist ghost town."

Beckett didn't mention the part about Evie fighting him like a wildcat or kicking him in the balls. Not because it would embarrass him but because it might embarrass *her*.

It didn't make a lick of sense given that they'd only just met, but Beckett felt extremely protective of this woman. More so than any other hostage he and his team had rescued in the past.

And he had no earthly idea why.

"Well, we can't ask for a better scenario than that," Shadow noted. "As for now, satellite imagery shows you're in the clear. There are still two tangos guarding the cave's back exit, but they appear to be oblivious to your presence...or the fact that their asshole friends are dead."

"Guess we should probably hit the road before they make that particular discovery."

The woman in his ear agreed. "If Miss Mitchell is good to go, then yes. Get your sweet heinies moving so we can get you all home and put this one behind us."

"Copy that, Shadow." Beckett confirmed. "The four of us are headed to the extraction site now."

"I'll keep an eye out from my end and let you know if there's any trouble along the way. Until then, no news is good news, so unless you hear otherwise, stay on course. I'll notify both Falcon and the pilot that you're on your way."

"Hard copy, Overwatch," Digger also gave confirmation he'd heard and understood the order.

With Shadow temporarily offline, Beckett finally had a moment to introduce his teammates. "Evie, I'd like for you to meet Digger and Apollo. Dig's our team leader, and Apollo, well...he's whatever we need him to be. They're both former

Navy SEALs and two of the best men I've had the pleasure of working with."

"Nice to meet you, Miss Mitchell." Apollo held out his gloved hand for her to take.

"Likewise." Evie shook Apollo's hand. "Apollo and Digger... I'm assuming those are nicknames?"

"You assume right." Apollo nodded.

"I'm also guessing you're really good at fighting, and you're really good at..." She turned her pointed finger toward Digger and guessed, "Digging holes?"

Beckett threw his head back and laughed as Evie handed him back the water bottle. He softened his tone when he told her, "That's a story for another day."

This wasn't the time to explain the other man's nickname stemmed from Dig's number of enemy kills, and it wasn't his story to tell. Aside from that, the woman had already borne witness to enough violence and death. He wasn't about to pile even more onto the haunting images she'd already be forced to live with.

"Do you have a nickname, too?" Evie glanced back up at him.

He nodded. "The guys call me Bones."

"Bones?" The light chuckle that shook her shoulders was like music to his ears. "Are you a doctor or something?"

"Or something." He shrugged. "Among my many, *many* other talents, I also serve as the team's medic."

"Bones." Her full lips curved, and her adorable twin dimples deepened beneath the moonlit sky. "I like it."

The woman was filthy and bruised, her clothes and hair in total disarray, and dried blood was still present beneath her cute as hell button nose and the corner of her mouth. And still, she was the most beautiful, intriguing woman Beckett had ever seen.

She's also just survived being kidnapped and held captive by a bunch of Taliban pricks. So maybe don't be a dickhead by thinkin' of her in ways you shouldn't.

As usual, his inner voice was right.

A few short moments later, they fell into a comfortable silence as the four of them followed the same path Beckett and his team had previously taken. As he studied Evie's attire, he considered how much cooler the desert had grown since he and his men had first arrived.

She was dressed in skinny jeans that were so dirty they looked more brown than blue, a stained white V-neck t-shirt that was torn at the collar and seam of one shoulder, and a pair of brown lace-up boots. But it was getting colder by the minute, and he worried she might be frozen by the time they reached their ride.

"Hey, hold up a sec."

Without question, both Apollo and Digger halted their forward movements. Beside him, Evie stopped in her tracks, her unspoken question in her furrowed brow.

"You're cold," he muttered low as he slipped his rifle strap up over his head.

Understanding erased the adorable lines between her brows, and Evie quickly tried to politely decline. "That's really nice of you, but I'm okay."

"You're shivering." Beckett motioned to her exposed limbs as he secured his weapon between his thighs before making quick work of his protective vest. With efficient movements, he removed the vest, and then the Multicam Crye G3 combat field shirt he was wearing. "It's dirty and probably smells like sweat" —he held it out for her to take—"but at least you'll be a bit warmer."

Evie's hazel gaze lifted to meet his. "You didn't have to do that." She slid her arms in the oversized sleeves. "Thank you."

With hurried movements, Beckett replaced his vest, securing the Velcro straps easily, before repositioning his weapon. The cool night air felt refreshing on his dampened skin, and though he knew he'd be cold by the time they reached the chopper, his muscle mass and natural body heat would be enough to get him there with relative comfort.

Regardless, knowing Evie would be more comfortable made being cold totally worth it.

Her hands trembled as she struggled to get the buttons through their designated holes. Without saying a word, Beckett stepped directly in front of her, moved her frigid fingers out of the way, and finished the task for her.

"Thank you," she whispered softly. "I guess I'm a little colder than I realized."

"Adrenaline dump doesn't help." He secured the top button near the shirt's collar. Rather than releasing it, he left his hands there as he stared down into her big, beautiful eyes. "I can only imagine what you've been through, but you're going to be okay. You and the girls are safe now."

"I feel safe." Evie held his gaze. "With you."

Beckett grinned, but her eyes grew wide. Almost as if she realized what she'd said could be misconstrued as something more meaningful—and crazy as it was, part of him wished like hell she had—she immediately slid her focus away from him and over to where Apollo and Digger waited.

"I feel safe with *all* of you," Evie clarified. "And I know it's not nearly enough, but I just wanted to say..." Those eyes found his once more as she uttered a heartfelt, "Thank you."

They were standing in the middle of an Afghanistan desert after leaving a slew of bodies in their wake, and damn if Beckett's heart didn't feel fuller and more alive than it had in maybe forever.

It was a simple act of kindness and appreciation from a woman he'd probably never see again. And that one thought—over all those racing through his mind—created a sense of disappointment and longing he couldn't begin to understand.

The fact that she was now wearing his field shirt only made matters worse. It was about three sizes too big, and she looked like she was swimming in the damn thing. But that didn't keep all sorts of uninvited fantasies from forming inside his sex-deprived mind.

His dick twitched behind the zipper of his BDUs as he imagined her wearing nothing but his shirt.

Down, boy. You're not out of the woods...or rather, the desert...just yet. Better get your ass moving before the terrorist's friends decide to show back up.

"Come on." Beckett listened to his inner voice, dropping his hands back down to his weapon before stepping away from her personal space. "Let's get you and the girls the hell out of here."

"Don't have to tell me twice."

The small snort that had bubbled up from somewhere deep in her throat sent a wave of humor and awe racing through him. From the moment he'd spotted her hiding in that literal hole-in-the-wall room to now, she continued to amaze him with her resilience and ability to overcome.

Most hostages they'd rescued—both men and women alike—usually broke down into a puddle of tears. Rightfully so, mind you. He found no shame in outwardly expressing one's relief and life-altering gratitude. But there was just something about this hostage...this *woman*...that spoke to him on a whole other level.

Whether it was her refusal to cower down to the men who'd taken her captive, the perseverance and inner strength she'd shown when she thought he was the enemy, or the fact that the first thing she'd thought of when she realized who he really was had been her young students, he wasn't sure. But there was one thing Beckett did know with utter certainty...

Evelynn Mitchell was one of a kind.

Staring down at her, he suddenly found himself wishing like mad they'd met under different—and much *better*—circumstances. But the simple truth was that all the wishing in the world wouldn't change the fact that they hadn't.

She'd been a hostage his team had been sent to rescue. They'd done their job, and once they got her and the girls back where they belonged, that would be the last he'd see of the pretty brunette with the bouncing curls and cute-as-hell dimples.

They fell back in line behind Digger, with Apollo taking up the rear. For a while, they walked in silence, carefully traversing the rough and uneven desert terrain. Several minutes in, Evie's sweet voice sounded again.

"Before, you said Apollo and Digger were *former* Navy SEALs. Does that mean you're no longer in the military?"

"All three of us served. Those two went Navy, and I chose Marines."

"But you're not a Marine anymore?"

Apollo let out a loud, exaggerated cough, but Beckett ignored his teammate and recited the old adage, "Once a Marine, always a Marine."

"Jesus, man," Apollo scoffed as they continued moving. "You can never just let that one slide by, can you?"

Evie's gaze turned a tad wary. "Did I...say something wrong?"

Before he could put her mind at ease, Digger grumbled his own version of the truth as he led them through the night.

"Bones always get butthurt anytime someone tries calling him a *former* Marine. As if those guys are above the rest of us or something."

Apollo chimed back in with, "To be fair, every branch always thinks they're the best. But we all know the truth."

Voice laced with a hefty dose of curiosity, Evie asked, "And what's the truth?"

"The Navy's the best there is. Although I bet our boy here could outdo any of us in a crayon-eating contest. Ain't that right, Bones?"

With his booted feet keeping the same, steady pace and his eyes still scanning their immediate area, Beckett lifted a hand and gave his teammate the bird. From his peripheral, he could see Evie's brunette brows arching high.

"Crayons?"

Digger grunted and Apollo began to chuckle, but Beckett ignored them and kept his focus on her.

"It's a running joke between the branches," he explained. "Marines eat crayons; Air Force is the Chair Force...because they don't do anything but sit on their asses in the cool AC... SEALs are squids..." His shoulders lifted in a light shrug. "You get the idea."

"What about the Army?"

He flashed her a grin. "They're like the Little League of the military. They take anyone willin' to join."

As if they'd somehow planned it ahead of time, both Digger

and Apollo let loose with a unified "Hooyah!" while Beckett went with the Marine's cry of "Oorah!"

The smile that spread across Evie's face seemed to light up the entire night sky. An impossibility, Beckett knew. Still, it did his soul good to know whatever those bastards had done, they didn't break her.

A few minutes passed before she spoke up again.

"If you aren't active duty military anymore, what are you?"

Normally, they'd work to keep as quiet as possible, but with Shadow serving as overwatch, if there were any heat signals nearby, she'd already have a bead on their location and would've given them the heads up.

Since their current threat level was low, and Evie was in the mood to talk, Beckett was more than happy to keep her mind occupied on something other than what she'd been through.

"In a nutshell?" Beckett glanced down at her. "We're hostage rescue specialists. We work for a company called Tac-Ops. It's short for Tactical Operations."

"So you guys just go around saving people who've been kidnapped?"

"Pretty much."

"Wow." The woman sounded impressed. "That's sort of...awesome."

"Hell yeah, it is," Apollo jumped back in.

Beckett's chest warmed as he thought of the man his team-mate had become. In just a few weeks' time, the badass operative had gone from grump to groom. And ever since Apollo and Nicki got married, the once-surly man was suddenly more smiles and a lot less snark.

Come to think of it, Falcon was pretty much the same. Though the man was never as moody as Apollo had once been, the former Ranger hadn't exactly been sunshine and rainbows, either. Not until he met Avery.

And Beckett was happy for both Falcon and Apollo. He really was. Though he had to admit, it was still pretty wild to think that two government-trained killers who still kicked down doors to rid the world of evil had fallen in love amidst danger and mayhem.

But they had.

Despite the circumstances in which they'd come together and the personal baggage each carried to the table, the two couples had somehow even figured out a way to build lives filled with love and happiness around a job as unpredictable—and dangerous—as theirs.

Yes, Falcon and Apollo had done it. They'd achieved the unachievable for guys like them. And if they could do it…

Maybe I can, too.

"I didn't even know a job like yours existed."

Evie's comment dragged him from his sea of wishful thinking.

"There aren't many companies like ours, but yeah." Beckett looked over at her. "We exist."

"Well, thank God, you do!" she exclaimed. "Although, I do have to ask…how did you know where to find us? Or that we'd even been taken?"

"We mostly take on private clients, but we also work the occasional government contract job."

And by occasional, he meant a fuck ton of off-the-books ops only a very select few—the President of the United States included—would ever even know existed.

"Which one was I?" She asked a few seconds later. "Was I government or…private?"

The question—and her overt curiosity over what he would normally think was moot at this point—gave Beckett pause. In his experience, most people knew if their families had the kind of personal safety travel insurance Tac-Ops offered. Policies that guaranteed his team would locate and extract a client if said client found themselves in a hairy situation.

Taken captive was the most obvious, of course. But they also got people out of hot spots or areas where violence unexpectedly erupted. Civil unrest. Riots. Attempts to overthrow foreign governments. That sort of thing.

From the file he'd read on the way here, Evie had no such policy, and neither did her father. Which begged the question... why the question?

Maybe she thought her dad got coverage for her while she was staying in Afghanistan.

"THIS OP WAS AN OFFICIAL ONE."

"So...government." Evie gave a curt nod before glancing out into the night.

Beckett watched her closely, wondering if he'd imagined the disappointment weaved within her soft tone. Feeling a sudden, inexplicable urge to give comfort, he did his best to cheer her up.

"I bet you're excited to see your dad again."

She turned his way and smiled. "Of course."

It was a perfectly appropriate response and one he'd expect from anyone who'd lived days thinking they'd never see their family again. But while her words said one thing, the look in Evie's weary eyes suggested something else entirely, which, much like the visceral reaction he felt toward the woman, made no sense whatsoever.

Why wouldn't she be happy to go home?

He thought back to what he'd learned from the intel Shadow had provided the team. According to her file, Evie's dad—Phillip T. Mitchell was the majority shareholder and CEO of Mitchell-Granger Investments. The prominent financial investment and advisory firm was built from the ground up by Mitchell's father, Evie's grandfather.

When the powerful patriarch died two decades before, he left the company, as well as the man's entire fortune, to his sole heir. Since taking over the family business, Phillip Mitchell turned what had been a successful and lucrative, multi-million-dollar business into a major financial conglomerate worth fifty-four billion and change.

As for Evie, from what Beckett could tell, the woman had

grown up with a silver spoon in her mouth and designer *everything* in and around her charmed life. A far cry and worlds away from the upbringing he'd had as a child.

Both of his parents were retired now. His dad had spent the better part of thirty years as a beat cop working the streets of Dallas while his mom had spent her tenure teaching second grade at a small suburban school.

They didn't have a lot, but as an only child, Beckett could never remember a time when he'd gone without. But when he compared his upbringing with what he'd read about the Mitchell family estate—including the massive mansion Evie had grown up in—he realized...

We couldn't be more different.

"Does my father know I've been rescued?"

Beckett swung his gaze in her direction. "I'm sure by now, someone with authority has been in contact with the girls' families. But you're an adult, and as far as our intel shows, your father hasn't put out a missing person's report or contacted anyone within the government about an abduction. Plus, this op was off-books, which means very few people will ever know what happened here."

She filled her lungs before exhaling slowly. "Okay. I was just curious."

"If you want, I can try to get permission to let you use our satellite phone to—"

"No, that's okay," Evie hurriedly cut him off. "I mean...it's probably crazy early there, and I'm sure he's still in bed, anyway."

The woman had been kidnapped at gunpoint, taken against her will, and held captive for days with minimal food and water. She'd also clearly been beaten and must have thought she was going to die. And yet, she was worried about waking up her dad to let him know she was okay?

His gut churned with the feeling that something was way off with this whole picture. But he didn't know Evie personally, and her family dynamics were not his concern. So rather than intrude on the part of her life that held no real influence on their mission, Beckett turned his focus back to...well...the mission.

"The men who took you," he spoke again. "Did they ever tell you why?"

"What do you mean?"

"They ever mention anything to you about plans for ransom demands for you and the girls? Or were there ever any conversations you might have overheard about why the five of you were targeted?"

"I have no idea why they took us." Evie gave a jerky shake of her head.

Her lips curved into a quick smile before she turned away, her focus homing in on the path ahead. Beckett had no reason to doubt what she'd told him, and there hadn't been any sort of noticeable change in her expression, but still there was *something* there he couldn't quite name.

Or maybe you're lookin' for somethin' that isn't even there.

Maybe. Or maybe there was more but she was too scared to say.

Fear could be a funny thing. Especially when it came in the form of terrorist assholes willing to kidnap—and often kill—anyone they believed could help with their cause.

Be it political, religious, or financial, it didn't matter. Men like the ones who'd taken Evie and the girls were soulless, selfish monsters who usually hid behind some sort of justifiable agenda.

And they would do whatever it took in their search for success.

But the danger had passed, and they were less than half-a-mile from their extraction point. Evie and her students had been rescued, and soon, they'd all be far away from the place where nightmares lived. And still, it seemed as if she were too afraid to share the whole of what she knew.

Maybe she just needs more time.

Maybe his inner voice was right. Hell, it had been less than an hour since they'd freed her from the cavernous prison. What he really needed to do was to cool his boots where she was concerned and focus on doing everything he could to ensure she truly felt safe.

"Don't worry," Beckett rumbled low. "You'll be back in the Hamptons before you know it."

Evie took three full steps before glancing up at him with that same frozen smile. "Great," she offered cheerfully. "I can't wait."

CHAPTER FOUR

Evie sat on the examination table with her legs dangling over the edge. The paper runner lining the black cushioned table crinkled beneath her every movement, the sound seemingly echoing in the otherwise silent space.

Unlike the sweltering desert heat they'd been forced to endure, the room she was waiting in now was cold to the point of being downright frigid. Of course, the gown she'd been instructed to change into didn't help matters any. But like most other times in her life, Evie followed the directions exactly as they'd been given.

Maybe you should've listened when Dad told you not to come here in the first place.

In hindsight, her subconscious thoughts were probably right. Maybe she *should* have gone against her own desires and taken heed to her father's stern warning.

To be honest, there was a small part that wished she had. The part that yearned for the memories of the last few days to disappear.

At the same time, Evie also couldn't bring herself to regret the fact that she'd been the one with the girls the day those men had come. That it was *her* who'd been there to offer words of comfort and solace during what was, without a doubt, the most terrifying moments of all their lives.

But thankfully, that time was over. And like Beckett had said during their hike through the Afghan desert, they'd all be going home very soon.

Too bad I no longer have a home.

Not the kind that mattered, anyway.

Evie blinked the disheartening thought away and forced herself to become hyper-focused on the room. It was equipped much like the emergency rooms at regular hospitals, complete with tiled floors, bright overhead lights, and the unmistakable scent of antiseptic.

The space was much larger than she'd expected to find on a ship, but that was probably because this wasn't just *any* ship. The chopper had flown them to a U.S. Naval hospital ship that was stationed a few miles off the coast of Pakistan. She and the girls were the crew's newest patients.

Thank God, they're safe.

Evie anxiously shifted her lower body, nervously kicking one of her feet back and forth in a slow, rhythmic motion. An hour had passed since they'd said their goodbyes just before her sweet, precious students left the ship for good.

Upon her insistence, they'd been checked out by medical personnel first. Each girl having been given a clean bill of health, minus some minor dehydration and the need for a few good, hearty meals.

Once they were good to go, they were escorted back onto the chopper, and under the watchful eye of what Evie could only assume to be four very capable Navy sailors, the girls were now on their way back home, where their parents were anxiously awaiting their arrival.

Be well, sweet girls. I'm going to miss you like crazy.

A sad smile lifted her lips as she recalled their last moments together. She'd forever remember the looks of pure elation that had spread across their smiling faces when she, Beckett, and his teammates had arrived at the helicopter hours before.

They'd been sitting in their designated seats but hadn't been buckled in. And when they saw her and the others crest the small hill leading to the valley where the massive metal bird sat waiting, all four had practically jumped from their seats to greet her.

Several hugs and tears later, they were in the air and on their way here. Evie couldn't remember a time when she'd felt such relief as she'd sat next to Beckett while they floated up and away from hell.

Her heart ached for what they'd been through, though she was grateful beyond words to know they hadn't suffered any physical abuse at the hands of those awful men. The fear and terror they'd all experienced the past several days were bad enough without adding that level of violence into the mix.

They're okay, now. Beckett's team got them out of there, and they're going to be okay.

Evie's thoughts turned to the man who'd saved her life. Beckett "Bones" Stone was tall. Strong. Kind.

Part of her still felt embarrassed by the way she'd gone all warrior princess on him back in the cave. But how the heck was she supposed to know he was a real life, honest to goodness American hero?

Pretty sure he tried to tell you that right before you kneed him in the goods.

Okay, fine. So there was that. Still, she couldn't bring herself to feel *too* guilty for the way she'd reacted. After all, in that moment, Evie believed she was fighting for her life.

If he hadn't stopped her—if she hadn't seen that American flag on his protective vest—there was no doubt in her mind, she would've continued the struggle until she was either unconscious...

Or dead.

Evie shuddered at the thought.

Lucky for her, the man she'd thought was a terrorist turned out to be someone completely unexpected. A hero in the midst of darkness. Her personal savior when she'd begun to think all hope was truly lost.

It didn't hurt that Beckett was also sweet and funny. And, as she discovered when they got inside the ship and beneath the vessel's bright lights, very, *very* handsome.

Yes, the former Marine-turned-hostage rescue specialist was the epitome of tall, dark, and mouthwateringly good looking. The whole package, really. One wrapped in camouflage, muscles, and a smile that awakened parts of her she'd long been ignoring.

Better stop that train of thought before it ever leaves the tracks.

Yes, she definitely needed to put an end to any notion of Beckett being more than what he was. A stranger who, by his own admission, was only in that cave because the government had paid his team to be there.

The government. Not my dad.

Evie's shoulders dropped as her spirit rapidly fell, like an abandoned hot air balloon that had deflated after being left alone in the middle of an empty, desolate field. She couldn't help but replay Beckett's words from earlier as they'd been making their way to freedom…

Don't worry. You'll be back with your dad in the Hamptons in no time.

She hadn't bothered asking how he knew where she was from. Guys like him probably had access to all kinds of personal information regarding the people they rescued.

Evie also didn't point out that she had her own studio apartment in Portsmouth, Rhode Island…where she'd lived since being hired to teach second grade right out of college. Granted, she'd subleased it to the young college graduate who'd been hired on as Evie's long-term sub for the semester, but still.

The thing that bothered her more—one bit of data Beckett couldn't possibly know—was that there wasn't anything left for her in the Hamptons…or anywhere else.

Sure she still had her job with the Portsmouth Public School District. And of course, there was Lo—her best friend from college. The two were as close as sisters, and before Evie left the States to come to the Middle East, they chatted by either text, phone call, or FaceTime nearly every single day.

But even if Lo—whose actual name was Lauren Davenport—

didn't live fourteen hours away in Charlotte, which she did, the other woman had decided to spend the summer with her sister, who lived all the way up in Michigan.

Since Lo's job was remote, she was able to work from virtually anywhere, making it possible for her and her older sibling to have some much-needed quality time together. Good for her friend.

Not so much for me.

So yeah, aside from some friendly-*ish* co-workers, there really wasn't much for her to look forward to. And sitting at the very bottom of that embarrassingly short list…

The conversation she would eventually have to have with her jerk of a father.

You could go back to work. Finish out the school year surrounded by familiar faces. Might at least help to keep the thoughts of being utterly abandoned at bay.

It was a plan Evie had considered as she'd listened to the steady thump-thump-thump of the helicopter's steadily whirling blades. But since there were only a few weeks left of the school year, and she had a long-term sub who'd already taken over her regular classroom, Evie had already decided to stick to her original plan of not returning until the fall.

Probably a good idea, anyway, given the horrors she'd experienced as of late. And if she were being honest with herself, taking a few months off to reevaluate her life—and process the fact that her father no longer wanted to be a part of it—may not be the worst thing in the world.

A fresh set of tears began to form, but thankfully the door opened at that exact moment, and the Naval Corpsman assigned to her care walked into the room.

"Miss Mitchell." The middle-aged woman dressed in government-issued camo moved with purpose in Evie's direction. "I'm Petty Officer Billings," she introduced herself with a smile.

"Nice to meet you," Evie offered quietly.

"You, too, although I think it goes without saying I wish it were under different circumstances."

She huffed out a breathy, "You and me, both."

"A member of the team who brought you in mentioned you'd been favoring your left side. If it's all right with you, I'd like to take a look. Nothing invasive, mind you. Just a cursory examination to make sure you don't have anything broken or any sort of internal bleeding we need to be aware of. After that, we'll get you cleaned up, get you some clean clothes, and a nice, warm meal. How does that sound?"

"Amazing, actually."

Well, not the examination part. But Beckett had explained it was standard operating procedure for situations such as hers, and honestly, Evie had been far too tired to argue.

Plus, the sooner you get this done and over with, the sooner you can see him again.

At least, she hoped to see Beckett again soon. He'd made her feel so safe during the trek to the chopper. But when they'd gotten to the clearing, she'd had her tearful reunion with the girls, and the next thing Evie knew, they'd landed on the ship's helipad.

The girls had been whisked away almost immediately by some of the brave men and women on board. Again, it was nothing she hadn't expected. Hell, she'd been the one to insist they get taken care of first. But hearing the plan and living it turned out to be two very different things.

Now all she could think of was whether she'd ever see them again.

Don't forget the man who saved you.

It was true. She *was* looking forward to seeing Beckett again. Just so she could tell him thank you one last time.

Sure, sure. You just keep telling yourself that, Eves.

"Your pulse is a bit fast," Petty Officer Billings spoke up again. "But that's to be expected, given what brought you here. You've been under a tremendous amount of stress, both physically and mentally. It's going to take some time to get back to feeling like your old self again."

Will I ever feel like my old self?

It was a valid question, and unfortunately one neither woman could immediately answer. And as Evie sat on the exam table, getting poked and prodded and thoroughly checked over, she began to wonder who her old self really was…

And who she truly wanted to be.

"Your zygomatic bones both seem to be intact, so that's good news." Billings carefully palpated Evie's cheekbones. She moved to the sides of her nose, adding, "Same with your nasal bones. But I would like to get an X-ray of your face and torso, just to be on the safe side."

"Okay." Evie did her best not to wince. "Whatever you think is best."

What was she supposed to say…no?

"I'll go check with the tech and make sure everything is ready to go, and then I'll come back here to get you." The other woman's brown gaze softened as she asked, "You okay sitting in here by yourself until I get back, or would you like for me to get someone to sit with you?"

Only if it's him.

"I'm good," she lied. "But thank you."

Billings gave a gentle nod and smiled. "I'll be back in few minutes. If you need anything before then, just pick up that phone there"—she pointed to a phone mounted on the wall to Evie's left—"and someone will be in here asap."

"Okay." Evie nodded. "Thank you."

"Just hang tight. I'll be right back."

Minutes later, the other woman returned as promised. Another hour and a half after that, Evie was showered, dressed in a pair of United States Navy sweats and matching crewneck, a brand-new bra, pair of underwear, socks, and her dust-covered boots.

She watched as the petty officer made her way across the room to the door. She swung it open but stopped short of shutting it completely behind her. Evie could hear her speaking to someone and assumed it was one of her fellow sailors.

When the door opened fully once again, it wasn't Billings' face she saw. It was—

"Beckett?"

Her heart gave a hard thud as a rush of heat began a slow

crawl up the back of her neck. Even to her own ears, his name had sounded all breathy and wistful. As if his presence was the one thing she'd been missing.

Is that such a bad thing?

"Hey." He stepped further into the room. Shoving his hands into the pockets of his BDUs, he stopped a few feet from where she sat. "How are you feeling?"

"Better." *Now that you're here.* "I'm just waiting on Petty Officer Billings to come back with my paperwork. But everything came back clear, so that's good."

"No broken ribs?"

"Not even cracked." Evie absentmindedly brought her right hand to her left side. "Who knew bruised ribs could hurt so bad?"

In a move that made her grin, Beckett raised his hand high in the air.

"Been there, done that." He huffed out a breathy chuckle. "A few times, actually."

An awkward silence passed between them. Fearing he'd leave if she didn't come up with *something* to say, Evie glanced around the room, desperate for a topic of conversation.

She spotted the clothes she'd been wearing when Beckett and his team had rescued her. Folded neatly on the seat of a nearby plastic chair was the shirt he'd been nice enough to let her borrow.

In an effort to resume even a modicum of conversation, she practically blurted out, "Your shirt is over there." *Oh, how I wish I could keep it.* "Thanks again for letting me use it."

"No problem." His gaze—which she'd recently discovered was an alluring dark brown—remained on hers. "You look good."

Her bark of laughter filled the air around them. "It's okay, Beckett. I've seen myself in the mirror, and *good* isn't exactly the word I'd use to describe...this." She waved a hand down the length of her own body.

His voice seemed to drop a full octave when he asked, "And how exactly would you describe yourself?"

"Uh...a mess." She chuckled incredulously. "Even with the days' worth of dirt and grime washed away, I'm still covered in bruises; my bottom lip is swollen, and I'm—"

"Beautiful."

Evie started to laugh at the ridiculous claim but then clamped her mouth closed when she realized he was being serious.

You heard him wrong.

That had to be it. It was the only logical explanation. She'd misunderstood what he'd said, and her hormone-driven mind had twisted his words into something they weren't.

She wasn't beautiful. Definitely not East Hamptons beautiful.

And definitely not while currently sporting a black eye, bruised jaw, and split lip on a face free of makeup and hair lying in limp, damp curls.

Evie knew she wasn't ugly, but she'd heard far too many comments over the years not to be fully aware of the way she looked to others...

Her face was too round, her dimples too deep, and her nose turned up at the end. She could still see the kids at school poking fun by pushing their own noses up, while running around the playground snorting like pigs.

In contrast to her olive skin, feminine curves, and thick brunette curls, almost all the girls she'd grown up with had been tall and thin with long blonde hair, high cheekbones, and perfectly straight noses. To be fair, most of those cheeks and noses had been paid for via their daddies' credit cards. And the blonde in their hair had only been the absolute perfect shade because it had come from a bottle.

But none of that mattered. Not when it came to kids. Especially not when dealing with a bunch of rich, spoiled teenagers.

Evie watched Beckett closely, awaiting his reaction to her blatantly honest self-assessment. She expected him to smile or give a little chuckle. Maybe even laugh at her silly, sarcastic remark regarding her current state.

But he didn't do any of those things.

What Beckett did do was slide his hands from his pockets and begin walking toward her. No, *stalking* was more like it.

She watched, the breath in her lungs becoming more and more frozen with each booted step he took. The expression on his chiseled, ruggedly handsome face was so intense it made her pulse race. And by the time Beckett came to a stop—mere inches away—Evie was pretty sure she'd completely lost the ability to breathe.

"Did you hear what I said, Evelynn?"

His voice…the use of her full name…the look in his enchanting eyes… All those things and more left her stuttering over her own words.

"I-I heard you, but…"

He moved in even closer, his gaze turning dark and fiery as he slowly lifted a hand toward her face. "There's no 'but' sweetheart," Beckett rumbled the low drawl. "I know beautiful when I see it. And mess or not"—he carefully tucked some wayward curls behind her ear—"you're right there at the top."

Evie stifled a gasp, her lower belly tingling from the electricity arching wildly within his touch. A rush of shivers raced down the length of her spine, and her heart kicked inside her chest with such force it felt as if it were trying to fight its way out.

"Thank you," she somehow managed to whisper back. "That's…really sweet of you to say."

The sweetest thing anyone's ever said to me, actually.

"They're not just words, Evie." Beckett gave a curt shake of his head. "I wouldn't insult you by blowin' smoke up your ass."

For some reason, that made her smile. "I appreciate that." She reflexively leaned into his touch.

Evie was surprised by how natural the intimate moment felt, given they'd only just met. Yet, somehow, being with him like this—him invading her personal space while cupping her cheek in such a warm, caring way—simply felt…

Right.

"Thanks for getting me and the girls out of that place," she offered for what felt like the millionth time. "If you and your team hadn't shown up when you did…" Her voice cracked with an unexpected jolt of emotion, preventing the formation of the remainder of what she'd been trying to say.

But Beckett understood, regardless. Like everything else with this man, he seemed to know exactly what she was thinking… and what she'd been feeling.

"You never have to thank me for that," he nearly growled. "I'm just sorry we couldn't get to you sooner."

"You got there." Her lids fluttered against a well of unshed tears as he began feathering his thumb across her uninjured cheek. "That's all that matters."

She looked up at him. He stared down at her. His heated gaze fell to her slightly parted lips as he leaned in closer. And then—

The door behind him opened wide as Petty Officer Billings entered the room with purpose. "Okay, Miss Mitchell. I have your discharge papers ready, and you're free to…oh! I'm so sorry. I didn't realize you still had company. I can come back if I'm interrupting."

Yes, please! Come back later. Much, much later.

But even as the thought crossed through Evie's mind, Beckett had already dropped his hand and was taking a giant step back.

"I-It's okay." She rushed to be the one to say it. "We were just—"

"Talking," Beckett finished for her.

Talking. Right. Nothing more…nothing less.

"Yeah. Beckett and his team were the ones who rescued me and my students," Evie explained needlessly. "He just came by to see how I was doing."

"That's very nice of you." Billings approached Beckett with a smile and an outstretched hand. "I'd like to extend my thanks for what you and your team did, as well. Doing this job…I've seen far too many situations like these end in tragedy. And with the military spread as thin as it is these days…let's just say, they need all the help they can get."

"Happy to help." Beckett shook the other woman's hand.

"Did I hear you're a Marine?"

"Yes, Ma'am."

"Well, thank you for your years of service."

"Likewise." He dipped his chin with a polite smile.

Evie's gaze dropped to their joined hands, and there was no denying the jealousy seeping into her veins. It was so stupid. Asinine, really. She held no claim on Beckett. They'd known each other what...like half a day's time?

But there was no mistaking the relief she felt the second Beckett released his grip and let his hand drop back to his side.

You're the one who needs to get a grip, girlie. It's not like you're ever going to see him after this.

The silent point was driven home when Beckett reached into his back pocket and pulled out what appeared to be a business card.

"My team's been called out to another job." He started back toward her. "I was hoping we'd be able to fly you home ourselves, but unfortunately, we have to leave." He glanced down at his watch and cursed under his breath. "Actually, I'm late to catch the chopper. But here." Beckett handed her the card. Glancing back at Billings, he dropped his voice, presumably to avoid being overheard. "My personal cell is on the back. You need anything...even if it's just to talk...feel free to text or call it anytime. If I'm available, I'll respond or pick up. If not, I'll get back with you as soon as I can."

Evie took the card, doing her best not to react when their fingertips brushed against one another's. "Thank you," she offered softly, never planning to call.

The last thing a guy like him needed was for a woman he'd once rescued to bug him after the fact.

"I don't give that number to just anyone," Beckett added. "And for what it's worth, I really hope to hear from you again soon. Even if it's just to let me know how you're doing."

Oh wow. Okay. So she wasn't quite sure what to do with that other than to say—

"Okay."

"You take care of yourself, darlin'." That bearded mouth of his lifted, sending her heart into a frenzy. "Talk soon, yeah?"

"Yeah." Evie nodded.

They shared a look that made her want to beg him to stay, but then she watched as Beckett "Bones" Stone turned around and walked toward the door.

Seconds later, he was gone, and Evie was still sitting on that exam table, wondering where she was supposed to go from there.

CHAPTER FIVE

Three weeks later...

"NICE SHOT." Beckett used the scope mounted on his rifle to study Digger's target. "Remind me not to get on your bad side."

"You're up."

He nearly smiled at his teammate's short, grumbled response. A man of few words, Dig was quite the enigma. The former SEAL hardly ever showed any emotion, and on the rare occasions that he did, it was almost always because he was pissed.

Beckett brought his own target into view. With the center of the paper silhouette balanced within his crosshairs, he released a slow and steady exhale. He pulled the trigger halfway through and...

Shit.

"That's three you've missed today," Digger was quick to point out. "Something going on?"

His gut tightened as he glanced over at his teammate, whose focus was on reloading the M4A1 Carbine assault rifle held securely in his hands.

"Like what?" Beckett asked, sounding far too innocent even to himself.

"You tell me."

"Nothin' to tell." He tried swallowing down the lie.

What was he supposed to do...tell Dig the truth? Admit that he was so completely and totally hung up on a woman he hadn't seen since their team had rescued her weeks earlier?

He couldn't do that. Because the truth was, he was distracted in a huge fucking way.

Of all his teammates, Digger would most likely be the least understanding in this particular situation. Hell, the man never even *dated* as far as Beckett knew.

How the hell could a guy like that get what it was like to be so overwhelmingly distracted by a woman he'd lost the ability to hit a damn target? The answer was, he couldn't.

So, no. Beckett would *not* tell Dig that his aim was off because he couldn't stop thinking about a woman he had no right to obsess over. There'd be no point.

Can't expect anyone else to understand this shit if you can't figure it out for yourself.

As if by design, Evie's smiling face invaded Beckett's mind. Just as it had since he first saw her picture during the team's initial briefing. Like it did every time he closed his damn eyes.

It had been three weeks since he'd left her on that ship, and he hadn't stopped thinking about her since. He even caught himself checking his phone multiple times a day in hopes that she'd finally sent him a text. Every time the thing rang, his heart filled with hope that it would be her on the other end of the line.

And with each new day that passed, he wondered if that would finally be the day he figured out how to let go of the fantasy world he'd created. One where Evie showed up on his doorstep to reveal she was just as obsessed with him.

"Christ, man. Why don't you just call her already?"

Beckett was pulled back to reality by the deep timbre of Digger's voice, but it took a few additional seconds for the grumbled words to fully sink in.

"Call who?" he asked flippantly, shrugging one shoulder for good measure.

There. That sounded casual enough. Right?

His answer came when Digger carefully laid his rifle on the

shooting platform before him and turned his steely gray-blue gaze Beckett's way.

"Really?" The other man groused.

"What?"

Almost as if in disgust, Digger huffed out a breath and gave a curt shake of his head. "Just know, my ass gets shot up on an op because you can't hit your fucking target, I'm going to return the favor...tenfold."

If his ass gets shot up...

"Dude." Beckett lifted his hands in defense. "Not sure what the hell you're goin' on about, but the only asses gettin' shot up on one of our ops are those belongin' to the bad guys."

Digger ran a hand over his face, muttering something that sounded an awful lot like, "Swear to Christ" before his chiseled face twisted into a deep scowl. "Would you please, for one second, drop the innocent, southern-boy bullshit charm and just admit you're still hung up on Evelynn Mitchell?"

What the...

Beckett's brows turned inward, his denial automatic. "I haven't talked to Evie since we were flown from that ship." *And it's fucking killing me.* "And that was like, what...three weeks ago?"

But who was counting, right?

"That's my whole point." Digger's expression remained as apathetic as ever.

"There's a point to all this?" He chuckled. "'Cause I sure ain't seein' it."

"You need it spelled out for you, fine. Here it is." The former SEAL's gaze intensified, becoming locked with Beckett's as he growled out, "Call. Her."

Beckett blinked, taking a few seconds to appreciate the moment.

"Holy shit. Are you..." He rolled his lips inward and gave a slight tilt of his head. "Are you actually giving me advice on my love life?"

"Don't be an asshole," Digger snarled. "I'm trying to tell you to do whatever it is you've got to do to get your head out of your ass and back in the game."

"The hell you talkin' about, back in the game?"

"You haven't been one hundred percent in since we got back from the HR op in Afghanistan. Your head's so lost in the clouds half the time that you're about two seconds behind the rest of us. And in our line of work, every fucking second counts."

"Bullshit, I've been in the clouds."

"I'm not the one shoveling bullshit here, Bones." Digger seethed. "Brother, I've *seen* it. So have Falcon and Apollo."

"Seen what?"

The pissed off man began reciting his list.

"You're quiet, for one. Only talking when you're spoken to. You don't smile or even try to act like you're enjoying yourself anymore. I mean, Jesus, man. You've even quit with those annoying as fuck jokes of yours."

The longer he spoke, the angrier Digger sounded. By the time his rant was over, the guy's face had taken on a light shade of red.

Beckett didn't say anything at first. He just stood there, staring back at his friend.

They'd worked side-by-side during some dangerous as fuck situations. Had witnessed cold-blooded murder, devastation, and heartbreaking loss.

And in all that time, no matter how dark things had seemed, Beckett couldn't ever remember seeing this man express his emotions with any of the team. About anything.

At. All.

Between his years of service with the United States Marines, and his time spent working for Tac-Ops, there wasn't a lot left in this world that took Beckett by surprise. But that right there…

That shocked the hell out of him.

"I'm not sure what to do with that, to be honest." Beckett blinked a few times. "Unless…" One corner of his lip curled slightly. "Dig…is this your way of saying you miss my jokes?"

Dig didn't smile. He didn't laugh. And like he'd recently pointed out, he wasn't one to shovel out bullshit.

Without a word, Digger turned away and began gathering up his things. Beckett waited for the other man to grumble the remainder of his big-brotheresque speech. Or, at the very least, call him some sort of well-deserved expletive.

But what he didn't expect, what Beckett could never see coming, was the look of vulnerability on the guy's face when he turned to him once again.

"Call her. Don't call her. Doesn't change my life in any fucking way. Just know, when the day comes that you realize you've lost the one thing you want but can never have...I will look you square in the eyes, just like I am right now, and I will remind you of this moment."

"You mean the moment when you lectured me like I'm some damn kid?"

"No, Beckett." Dig's expression fell flat. "I'm going to remind you of the time I fucking told you so."

The other man turned away once again. And this time, he didn't look back.

Beckett didn't move. He didn't utter a single word. He just stood there, watching his teammate cross the graveled stretch toward where he'd parked his truck.

A full minute later, he was *still* standing there like an idiot, wondering what the ever-lovin' hell had just happened, when he remembered...Digger was his ride.

Well, fuck.

"Hey!" He kicked his own ass in gear and started grabbing his guns and ammo. "Wait up!"

In a rush of hurried movements, Beckett went to his designated shooting platform, holstered his pistol, and slung his rifle over his shoulder. With both hands filled with matching ammo boxes, he spun on his heels and walk-jogged to where Digger sat waiting.

A short stretch later, they were leaving what their boss referred to as his "farm". In reality, the expansive property bolstered 400 acres of secured land purchased exclusively for company use.

Well, almost exclusively.

Between the state-of-the-art fencing, home security systems, the outdoor shooting range, an impressive indoor range—complete with a simulator marksmanship training room, and an enormous underground shelter that could withstand a nuclear war—the place seriously had it all.

Through the passenger sideview mirror, Beckett watched the property's massive plantation-style home grow smaller with every turn of Digger's tires. He nearly smiled to himself as he thought of their boss's choice to refurbish the place rather than tear it down.

Impressive in size, the centuries-old home was a classic white, showcasing several tall, thick pillars along the length of a wrap-around porch. About a billion windows could be seen throughout, each one framed with the traditional black shutters.

As they passed through the security gate at the end of the drive, Beckett imagined what the house had been like in the past. Whether it had been filled with love and laughter...or loneliness and pain.

Square footage doesn't make a place lonely, Beck. It's the lack of company within its walls.

The first ten minutes of the drive back to Charlotte were filled with a thick, awkward-as-hell silence. As he stared out the window at the rural scenery blurring past, Beckett realized he'd all but lost the torturous inner fight to keep his mouth shut until he was home.

With the proverbial white flag waving high in the air, he turned his attention to the man behind the wheel and begrudgingly admitted, "You're right, okay? Are you happy?"

"Do I look fucking happy?"

A quick glance showed Digger's fists were both white knuckled as he kept his shaded gaze locked on the road ahead.

Definitely not happy.

"I can't call her, Dig," Beckett muttered low. "Evie, I mean. I never..." He shook his head and turned away, pissed as hell at himself. "I never got her new number. I only gave her mine."

During the team's after-action debriefing upon returning to the States, he'd read over Evie's classified statement. In it, she mentioned how the men who'd taken her had destroyed her phone. According to the transcript, the agent questioning her at the time suggested she change her service provider and number, just as an added precaution.

Having picked up Evie's penchant for following directions, she'd presumably changed the number weeks earlier.

"I thought we were past the bullshit," Digger grumbled. "You know all you'd have to do is ask, and Shadow would have the woman's number for you in a handful of seconds."

"Okay, fine." He blew out a breath. "You want the truth? Here it is. I gave Evie my number three weeks ago, and she hasn't texted or tried to call even once."

"So?"

Beckett frowned. "So...if she wanted to talk to me, she would've reached out by now."

And damn if that annoying little fact didn't burn his ass far more than it should.

"Maybe she's been waiting for *you* to make the first move."

"Kind of hard to do if I don't have her number."

"Call Shadow right now and ask for it."

"I can't."

"Why the fuck not?"

"She was a hostage, Dig," Beckett practically yelled. "The woman was held captive in that fucking cave by those sadistic assholes who thought it was perfectly acceptable to beat her, starve her, and treat her and those little girls worse than fucking dogs. I'm sure the last thing she wants is to talk to a guy who's a constant reminder of the worst experience of her life."

The truck's interior grew quiet as they covered another half mile of pavement. When Digger decided to resume speaking, the former SEAL surprised the hell out of Beckett yet again.

"Do you like this woman, yes or no?"

"I barely know her."

"Not what I asked."

The man was like a dog with a freaking bone. "Sure. Yes. I like her."

"Then you should tell her."

"It's not that simple."

"Actually, it is." Digger waited a beat. "The phone number, the fact that she was a hostage, or even that it was our team who rescued her...those are all just a bunch of excuses. The truth is, you're scared of being rejected, so you're choosing to reject the notion altogether. But I'm telling you, if you don't at least try, you'll regret it for the rest of your life."

Beckett studied his friend closely. There was an unmoving expression spread across Dig's masculine, scruff-covered face. His taut, sinewy forearms shifted with the slight twists and turns of the wheel. And the man's gray-blue eyes stared through the lenses of his tactical shades.

From the outside, the guy looked like the same crabby-assed Digger he and the others knew and loved. But for the first time since knowing the surly bastard, Beckett began to realize there was much more beneath his friend's cold and calculated exterior.

There's a story there, somewhere. And one of these days, I'm going to pry it free.

"You don't think Owens will be pissed if he finds out I used company resources for personal business?"

"Another excuse." Digger turned his disappointed stare Beckett's way. "Seriously, Bones. Do you not remember Falcon and Apollo both going apeshit and doing whatever they could to find their women when they were in trouble?"

"Well, yeah, but that was different. Both Avery and Nicki had gotten snatched up again. Of course, Boss is going to let us use whatever means necessary to rescue the innocent. I mean, it's kind of what we do. But Evie hasn't been kidnapped again, so this would purely be me wanting to contact her for my own personal interest."

"Don't be a smartass, and who the fuck cares? So you want to check up on a woman you rescued. Make sure she's doing okay after having the shit scared straight out of her. You really think Owens will have a problem with that?"

The man had a point. And the more he talked, the more Beckett began to really listen.

"So it'd just be like a follow-up call," he mused. "Good customer service."

"Exactly. Besides..." Digger flipped his blinker, checked the rearview, and quickly changed lanes to take the next exit. "What's the worst that could happen?"

Uh...she could start laughing hysterically before telling me to kick rocks.

Or Dig could be on to something.

"Maybe you're right."

"I know I'm right."

"And so modest, too." Beckett joked. "But just out of curiosity, what's your take in all this?"

"My take?"

"Yeah, you know. Why the hell do you even care?"

"I don't," Digger growled.

His lips curved as he stared across the truck's broad center console at the former SEAL. With a semi-serious tone, Beckett asked his friend, "Now, who's shovelin' bullshit?"

The same thinly veiled vulnerability seemed to fall over Dig as he said, "I'd just hate to see you always wishing you'd tried, that's all." A beat later, that same veil lifted, and the old Digger returned with a gruffly added, "And I'm getting damn tired of worrying about getting a bullet in my ass because you're off somewhere thinking of her."

Well, shit. What he *thought* would be a day of shooting targets and talking guns had turned into a bizarre—yet surprisingly encouraging—dose of romantic advice from the last man on the team Beckett ever would've expected.

And now he had a choice. Continue pining away for a woman who may have already forgotten all about him or...

Call her.

Maybe Digger really was right on this front. And maybe, just *maybe*, when Evie hears his voice again...she'll be happy to hear it.

CHAPTER SIX

Later that same night...

"OKAY, so be honest. Does this dress make my ass look big?"

Evie rolled her eyes with a chuckle and smiled at the woman filling her computer's screen. "You look amazing, Lo." She gave her best friend's fashion choice an honest review. "As always."

The two women had been friends since attending the same college orientation course their freshman year at Columbia University. Right away, Evie had appreciated Lo's down-to-earth vibe. She'd also recognized how, despite the other woman's wealthy upbringing—which practically mirrored her own—the sweet and sassy Lo acted as much like a regular Joe as anyone Evie had met since.

And she hadn't lied when she told her friend she looked amazing. Even from this side of her laptop's screen, it was plain to see the little black, strapless dress Lo had purchased for an upcoming date hugged the woman's toned curves with perfection.

It didn't hurt that the garment's hem stopped a few inches above the knees, perfectly showcasing Lo's long, former-model legs.

Subconsciously, Evie glanced down at her shorter, curvier

legs, which were currently outstretched atop Lo's plush white comforter. With her laptop balanced on her jammie-clad thighs, she wondered not for the first time what it would be like to be five-ten rather than only reaching her God-given height of five-five.

"That's what you always say." Lo's long, wavy blonde hair swayed across the woman's bare shoulders as she spun back around to face her computer's camera.

Evie simply grinned as she responded with, "That's because you always look amazing."

"Whatever. Honestly, I don't even know why I'm putting so much effort into this date. It's not like anything will come of it."

"You don't know that."

"Uh…yeah. Actually, I do."

Evie's head tilted slightly to the side as she pretended to reach deep inside her memory bank. "That's odd. I don't remember seeing 'psychic' listed on your website bio. And I'm pretty sure I'm the one who proofed it for you, so…"

"Hardy har har." Lo rolled her pretty blue eyes. "Seriously, Eves. This is such a waste of time. I'm only going to be in town for a couple more weeks. After that, I'll be back home to, hopefully, hang out with you before you have to go back to Portsmouth. So it's not like there's even enough time to get to *know* the guy, let alone try to start something serious."

"Who says it has to be serious?"

"Plus, there's the whole long-distance thing," Lo continued as if Evie hadn't spoken. "Which, as you know, I've never been a fan of. And then there's—" She cut herself short before releasing a fairly loud sigh. Lo's gorgeous face filled the computer's small screen as she reached for her previously propped-up phone. "God, I'm such a shit friend."

The unexpected comment sent Evie laughing. "You're not a shit anything, Lo." *Far from it.* "Where the heck did that come from, anyway?"

"We've been on the phone for like twenty minutes, and I've been whining this whole time about going on a date with the hottest guy I've met in like…forever. Meanwhile, you're stuck watching my place, twelve hours from your own home, and you have nothing but my plants to keep you company."

"Well, first of all, you can always whine to me about anything. You know that. Second, the whole point of my *offering* to house-sit for you while you're gone was so that I *could* be away from home for a bit."

"I guess so." However, Lo didn't sound convinced. "I still don't get why you wanted to stay at my place in Charlotte after having already been out of the country for two months. Speaking of which, did you ever find out why they cut your teaching program over there short?"

Shards of guilt assaulted her in droves, and Evie's chest tightened from the knowledge of the lie. She hadn't told Lo anything about what had happened in Afghanistan, but that was because she'd been...*encouraged*...to sign an NDA, or Non-Disclosure Agreement, upon returning to U.S. soil.

Apparently, the U.S. Government wanted to keep Tac-Ops' rescue mission top-secret. At first, Evie had been completely thrown by the suggestion that the team responsible for the save be kept quiet from everyone. Including her best friend. But after hearing Homeland Security's explanation for the secrecy, she better understood...

Tensions between the Taliban and the United States are already at an all-time high, Miss Mitchell. If those currently holding power over the citizens of Afghanistan were to discover we sent Americans into their country, and those Americans caused the deaths of their members —regardless of their extreme beliefs and actions—they could see it as permission to retaliate in an even larger fashion. And by signing this, you'll also be protecting the identities of the men who saved you and those little girls.

Evie probably would have agreed to the NDA even without the bureaucratic explanation because that's what her government had asked her to do. After all, going down in infamy as the woman who started World War III wasn't exactly on the list of things she hoped to accomplish in life.

But it was that last part of the Homeland agent's speech that had put her hand in motion. The minute that guy began talking about why it was safer for Beckett and his teammates if she never mentioned their existence or the "incident", as he'd referred to the kidnapping, Evie had already begun signing her name.

Beckett had literally risked his life to rescue her and the girls. Same with Digger, Apollo, and Falcon. So if keeping her mouth shut about them and their heroic actions would help to ensure *their* safety, then that was exactly what Evie would do.

Even if it meant lying to the only real friend—the only *family* —she had left.

"Budget cuts," she forced out the untrue words.

"That sucks."

"Yeah, maybe. But I was okay with coming home when we did. It was just such a different world over there." She kept her additional comments vague. "I don't know. I guess it was just a much bigger culture shock than I expected. And going from rooms with dirt floors and wearing a burka every time I went out into public back to having all the luxuries of home..."

When Evie's voice trailed, Lo astutely pointed out, "But you have those same luxuries at my condo, right? So, what's the difference?"

Her gut tightened as she attempted to defend what she'd hoped was a plausible excuse for having yet to return to her own apartment in Rhode Island or, God forbid, her father's home.

"I know it doesn't make much sense, but I just wasn't quite ready to return to my normal life." She used air quotes for added effect. "Not to mention, the teacher who's subleasing my studio will still be there for weeks, so I wouldn't be able to stay there, anyway." Not unless she kicked the other gal out early, which wasn't something Evie would even consider doing. "This way, you can rest assured that your plants will all be lush and green and still living when you get back."

With a soft chuckle, Lo thankfully seemed to take the lame excuse at face value. "Well, thanks, but I can't promise I'll be able to *keep* them alive after you leave." She twisted her face into a humorous look of discouragement. "I really do appreciate you watching over things for me while I'm gone, though. It's a great neighborhood, and nothing bad ever happens there. But I still feel better knowing it's not just sitting dark and empty and ready for the taking."

"I totally get it." The tension in her shoulders started to ease. "Now. Back to this date…"

Lo groaned, falling dramatically back onto her bed. *"Fiiiine…"* She drew out the word. "I'll go. But if I fall totally and completely in love with this man just to have to leave him behind when I come back in two weeks, you're on the hook for the obligatory ice cream and wine."

"Deal," Evie agreed with a laugh. "What time is this mystery date picking you up?"

"He's not." Lo pushed herself back up into a sitting position. "I'm meeting him at the restaurant in…" She gasped when she saw the time on her watch. "Shit. I have to go. I'm supposed to meet him in less than an hour, and I still have to do my makeup and hair."

"So you'll be fashionably late. I hear that's making a comeback."

An unladylike snort rose from Lo's throat as she jumped up from the bed and rushed into the attached guest bathroom. "Thanks again for keeping an eye on things while I'm away. And…" Her friend stopped what she was doing to focus solely on the screen. "It wouldn't hurt you to get out there, too, you know?"

Evie's brows bunched together with confusion. "Get out there?"

"You know…date."

"I date," she countered defensively.

You're getting pretty good at stretching the truth, eh, Eves?

"When was the last time you went out with a guy?"

"It's not as easy for me as it is you," Her defenses remained engaged. "You work for yourself, so you can set your own schedule. It's kind of hard to meet someone when I spend all my days at school and my evenings grading papers or making lesson plans."

It sounded like a plausible enough excuse for not putting herself *out there*. Lo, however, wasn't buying it.

"This is me you're talking to remember?" Her friend's expression went totally deadpan. "I know for a fact you could very easily carve out a couple of hours a week to go out and do something fun. Or better yet..." A corner of Lo's full lips curved upward. "You could go out and do some*one* fun."

"Lo!"

"I'm serious. I bet you haven't even slept with anyone since Preston."

Now it was Evie's turn to let her face fall dramatically flat. "I thought we agreed never to speak of him again."

"Sorry, sweetie." Lo brushed her broken promise away. "We're in desperate times, here, and that calls for desperate measures." The other woman gave a slight pause and then, "Look, Eves. I know that whole thing with...*He Who I Shall Not Name*...ended badly, but dumping his pretentious ass was the best decision you ever made."

"You'll get no argument from me on that front."

"That being said, you dumped him because you wanted better for yourself, right? That's what you told me, anyway. You said you wanted more out of life than some hoity-toity husband dragging you off to the same kind of fancy-ass parties our parents always forced us to attend."

"Your point?"

"My *point* is, you'll never find more if you don't look. And... now, I mean this with nothing but love, but...I'm pretty sure you weren't going to find your happily ever after in some desert village that's halfway around the world."

The comment hit her square in the gut, and it took every-thing Evie had not to outwardly react. Lo had been less than thrilled about Evie's decision to go to Afghanistan, and now she understood why.

Not only was her friend worried about the obvious risks to an American woman traveling to that part of the world, but apparently, Lo was also convinced the trip had been a way for Evie to avoid facing her newly single status.

Well...is she wrong?

Regardless, Evie insisted, "I didn't go to Afghanistan because I was running from something. I went because I believed in the cause and thought I could help."

And yeah, okay. So maybe she was also hoping to find some sort of clarity on where the rest of her life was headed.

Instead, I almost ended up dead.

"If you say so." Lo didn't sound convinced. "As I was saying, this is the perfect time to go out and try something new. In fact..." Her friend cleared her throat and changed her tone to one far more formal and pretended to straighten a necktie that didn't exist. "I hereby challenge you to go on at least one date before I get back into town."

"What?" Evie stared back at her friend as if the other woman had lost her damn mind. "That's in like two weeks, Lo. You can't seriously expect me to meet a single, non-creepy, self-sufficient, halfway-decent-looking guy *and* go on a date with him that quickly."

If I was tall, blonde, and supermodel gorgeous like you, maybe. But not this chick.

"Oh, come on, sweetie. It's not like it has to lead to anything serious. Hell, you could even start the whole thing off by letting him know up front that you're not looking for strings. It could at least get you over that dreaded rebound hump. And then maybe, after a few good, sweaty rolls in the hay with some massively hot stranger, you'll be ready for something a little more serious when you *do* meet a man you really like."

Evie couldn't help but laugh at the "roll in the hay" bit. But on the inside, her heart ached with the urge to tell her friend the truth...

That she'd already met someone she was interested in, and he was tall, dark, muscular, and sexy as sin. Yes, the man she was thinking of—the man she *always* thought about—was the epitome of strength and masculinity.

A true hero in every sense of the word.

But she couldn't tell Lo about Beckett "Bones" Stone. She couldn't tell...anyone.

Right on cue, Beckett's handsome face suddenly filled her vision. It was the same face that had occupied her thoughts to the point of distraction ever since she'd last seen him.

The car. The kitchen. The shower... It didn't matter where she was or what she was doing. Out of nowhere, a barrage of questions would hit without warning. And Evie was defenseless against them.

Where is he?
What's he doing?
Is he okay?
Is he on another rescue mission?
Is he in danger?
Does he already have a woman he loves?

Not a single day had gone by since they'd parted ways that she hadn't found herself thinking about the man who'd saved her life. Not a single night had passed when he hadn't been present in her dreams.

The man gave you his number. You could just shoot him a text. Or, you know...call him.

"I'll think about it," she spoke to both her inner self and to Lo. "In the meantime, have fun tonight, and be careful. Oh, and promise to tell your sister I said hi."

"Okay, I will, and I promise." Lo grinned. "Don't worry. I'll call you tomorrow to share all the deets."

"Not sure I want to know *all* the deets." Evie chuckled. "Just kidding. I can't wait to hear how your first official blind date went."

A stretch of silence passed before the other woman asked, "Seriously, Eves. Are you doing okay? You seem...I don't know... different somehow."

"I'm good." The positive response was automatic. "Just tired."

Though she looked like she wanted to say more on the subject, Lo ended the conversation with a soft, "Love ya, sweetie."

"Love you back."

The two shared a parting smile before Evie reached up and pushed her laptop closed. Letting her head fall back against Lo's cushioned headboard, she closed her eyes and blew out a long, slow exhale.

She really hated having to lie to her best friend. Or anyone, for that matter. Aside from the nightmares she still suffered on a nightly basis, that had been the worst part of the whole ordeal.

Now, more than ever before, Evie needed to talk. She was still trying to process what had happened and working to make sense of everything.

Deep down, she knew she probably never would. Not fully, anyway. But it sure would be nice to be at least able to talk through some things with someone who'd understand.

Her lids lifted, and she glanced at where her purse hung from a decorative wall hook near the door. She thought about the small, rectangular business card still tucked safely away inside. Thought about the number that had been hand-scribbled in black ink on the back.

Evie recalled the moment Beckett had handed her that card, and then she thought about what he'd said…

My personal cell is on the back. You need anything…even if it's just to talk…feel free to text or call it anytime.

She could still hear the deep rumble of his voice. Could still feel the tingling in her lower belly the arousing sound had created.

I don't give that number to just anyone. And for what it's worth, I really hope to hear from you again soon. Even if it's just to let me know how you're doing.

At first, she'd been incredibly flattered by the gesture. After all, there'd been a moment there—right before Petty Officer Billings had walked back into the exam room—when she was almost certain he'd been about to kiss her.

You take care of yourself, darlin'. Talk soon, yeah?

Those were the last things he'd said to her, and then…he was gone.

At the time, Evie had fully intended to text him when she returned to the States. Just to let him know she'd made it back into the country safely and that she was doing okay. But then she remembered those bastards had purposely crushed her phone, and she'd been forced to leave it behind when she was taken.

The more time that passed, the more Evie became convinced that she'd imagined the heat in Beckett's eyes and the electricity that had arched from his soft, sweet touch. Soon, the fear of rejection had become so real she decided it was best to put it all behind her—including him.

If that's really true, why do you still have his card?

Evie glanced at her purse again. It was just a text, right? There wasn't anything scary about one of those. It would just be a few simple, typed-out words to let Beckett know she was still alive.

There was no harm in that, right? No suggestion of expectations or anything remotely romantic. Just a simple, purely platonic-intended text.

She could practically hear Lo's voice in her head now...

Come on, Eves. What's the worst that could happen?

What was the worst, indeed?

Before she could change her mind, Evie set her computer on the mattress beside her and swung her legs over the edge. She stood, her bare feet sinking into the room's plush white carpet as she marched toward her hanging purse.

Once there, she unzipped the brown leather crossbody, stuck her hand inside one of the bag's interior pockets, and found the card right where she'd left it. Purse forgotten, Evie flipped the card over on her way back to what was her bed for the next couple of weeks.

When she settled back in, with her back against the headboard like before, she reached for her new cell phone resting on the nightstand to her right. Nerves danced in her belly as her thumb brushed lightly across the penned digits.

It's just a text. A simple, friendly, no hidden-meaning text.

Evie drew in a deep breath, filling her lungs to their capacity before exhaling the steeling breath and tapping her phone's slick screen. She brought up the messages app and began entering the number as it was written on the card.

Her right foot bounced anxiously as it lay over her left ankle, and Evie's lower lip became trapped between her front teeth. She stared at the empty space and the blinking cursor, trying to figure out exactly what she should say. After a few seconds of thought and another forced breath, she brought both thumbs to the screen and began typing out the message...

Hey, Beckett. It's Evie Mitchell. I was just sitting here, thinking about you and—

No. That sounded far too personal.

Evie deleted the last chunk of words and started that part over.

I know it's been a bit, but I thought I'd let you know I'm still alive and kicking. Hope all is well with you and the team. Thanks again for all you did.

She read over the message as a whole, double-checking for any typos or parts that required revision. Deciding it sounded perfectly friendly and not at all like how she felt—like a desperate woman in lust with a man she barely knew—Evie threw caution to the wind and hit "send."

And then...she waited.

At first, she kept sitting there, staring at the phone as if she could mentally force him to respond. When the waiting became too nerve-wracking, she set the phone down and went into the bathroom.

Evie began her nightly routine of washing her face and applying her preferred skincare. She'd showered earlier, so she'd already changed into her PJs. But then Lo had called, so she'd put off the rest, and since there wasn't anything else to do at the moment...

She grabbed her toothbrush and the tube of toothpaste and proceeded to brush her teeth with vigor. Once that task was completed, Evie glanced around the room, tidying up whatever messes she'd made before turning off the light and walking back into the other room.

When she was halfway between the bathroom and the bed, Evie heard the telltale dinging coming from her phone.

A new text.

Recognizing the notification as the receipt of an incoming

text, Evie picked up the pace and hurried to where she'd left her phone. She stopped short of reaching for it, hating how badly she wanted it to be him.

It's probably just Lo.

The new mantra was her lame attempt to avoid getting her hopes up. But when Evie finally picked up the phone and looked at who the new message was from, her heart nearly leaped into her throat.

It's him! He wrote back!

Despite her thirty-one years, Evie felt like a teenager experiencing her first major crush. Her heart was racing, her palms felt sweaty, and a million butterflies danced wildly in her belly.

Unable to wait, she opened the message and began to read what Beckett had sent…

Hey, Evie! Good to hear from u! How r u? Bet ur glad to be home.

Her lips spread into an instant smile. The teacher in her rarely allowed for slang spellings or improper grammar. Occupational hazard and all that. But for some reason, seeing it come from Beckett made her smile grow even wider.

Definitely.

She hit send. Belatedly, she expanded her response with a quickly typed out…

Technically, I haven't actually been home yet. I flew a bit south instead. I'm house-sitting for a friend.

Three little dots appeared inside the tiny bubble at the bottom of the feed. They moved in waves, letting Evie know Beckett was typing back.

Really? Figured u would go straight to ur dad's.

Evie's thumbs hovered over the screen as her mind raced to create a valid reason to explain why she hadn't. Something other than the heartbreaking truth.

He's out of town on business.

She quickly deleted that and started over.

He's out of the country on business.

Before she could convince herself otherwise, Evie sent the bold faced lie to Beckett, praying he didn't press the topic further.

Those three little dots appeared once more. Seconds later, his return text came through.

This place ur house sitting. Anyone else there with u?

It wasn't the question she'd expected, but he hadn't asked anything else about her dad, so Evie took it as a win and started to type.

Nope. It's just me. Safe neighborhood, though. Quiet, well-kept, and virtually no crime.

He wrote back almost immediately.

Good deal. But still be careful, ok?

Evie's heart melted just a little.

I will. Don't worry.

More dots appeared, but then they vanished. A breath later, they were back, as if he'd started to type something out again. And again, they disappeared.

The pattern repeated itself twice more before another text finally came through.

Where in the south?

Evie frowned.

Huh?

Beckett immediately wrote back…

U said south. What city?

Which city. Right. Of course, that's what he'd meant.

Charlotte.

Evie sent the text and waited.

At first, there was nothing. No bubble. No typed words. But then those three little dots reappeared, and after what felt like an excruciatingly long wait, Beckett finally sent another message.

Can I call?

The breath in her lungs ceased to exist, and her eyes remained glued to the screen. He wanted to *call* her?

Her pulse spiked, and her stomach twisted itself into knots.

Evie was torn between elation and trepidation. For weeks, she'd wanted nothing more than to hear that deep, masculine, slightly southern voice. But in order for that to happen, she'd have to actually talk back.

The nerves firing deep inside left her momentarily frozen.

Apparently Beckett grew tired of waiting, because her phone notified her once again of a new incoming message.

U still there?

The question kickstarted her brain back into motion. With her thumbs moving rapidly across the screen, Evie quickly typed out her response.

Sorry. Still here. And yes, you can call.

She hit send and blew out a breath, letting her back fall against the soft headboard mounted to the wall behind her. There. It was done. Now there was nothing left to do but—

Her phone began to ring. The sound seemed much louder than normal, making her jump as the default tone echoed off Lo's bedroom walls.

She pulled in a deep breath to calm her erratic nerves and then…she answered the call.

"Hello?" Her greeting was soft and a bit unsure.

"Well, hello to you, too."

Evie's eyes fell shut, and she reveled in the man's drawled greeting. God, it was good to hear his voice again.

It was as deep and rumbly as she remembered. Like a gentle balm to her restless soul, just hearing him again immediately putting her more at ease.

"H-How…" Her words became stuck, and she was forced to clear the sudden dryness from her throat and tried again. "How have you b—"

"Are you really in Charlotte?"

The unexpected question took her by surprise. "Uh…yeah. It's where my friend lives. The one I'm house-sitting for. Why?"

There was a noticeable pause, and for a moment, Evie thought maybe the call had been lost. But just as she was about to pull the phone away to see if that was the case, she heard—

"Because, darlin'. I'm in Charlotte, too."

CHAPTER SEVEN

The next afternoon...

BECKETT CHECKED his watch for the third time in as many minutes. He was early, and Evie had promised she'd be here. So why the hell was he obsessed with watching the time?

Could it be you're afraid she won't show?

The thought may have crossed his mind a time or two. Or twenty. But Evie didn't strike him as the type of woman to stand someone up.

There's a first time for everything.

Wanting to kick his inner thought's imaginary ass, Beckett took a drink of his water just to give himself something to do. Damn, he needed to relax. It was just lunch, for Christ's sake.

Even so, he hadn't been this nervous in forever. And it wasn't even a date. Just two people taking time out of their day to reconnect, share a meal, and hopefully get to know each other a little bit better.

Pretty sure that constitutes a first date, dumbass.

No, it constituted him getting the chance to see Evie with his own eyes and verifying himself, she really was doing okay. And yeah. Maybe a part of him was curious to see if the undeniable connection he'd been obsessing over since Afghanistan actually existed or whether it was a figment of his hormone-driven imagination.

The minutes ticked by, and the longer he sat and waited, the more convinced he became that this was all a huge mistake. He never should've listened to Digger. What had he been thinking, taking romantic advice from a guy like that?

Falcon, sure. Apollo, no problem. But those two had already found the loves of their lives. But Dig? That man wouldn't know love if it kicked him square in the—

A flash of red caught his attention from one corner of his eye. Turning his focus to the source, Beckett was instantly thrown into a parallel universe. One where everyone and everything suddenly ceased to exist. Everyone except...

Evie.

Dressed in a long, flowy, belted red dress and matching fedora, the woman literally took his breath away. And the closer she got to where he was sitting, the clearer Beckett's answer to his earlier question became.

Oh, yeah. Definitely still there.

He shot to his feet, nearly toppling over his chair in the process. After repositioning it to ensure it wouldn't fall, he stepped around the table's edge to greet her.

"Aren't you a sight for sore eyes." He flashed her a grin and raised his arms out to his sides, offering her a friendly hug.

Evie approached him with the same dimple-dipping smile he'd longed to see. "Hi, Beckett." She went willingly into his arms. "It's great to see you again."

Beckett closed his eyes and savored the moment, subtly inhaling her intoxicating scent. She smelled of warm vanilla with a hint of strawberries, making him wonder if she tasted just as sweet. And it was in that moment when Beckett knew...

I'm in deep, deep trouble.

"You, too, darlin'. You look...amazing." He gave another small squeeze before begrudgingly letting her go.

"Thank you." A light hue of pink filled her porcelain cheeks as Evie tucked a few curls behind her ear. "So do you."

She moved toward the empty seat across from his, but

Beckett beat her to the punch. Pulling it out for her—as any true gentleman would—he waited for her to sit before gently aiding in her efforts to scoot closer to the table.

"Thank you," she offered again, taking her hat off her head and setting it in the empty chair to her left.

As he walked back to his seat, Beckett noticed Evie lightly running a hand through her brunette strands. His fingers itched with the urge to reach out and do the same. Instead, he sat across from her, adjusting his chair before resting his forearms on the table's edge.

"This is so surreal." Evie stared back at him with an almost awe-like expression. "I can't believe you live here."

"I still can't believe *you're* here. I mean...what are the odds, right?"

About a billion to one, if I had to take a guess.

"I know." Her thick curls feathered across her shoulders with a gentle shake of her head.

With the rest of the restaurant almost completely tuned out, Beckett began the conversation he'd rehearsed endlessly in his mind ever since she agreed to meet him for lunch.

"You said you're here for a couple more weeks?"

"Yep." Those dimples caved in a smidge more. "My friend Lo...short for Lauren...is spending some time with her sister in Michigan. Since my place is still being subleased for another few weeks, I offered to house-sit for Lo while she's gone. And thanks to online banking and shopping, I was able to replace my phone, and debit and credit cards, fairly quickly. I also ordered a few things I was forced to abandon overseas. Clothes, toiletries...that sort of thing."

"So you're doing okay, then? There's nothing you need while you're in town?"

Name it, and it's yours.

"Nope." She shook her head. "I'm good. Well...better, anyway."

Beckett's lips parted with the intention of asking why she hadn't chosen to stay with her father. But their server picked that exact same time to approach the table, so he clamped his mouth shut and decided to wait.

"Hi, I'm Adam." The twenty-something man smiled down at Evie. "Can I bring you something to drink?"

"Water's fine, thank you." She grinned. But almost as quickly, she said, "Actually...can you please change that to a Diet Pepsi, instead?" To Beckett, she added a quieter, "I'm feeling like having some bubbles."

Damn, if she isn't the cutest thing I've ever seen.

"Sure thing. Are you two ready to order, as well, or do you need more time to look over the menu?"

"Oh, um..." Evie glanced across the table at him and back to Adam. "If you could give us a couple more minutes, that would be great."

"No problem. I'll be right back with that Diet Pepsi."

"Thank you."

The young man gave them a nod before turning and walking away.

"I guess I should figure out what I'm going to eat." Evie picked up the laminated menu that had been placed nearest her. "I've never eaten here, so I have no idea what's good."

"Everything."

She glanced up at him and blinked. "Everything?"

"There's a reason I suggested this place. The guys and I come here all the time. I've literally had just about everything they offer, and I've never been steered wrong."

"Hmm..." She took a moment to peruse the items listed. "The lasagna sounds good, but I'm thinking that might be a bit too heavy for lunch. I think I'll go with the grilled chicken panini and a small Tuscan salad."

"I've had the panini." Beckett nodded in approval. "Good choice."

"What are you getting?"

"My go-to is their meatball sub and parmesan-parsley fries. But make sure you save room for dessert," he suggested. "You gotta try the chocolate cake."

Evie set her menu to the side and grinned. "Chocolate cake is my favorite."

A girl after my own heart.

"So." Beckett attempted to resume their earlier conversation. "You said you flew straight here after—"

"Here ya go." Adam returned with Evie's drink. He set the glass of bubbling Diet Pepsi on a round, thin coaster. "Did you have enough time to look at your options, or…"

"I think we're ready," Beckett informed him.

Ready for you to skedaddle so I can finish a fucking thought.

"Great." The young man pulled a small order pad and pen from the small, pocketed apron tied around his waist. After taking their orders, he promised it wouldn't be long for the food to arrive before turning and leaving again.

Evie took a sip from her straw before carefully setting the glass back onto the provided coaster. "Sorry. You were saying?"

You're perfect in every way, and I want to marry you and have babies with you and—

Beckett put a fist to his mouth before coughing the ridiculous thoughts away. "Excuse me." He coughed again for good measure. "What was I saying? Oh, yeah. I know you said someone else is staying at your place, but what about your dad?"

Evie's expression remained frozen in place, her voice a bit too casual when she asked, "What about him?"

There it is again.

He'd damn near convinced himself he'd imagined her strange reaction when he'd brought up her father the night of the rescue. Now he had no doubt.

She'd gone from acting perfectly normal to wearing that same almost forced expression of casual coolness. And both times he'd noticed the change was when Beckett mentioned her dad.

Something was definitely up there, and he felt compelled to uncover the truth.

"Have you even *seen* your dad since you got back?"

Evie's fake-as-hell smile began to falter. "I told you. He was… out of the country."

"On business."

She gave a jerky nod but said nothing.

Oh, sweetheart. Don't you know you can't bullshit a bullshitter?

Beckett leaned forward, resting his upper body on his forearms once again. Fixing his empathetic gaze with hers, he prayed she could see his only intention was to do what he could to help.

"Look, I...I know it's none of my business, and you are certainly within your rights to tell me to kick rocks, but..."

"But?" Evie prompted, taking advantage of his momentary hesitation.

"You and your dad. Are there problems there?"

Her flawless skin seemed to pale before his very eyes. She glanced away, just for a moment, and when her gorgeous hazel gaze returned to his, he could've sworn they showed evidence of a touch of unshed tears.

"My father is a very busy man. I mean, he runs a multibillion-dollar corporation, so there's always some sort of important meeting or—"

"Not askin' about his job, darlin'. I was askin' about how things were between the two of you."

Evie's full, ruby lips parted as if she were about to speak. But then she closed her mouth and looked down at her hands, which had become balled together on the table before her.

Way to go, dipshit. Now look what you've done.

"I'm sorry," Beckett apologized. "Your relationship with your father is none of my business, and I never should have—"

"I'm the one who owes you an apology," Evie whispered, focusing on her fidgeting hands.

"You?" He frowned. "What the hell do you have to apologize for?"

"I um..." She brought her saddened eyes back up to his. "I lied."

She'd what?

"Lied to who, sweetheart? Me?"

"You. Your team." A quick lick of her lips. "Homeland Security."

Okay, now *that* definitely got his attention.

"What did you lie about?" When she remained silent, he reached across the small table and covered her hands with one of his. "It's okay, Evie. Whatever it is, you can tell me." Then, because he needed to be absolutely sure she knew it, Beckett added a soft, "You can *trust* me."

So many thoughts raced through his mind as he sat there, waiting for her to reveal whatever had her feeling so obviously ashamed. Endless scenarios involving the men who'd taken her captive began to play like a bunch of sick, twisted movie clips in his mind.

Them beating on her.

Interrogating her.

Doing things to her no man ever had the right to do.

Ah, hell.

Was that it? Had she been sexually assaulted and was too afraid or ashamed to let anyone know?

You were talking about her dad, nimrod. Not the men who took her. Whatever this is, it has to do with him.

"My dad isn't out of the country on business." She finally came clean. "At least, I don't think he is."

"Okay…" Beckett studied her closely. "Why did you feel you had to say that he was?"

"Because it's easier than admitting the truth."

"Which is?"

"Those men who took me and my students…" Evie kept her voice soft and low, presumably so only he could hear. "They did put out a ransom demand."

Beckett's muscles tensed with the unexpected revelation, but he did his best not to react in a way that was noticeable. "How can you be so sure?"

"The second day I was there, they took me to another room, away from the girls. There was a small desk, and the only things on top were a small piece of paper and a pen. They forced me to sit and write down my father's personal cell phone number."

The fuck?

"Did they call it?"

Her head bobbed with another jerky nod. "After I was taken back to the room."

Beckett took a beat to pause, knowing he'd need to tread very lightly. She was finally starting to open up to him. To reveal potentially serious and vital intel about a Tac-Ops mission. The last thing he wanted to do was shut her down by saying the wrong thing.

"Did you hear the phone call?"

"Not that one." She shook her head, pulling her bottom lip between her teeth.

"That one?" He frowned. "But you did hear *a* conversation between the men who took you and your father?"

"I'm not explaining this very well." Evie blew out a breath and sat back in her chair. When she did, her hands slipped free from where they'd been held beneath his. "About an hour before your team showed up, I was taken away from the girls and into a different room. Not the one with the desk. This one was further down the tunnels. Anyway, the man shoved me inside, then he hit me." Her hand absentmindedly went to her unblemished jaw.

Flames of anger ignited within him, sending both of Beckett's fists into tight, white-knuckled balls. "Then what?" He purposely kept his tone rock steady.

"He started yelling at me, claiming the number I'd given them was wrong."

"Was it?"

It wouldn't have been the worst move if she were trying to buy herself some time.

"It was my father's number," she insisted. "That man...he started to hit me again, but I finally convinced him to let me make the call. I thought..." Her voice cracked. "I thought maybe if my dad heard my voice, then he'd know the situation was real. That it wasn't some sort of scam, and the girls and I really were in danger."

"That was smart." Damn smart.

But from the look on Evie's face, her idea must not have gone as planned.

"The man handed me his satellite phone, and I dialed the number. At first, I didn't think my father was going to pick up. But then…he did."

Once again, Beckett had to call upon his training not to react to the what-the-fuck bomb she'd just dropped. He knew for a *fact* someone from Homeland had been in contact with her father post-rescue. Hell, he'd read the classified—and appropriately redacted—report himself.

Including the sworn statement from the agent who'd spoken directly to Phillip Mitchell…

Hostage A's father denied any knowledge of the abduction and/or subsequent rescue carried out by the unnamed tactical team.

Hostage A. That was the anonymous title assigned to Evie for the purpose of the official reports.

Beckett had read dozens just like it, but never before had the label ever angered him as it had with that one. The hostages discussed in those reports were human beings with lives and fears, and people who loved them. However, the powers that be reduced them down to little more than letters in the alphabet.

Evie's so much more than that.

"What did your father say when you told him about the ransom?"

Evie blinked, and this time, there was no mistaking the tears rushing to fill her eyes. "He said he didn't have a daughter and demanded we stop calling."

Beckett couldn't have been more shocked—or more enraged —than he was at that very moment.

"Are you fucking *kidding* me?" he seethed loudly. Several nearby customers immediately stopped their conversations and turned their way. Realizing he'd pretty much just blurted that shit out for all to hear, he leaned forward and reverted back to his calmer, more in-control self. "Sorry. You were saying?"

"That's it." A tiny shrug. "I told my dad what had happened and that those men were going to kill me and the girls if he didn't send the money, and he basically denied my existence altogether."

Mental note: Find Phillip Mitchell and beat his fucking ass.

"And after that?"

The devastation in her big, round eyes as they met his tore at his heart when she stared back at him. Evie released a humorless chuckle and sighed.

"After that, my father hung up."

So many curse words flew through Beckett's mind at once. The rage he felt toward Evie's piece of shit dad was unprecedented to the point of becoming downright murderous.

Alternate plan: Find Phillip Mitchell's selfish, money-lovin' ass and fucking kill him.

A memory shot to the forefront of his thoughts. One from when he, Digger, and Apollo had been escorting Evie away from the cave to their exfil spot.

"That's why you asked if your rescue had been government-sanctioned or private pay," he surmised.

She nodded, swiping angrily at a tear that had escaped. "When you said your team took on government and civilian contracts, I thought maybe that was why my father refused to pay. I thought…no, I'd *hoped* you were going to tell me my father had hired your team to find me, and *that's* why he'd said the things he had on the phone. Because he already knew I was being rescued, and he didn't want to play into the kidnappers' hands." Sadness filled her gorgeous stare. "Obviously, that wasn't the case."

"I'm so sorry." Beckett's heart broke for what that must've been like for her. "I see now why you didn't run straight to him when you got back to the States."

"Didn't see any point in going to him." She shrugged. "And the suckiest part is I can't even talk about it. Not the kidnapping. The rescue." Her mesmerizing eyes lifted back up to his. "You. I mean, Lo's really the only friend I have, but still. It's hard, you know?"

"I do." He nodded. "I'm guessing Homeland saddled you with an NDA?"

"They said it would protect me, as well as you and your team."

More like covering the government's bureaucratic asses, but whatever.

"Some government ops are like that," he shared. "A lot of them, actually."

"On the flip side, while it sucks not being able to talk about it with Lo, it's also been nice not having to worry about getting bombarded by the press. I've seen those kinds of stories and always felt so bad for those involved. Going through something like I did was bad enough. Having to rehash it for reporters every time you step out the door..." Evie's spine straightened a tad with a more confident shake of her head. "I'll pass."

The table grew quiet for a stretch before Beckett decided to risk asking another prying question.

"Your dad," he began. "Do you know why he would refuse to pay for your freedom?"

"Money." Her bitter response was instant. But then, "I should back up. My dad and I have never really been close. Actually, we're absolutely nothing alike. My mom, on the other hand..." Sadness filtered into her multi-hued gaze. "She did her best to be a good mother. But she died when I was young, and I'm an only child, so..." Evie sighed. "The fact of the matter is, I've never been what you'd call a Daddy's girl."

"Because of his job?"

"Partially. With my father, work always comes first. No, that's wrong," she quickly amended. "Money. *That's* what always comes first. Which is why he refused to pay the ten million for our release. But even with money aside, our personalities and interests have just never really aligned."

"Ten million?" Beckett considered this. "I gotta be honest, Evie. I've seen your father's financials. To a guy like him, ten mill is—"

"Less than the amount he spent on his last charity event," she finished for him. "Yeah. I know."

"Jesus." He fell back in his chair and ran a hand over his jaw. "I don't even know what to say."

What could he say?

Sorry your dad's a money-hungry douchebag who'd rather foot the bill for your funeral than keep you alive?

"It's okay, Beckett." She brushed his concern away. "I knew he was all but done with me when I went against his wishes and signed up for the trip to Afghanistan. I just have to face the fact that my father saw an opportunity to finally be rid of me, and he took it."

But why? Why, in God's name would a father do that to his only child?

Evie was obviously still dealing with the fallout of such a crushing blow, and it broke his heart to see. It was also clear that the woman was trying her damnedest to not only deal with all that she'd been through but also accept the severed relationship with her father and move on in her own way.

And for that, he couldn't be prouder.

Minutes later, their food was delivered hot and ready to eat. The pair spent the rest of their lunch in a carefully balanced dance of consuming their delicious lunch and changing the conversation to a more normal, casual tone.

Over the course of the meal, Beckett learned all about Evie's friend Lo and how the two had been best friends since college. Evie shared that Lo had started out as an education major but then switched to journalism and photography mid-semester of their junior year.

By the time dessert came, Evie insisted they talk more about him. Sensing she needed the focus to be off of her, Beckett gladly obliged.

Over a massive piece of shared chocolate cake, he told her a little about his parents, where he'd grown up, and even a couple short stories from his days with the Marines.

By the time the check came, he felt like he'd learned so much. And yet, at the same time, he was desperate to think of something else to discuss just so their time together wouldn't come to an end.

"That was amazing." Evie stepped past him as he held the door open on their way out of the restaurant. "And thanks, again. You didn't have to pay for my meal, too."

"You kiddin'?" Beckett followed her out onto the sidewalk. "My mom would have my hide if she heard I'd made you buy your own lunch."

Evie looked up at him with a beautifully wide smile and said, "It sounds like your mom did an excellent job raising you."

"Most days." He chuckled. "I mean...nobody's perfect, right?" Beckett sent her a quick wink and a grin.

"Well, I think you're pretty perfect." Evie's cheeks reddened with an obvious flush of embarrassment. "I, uh...I only meant that you're—"

"It's okay, darlin'." Beckett winked at her again. "I know what you meant."

The two shared a look, and if they'd been in private and not on a busy downtown street, he would've pulled her to him right then and there and kissed her to his heart's content.

But they *were* on a busy street, and he wasn't about to assume she'd be receptive to that sort of behavior. So, like the good southern boy he was, he offered to walk her to her car instead.

"Where'd you park?" Beckett asked. "I'm down the way a bit, but I'm happy to walk to wherever you're—"

"I didn't drive here," she announced as she pulled her phone from a pocket he hadn't realized her dress possessed. "I mean, I appreciate the offer, but I used one of those ride-share apps. So I can just—"

"I'm not walking off while you get into a car with a stranger."

When Evie's eyes jumped back up to his, Beckett realized how overbearing his declaration must've sounded. Clearing his throat, he quickly backtracked and tried again.

"What I meant to say, was that I'm happy to give you a ride to Lo's. But only if you're comfortable with that."

"You saved my life, Beckett. Of course, I'm comfortable with that. I just don't want to put you out, that's all."

In that case...

"You're not. I'm off today, remember?" He'd made sure to slip that little fact into the phone conversation they'd had the previous night. "So unless the team gets called in for an unexpected job, I've got time to give you a lift."

111

Evie studied him a moment before sliding her phone back into her dress pocket. Placing her cute as fuck hat back on her head, she motioned to where he'd indicated he'd parked. And with a smile on her face, she looked up at him and said, "Okay, then. Lead the way."

* * *

"WHAT THE FUCK do you mean you don't have the money?"

Beads of sweat formed on his nervous brow. He'd expected the man on the other end of the burner phone to be pissed. He'd even gone over the conversation in various forms multiple times in his head before making the dreaded call.

No amount of preparation, however, could truly prepare him for the gut-twisting fear churning deep within.

"I know we agreed on this week, but—"

"But nothing!" The powerful man's angry voice blasted through the phone's speakers. Several seconds passed, and when he spoke again, his tone was once again steady, to the point of nearly sounding calm. "You said this wouldn't be a problem. That you had a fool-proof way of getting the cash."

"And I will get you the cash. I just need a little more time."

The silence that stretched on put him even more on edge than he already was.

"You've had time. In fact, if memory serves, this is the second extension I've already allowed."

"Please." He sounded as desperate as he felt. "You have to understand. Ten million is a lot of money to move undetected."

"You said your plan would work, and quite frankly, I've grown tired of waiting."

"Everything was in place, and there was nothing to suggest things wouldn't go according to plan. I had no way of knowing they'd end up—" He caught himself in time to prevent revealing too much. "Look, I know this is less than ideal. Trust me, I was just as pissed as you are when I discovered there'd been a problem securing the funds. But I'm already looking into another avenue, and—"

"Another avenue, another excuse."

That churning in his stomach had turned to full-blown nausea. You didn't cross a man like the one on the other end of the line, and you damn sure didn't come between him and his money.

He'd just as soon kill you as wait another minute for his cash.

The thought wasn't one of exaggeration. It was a fact. Either he got this man his money, and soon, or his ass would be just as dead as those incompetent terrorists he'd hired.

"I've always come through for you in the past, haven't I?" His question was rhetorical.

"It's the only reason you're still breathing."

Breathing is definitely good.

"Okay, so I just need you to trust in the relationship we've built and consider my past performance as proof that I am a man of my word. Trust me, I *will* get you your money."

The sooner, the better.

"I don't trust anyone," the man nearly growled. "However, you have always done right by me in the past, so I will give you one last extension. Just know that if you fuck me over on this again, there will be no additional chances. And remember… I, too, am a man of my word."

Yes!

"Thank you!" He wanted to cry with relief. "You won't regret this. I promise."

The line remained silent, and it took him a moment to realize the other man had already ended the call. He blew out a breath and shut the burner phone as he rounded his large cherry mahogany desk.

Pulling out the bottom left drawer, he dug beneath the stack of folders and lifted the plywood panel designed to keep the small space hidden from view. He dropped the phone inside and replaced the drawer's false bottom, rearranging the file folders so they appeared to have been left undisturbed.

After shutting the drawer, he secured its lock with the small key attached to his personal keychain. He then slid the keys back into the pocket of his dress pants before returning to where he'd been standing at the front of his desk.

He stared down at the near-empty double old-fashioned glass he'd abandoned early into the call. Picking it up, he brought its smooth edge to his lips before tipping his head back and downing its remaining contents.

His legs trembled slightly as they carried him over to the impressive stone fireplace taking up much of his office's west wall. With the glass still in his hand, he lifted it out in front of him. Turning it slowly, he appreciated its intricate dips and grooves as the sun's natural light shone upon it from the room's floor-to-ceiling windows behind him.

Made of the finest Waterford crystal, the glass was like everything else he possessed. Expensive, high-end luxury that screamed *I have money*. And those with all the money, well...

We hold all the power.

Problem was he didn't have any money. Not really. Every cent he had belonged to someone else.

It was how the game was played, and he was perfectly fine with it. As long as the score remained in his favor, that is. And unless he came up with another way to get the ten million he owed, he'd lose everything he'd worked his entire life to achieve.

Who are you trying to kid? You don't find that son of a bitch's money, your ass will be dead.

In an explosion of maddening rage, he lifted the empty glass into the air and threw it as hard as he could into the fireplace's brick-lined firebox. Shards of crystal shattered on impact, scattered around the unlit logs and wrought iron grate.

Damn you, Evelynn. You were supposed to be my ticket out.

The beads of sweat returned as his mind raced to come up with another way to get the money. He had no idea where the spoiled bitch was or who had helped her escape. But it didn't matter.

He needed a new plan. A foolproof way that wouldn't end with a bullet in his head.

There wasn't time to reinvent the wheel, so he'd have to adjust his original plan. He'd have to kidnap Evelynn again. He'd found her once. He could do it again. And this time, he'd make sure she was kept in a place that was inescapable.

Once the ransom money was paid and he had the cash in hand, he'd dispose of Evelynn to avoid leaving behind a witness, pay off his debt, and then...

And then, I'll be home free.

CHAPTER EIGHT

Evie moved along the small walkway leading from Lo's paved driveway. The condo's entrance was sufficiently covered with a modest porch roof, and her friend had decorated the jutted space with a modern farmhouse feel.

The door was painted a dark hunter green, and a wooden sign that read *Welcome* sat balanced against the light gray siding nearby. Rested on the concrete below was an overflowing pot filled with gorgeous pink begonias, and to her right was a small accent table with a colorful mosaic top.

Evie's attention, however, wasn't really on her friend's decorative front stoop, but rather on the man who'd been sweet enough to walk her to the door.

Aside from the nightmares she'd come to expect, there had also been good dreams since returning to the States. Ones starring none other than her very own personal hero.

Hot. Passionate. Soul-enchanting dreams that had left her craving.

But as good as Evie's fantasies about Beckett were, the fictional images locked in her brain were nothing like the real-life man.

He'd been mouthwateringly handsome when dressed in head-to-toe camo and covered in military-grade gear. But put the tall, dark, and deadly man in a pair of well-worn jeans, a dark gray henley—that hugged his muscular upper body like a glove, no less—and a pair of brown lace-up boots lightly scratched and worn on the tips...

Holy mother of hotness.

She stopped and turned to face him, trying not to drool. "Thanks again for lunch. It was really great seeing you again."

So, so great.

"You, too," he replied with his usual male rumble.

God, she loved his voice.

"And thanks for the ride," she offered, not quite ready to say goodbye. "I really appreciate it."

"Any time. And I mean that," Beckett drawled. "You need anything while you're in town, I'm your man."

If only that were true.

Her inner thoughts—and overactive hormones—left her feeling flushed and a little out of sorts. When it came to the opposite sex, she wasn't typically one to flirt or show interest. Not until she'd at least been given a sign that the other person was interested in *her.*

So far, Beckett had been a perfect gentleman. Which was great, except...

I kind of wished he wasn't.

Oh, she appreciated the polite gestures like pulling out her chair at the restaurant or opening her car door. But sometimes, even *she* preferred a more take-charge attitude regarding her romantic interests.

And so far, Beckett had been completely and totally hands-off.

Maybe that's because he's not romantically interested in you.

A memory flashed even as the thought crossed through her muddled mind. She was back in the exam room on the ship. Beckett was standing before her, much like he was now. They were talking about her state of dishevelment, and then...

He said I was beautiful.

"Hey, about the thing with your dad..."

His trailed voice pulled her back into the present.

"It's okay, Beckett." She shook her inappropriate thoughts away while meeting his gaze. "I know what you're going to say."

"Yeah?" One corner of his kissable lips turned upward.

Evie nodded. "I know I need to just forget about him and move on with my life. And I will."

I hope.

"Actually…" He took a step closer, shoving his strong, masculine hands into the pockets of his jeans. "I was gonna say if you ever decide to confront the son of a bitch, I'd be happy to tag along." One of his broad shoulders lifted in a shrug. "Wouldn't mind lettin' him know what I think about what he did to you and the girls."

Part of her never wanted to see her father's face again. But the other part…

"I just want to ask him why, you know?" A ball of emotion grew thick at the base of her throat. "I want to look him square in the eyes and ask him why my life isn't worth him spending even a tiny portion of his precious money."

Something flashed behind Beckett's eyes. A hefty dose of anger was there, of that she was certain. But there was also something else. Something darker. Deeper.

And as he slid a hand from his pocket and placed his palm against her cheek, the source became suddenly clear…

Desire.

"You're worth it, darlin'." He inched even closer. "You're worth every fuckin' penny that man has, and don't you *ever* let him or anyone else make you think you're not."

The unexpected words drove the air straight from her lungs. No one had ever said anything like that to her before. Or about her, for that matter. And the fierceness in his tone—along with the sheer intensity in his unwavering stare—left her feeling more confused than ever before.

"I don't…" she began on a whisper. "I-I don't understand."

"What don't you understand?"

"You."

Beckett's dark brows dipped together in the center as one corner of his lips curved into a grin. "Me?"

Evie nodded. "We met once, nearly a month ago. In the middle of madness and chaos, no less. But then I see you again today, and we share one meal, and it's like…" A look of bewilderment fell over her. "It's almost as if I've known you—"

"Forever."

She nodded again, comforted by the knowledge that she wasn't alone. "You feel it, too," she boldly proclaimed, her gaze remaining fixed on his. "Don't you?"

Please don't let me be the only one.

Beckett's Adam's apple bobbed with an audible swallow as he stared down at her in an unbearable silence. For a long, torturous moment, she was convinced she'd made a terrible, humiliating mistake.

But then…

"Oh, I feel it, sweetheart." He leaned in, his lips coming within a hair's breadth of hers. "Question is, what do you want to do about it?"

Evie knew *exactly* what she wanted to do. And so…

She closed her eyes, rose up onto her tiptoes, and brought her mouth to his. She didn't have to go far, given he'd already filled her personal space. And when their lips met for the very first time, it was as if the stars aligned, and the angels began to sing.

Okay, so maybe there wasn't any actual singing, and the stars wouldn't shine for another few hours. But damn, if there wasn't *some* sort of profound shift in her existence. And when she got her first real taste of the man she'd fantasized about for weeks, Evie realized her world as she knew it would never be the same again.

Beckett deepened the kiss, his tongue sliding across the seam of her wanton mouth in a seductively enticing invitation she couldn't refuse. Her lips parted, their tongues met, and just like that…

Evie. Was. Lost.

He tasted of chocolate and sin, and as they stood kissing on the slight stoop for God and everyone else to see, she couldn't bring herself to care. Not about the cars driving past or any neighbors who may walk out their door at any moment.

Nothing else mattered aside from her...and him.

Beckett.

His name whispered through her mind as he held her body close. Her chest pressed against his, her hands clutching the thin shirt covering his broad, masculine shoulders. And when Beckett's movements slowed, and he began to pull away, it took everything in her power not to beg him to stay.

"Damn." He licked his lips, curling them into a crooked grin that made her heart race and her sex ache with need. "I know the gentlemanly thing to do would be to apologize for that."

"Why?" Evie challenged lightly. "Are you sorry you kissed me?"

Technically she'd made the first move, but Beckett had kissed her right back, so...

"Only if you are." The hypnotic rumble of his low voice captured her. "And to be perfectly honest..." He ran a hand over the dark stubble covering his jaw. "I'm not so sure I'd be sorry even then."

"Good." She smiled at the man's unabashed honesty. "I'm not, either."

If she hadn't been staring straight into his eyes, Evie would've missed the sliver of relief shining briefly behind his darkened gaze. But then another thought struck.

"I do have one question, though..."

"You can ask me anything you want, darlin'."

Oh, how she loved it when he called her that.

"I just thought...just in case, I figured I should make sure that you aren't..." *Good lord, Eves. Just ask the man already.* "You're not seeing anyone at the moment...are you?"

Please say no. Please say no. For the love of all that's holy, please say—

"No." Beckett put her out of her silent misery. "And just so you know, if I weren't single...that kiss never would've happened."

Meaning he wasn't the type of guy to cheat.

Good to know.

"I didn't think so," she responded honestly. "I guess I just needed to hear you say it."

Preston had cheated on her back when they'd been dating. More than once, actually. Something Evie had discovered in the last days of their so-called relationship.

In hindsight, it wasn't the cheating that had ended things between them as much as the fact that she'd never truly loved him. If she were being totally honest with herself, she wasn't so sure she ever really even *liked* him.

She'd tried, of course. Because that's what Mitchells did. They did what they were told...and what was best for the family name.

Even more importantly, she'd been raised to always think of the family—and its lucrative business—first, above all else. Including her own hopes and dreams.

My own happiness.

Since Preston's father was one of Mitchell-Granger's largest clients, Evie and Preston's coupling had resulted in a multi-million-dollar deal. One her father had immediately celebrated with two hundred of their closest family and friends.

Close, my ass. The man dropped twenty grand on a party to hobnob with the wealthiest and most influential names in East Hampton.

"Hey." Beckett lifted Evie's chin with the softest of touches. "Where'd you go just now?"

"Nowhere." She met his gaze once more. "I'm still right here." *With you.*

But he was already shaking his head. "Only way this works is if we're honest with one another." He brushed his thumb lightly across her skin.

"This?"

"Us."

Her heart thudded hard against her ribs. "There's an us?"

Oh, she really, *really* liked the sound of that.

"I think there could be." Beckett dipped his head in a barely-there nod. "A minute ago, you asked if I felt the same things you've been feeling. Now, unless I'm way off base with all this—

or you're hiding a secret boyfriend or husband I don't know about—I think that kiss just gave us both the answer we've been searching for."

Evie was beginning to think maybe *he* was what she'd been missing all along.

He was tough and gentle. Sweet and incredibly kind. And so very different than any other man she'd ever met.

Growing up, Evie had always assumed she'd end up with someone like Preston. Rich. Preppy. Well-connected within the circles of the elite.

Not because those things were what *she* deemed most important in a life-long mate. But because her father did.

For as long as she could remember—especially after her mother's passing—the one thing Evie had wanted most in the world had been her father's approval. Lucky for her, she'd eventually grown out of that fairytale stage.

She'd not only dumped the only man to have ever garnered her father's approval, but she'd also changed career paths to follow her true passion. And then...

Then she'd gone and gotten herself kidnapped in Afghanistan.

Despite the terror she'd been forced to endure when she'd been sitting in that carved-out prison cell—when the girls were asleep, and all she had to keep herself company were her thoughts—Evie had allowed herself to dream.

She'd imagined the life she'd been terrified of losing. The one she had yet to even have a chance to live.

And in those dreams, the kind of man she'd always imagined building a life with wasn't some privileged, silver-spoon brat who'd been handed everything to him on a silver platter.

He was warm and caring. Funny and kind. And rather than the skinny-jean metrosexual type who always seemed prevalent in her father's circles, the man of Evie's dreams was always muscular and manly. Masculine and strong.

Someone who could protect her from the evils of the world while also creating the kind of love and passion her heart and body craved. Someone just like...

Beckett.

"There's no husband." She finally found her voice again. "Or boyfriend, for that matter. And you're right. I think…" A quick, nervous lick of her lips. "There's definitely something between us. It's crazy, and I can't even begin to explain it, but—"

"But?"

"I'm only in town for a couple more weeks, Beckett."

"So?" He blew off her worry. "We make the most of our time together while we can."

"And after that?"

Beckett's dark, heated gaze remained fixed on hers as he sent her a smile that left her toes curling. "The after is up to you." His hand slid to cup one side of her face. "So what do ya say, darlin'? Wanna see where this thing takes us?"

Her belly tingled with anticipation.

"I do." Evie smiled up at him. "But…there's something I need to take care of first." Something she knew deep down she needed to face head-on, once and for all. "I need to see my father. I lied about him not being available earlier because I was too afraid to face the truth."

"But you're not anymore?"

"No." She shook her head. "At least, I don't think I am."

"What changed?"

You.

"What you said earlier. About confronting him?" She swallowed nervously. "I'm going to do it."

First chance I get.

Concern flittered behind Beckett's dark eyes. "Evie, I wasn't trying to push you into doing somethin' you're not ready to do. I only meant—"

"I know what you meant, and I promise you aren't pressuring me into anything. I just know I won't be able to focus on building a future for myself, let alone one that includes…anyone else." Her gaze bore into his. "Not until I face what happened head-on. And a big part of that…maybe even the *biggest* part…is getting answers from my father."

Answers she damn well deserved.

"Done." Beckett's response was instant. "Tell me when and where, and I'll be right by your side."

Evie's heart swelled, and her eyes burned with a rush of unshed tears. This man...this incredible, amazing man was offering to support her through what was sure to be an excruciatingly painful conversation with her father.

But as much as she loved the idea of Beckett being by her side—in more ways than one—this fight was one she needed to take on alone.

"I appreciate that, Beckett." Evie rested her palm against his chest. "More than you'll ever know. But I need to do this on my own."

"You sure?"

She nodded. "My relationship with my father was complicated long before Afghanistan. We have nothing in common, we rarely see eye-to-eye about, well, anything...we don't even look anything alike."

"You take after your mother."

"I've often wondered if that's why he resents me as much as he does."

"Because you're a constant reminder of what he lost?"

Another nod. "There are a lot of things I need to clear the air with as far as he's concerned. His source of contention toward me is one of them. And honestly, I'm not sure I'd be able to discuss everything as openly as I need to if you're there. I hope you can understand that."

"Of course, I understand." Beckett covered her hand with his and gave her a gentle squeeze. "I just hope *you* know I'm here. For whatever you need...whenever you're ready."

Evie felt absolutely awe-struck. There was no other way to describe it. This man...this honest-to-goodness American *hero*... was like a dream come true.

Is he? Too good to be true?

The intrusive thought was more than a little unsettling. But while the answer still remained to be seen, she chose not to borrow trouble.

She'd had more than her fair share of that lately, not to

mention her impending visit with her father. Plus, there was just something about Beckett. A deep-seated goodness that shined brightly within him.

And every instinct Evie had said this was a man she could unequivocally trust.

"Okay, so that's it," she announced. "I'm going to book a flight to East Hampton tomorrow. If my father truly wants me dead, he's going to have to tell me that to my face."

A set of lips she could still taste on her own curved upward with Beckett's slow-forming grin. "That's my girl."

His girl.

Boy, that sure had a nice ring to it.

CHAPTER NINE

Mitchell Estate
East Hampton

EVIE GAVE her driver a generous tip and sent him on his way. She took a moment to breathe in the fresh sea air before turning and facing what had once been her childhood home.

Only it had never felt like a home. Not a real one, anyway. Definitely not after her mother's untimely death.

She would've paid the ransom. She would have loved me enough to save me.

Regret momentarily flourished as Evie took those first tentative steps toward her family's estate. As she did, Beckett's voice rang clearly through her ears…

You're worth every fuckin' penny that man has, and don't you ever let him or anyone else make you think you're not.

Her father's actions—or lack thereof—had left her questioning that very thing. For weeks now, she'd sat at Lo's. Alone and soaked in tears and heartache, wishing with all she had that it was all some sort of horrible mistake.

Deep down, however, she knew the awful truth. And it was that truth that had brought her here today.

You came all this way. May as well get it over with.

The soles of her sandals slapped loudly against the paved circle drive. Evie cringed as she gazed up at the three-story monstrosity, wondering how anyone could consider making a place like this their home.

It was too big. Too pretentious. And far too cold to be cozy.

Evie liked cozy. Almost craved it, really. She had since she was a little girl.

When she'd envisioned her future, the one thing that remained consistent was her desire to establish roots in a place that felt warm and inviting. Like the way she'd felt while wrapped snuggly in Beckett's arms.

I want to be there again. I want to feel his warm embrace. I want to feel safe and protected and...loved.

It was far too soon to be having those kinds of thoughts. Especially for a man she barely knew. But Evie also understood the faster she got her ass inside and said her piece, the sooner she'd be back in Charlotte—back with *Beckett*—again.

She wasn't doing this for him, however. Coming here... finally facing her personal demons...

This is all for me.

Shoulders squared, Evie straightened her spine and picked up her pace. Taking the elaborate split staircase, the smooth, white stone steps carried her up to the structure's massive double doors.

She started to press the doorbell but stopped mid-reach. After a brief moment of careful consideration, she decided it best to keep with the element of surprise.

This was still her family's estate, after all. And as her father's sole heir...

Like it or not, this is your legacy, Eves. You have every right to be here.

Rather than announce her arrival, Evie used her key to unlock the secured door. After slipping her keys back into her purse, she drew in a steeling breath and pushed against the door on the right.

A blast of cool air struck her as she crossed the threshold of her childhood home, carrying with it the familiar scent of roses and lemons. The nauseating combination was derived from the ever-present array of fresh-cut flowers her father insisted be on constant display, combined with the very specific line of cleaning supplies he demanded his cleaning staff use.

It always comes down to money and appearances, Evelynn. In our world, that's all that matters.

Her father's words of so-called wisdom filled her ears as Evie studied the expansive, two-story foyer.

Large squares of polished white marble led guests to the home's grand staircase. With its ornate spindles and hand-carved mahogany railing, the design was in keeping with the exterior split stairs leading to the mansion's front doors.

Along with expensive paintings and a massive crystal chandelier hanging overhead, the curved staircase offered those who entered a glimpse into her father's luxurious taste. For Evie, however, the impressive showcase of wealth wasn't so much breathtaking as it was a stark reminder of her childhood.

One filled with hollow dreams and wishes that would never come true.

"Evelynn?" A voice sounded from Evie's left. "My goodness, is that really you?"

She turned her attention in that direction, her lips already lifting into an automatic—and genuine—smile. "Helen." Evie made her way to the woman who'd practically raised her. "It's so good to see you again."

Helen O'Brien had worked for the Mitchell family since before her grandfather's passing. Born to Irish immigrants—who'd also worked for Evie's family until they were too old to carry on with their duties—the sixty-two-year-old woman worked harder and with more pride than anyone Evie had ever known.

She felt herself being pulled into a giant bear hug.

"Oh, how I've missed seeing your smiling face around here." Helen's familiar accent was prominent and...oddly soothing. "But I thought you were over in that dreadful place for another week or so. Did they send you home early? Your father didn't mention you were coming home."

That's because he thinks I'm dead.

It took everything in Evie's power not to react. Clearly, her father hadn't mentioned the kidnapping or the ransom demand to his most trusted employee. But why would he?

If Helen ever found out what he did, she'd quit his selfish ass and never look back.

A sliver of vengeance began to weave its way through her veins, and though it went against her very nature, Evie couldn't deny the overwhelming temptation to tell Helen the truth. One simple story is all it would take, and her father's entire world would come crashing down around him.

Helen was the closest thing to a mother Evie had known after her real mother's untimely death. And if there was one thing she knew about Helen's fiery Irish spirit...

She'd always, *always* stood up for Evie. Like a mama bear protecting its cub.

NDA, remember? You tell her about Afghanistan, your world will be the one that crumbles.

Evie nearly groaned because her inner voice was right. There was a non-disclosure agreement in place. One that was signed, notarized, and stamped with the Homeland Security seal.

Rather than risk a hefty fine—or worse, a prison sentence—Evie looked down at the woman she'd entrusted to keep her deepest, darkest teenage secrets and did her best to keep the lies to a minimum.

"I *did* get back earlier than originally planned." A careful truth.

"And you came straight here," Helen assumed with a beaming smile. "You know, I have to admit...I feared the last time I saw you it would be for the very last time."

You have no idea.

"Why do you say that?" Evie's pulse raced a bit faster.

Helen didn't know about the refused ransom. She couldn't possibly—

"I heard you and your father going at it that day," the sweet woman admitted. "I assure you, I wasn't purposely eavesdropping. But your conversation grew quite loud toward the end, and I happened to be walking by his den."

"He didn't want me to go."

"Yes." Helen's thin lips curved into a knowing grin. "I gathered as much."

Memories from that day threatened to overwhelm her, but she pushed them aside and forged on. "Is he here?"

"Your father's in his den, dear."

Of course, he is.

Leaning in, Evie kissed the sweet woman on the cheek before pulling away. "It was great seeing you again, Helen."

"Will you be staying for dinner? I'd be happy to set out an extra plate for y—"

"I'm not staying." *Not a second longer than I have to.* "I just came to ask my father about something."

"Must be important for you to come all this way."

"It is." Evie nodded.

More important than you'll ever know.

"Well. It was such a nice surprise seeing you again." Helen pulled her back in for a parting hug. "If you change your mind about dinner, you know where to find me."

I won't.

"Thanks, Helen." Evie smiled fondly. "It was really good seeing you, too."

The other woman's gaze held steady as she took Evie's hands in hers. After a tense few seconds, Helen gave her a gentle, loving squeeze before turning around and walking away.

As far as reunions went, the moment was bittersweet. She loved the older woman and had always considered her family. But after decades spent as a trusted Mitchell family employee, she feared that if push came to shove, Helen would choose loyalty over love.

Which meant once again, Evie was on her own.

No time like the present.

She turned to her right and walked toward the open space beneath the elaborate staircase. If she continued going straight, the marbled path would have taken her through the Great

Room, past the professionally designed chef's kitchen, out the back doors, and onto the home's expansive covered porch.

Evie didn't go straight.

Once clear of the overhead walkway hovering up above, she took an immediate right. Her heart beat a little harder with every step she took as her trembling legs carried her down the long, narrow hallway.

Toward her father's office.

Toward the man who'd so easily been willing to let her die.

Her footfalls slowed as she approached her father's office door. It was shut, of course. He rarely left it open.

Evie considered knocking but decided against it. He didn't deserve the courtesy a knock would provide. After all, he'd afforded her far, far less.

Lifting her chin, she pushed back her shoulders and filled her lungs with a long, cleansing breath. She turned the knob on a slow exhale before pushing the door wide open.

Not bothering to look up from the papers in his hands, her father stated gruffly, "I thought I said there were to be no interruptions."

"You also said you didn't have a daughter." Evie shut the door behind her. "And yet, here I am."

His head shot up, his widened gaze giving away the man's obvious shock.

"E-Evelynn?"

She walked steadily toward the man who'd so grossly betrayed her. "Surprised to see me, Father?"

"You're..."

"Still alive?" Her lips curled into a smirk. "Very much so, no thanks to you."

According to the NDA she'd signed, discussing her kidnapping and subsequent rescue with anyone who wasn't already privy to the "incident" was strictly prohibited and punishable by the law.

The U.S. government may not be aware of her father's involvement—or rather, non-involvement—but he was very much aware of the danger she'd been in.

And the death sentence he'd personally delivered.

"I thought—"

"I was dead. Yeah, I get that." She casually plopped down in one of the two chairs facing her father's desk. "But as you can see, I'm not."

"I don't…" He shook his silver head. "I mean, I'm…"

"Speechless?" She settled back into her chair. "That's okay. I'll start. Which part would you like to hear first? Where the Taliban extremists barged into my classroom and forcibly took me and four young girls hostage? Or would you prefer to start with the cave we were imprisoned in for days with hardly any food or water?" The more she spoke, the louder her voice became. "Or maybe you'd like me to tell you about the time one of them beat me within a hair's breadth of unconsciousness because he believed you when you told him you didn't have a daughter!"

"Evelynn, please. I know what you must think, but—"

"What I think?" Her humorless laugh echoed off the room's stately wood-paneled walls. "What I *think* is that you're sitting there, going on about your day as if none of what I went through ever happened. As if you didn't receive a call weeks ago with a demand for money in exchange for my life and the lives of those four precious little girls."

She stood, placing her hands on his desk and locking her elbows as she leaned in closer. Rather than yell, Evie kept a tight leash on her overzealous vocal chords, dropping her tone to a deeper, deadlier level.

"And I think"—she continued—"your clients would be very interested in hearing about how the man to whom they've entrusted their entire life savings could be such a cold-hearted, uncaring *bastard* as to let your only child, along with four sweet, innocent little girls, die at the hands of those monsters. *That's* what I think."

The bluff was just that.

A bluff.

If she blew the whistle on her father's horrific act, he'd be eviscerated by the court of public opinion. His so-called friends would just as soon disavow him rather than be saddled with a scandal none of them could afford. Many of his clients would leave his firm to avoid being associated with such a public pariah.

As for his staff, that was tricky. Her father may be a ruthless son of a bitch, but he paid his staff well, and they knew it. They earned every penny, mind you. But they knew which side their bread was buttered.

And good luck finding a job when you worked for the guy who could've easily paid the ransom and been done but instead was willing to let his only daughter die.

But...thanks to the NDA, her threats were as empty as her father's love for her.

"How dare you." Her father stood as well. "You barge in here, unannounced, I might add, and you—"

"Are you kidding me right now?" Evie stared back at the man as if he'd lost his damn mind. "I was kidnapped, Dad! Those men...they took us against our will. They starved us, they hurt me..." Her voice cracked, but she cleared her throat and forced herself to continue, "I just want to know why, okay? Tell me why, and I'll walk out of this house and never bother you again."

"As I was trying to say before. I thought the phone call was a scam. A ruse to steal my money. It wouldn't be the first time someone attempted to rob me of what's rightfully mine."

"What's rightfully *ours*," she corrected. "Half of the estate is mine, remember? Also, I might buy the whole scam excuse if I hadn't spoken to you myself. I talked to you, Dad. *Me.* I begged you to send the money to save us, and you hung up on me as if I were nothing. As if the five of us were...nothing." A set of twin tears streaked down her flushed cheeks before she could stop them. "I told you *exactly* what would happen to us if you didn't pay, and yet, you still want to stand there and tell me you believed it was all a scam designed to steal your precious—"

The rest of Evie's words became lost in a startling realization. One that was almost as painful to accept as believing her father was fine letting her die.

"Oh, my god." She pushed herself off the desk and stood straight once more. "You thought it was me."

"Evelynn—"

"That's it, isn't it? You thought I set up the whole thing. That I orchestrated some big, elaborate kidnapping scheme to steal ten million dollars from you."

"I…" Her father began but paused before trying to explain himself. "If you'll recall, I warned you the last time you were here."

"You told me I was done." Evie stared back at a man she felt she barely knew. "That was your warning to me, right? You said if I went against your wishes and joined the semester-long program in Afghanistan I was done." Her heart began to shatter where she stood. "And you what…thought I went over there and decided to get *even* with you? You think I hired members of the Taliban to extort money from you, despite knowing my portion of Mom's inheritance will be mine in less than a year, anyway?"

According to her mother's will, half the value of her life insurance policy would go to Evie on her thirty-second birthday. The other half had already been awarded to her father years before, shortly after her mother's death.

"I think I've explained myself quite enough." Her father rounded his desk and came to where she stood. "As for your threat to air our dirty laundry to my friends and clients…I'd tread very carefully if I were you."

"Or what?" She arched a defiant brow. "You'll abandon me to die? Oh, wait. I believe that box has already been checked off your to-do list."

Evie had never been so utterly spiteful with her father…or anyone else, for that matter. But the longer she stood there listening to him brush away what he'd done as if it were nothing —as if *she* was nothing—the more she questioned how they could even be related.

"You've always had such a smart mouth."

"And you've always been a heartless jerk."

Her father raised a hand as if to strike her, but Evie was ready. On reflex, she grabbed his wrist, stopping him mid-swing.

I've had enough of men thinking they can manhandle me into submission.

"Do it," she challenged. "I'll have you arrested so fast, your head will still be spinning when they take you into booking."

Evie shoved his arm away and took a cautionary step back. Her chest heaved, and her heart felt like a sledgehammer pounding against her ribs.

For all his faults, her father had never laid a hand on her in anger. Not even once that she could remember. But now…

His face turned red, and the vein in his forehead seemed to bulge with fury. Rather than cowering beneath the weight of her most recent statement, her father appeared to bolster his emotions into barely controlled anger.

"You think you can come into my office…into *my* home…and disrespect me like this? You think you can *threaten* me?"

"I think I've more than earned the right to know how you could so easily let me die."

"The only thing you've earned, young lady, is an invitation to leave."

"I'm not a young lady. I'm an adult," Evie seethed. "And I'll leave when I have an answer. A *real* answer. Not some bullshit excuse about a contrived scam that makes absolutely no sense."

"I've said my piece on the matter, and I have nothing more to add." He turned away with the clear intent of returning to his seat.

Refusing to be so easily dismissed, Evie made a tsk sound with her tongue and gave her head a disappointing shake.

"You know, Dad…you've been a lot of things over the years. Serious. Driven. Ruthless. Absent. But a coward?" She stared straight at him. "I have to admit, I never saw that one coming."

"How dare you—"

"You know, this is the first time since Mom died that I'm glad she isn't here. Because if she were…if she could see the kind of father you turned out to be…" A huff of a humorless chuckle escaped. "She'd be so ashamed."

Her father's gray-blue gaze became enflamed with fury. He stormed across the room to one of three mahogany file cabinets.

Evie watched as he unlocked the top drawer and began skimming through the folders inside.

"You still think your mother was so perfect?" His movements were rough. Angry. "What am I saying? Of course, you do. But that's only because she never told you the truth."

"Wow." Evie crossed her arms at her chest. "Typical Mitchell patriarch fashion. I point out your shortcomings, and you start trying to turn the conversation around to the only parent who ever seemed to care about me. A woman who isn't even here to *defend* herself."

"Your mother wasn't as perfect as she led you to believe." Her father yanked a folder free and slammed the cabinet drawer shut. "Not even close."

He tossed the folder down onto the desk. It slid to a stop directly in front of where Evie was standing.

"Go ahead." The infuriated man motioned for her to pick it up. "See for yourself."

CHAPTER TEN

Uncertainty caused Evie to hesitate to do as directed and open the folder. Whatever was inside couldn't be good—not if her father saw it as ammunition against her own mother.

But if there was one thing she'd learned in recent weeks, it was that she was a hell of a lot stronger than even she gave herself credit for.

You survived being held captive by monsters. Surely, you can handle whatever he thinks he has in his corner.

Evie opened the folder and looked inside. At first, she wasn't sure what she was seeing. But then...

"These are DNA test results." She glanced back at the top of the page and frowned. "From thirty years ago."

Her stomach churned with dread as her father began to explain.

"You'd just turned two. You had a head full of short, dark curls, and your eyes were too big for your face. In fact..." He shoved his hands into his dress pants pockets. "The only real noticeable difference between pictures of your mother at that same age and you are those dimples of yours."

My dimples?

"I don't understand." Evie stared back at him. "What does any of this have to do with—"

"Your mother didn't have dimples. No one in her family did.

Obviously, I don't possess that particular trait, nor does anyone I know from the Mitchell side."

When he didn't continue, she exhaled impatiently and started to close the folder. "I'm not sure what it is you're rambling about, or what point it is you think you're making, but—"

"Those men who took you." Her father slowly brought himself closer. "They called and demanded I buy my daughter's freedom."

"And you lied," she bit back. "They told you they would kill me...I told you they were going to kill me...and you *lied* and said you didn't have a daughter."

"See, that's where you're wrong." He removed his hands from his pockets and shook his head slowly. "I spoke the truth."

Her father had gone mad. That was the only explanation for his confusing rant. Of course, he'd lied. And how he could stand here and even attempt to say otherwise—

Evie glanced back down at the decades-old DNA test. Studying it closely, she took the time to read the details she'd previously ignored.

According to the report, the primary sample tested had come from her biological father. And the name listed by the results from the sample that had been tested...

It can't be true. It can't—

Her eyes flew back up to a man who, up until two seconds ago, she'd believed was her father. The paper held tightly in her hands suggested otherwise.

"You're lying."

"No." His unwavering stare became void of emotion. "I'm not. The proof is right there in your hands." He motioned to the printed test results. "The percentage of DNA you and I share is—"

"Zero," Evie whispered, shocked to her very core. "How is this...if this is true...if you really aren't my biological father, then...w-who is?"

"A man named Denny Prescott. He and your mother were

high school sweethearts. They dated through most of college, too. Until I came into the picture."

"You broke them up?"

"Your *mother* broke them up. She finally came to her senses and realized they never should have been together in the first place. Everyone knew it. Her parents. Mine. We all knew I was better suited for your mother than Prescott."

"Why do you say that?"

"He was a scholarship student, for one." Her father—or whoever he was—said this as if it were the ultimate sin. "He had no money. No chance of a real future. Not the kind of future a woman like your mother deserved."

Evie was starting to understand. Denny Prescott didn't come from a wealthy family, therefore he wasn't worthy.

Typical East Hamptons attitude.

"So you what...swooped in and saved Mom from a life of despair?" Her sarcasm was more than a little obvious.

"I saved her from a life that would have been mediocre, at best. And I didn't want that for her."

"Let me guess, because you loved her." Evie's comment came out as a sarcastic quip, rather than a question.

"You're damn right I loved her!" He took a storming step toward her. "Don't you get it? Your mother was my everything. My *everything!* And when she told me she was pregnant with you, I was over the moon with joy. I took time off of work and was at every single doctor's appointment...and the day I saw you for the very first time on that ultrasound screen, I thought, 'My god. My life is perfect'. Only it wasn't perfect. It was all a façade. A joke created by your lying, cheating mother, and I..." Real emotion seemed to thicken her father's throat. "I was the goddamn punchline."

"You're saying Mom cheated on you with this Denny Prescott guy?"

"She swore it was a one-time thing. A moment of weakness that just happened to result in your conception."

"You think it was more than that." Evie effortlessly surmised.

"You think they'd been seeing each other behind your back for a while."

"Wrong again, dear daughter." His last word was an apparent dig. "I don't think they ever *stopped* seeing one another."

The room began to spin, and it was becoming harder and harder to breathe. Feeling sick to the point of nearly vomiting, she was forced to support herself with a hand on the edge of her father's desk.

Except he wasn't her father. A man named Denny Prescott was her father. The proof was clutched tightly in her white-knuckled fist.

Her mother had lied to her. The basis for Evie's entire *existence* had been one giant lie.

It was no wonder the man standing before her never acted the way a father should. All those years of him being disinterested and distant. The times she'd tried over and over to gain even a fraction of his attention. Or a sliver of his love.

He hadn't dismissed her because she'd been born a girl rather than a boy. She couldn't even blame his presumed disdain on the stresses of his job or that maybe he hadn't wanted children to begin with.

Phillip Mitchell was many things, but even she had to admit he was no liar. Sure, he'd initially tried excusing his claims of not having a daughter as his belief her call from the cave had been a scam. But now Evie understood why.

He'd been protecting her from the truth. Or, more accurately, he'd been trying to protect himself...and the Mitchell family name.

"That's why you never said anything." She glanced back up at her father. No...at *Phillip.* "You never told me the truth about this...about us...because it would sully your precious reputation."

"It also would have sullied your *mother's* reputation." A hint of real emotion flared behind his otherwise cold eyes.

"Did you ever tell her you knew?"

"I confronted her with that same piece of paper the day I got the results."

"And?"

"And we both agreed it was in all our best interests to keep the truth a secret."

"From me?"

"From everyone."

Everyone...

"Does that mean Denny Prescott has no idea I'm his daughter?"

The man had the right to know he had a child.

"Prescott is dead." He blurted out the news. "Car accident. It happened before you were ever born."

And the hits just keep coming.

"If Denny died before I was born, how can you be so sure he was my biological father?"

"There's something else in that folder. A photograph in the very back."

Evie's hands trembled as she reached inside the folder. As promised, she found a picture. And when she studied the frozen image, any doubt that Phillip was telling her the truth vanished in an instant.

The photo showed a woman and a man. They were standing on the beach. Smiling at the camera as they held each other close.

"This is Mom," she whispered softly.

"And that's Denny Prescott."

The deep rumble held what she guessed was years of pent-up resentment and jealousy.

"He looks like—"

"You." Phillip nodded. "Or rather, you look just like him."

Evie studied the deep caverns Denny Prescott's smile had created. Twin dimples that looked just like...

Mine.

"Your mother didn't even bother denying the affair," he continued. "And the test results are irrefutable, so even if she had..."

His voice trailed off, and Evie understood why. There wasn't much more to be said on the matter. The proof of what he'd said was printed in black and white.

"I always felt like you resented me," she finally spoke up again. "I just never understood why."

"I loved your mother," Phillip announced as a matter of fact. "I would have done anything for her."

"And I was a constant reminder that she didn't love you back."

When he didn't argue the fact, Evie knew she'd finally gotten the answer she'd been searching for. And as much as it shredded her to know she'd spent her entire life desperately seeking her father's approval and love, there was a part of her that felt almost...relieved.

Phillip Mitchell's disdain for her wasn't a result of anything she had or hadn't done. It stemmed from a deep-seated pain that her mother had caused.

If his claims were to be believed, then he'd truly loved her mom. But it was becoming clear that, despite his feelings, her mother's heart had belonged to another.

Evie had been lucky enough to get out of her relationship with Preston despite massive pressure from both their families to solidify their coupling through marriage. Looking back now, she couldn't help but wonder if her mother hadn't felt the same sort of pressure. And maybe that's why she chose to marry Phillip rather than the man she'd truly loved.

Oh, Mom.

"I'd like to keep this if you don't mind." She held up the photo in her hand.

The man standing before her nodded but said nothing.

Evie slipped the picture into her purse and then faced the man she'd called her father for what she assumed would be the very last time. Tears filled her eyes, but she ignored them and forged on. There was one more thing she needed to make crystal clear.

"I'm not going to blackmail you or use the truth about us or your refusal to help me and those girls to try to ruin your repu-tation." Her solemn gaze returned to his.

He blinked, almost as if this caught him by surprise. "Then what is it you want?"

"From you?" She shrugged. "I don't want anything from you. But even if I did, it's not rightfully mine now, is it?"

Not anymore.

A knowing expression spread across the man's hardened face. "You could fight your right to the Mitchell family inheritance. And, given that you were raised as if you were my child, you'd most likely win."

Didn't he get it?

"No one wins here, Phillip." Evie purposely used his given name. "Not me...and certainly not you."

Evie turned her back on him and walked out of the room. Moving with hard, purposeful steps, she kept her chin up and her emotions in check as she made her way down the hall and through the home's elaborate foyer.

She reached the front doors. Yanking open the one on the right, Evie started to cross the threshold but was stopped by an unexpected wall of muscle.

A familiar deep voice accompanied a set of steadying hands. "Whoa, there. Where's the fire?"

"Oh!" A tiny squeal of surprise escaped Evie's throat. "Excuse me. I'm so sorr—" She blinked as recognition belatedly sank in. "Mr. Granger?"

"Evelynn?" Her father's years-long business partner stared back at her with obvious surprise. "I didn't realize..." He glanced back at the circle drive behind him. "I didn't see your car. And since when do you address me in such a formal manner?"

At fifty-four, the middle-aged financial genius was one of the very few people in her parents' circle Evie actually liked.

"Sorry, Landy." The smile lifting her lips was genuine. "And I only flew in for the day. My ride's on the way to take me back to my hotel."

Well, her ride *would* be on its way. Just as soon as she could get on the app and arrange for one to pick her up.

She should probably feel guilty for the harmless, little white lie. But the fewer the questions Landy asked, the sooner their unexpected reunion would be over.

Exchange a few pleasantries. Leave this place with as much dignity as possible. Fall apart in the privacy of my hotel room.

That was her plan, and as hard as it was becoming to keep herself together, Evie was bound and determined to follow through.

"Hotel? Why aren't you staying…" His friendly blue stare slid to the house behind her and back again. "Let me guess. Your father's still being his stubborn, pig-headed self?"

Apparently my father's already dead.

"I wasn't sure what his schedule was, so I played it safe and got a room in town."

His broad shoulders shook with a chuckle. "You're the only multi-millionaire I know who prefers basic to luxury."

"It's a perfectly lovely room, and I'm not a multi-millionaire yet," Evie reminded him. "My birthday isn't for another four months."

"The trust." Landy nodded. "I remember, now. But listen, why the whirlwind trip? I assumed when you returned from your little trip overseas, you'd stay here for at least a few weeks."

"You mean, you thought I'd spend my time away to reflect on how I left things the last time I was here, and I'd do what I always do and try to make amends."

"Such a smart little cookie." Landy's familiar smile momentarily eased the aching in her broken heart.

Evie chuckled at the forgotten nickname. "I don't think you've called me that since I was a child."

"Yes, well…I do suppose I should abandon the silly notion. After all, you are clearly no longer a child."

No, I'm not.

She was an adult who was free to do whatever she wanted. And right now, what she wanted to do more than anything was to leave.

"It was great seeing you again, but my ride will be here any moment. If you're looking for my—" Evie caught herself, correcting the near-miss with a quick shift in her choice of words. "He's in the den."

"Where else would he be?" Landy pulled her in for a hug. "Don't be a stranger, yeah?"

"I won't." Another lie. "Take care, Landy."

"You, too, honey." With a parting grin, he disappeared inside the house.

Finally alone once again, Evie drew in a cleansing breath and made her way down the mansion's front steps. She pulled her phone from her purse and quickly ordered a ride from the previously used app before embarking on a reflective walk down the quarter-mile paved driveway.

Less than ten minutes later, the expected blue sedan arrived at the property's wrought-iron gate. And as she left her family home—and a lifetime full of lies—behind, Evie realized she was finally and truly...

Free.

CHAPTER ELEVEN

Four hours later...

"ARE you sure this is a good idea?"

"Nope." Beckett kept his chin up and his shoulders back as he made his way through the hotel lobby. The confident stature creating an appearance of belonging, despite the answer he'd just given.

"She may not want you there, you know." Shadow didn't pull punches. "Going toe-to-toe with her father about what he did... that couldn't have been a pleasant conversation."

His grip tightened around his phone at the thought of Evie's piece of shit dad. "Why do you think I'm here?"

"You're there because you care about this woman. But as someone who cares about *you*, I want you to be prepared for the possibility that she may not be elated when you show up at her hotel room unannounced."

"Who wouldn't be happy to see me?" Beckett teased, boarding the elevator and pressing the button to Evie's floor.

"Bones..."

The brilliant woman's warning made him grin. "It's like I said earlier, when I first called. I just need to see for myself that she's okay. Once that happens, if Evie wants me to leave, I'll be on the next flight back to Charlotte."

"Mmm hmmm..." She sounded less than convinced. "Well, unless Owens says otherwise, the team's in-house the rest of the week. Oh, and your five-day vacation request was submitted and approved before your plane ever left the ground. You know, just in case you do decide to stay."

The corners of his lips curved even higher. "One of these days, you'll have to tell me how you do that."

"Do what?"

Her overtly innocent tone didn't fool him for a second.

"How you seem to know exactly what we need at the exact time we need it."

"What can I say?" Shadow asked rhetorically. "It's a gift, really."

It sure as hell was.

"You're one of a kind, you know that?"

"Of course, I do." The woman didn't miss a beat. "The world couldn't handle two of me."

Beckett's chuckle echoed off the elevator's reflective walls as the cart came to a stop and the doors slid open. "Bye, Shadow. Thanks again."

"Good luck, Bones. And, for what it's worth, I really do hope she's happy to see you."

The line went dead before he could respond.

He stepped out into the elevator lobby. Taking his cue from the signs mounted on the wall opposite from where he stood, Beckett turned right and began making his way down the long, empty hallway.

His footfalls were swallowed by the hotel's soft, patterned carpet as he passed by several numbered doors. The closer he got to room four-fifty-three, the more he began to question his impulsive decision to come here.

What if Shadow was right? What if Evie isn't happy to see me?

Beckett had been so confident when he'd first made the call to Shadow. And he hadn't felt even the slightest twinge of guilt over asking his team's tech goddess to use her hacking skills to find the name of the hotel where Evie was staying.

As a matter of fact, it wasn't until this very moment that he really and truly considered how insane his being here would probably seem.

You sure this is a good idea?

Shadow's earlier question whispered through his mind as he approached her room. Nerves twisted themselves into knots, adding to his present state of uncertainty.

Not one to let fear deter him from his goal, Beckett covered the remaining distance between him and that damn door. He pulled in a breath, raised his fist, and then...

He knocked.

Guess if she slams the door in my face, I'll have my answer.

Beckett shifted his weight from one booted foot to the other as he did his best to put a lid on his rising anxiety. Shadow was right to question his impulsiveness. What was he thinking, showing up here unannounced...and uninvited?

You could still leave. If you move your ass right now, you might make it to the stairs before—

The door swung open, the woman standing before him literally stealing the breath from his lungs.

Having washed her skin free of makeup, Evie appeared even younger than her thirty-one years. Her thick brown curls were piled high on her head with a few delicate locks left loose, framing her gorgeous face and brushing along the nape of her neck.

And though it probably didn't make much sense, the woman's casual choice of dark gray leggings, white, fitted t-shirt, and white, no-show socks were even more of a turn-on than the cute red dress and matching hat she'd worn the day before.

Damn, she really is beautiful.

"Beckett?"

The shock in Evie's voice ripped his attention back into focus.

"Surprise!" He smiled like the idiot he was.

Surprise? Really?

The lame greeting made him want to kick his own ass.

"Wha...what are doing here?"

Suddenly feeling like the biggest dipshit in the universe, Beckett offered her a rambling explanation.

"I woke up thinking about you and what you were coming here to do today. I also couldn't stop thinking about what you said before about not being able to talk to Lo or anyone else about, well, *any* of this, and I thought...." He shoved his hands into his pockets, exhaling slowly. "I guess I thought you might need someone to vent to or a shoulder to cry on. And I know what you're going to say. I could've just texted or called rather than flying standby to get here. But the thing is, it's not always easy to decipher true emotion through text, and even if I'd called and you swore you were doing okay, I still would've spent the rest of the day worrying regardless. So...here I am."

Those round eyes locked with his in an unreadable, immovable stare. Evie didn't say anything at first, and he was almost certain she was going to slam the door in his face and never speak to him again.

Thankfully, she didn't do that. Instead, Evie opened the door wide and stepped aside, giving him room to pass.

Beckett's heart thumped hard with relief and...yeah, okay. He was man enough to admit it. Excitement. Not because he thought he was going to get lucky but because her silent invitation to join her in her room meant getting to spend more time with her.

So I enjoy just being with her. Sue me.

As he entered the room, however, his focus wasn't on his own selfish desires, but rather Evie's wellbeing and current state of mind. After all, that was the whole reason he was here.

"How did you know where I was staying?" The door behind him snicked shut before the beautiful woman turned to him once again.

Yeah...about that...

Silently praying she wouldn't kick his ass right back out into the hallway, Beckett told her the truth. "After you texted earlier saying you'd landed and were checking into your hotel, I asked my team's technical analyst to ping your phone."

Her dark brows bunched together with a tilting of her head. "He can do that?"

"She, actually," Beckett corrected with a lopsided grin. "And yeah. Shadow's one of the best in the business. But I can assure you, she doesn't make it a habit of invading people's privacy."

Not the innocent ones, anyway.

The guilty, well…that was another story.

"So let me get this straight. You had your team's tech guru access the GPS on my phone, so you'd know which hotel I was staying at. Something I'm pretty sure is illegal, by the way. Then you dropped everything to hop on a plane and fly here from Charlotte, all because you were worried about me?"

"That pretty much sums it up, yeah." Beckett shrugged. "Although hearing you say it out loud makes me realize how stalkerish it probably seems. In fact…" He turned and started for the door. "Just promise me you're good, and I'll call for a ride back to the airport and—"

"Wait!" Evie grabbed hold of his forearm.

His gaze fell to her hand before lifting back up to meet hers. "Why? You need me to stick around and wait for the cops to come by and serve me with a restraining order?"

The lighthearted tease was awarded with the tiniest of grins. "I don't want to get a restraining order against you, Beckett. And I don't…" She pulled her bottom lip between her teeth. "I don't need you to leave."

Thank God.

"No?" One of his brows arched playfully high.

Evie's dark curls bounced with a shake of her head.

"What *do* you need?"

"This."

She went to him, wrapping her arms tightly around his midsection. It took the span of a single heartbeat to process the fact that Evie wasn't kicking his ass out. Instead…

She's hugging me.

Beckett embraced her fully, holding her body flush with his.

The woman clearly needed some serious comfort, and he was more than willing to give it.

"You okay?" he asked softly as he tucked her head beneath his chin.

The scent of strawberries enveloped him, and he had to fight the urge to sniff her silken hair.

"I will be." Evie's sweet voice was muffled. "But I'm better now that you're here."

His eyes fell shut as the tension in his neck and shoulders eased. Beckett rested his cheek on the top of her head, and for the first time since he'd last seen her, Beckett felt as though he could truly breathe.

"Does this mean you aren't plannin' on callin' the cops?" he teased.

Her soft chuckle filled the air around them. "No cops." Evie pulled away enough to look up at him. "It was really sweet of you to be worried. Although, I still can't believe you came all this way just to check on me."

"Like I said, I was worried."

"But why?" Evie stared up at him as if he were a puzzle she was trying to solve. "I mean, I know we agreed to start seeing each other, but that conversation was just last night, so I—"

"Darlin', if you're asking why I feel the need to protect you in every way I possibly can, I'm afraid I don't have an answer for that." Beckett reached up, tucking a few curled tendrils behind her ear. "What I *can* say is the thought of you hurting, physically or otherwise, tears into me like nothing ever has before."

Evie's gaze shimmered behind a well of unshed tears. "Beckett..."

"But if you don't want to talk about it, I respect that, too. I just thought you might need to."

"You have no idea." She turned and began walking further into the room. "I just opened a bottle of wine. It's a sweet red from room service. But if you prefer beer or soda or something—"

"Wine's fine." He followed her steps.

"I hope the balcony's okay. It's such a nice day, and I thought some fresh air would do me some good."

"Balcony's perfect."

But not as perfect as those mouthwatering curves of yours.

Speaking of curves…

Beckett's dick twitched behind his zipper as focus lowered to her luscious ass. Evie wasn't rail thin like some of the women he'd dated. She had that whole Marilyn Monroe hourglass thing going on, and those curves—in those tight, can't-hide-a-thing leggings—made his fingers twitch and his mind race with thoughts of all the naughty things he wanted to do to her.

So many, many things.

"Make yourself at home." Evie motioned toward the French doors leading to the balcony. "I'll get you a glass and meet you out there."

His attention snapped back up to where it belonged, and he quickly reminded himself of why he was here. He'd flown here to talk. Listen. Comfort.

Not ogle the woman's luscious ass.

"Sounds great," Beckett practically blurted.

Evie turned right and headed for the room's small kitchenette area. He continued toward the French doors, unable to keep from stealing a final glimpse of her tempting backside as he walked past.

So very, very tempting.

Minutes later, the two were seated at the small patio set with their wine glasses in hand and a magnificent view of the Atlantic. A cool breeze blew past, carrying with it the calming scent of the salty sea air.

Beckett turned his head toward Evie, who was sitting in the cushioned chair to his right. She reached up to brush away some strands blowing in her face as she stared out onto the rolling waves.

Goddamn, she's beautiful.

"He lied." She didn't take her eyes from the water.

"About not having a daughter? Yeah, sweetheart," Beckett let the endearment slip. "I know."

But a humorless chuckle shook her feminine shoulders. "Ironically, no. As it turns out, *that* part was actually true."

What?

He frowned, shifting in his chair to face her more fully. "What do you mean, that part's true?" When she didn't respond right away, he prodded with a soft, "Evie?"

She turned to him, then. The sadness dimming the shine in her eyes breaking his fucking heart.

But by the time she was finished sharing the unbelievable tale of the bombs Phillip Mitchell had dropped at the poor woman's feet—her mother's affair, DNA tests, and a man so selfish he didn't hesitate to wipe his hands of the child he'd spent three decades resenting—Beckett's empathetic heartbreak had morphed into a burning, raging fury.

With a muttered curse, he shot up from his seat and stormed back into the room.

"What are you..." Evie was hot on his trail. "Where are you going?"

"I think it's time Phillip Mitchell and I had a talk."

"What? Beckett, no!"

"Sorry, darlin'. But this isn't somethin' I can just let go."

She rushed past him before sliding directly into his path. "Yes." She put a hand to his chest, forcing him to stop. "You can."

"Evie—"

"Please, Beckett. I get that you're trying to help, and I can't even begin to tell you how much that means. But this isn't your fight. And really, at this point, it's not even a fight at all."

"Like hell, it's not." His back teeth clenched together. "From what you've said that man—a man who should have loved, nourished, and protected you—made you feel as though you were a thorn in his side, rather than a daughter who simply wanted to be loved. Now, after learning those terrorist bastards failed to rid him of his burden, he drops this DNA bullshit on you and all but tells you to have a nice fucking life!"

Shaking his head in anger, Beckett reached back and began rubbing the tense muscles in his neck. *God,* he wanted to beat

Phillip Mitchell's ass. He would have thought Evie would want that, too.

But instead...

"What my fath..." she started, quickly correcting her mistake. "What *Phillip* did is unforgivable."

"Which part?" he scoffed.

A sad smile lifted her ruby red lips as she let her hand fall back to her side.

"All of it," Evie answered softly. "And trust me, if you'd shown up here a couple of hours ago, you would have found me in a puddle of tears. But once I got past the initial shock and over-whelming feelings of consternation and betrayal, I realized...it finally makes sense."

The pain and rejection reflected in her glossy eyes tore at his very soul. But there was also a sliver of peace there. One Beckett hadn't seen there before.

"What makes sense, sweetheart?"

"I've spent my entire life trying desperately to gain my father's love and affection. But no matter what I did, no matter what I accomplished, it was never good enough. *I* was never good enough." That sad smile of hers returned. "I got into three different Ivy League schools, you know? But even then, either my scores weren't high enough or the comments from my essays and interviews weren't positive enough. That's when it finally hit me...it didn't matter what I did, it would never be enough. I was never going to be good enough."

"That's when you decided to go into teaching," he surmised.

Evie nodded. "And when I decided to follow my passion and teach in the public school system, rather than some hoity-toity private school run by politics and money, rather than the best interest of its students."

"I'm happy as hell that you followed your dreams, but that doesn't make me want to kick his ass any less."

Her expression softened as she reached up, cupping one side of his rugged cheek. "No one understands that desire more than me. But don't you see? This is actually a *good* thing."

"I'm sorry?"

"Phillip didn't spend my childhood treating me like I was a thorn in his side because of anything I did or didn't do. And it wouldn't have mattered what I did or where I worked or what country I chose to travel to. Nothing I ever do will make him love me because I'm not his."

Understanding finally began to sink in. "You're glad he's not your biological father because that means his disdain had nothing to do with you."

"Exactly!" Genuine relief shone behind her hazel gaze. "I've spent my entire life thinking I was a constant failure in that man's eyes, when the truth is, he'll *never* be able to love me because I'm—"

"Another man's child."

She nodded again. "Does it hurt to know he'd just as soon see me dead than claim me as his own? Of course, it does." A fresh set of unshed tears filled her round eyes. "But the way I see it, I have one of two choices. I could sit around mourning the loss of a man who's done nothing but ridicule and lie to me, or I can see the situation for what it really is."

"And what is it?"

"A chance to start over. To sever all ties without a stitch of guilt or obligation and live my life without fear of condescending lectures or rants designed to point out my many failures and disappointments." Evie's shoulders visibly relaxed. "I love that you want to defend my honor, Beckett—"

"I can't stand that he hurt you."

"—but as much as I'd love to see you knock him on his pretentious ass, the fact that I'm not Phillip Mitchell's biological daughter means I'm finally *free*. I can do what I want..." She inched her body closer to his. "With whomever I want. And there's not a damn thing Phillip Mitchell can do about it."

Beckett's dick grew hard, and his heart felt like it would pound straight out of his chest. Unless he was reading Evie all wrong, the sexy brunette was coming on to him. And while he wanted nothing more than to strip her down and finally take what he'd been craving, his need to protect her—even from himself—was even stronger than his desire.

"I want you, darlin'," he stated bluntly. "More than I've ever wanted anyone else."

"But?"

Cradling her beautiful face with both his hands, Beckett held her stare and told her the truth. "You've had one helluva day," he rumbled low. "The very last thing I'd ever want to do is take advantage of you or your situation."

"And they say chivalry is dead," Evie teased, her tempting breasts pressing against his chest. "Lucky for you, there's nothing to take advantage of."

"Evie…"

"I'm serious, Beckett. Have I had an emotional day? Sure. Will I still have moments of sadness or heartache along the way? Of course, I will. But am I such an emotional mess I can't make thoughtful, rational decisions?" The curls gathered on top of her head swayed back and forth with a slow shake of her head. "I know exactly what I'm doing…" She lifted onto her tiptoes and feathered her lips along his. "And I know exactly who I'm doing it with."

Beckett knew he should walk away right now, but his feet felt as if they were immersed in unbreakable concrete. Momentarily frozen in place, he couldn't seem to do much of anything other than hold her close and lose himself in her soulful stare.

"I don't ever want to hurt you," he whispered the solemn vow.

"So don't."

"Evelynn—"

"You said you wanted me." Her lips touched his again. "Did you mean that?"

"You know I did."

Evie pressed her body impossibly closer to his. Her gaze became fixed with his, the heat there unmistakable. And as she pulled his bottom lip playfully between her teeth, she whispered back a taunting…

"Prove it."

CHAPTER TWELVE

Evie wasn't sure who moved first, and she didn't care. All that mattered was that Beckett was here, and his lips were on hers.

Lord, have mercy!

She took the kiss deeper, her tongue meeting his in a feverish dance. A low, almost animalistic growl reverberated from Beckett's throat as his hands lowered to grab hold of her hips. And in the span of her very next heartbeat…

"Ah!" Evie couldn't stop the tiny cry of surprise as she was suddenly hoisted into the air. On reflex, she wrapped her legs around his narrow waist while locking her hands behind his neck to keep herself from falling.

At the same time, she could feel his strong, steady arms wrapping around her back and holding her safely in place.

"Don't worry," Beckett spoke between kisses as he began walking them toward the suite's only bedroom. "I've got you."

Boy, did he. And in more ways than one.

His mouth returned to hers, their combined breaths becoming heady with passionate desperation. A man true to his word, his protective hold on her didn't falter, and soon, Evie found herself being lowered onto the king-sized bed.

Beckett followed her down, letting his body lay half on hers and the mattress beside her. His kiss was like the man himself…a wonderfully conflicting measure of strength and gentleness she'd only ever felt with him.

Only him.

It wasn't as if she were an expert when it came to men and sex. But Evie also wasn't a novice.

She knew desire when she saw it. When she *felt* it. And knowing a kind, sexy, hero of a man like Beckett Stone wanted her as desperately as she wanted him made everything else going on in her life seem almost insignificant.

As if simply being with him could right all the wrongs in her world.

"You're so fucking beautiful," Beckett's deep whisper filled her ear as his lips and tongue teased her delicate lobe.

Evie sucked in a breath, his sweet words and tantalizing touch sending waves of goosebumps racing across her skin. Determined to make the most of the precious moment, she let her lids fall shut, allowing herself to become lost in his touch.

Her head fell to the side, the comforter's cool material against her cheek a stark contrast to the inferno raging within her. Hot, wet need pooled between her legs as her body ached with unprecedented longing.

Beckett's lips left a fiery trail of short, tantalizing kisses as he followed an invisible path along the side of her neck. He gave her delicate skin a playful nibble, followed by a quick lick with just the tip of his tongue.

Evie's sudden gasp morphed into a pleasurable moan. And when he leaned up and took her mouth in his once more, she knew this once would never be enough.

"Beckett..." His name lingered in the air like a warm summer breeze. "I need you."

"Don't worry, darlin'." He nipped at her bottom lip. "You've got me."

Her heart kicked a hard staccato against her ribs. This thing that was happening between them was all still so very new. And yet, Evie felt the abyssal depth to which those sweet words reached the moment they fell from his lips.

She did have him. And whether Beckett knew it or not, he had her. For as long as the mouthwatering man wanted.

Speaking of mouthwatering...

Evie reached for the hem of his black crewneck t-shirt and began hungrily pushing it up his sculpted chest. Understanding her obvious intent, he tore his mouth from hers, sat up, and reached back behind his head.

In one smooth, seamless motion, Beckett pulled the garment up over his head and off his arms. With his eyes locked with hers, he then bunched the soft cotton into a ball before tossing it somewhere to the side.

Her mouth watered as a rush of arousal left her sex swollen and heavy with lust and need. Damn, the man was perfect. A beautiful, perfect male specimen whose body was a work of pure, tanned, unadulterated art.

Beckett's muscles contracted beneath her touch. She could hear his breath hitch as her greedy hands began their slow, sensual exploration, and she smiled. Knowing he was every bit as affected by her touch as she was his gave Evie a sense of encouragement, so of course...she kept going.

Working her way up his toned pecs and brawny shoulders, she took time to memorize as much as she could. Every crevice. Every dip. Every curve.

Every inch she could see was a destination to discover, and she made damn sure to commit them all to memory. Because something Evie knew better than most...

Tomorrow is never guaranteed.

"My turn." Beckett practically growled as he gently wrapped his hands around her wrists and eased them from his body. With slow, careful movements, he guided her arms up so her hands were high above her head before ordering a low, "Don't move."

She obeyed the command, keeping her arms up just as he'd positioned them. It didn't take long for her to realize his motive.

He reached for the hem of her t-shirt. Evie's breath caught in her throat as his knuckles brushed against the skin at her lower belly, but still, she didn't move.

Beckett pulled the shirt up over her head and tossed it to the side. His dark gaze lowered to her lace-covered breasts. He reached out, slowly sliding her bra straps down her shoulders—first one and then the other—before expertly undoing the front clasp nestled snugly in the lacy center.

Her breasts spilled free as Beckett removed the delicate white item altogether, and for a moment, Evie felt as if she were the most desired woman in the world. But then...

A sudden sense of uncertainty began pushing its way through, bringing with it a slew of self-sabotaging questions. Were her breasts too big? Her nipples too dark? Was her belly not toned enough, or her hips too wide?

At a size twelve, Evie knew she wasn't exactly runway model material. And she'd always been perfectly fine with that. But now...

Now I want to know what Beckett's thinking.

Or maybe she didn't. Maybe it was best if she just *pretended* his opinion of her didn't matter. Or better yet, maybe she could pretend he thought she was absolutely—

"Perfect."

Evie's eyes flew up to Beckett's, and for a split second, she was certain he'd just read her mind. But in her attempt to search his dark brown gaze, she realized he wasn't looking into her widened eyes at all. Instead, he appeared to be eagerly soaking in the rise and fall of her exposed breasts.

Guess he's not a mind reader, after all.

Emboldened by his obvious physical desire, Evie reached for his belt. But before she could make a move to release it, Beckett slid out of arm's length and stood at the side of the bed.

"What are you—"

"Figured taking off my pants would be easier if I was standing." He arched an expectant brow.

Fair enough.

She followed his lead, scooting her body to the edge of the mattress so she was sitting directly in front of where he stood. Evie went for the belt a second time, her eyes remaining fixed with his as she pulled the thick leather strap free.

With his buckle undone and his belt straps hanging loose, she was able to easily free the button at the waist of his well-worn jeans. The zipper came next, and though it wasn't easy, Evie forced herself to go slow.

This was their first time being together...like this. She wanted to make it as good for him as she could. She also, selfishly, wanted to make it last.

"You're killin' me here, you know?" Beckett's deep drawl teased.

A wicked smile formed on her uplifting lips. "Am I?" Evie asked far too innocently.

And then she purposely let the back of her knuckles brush against the solid bulge stretching the denim alongside the zipper's teeth.

He sucked in a breath, his six-pack tensing at the same time the impressive erection twitched beneath her touch. "You're playin' with fire, Evelynn." Beckett rumbled the warning. "Just remember what they say about paybacks..."

Evie's soft chuckle filled the air around them. "That a threat, cowboy?" she teased, pulling the zipper's metal tab down the rest of the way.

The stuttering sound of the metallic teeth seemed almost deafening in the otherwise silent room.

"No, darlin'." His fingers slid into the curls at one side of her head before he gently guided her focus back up to his gorgeous face. "That's a promise."

The expression on his face left her breathless, sending Evie's heart skittering deep inside her chest. Beckett's brown eyes appeared almost blackened with desire. A desire she understood all too well.

Despite her recent thoughts about savoring the moment, Evie's ferocious need for him far exceeded her inner strength. She'd never wanted a man more, and it was that very same primal need pulsing through her veins that was the driving force pushing her closer and closer to paradise.

Evie reached up, pushing his jeans down the length of his strong, masculine thighs. Keeping her eyes on his, she gave his black boxer briefs the same treatment.

Seconds later, Beckett's erection bobbed free.

She did her best to school her reaction, but the tantalizing movement still managed to pull her focus straight to its source. Heat curled down her spine as she caught her first sight.

Long. Hard. Ready.

Oh, my.

He was even bigger than she'd imagined, though she shouldn't have been surprised. The man looked like a sculpted god with his lean, muscular physique. A tall, dark, and ruggedly handsome deity whose sole purpose for walking this earth was to bring her pleasure.

And though she was fully aware of how fantastical her recent thoughts were, she was nothing if not a dreamer.

Speaking of dreams...

Intent on fulfilling one of hers, Evie reached out, wrapping her fist as far around his swollen cock as she physically could. Beckett's low moan spurred her into action, and she began stroking his hot length in slow, calculated movements.

He sucked in another breath, and her inner muscles clenched with anticipation. His erection was so full, almost angry in appearance. But if the drop of moisture coating the tip was any indication, he was enjoying every slow, methodical stroke.

Bet he'll enjoy this, even more...

Evie leaned forward, keeping her movements slow enough to give him plenty of time to change his mind. But Beckett didn't try to stop her, and if he had any reservations about where things were headed, he didn't let it show.

"*My* turn," she whispered a repeat of his earlier sentiment.

She leaned down, sucking him deep into her mouth. A deep, almost primal moan escaped from his lips as she used hers to torture him in the most delicious way possible.

"Jesus, Evie," Beckett breathed.

His hand went to the back of her head, his fingers filling with her hair. Evie began sucking him in harder, while continuing the slow, torturous slide of her fist.

A slight sting registered in her scalp, but the pain was surprisingly pleasurable...and erotic as hell. Struck with a feeling of feminine strength and sexual prowess, she reached up, cupping the delicate area below his shaft as she pumped him in and out of her mouth in a sensual rhythm.

"Christ Almighty." He panted. "That feels..." Another pant. "Fucking...amazing..."

His deep, even breaths came faster and shallower as the seconds ticked past. Evie could feel his balls tightening against her palm, and she knew the delectable combination of her mouth and her fist were getting Beckett closer and closer to where he needed to be.

But just as she was certain he was about to explode into a fireball of orgasmic bliss, she found herself being carefully pushed away.

"Hey!" Evie admonished with a frown. "I wasn't finished."

"Maybe not, but I just about was." He shot her a knowing glance. "And as much as I enjoyed the hell out of your mouth, that's not how our first time is goin' down."

Going down...no pun intended, right?

Before she could point out the man's double entendre—or inquire about his "first time" comment—she found herself lying flat on her back against the mattress. As for Beckett, well...

He deftly began removing his boots and socks before finishing the job she'd started with his boxers and jeans. Evie lay still in the center of the bed, soaking in the magnificent view.

Beckett reached for her, dipping his fingers between her hips and the waist of her leggings. Not bothering to play coy, she lifted her lower body from the mattress with a smile.

The leggings went first, immediately followed by her white lace panties. Letting the clothing fall near his feet, he positioned himself between her slightly splayed feet. And when Evie looked deep into his heated gaze, she found him staring down at her as if she was the most desirable woman in existence.

"Remember that payback I mentioned earlier?" His fingers caressed her ankles as he spoke.

"Go ahead and do your worst." Evie stretched her arms up high above her head, letting her hands rest loosely on the covers. "I'm not scared."

A slow, deliciously evil grin lifted one corner of his mouth as he rumbled back, "You should be."

Without warning, he used the grip on her ankles to slide her entire body closer to his. Beckett positioned himself between her legs as they dangled over the mattress's edge. And then, as he stared down at her as if he were a starving man preparing to feast, he dropped to his knees and brought his mouth to her sex.

Passion and lust took hold as Evie's head flew back, and her eyes fell shut. She reached blindly between her legs, hungrily raking her fingers through Beckett's short, dark hair.

The man's primitive growl vibrated against her as his lips pressed against her very core. Time around them stood still, and she felt an almost euphoric high as she lost herself in the pleasure he so selflessly gave.

Her lower body lifted of its own accord, as if instinctively searching for more. More of his tender, bearded lips. His masterful tongue. His...*Oh, God!*...his fingers.

She moaned and writhed beneath his erotic musings as Beckett licked and laved her sensitive, swollen sex. At the same time, he thrust a slow, steady finger in and out of her welcoming heat.

Every move he made brought her closer to Heaven, and Evie knew it wouldn't be much longer. And when he brought his mouth higher and began pleasuring her clit, it was only a matter of time...

"Ah!" Evie cried out, her fingers gripping his hair tightly as the tip of Beckett's tongue flicked her swollen bundle of nerves.

Her body trembled uncontrollably beneath his incredible touch. As the insurmountable pressure continued to build, Evie felt as though she were drowning in a sea of wanton pleasure.

There was only one lifeline she could throw. Only one man who was capable of saving her. But she feared if he didn't get her there soon, she may not be able to survive.

"Please," she begged him shamelessly. "I need..."

Her breaths came faster and with more force.

"Hold on tight, darlin'," Beckett rumbled from his kneeling

position between her splayed thighs. "I know exactly what you need."

And in the span of the next few seconds, her real-life hero proved he was a man of his word.

He added a second finger. Pressed his tongue harder against her clit. Beckett's hand moved faster, his fingers curling inside her with expert precision, and when he pulled her sensitive bundle between his lips and began to suck—

"Beckett!"

His name echoed throughout the entire hotel suite as Evie came longer and harder than she ever had before. A low, almost carnal keening sound echoed through her ears, and it took her a moment to realize it was coming from her.

"There ya go, sweetheart," Beckett drawled as his fingers continued to pump. "Just let it all go…"

And let go, she did.

Her fingers clutched the hair still filling her fists as her entire body arched high off the bed. Wave after wave of pleasure rolled through her before she finally felt herself feathering back down to earth.

By the time she managed to reopen her eyes, Beckett was back on his feet with a smug smile on his face and a foil wrapper in his hand.

When did he have time to—

He leaned down and pressed his lips to hers. "Ready for more?" he whispered low.

She may not survive it, but oh yeah. She was definitely ready.

Evie nodded, watching him through a set of heavy, sated eyes as he ripped open the foil square and donned the thin, protective sheath.

"This is going to go fast." The mattress dipped beneath his weight.

"That's okay." She smiled up at him. "I don't need slow."

I just need you.

Beckett held his weight on his elbows while settling himself between her opened thighs. His eyes became fixed on hers as he reached between their bodies and lined himself up to her entrance. Then...he paused.

"This is more than just sex for me, Evie."

A flash of vulnerability crossed over his heated gaze, and her heart melted inside her chest.

"For me, too, Beckett," she whispered back, bringing a loving hand to one side of his ruggedly handsome face.

His whiskers tickled her palm as they moved with the man's sweet smile. And with the very next beat of her heart—

He thrust forward, filling her in one long, slow push. A low groan vibrated within as Beckett's eyes nearly rolled into the back of his head.

"Jesus, you feel amazing."

Evie's breath caught from the sudden intrusion, and it took her body a moment to fully accommodate his larger-than-average size. He must have mistaken her momentary hesitation for something else, because the next thing she heard was—

"You okay?"

The soft whisper of concern made her smile. "I'm better than okay." She leaned up, giving him a soft, sweet kiss. "Much, much better."

"Thank God." He kissed her back.

She giggled but then...Beckett began to move.

The next several minutes passed in an impassioned blur. She took. He gave. Each thrust growing harder and faster than the ones before.

Their bodies moved in synch, as if they were two parts of a perfect whole. And as Beckett made love to her in a way no other man had, Evie wondered how she'd survive if he ever decided to walk away.

Don't think about that now. Just...feel.

His tongue danced with hers as his cock surged forward once again. The man's kiss was as demanding as his powerful thrusts, and yet Evie had never felt more cherished.

"Ah, fuck..." Beckett bit out as his body pushed in and out of hers.

She could feel him growing impossibly harder and knew that

he was close. Tilting her hips, she moved her body in perfect rhythm with his. And when his movements started to become jerky and uneven, she was ready to fall right along with him.

"Evie…" He panted out her name as if she were a lifeline he was desperate to reach.

I'm here, Beckett. I'll always be here.

The presumptive thought had barely driven past her mind when the telltale signs of her second climax made their presence known. She was almost there. Just a few more seconds and…

A deep, guttural groan roared above her own cries of pleasure as they simultaneously found their release. Evie's eyes squeezed shut as she started to come again.

She felt an overwhelming sense of primitive satisfaction rolling through her as she continued riding the waves of her orgasm until the very end. And Beckett—bless the man's giant, selfless heart—made sure to pull every ounce of pleasure he could for them both.

Time passed in a rapturous blur as they eventually fell into an unmoving peace. Him on top of her. Her legs lazily wrapped around him.

When the electrical currents called a cease-fire and her body grew limp, Evie had the fleeting thought that she wanted the moment to last forever. But all-too-soon Beckett lifted his heaving chest from hers and stared down into her contented gaze.

"That was…amazing." His voice was lower and slightly rough, making him sound even sexier than normal.

"Yes." Evie lifted her head from the mattress and gave him a kiss. "It was. Thank you." She brought a hand to one side of his face.

"Pretty sure I'm the one who should be thanking you."

She smiled, pressing her lips against his for the second time. "Call it even?"

Beckett brushed the tip of his nose against hers and grinned. "Only if you promise for a rematch in the very near future."

She gave a teasing nibble of his bottom lip before whispering back, "Done."

The joke was on her, however, when he reached out, cupped the back of her neck, and slammed his mouth to hers. By the time the kiss was over, they were both breathing heavily once again.

"I meant what I said, Evie." His tone became serious. "This… you…it means something to me."

"It means something to me, too, Beckett," she responded honestly.

So much more than you'll ever know.

"There's one more thing," he added softly. "I'm a selfish asshole."

Evie frowned, not having seen a single speck of evidence to back up the man's surprising claim. "You're not an asshole, and I can't begin to picture you being selfish about, well, anything."

A soft chuckle left Beckett's bare shoulders shaking. "Oh, I can be a dick if the occasion calls for it. Just ask my teammates." His incredible lips flattened, and his serious tone returned. "As for the selfish part, you're right. That's not usually me. But things are different with you."

"They are?"

He nodded. "Everything's different when it comes to you, sweetheart. And I may not know where this thing with us is headed, but I do know I want you all to myself for as long as it lasts."

Her heart skittered inside her chest as understanding finally sank in. "You're talking about exclusivity."

"Damn right, I am." He gave her lip a playful nip. "I want you all to myself, Evie. And I know you've still got shit to work through from what happened, not to mention that asshat you used to call your father, but I'm here." A sweet kiss that time. "And unless you tell me otherwise, I plan on staying right here. By your side."

Too soon or not…too crazy or not…it didn't matter. It was too late. *Evie* was too late.

She'd already started to fall in love.

CHAPTER THIRTEEN

"Are you sure this is a good idea?"

Beckett looked over at Evie and smiled. Her question was the exact same one Shadow had posed to him three days earlier, when he'd decided to make his impromptu visit to Evie at her East Hampton hotel.

At the time, his answer had been no. Truth was, he'd been nervous as hell showing up unannounced the way he had. But this...this was different. Here, he knew they'd both be safe from judgement or ridicule because they'd be surrounded by his teammates and closest friends.

Beckett reached for her hand and linked their fingers together. "It's going to be fine," he promised with a wink. "Trust me."

"I do trust you, Beckett." Evie curled her fingers around his and smiled. "With my life."

Warmth spread throughout his chest as he experienced an overall feeling of weightlessness. Beckett was happy. *Truly* happy. And it was all thanks to the woman walking hand-in-hand by his side.

The last three days had been the best of his entire existence. Between that first magnificent night spent in the hotel and the last two days and nights spent with Evie at her friend's place here in Charlotte, he couldn't remember a time when he felt this alive.

Alive.

Happy.

In love.

Truth was, he was completely and totally head-over-boots in love with the woman. And anyone who wanted to debate his newfound feelings, well...

They can eat a bag of dicks.

It didn't matter that it was fast, and he sure as shit didn't care what other people would think. Beckett knew what he felt, and he damn well knew it was real.

The mind-blowing sex was merely a bonus.

"Relax, darlin'." He gave Evie's hand a gentle shake as they made their way up the sidewalk to Falcon and Avery's home. "You've already met the team, and they love you."

"They hardly know me, Beckett."

"They know enough." His lips curved upward. "Listen, the guys all know you're comin' and that we're together. And they're cool with it."

"You really think so?"

"I *know* so." He gave her shoulder a playful nudge. "Just like I know the wives are gonna love you."

"Well, let's hope you're right." Evie crossed two fingers on her free hand. "Otherwise, this is going to be a very long, very *awkward* afternoon."

With a chuckle, Beckett followed the sidewalk's curve up to the home's front porch. Thanks to Avery's decorative eye, the vinyl and rock sided arts and crafts-style home appeared as warm and inviting as he already knew it to be.

Located on a quarter-acre lot near Charlotte's northeastern city limits, the secluded piece of property offered its owners a private backyard and patio perfect for casual gatherings. And since the men of Tac-Ops used any excuse they could to hang out and shoot the shit, this had become the team's unofficial cookout headquarters.

Not bothering to knock, Beckett opened the front door and

stepped to the side, motioning for Evie to enter. Once inside, he took the lead again, guiding her through the small foyer, past the home's impressive kitchen, and through the open living room space to the back patio doors.

Beside him, he noticed the long, deep breath Evie had just pulled into her lungs. Knowing she was steeling herself for her first social interaction with the group, he paused long enough to give one final reassurance.

"Come here." He pulled her to him. Releasing the grip on her hand, he brought both of his to each side of her flawless face. "Everything is going to be fine."

"I know."

Her words said one thing, but the greens and browns in her gorgeous hazel eyes were a dead giveaway that she was more than a little nervous. A sudden need to ease her unnecessary anxiety about getting together with his friends had Beckett leaning in for a kiss.

He pressed his lips to hers, keeping the contact publicly appropriate in case they were spotted. For her sake, only—because he didn't give a fuck who saw them—he gave her a sweet, chaste kiss before pulling back and staring deep into her eyes.

"I know it won't happen, but if at *any* time, you decide you want to bail, all you have to do is say the word, and we'll go."

"I'm good, Beckett." Evie visibly shook her worries away. "It's just a small case of the jitters, that's all. Promise." She rose to her tiptoes to give him a kiss of her own.

"Okay, then." He slid the patio door open and held out his hand. "After you."

The bottom portion of her light pink sundress blew against her legs with a passing breeze. In the back of his mind, Beckett had the fleeting thought that he was glad she'd decided to add the cropped denim jacket at the last minute.

He didn't want her being cold, after all.

Dude. Pushing the protective bit a tad far, don't you think?

No. No, he didn't. The way he saw it, now that they were officially a couple, his job wasn't solely about keeping her safe from terrorist pricks or asshole pseudo-fathers. He wanted to protect her from everything he could...for as long as he could.

Because he loved her.

"About time you showed up!"

Beckett looked up to see Falcon headed his way. The six-three sniper had two amber colored bottles in his hand. One with the cap still on, and one without.

"Dude, we're like ten minutes late," he told the former Army Ranger. "And"—he glanced over their host's shoulder to the smoking grill several yards away—"Apollo just put the burgers on the grill, so the food's not even ready yet, anyway."

The man's blue eyes gleamed with humor as he held out the unopened bottle and grinned. "That all you came here for? The food?"

"Don't forget the beer," Beckett teased, taking the offered beverage from his friend's outstretched hand. "Thanks. You remember Evie..."

"Of course." Falcon hurriedly wiped the condensation from his right hand before offering it to Evie. "Bones said you were in town and that the two of you had...reconnected." He sent Beckett a knowing grin before refocusing on her. "How are you?"

"Better than the last time you saw me." Evie chuckled and shook the man's hand. "And thanks for letting me crash your party. You have a lovely home."

"Thanks. We like it. And you're not crashing anything. You know me and the guys..." The other man turned and pointed to the three women sitting around a stone firepit. "And that's my wife, Avery, in the white sweater. The brunette to her right is her sister, Alex, and the blonde to her left is Nicki. She's married to Apollo." Falcon looked back at Evie. "They're excited to meet you."

"I'm looking forward to meeting them, as well."

Beckett could tell she was still a bit nervous, but he knew without a doubt she'd fit right in.

No time like the present...

"Come on." He jutted his chin toward the ladies. "I'll introduce you."

Another breeze blew past, lifting several of Evie's curls. Still smiling, she reached up and brushed them from her eyes, tucking the unruly locks behind one of her adorable ears.

Beckett's breath was literally stolen by her beauty, and he couldn't seem to take his eyes off her. That was until he nearly tripped over a patio chair he'd missed seeing while under her spell.

"You good?"

Evie's laugh was the sweetest of symphonies, and one he couldn't wait to hear again.

"Always," he drawled, wearing an unabashed smirk.

Then he turned his head to keep from falling on his ass.

He surveyed the pleasant scene before them as they walked toward the other women in attendance. They talked and laughed as they sat around the stone fire pit, their glasses of wine in various stages of consumption.

"Hey, Beck!" Avery Morgan shot up from her seat to give him a hug. "Glad you could make it."

"Wouldn't have missed it." Beckett hugged the sweet woman back.

Before he got the chance to do it himself, Avery pulled away and turned her pretty brown eyes Evie's way.

"You must be Evie." She held out her hand. "It's so nice to meet you. I'm Avery, Garrett's wife. Of course, you probably know him as Falcon."

"It's nice to meet you, too." His date for the afternoon smiled. "I was just telling your husband how great this place is."

"Thanks." Avery's smile grew as she glanced around the peaceful backyard. "It's a work in progress, but we really like it here. Oh, sorry." She looked back at Evie. "Where are my manners? This is my sister, Alex." She pointed toward the woman still sitting in the chair to Avery's right.

"Hey," Alex held up the glass in her hand and flashed Evie a friendly grin.

"Hi."

"And that's Nicki." Avery motioned toward the attractive blonde to her left. "She's married to Ethan."

"And Ethan is…Apollo. Right?" Evie guessed.

"That's him." Nicki stood and gave her hand to Evie. "It's nice meeting you."

"You, too."

"If you've got the nicknames down, you've already won half the battle," Alex quipped.

Laughter came from them all, including Evie.

"I'm not sure I have the team names mastered, but I do have to ask…" Her gaze focused on Alex. "What's the other half of the battle?"

Rather than answer the question directly, Avery's sister leaned down, grabbed a clean wine glass from the handful waiting to be chosen, and handed the glass to Evie. "Pull up a chair and pour yourself some wine." The extroverted artist gestured toward the empty seat to her right. "This is going to take a while."

Everyone laughed, including Beckett. It wasn't as if he could argue the woman's claim.

"Sounds like that's my cue to leave," he half-joked. To Evie, he quietly asked, "You good here?"

If she wasn't, he wouldn't even think about leaving her side.

"I'm good." Her dimpled smile was as genuine as it was beautiful. "Besides, from the looks of things, I think they might need some help."

Beckett followed her line of sight, turning just in time to see Apollo and Falcon moving hastily in front of the grill. Flames shot up from beneath the appliance's metal grate, and it was clear the two men were moving quickly to avoid burning their food to a crisp.

Standing a few feet away—and looking cool as a fucking cucumber—Digger took a sip of his beer while watching the humorous scene unfold. With a slight shake of his head, he shoved his free hand into the front pocket of his jeans as Falcon began dousing the flames with what Beckett assumed was clean water.

"I think you're right." Beckett's gaze slid back to Evie's. "Better go help put out the fire...literally." He leaned in for a quick peck on her lips...just because he could. "You know where to find me."

"I'll follow the smoke."

He laughed as he turned and walked away, laughing as he crossed the patio to offer aid to his barbeque-impaired friends. Beckett didn't look back or second-guess his decision to leave Evie with the girls. He could already tell she was going to fit right in.

"Are you *trying* to turn those burgers into hockey pucks, or do you just prefer your meat overdone?" He couldn't resist the dig.

"You think you can do better, be my guest," Apollo groused back. "Damn thing got too hot too fast."

"No shit," Beckett snorted sarcastically as he held out his hand palm-up toward Falcon. "Give me the bottle and step aside."

Falcon did as he was asked, grumbling something under his breath about Texans and their barbeque. In response, Beckett brought the plastic nozzle closer to the grate and sprayed.

"Say what you want, city boy," he swiftly began extinguishing the unruly flames. "If it's one thing I know, it's how to work a damn grill."

"Looks to me like you've been working something else." Falcon jutted his chin in the ladies' direction.

"And?" Beckett didn't bother looking. "I already told you Evie and I were together."

"Oh, I know." Falcon took a swig of the beer he'd just opened and shrugged. "I just try to give you shit every chance I can."

"Yeah, well...maybe next time you should try harder, 'cause that was totally lame."

"My ass, it was lame. And you aren't the only one on this team who can make a joke, you know?"

"Yeah, but...does it really count if nobody laughs?" Beckett pointed to Apollo as the other man began to chuckle. "See? Now *that's* the reaction you want when telling a joke."

"Fuck you, Bones." Falcon flipped him the bird before changing to a more genuine tone. "Seriously, though. I like Evie, and I truly hope things work out for the two of you."

"Yeah?"

The other man frowned. "You act like that surprises you. Told you on the phone the other day that I'm cool with it." His gaze slid over to Apollo and Digger before bringing it back to Beckett's. "We all are."

"No, I know." Beckett set the nearly empty water bottle down before grabbing the long, metal spatula to flip the burgers. "And I told her as much. I guess I just expected more blowback, what with Evie being a former rescue, and the fact that we haven't known each other very lo—"

"I fell in love with Avery damn near the moment I met her," Falcon cut him off. "And need I remind you that she was also a Tac-Ops rescue...*twice?*"

"So was Nicki," Apollo chimed in. "Granted, she and I had a history before that fucker Beňová tried to kill her. But still..."

The small group of men fell momentarily silent as memories from that tumultuous time came rushing back. Not long after, Falcon turned his blue eyes Beckett's way.

"Time frame doesn't matter when it's right." The former Ranger looked as serious as ever. "She handled herself damn well with those asshole terrorists, which means not only is she smart, but she's tough. And there isn't a person here who'd judge you for falling in love with a woman you rescued. I mean, at this point..." His intense expression gave way to a smirk. "It's kinda what we do."

Both Apollo and Falcon joined Beckett in a sudden state of laughter because...well...Falcon was right. Both he and Apollo had found the love of their lives in the midst of rescues and danger, and if this thing worked out with Evie, it would mean he had, too.

Three down, one to go...

His focus shifted to Digger, who wasn't laughing or flashing so much as a smirk. While remaining as stoic as ever, the former

SEAL gave a simple shrug of a shoulder. And for Dig, that was almost as good as a smile.

One of these days, I swear, I'm gonna figure out what it is that makes that man tick.

But until then…

He turned and looked to where Evie was sitting with the girls. Alex said something to the group, and they all burst into hysterical laughter.

Including Evie.

"See?" Falcon gave Beckett's bicep a friendly slap. "What'd I tell you? She fits right in."

As if she could sense he was watching her, Evie glanced his way. She gave him a tiny wave, and Beckett smiled back, his entire chest filling with warmth as his heart began to swell.

He'd assured her she'd get along with Avery, Nicki, and Alex, so it really came as no surprise. But seeing the proof behind that beautiful wide smile of hers, and Beckett knew…

I'm never gonna let her go.

* * *

"Uh oh. I know that look."

Evie tore her gaze from Beckett to find Nicki looking at her from across the fire. Realizing the other woman was referring to her, she asked the pretty blonde, "What look is that?"

"The one currently plastered all over that pretty face of yours." Apollo's wife shot her a knowing smile.

I have a look?

"I don't know what you're—"

"She's right, you know?" Avery's expression matched that of Nicki's. "You look at Beckett the same way Nick looks at Ethan, and how—"

"Avery looks at Garrett," Nicki finished for the other woman.

Evie glanced over at Alex, who was taking a sip of her wine. "Don't look at me." Alex sat her nearly empty glass onto the small accent table between them. "I live a perfectly contented single life. But…"

"But what?" she was almost afraid to ask.

After a quick glimpse at both Avery and Nicki, Avery's sister looked back at Evie and grinned. "They're both right. And, for what it's worth, Beck looks at you the exact same way."

He does?

Unable to keep from it, she stole a quick glance Beckett's way. Her heart leaped and butterflies flourished when she saw what the other three meant.

He does.

"Oh, yeah." Alex's confident tone pulled Evie back to the conversation. "Stick a fork in her, girls. She's done."

Not pretending to misunderstand the other woman's meaning, Evie simply lifted her glass to her smiling lips, letting the sweet red vino pass slowly over her tongue. They weren't wrong in their astute assessment of her feelings toward Beckett. She was far too gone where the hostage rescue specialist was concerned.

The last few days had been absolutely incredible. They'd talked and laughed... Evie couldn't remember the last time she'd laughed as much as she had with Beckett. But they also had more important, more serious conversations, too.

Evie had told him all about her mother and how she'd lost her when she was eight. Bad weather and unsafe speed had been the official cause of the accident, but what Evie remembered most was how she'd felt so utterly and completely alone.

She told Beckett what it was like growing up surrounded by a bunch of snobby, spoiled, rich kids. And how, as she'd grown older, she couldn't wait to get away from East Hampton and out on her own.

The best parts of their conversations were when he'd do the sharing. How his voice grew soft with affection when he spoke of his mom. The way his tone filled with pride when Beckett told her about his dad.

She loved that his mom was a retired schoolteacher, and that Mr. Stone had spent his youth protecting the citizens of his city. Beckett swore she'd love them both, and from what the man had already shared, Evie couldn't agree more.

So yes, she was "done", as Alex had put it, and there wasn't a single part of her that was sorry. The only thing left for them to figure out now was how to make a long-distance relationship work.

A phone began to ring, the peeling sound cutting through the afternoon air. At first, Evie paid it no attention until another phone rang. And then...

Another.

She and the other women all turned and looked at the guys. All four had their cells to their ears, and from the expressions on their handsome faces, it wasn't good news.

"Well, Evie," Nicki spoke to her from across the flickering flames. "It looks like you're about to get your first real test."

"Test?" Evie's brows bunched together. "What do you mean, test?"

"She means, the guys just got called up." Avery pushed herself to her feet and sighed. "And *that* means, you're about to see if you can handle being with a Tac-Ops man."

Her gaze slid back to where he was standing, and her chest instantly grew tight. A giant fist reached inside and squeezed her heart as she thought of him running headfirst into danger.

A few days of awesome sex and in-depth conversations was one thing. But staying behind while the man she loved went to places unknown to risk his life for God only knows what...

If he and his team didn't do what they do, you and the girls would be dead.

It was that thought that had her rising to her feet to make her way across the patio to where Beckett stood. As hard as it was to think of him risking his life, she understood better than most what an impact he and his team could make.

Besides, Nicki and the others were right. This *was* a test of epic proportions. And she intended to pass with flying colors.

CHAPTER FOURTEEN

Thirty-six hours later...

"On a scale of one to not a fuckin' chance, what are the odds these guys are actually gonna show?"

Beckett sat in his designated seat on the private jet owned by his boss and waited. The last time Tac-Ops had been slated to buddy up with another team, Beckett and the guys had been left high and dry right at go-time.

Not that it was the other team's fault. They'd simply been following Uncle Sam's orders.

Regardless of the reason, however, any major last-minute op changes—like the one they'd faced in Afghanistan—risked screwing the whole damn pooch. Luckily the mission to rescue Evie and the girls had gone off without a hitch, despite the unexpected change in plans.

Lucky for Evie and her students. And damn lucky for me.

"That hurts, Bones." A teasing female voice sounded throughout the luxurious cabin from the jet's state-of-the-art telecom system. "After all this time, I thought you trusted in the genius that is Shadow."

Beckett grinned. "Oh, I trust you plenty, darlin'. It's the

random team we know squat diddly about that's got my knickers in a twist."

"Well, get ready to iron out those pesky wrinkles of yours because these guys are the real deal. And I've already been in contact with Mustang, and he and his team are at the airstrip, and they're waiting for *you* to arrive."

"Mustang?" He frowned. "Who the hell's that?"

"Uh...the leader of the SEAL team you're working this op with. They use nicknames in the field, just like you guys. There's Mustang, Midas, Aleck, Pid, Jag, and Slate." The woman paused a beat before asking, "Wait. You said you don't know anything about them, but I personally sent each of you a detailed file on each of the six SEALs running assist on this one. Did you not get it?"

A purposeful silence stretched on for a handful of seconds before Beckett let her know, "Oh, I got it, and I read it. I just wanted to see if you'd take the bait, is all."

"Always the comedian, aren't you Bones?" Shadow's lack of actual amusement was obvious. "But you know, one of these days, you're going to need my help, and I just might not pick up the phone. Then what will you do?"

"Ah, come on, now, darlin'," he crooned. "You shouldn't even joke about a thing like that."

"Hey, you started it."

"Fair enough." Beckett's grin lifted into a full-blown smile. "My apologies."

"Thank you. Now, let's go over the plan one last time, shall we?" Her focus shifted as the tech genius got down to business. "In about twenty minutes, you'll land at the private air strip our fearless leader's friend was kind enough to let us use. Once there, both teams will drive to the launch site on the island's northern beach where you guys and the SEALs will suit up and swim to the target's location."

"Quick question..." Apollo got the mysterious woman's attention. "Hypothetically speaking...what would happen if I forgot to pack my wet suit?"

There was a stark pause and then, "Ethan Michael McAllister, please tell me you aren't serious."

"Whoa! Why you middle naming me?"

"Apollo, the entire *premise* of this mission's success begins with your team swimming to the island one mile northwest of the one on which you're about to land. And you just told me you forgot your freaking wet suit! *That's* why I'm middle naming you."

"Actually, I posed a hypothetical question. You assumed I was making an admission of guilt."

Shadow waited a beat before asking, "Et, tu, Apollo?"

Beckett laughed along with Apollo and Falcon before doing his best to ease the sweet woman's damaged ego.

"Look at it this way, Shadow." He softened his tone. "You're like our little sister, and as such, it's our big brotherly duty to tease you every once in a while."

"You really expect me to buy that line of cra—"

She started to call him on his shit, but Shadow never got the chance thanks to Digger's growled interruption.

"She's not our sister, and this isn't a fucking family reunion. So how 'bout you guys shut the hell up and let the woman do her job so that we can do ours."

The cabin grew silent as Beckett and the others shared a collective *what the hell* look. The guy had never been the happy-go-lucky type, but this felt like something else. And unfortunately, Beckett couldn't catch a bead on what that something was.

"Sorry about that, Shadow," he offered sincerely. "Please...continue."

"Thanks, Bones." She cleared her throat and resumed their mission review. "As I was saying, after you swim to the target location, both teams will work together to eliminate the threat and ensure the safety of the hostage. And in case any of you need a refresher on him, too, the hostage's name is Isak mar Rahal. He's a billionaire software designer who happens to be the tenth richest man in the world, and he's also one of our clients."

"Exfil still on as planned?" Falcon double-checked with their resident genius.

"Affirmative," Shadow confirmed. "Once the property has been secured, the other team will swim back to point A, get their chopper, and then fly back to pick you guys up. After that, you and Mr. Rahal will bring that bougie jet of yours back home. Any questions?"

"I have one." Beckett decided to go for one more playful shot before the woman disconnected the call. Sitting up a bit straighter, he asked her, "You ever gonna tell us your real name, or do you plan on keepin' us guessin' forever?"

Digger's intense gaze shot his way about a half-second before those of his other two teammates. They didn't really talk about the fact that no one knew who Shadow was. It was like this unwritten rule or some shit.

But one of these days...

"Nice try, Bones." Shadow sounded more amused than anything. "But it's gonna take a whole lot more than some smooth-talkin' cowboy to uncover my deepest, darkest secrets."

"Yeah, Bones," Falcon joined back in. "Besides, if she was going to tell anyone on the team her real name, it would be me."

"You?" Beckett shot the man an incredulous stare. "Why the hell would she tell you over me?"

"Or me?" Apollo looked over at them both.

From beneath his breath, Digger released a few grumbled curses as he shook his head in obvious frustration. He opened his mouth, probably to chew their asses for starting shit again, but Shadow never gave the man a chance.

"You know, Falcon," she spoke to their lead sniper directly. "I get that you and Apollo were just following Bones' lead at the beginning of this cute little game of yours. But while I expect that kind of boyish and immature behavior from the likes of those two, hearing you join in is just..." A click of the woman's tongue preceded a dramatic exhale. "Well. I'd be lying if I said I wasn't disappointed."

The steady humming of the plane's high-tech engines was the only sound filling the otherwise silent cabin. Two full seconds passed before Beckett lost the fight and started to laugh. Apollo and Falcon joined in almost immediately.

Digger refrained, as usual. But even though the big grump didn't laugh, Beckett could've sworn the man's lips twitched with a ghost of a smirk.

Maybe there's hope for him yet.

"All kidding aside"—Shadow got back down to business— "you'll be landing in like fifteen minutes. Does anyone have any *real* questions before your wheels touch ground, or are you good with the plan as it sits?"

Sitting up a little straighter, their team leader asked, "What about the pirates? Any change where they're concerned?"

"Satellite feed is still showing a total of eighteen active heat signatures in and around the targeted location," the woman who served as Tac-Ops' overwatch shared. "Twelve are positioned around the perimeter of Rahal's mansion…two tangos at each of the structure's four main corners, two at the front door, and two in the rear. According to the blueprints, the others are inside the mansion near the home's great room. As of right now, I'm not picking up anyone else on or around the entire island, so between the ten of you, it should be a quick in and out."

Famous last words.

Apollo shot Beckett a quick glance before sliding his gaze across both Falcon and Digger. "This thing has to be an inside job. No way it's anything else."

"I agree." Beckett nodded.

"Oh, yeah," Falcon joined in. "I'd bet my next paycheck this shit was orchestrated by someone on the inside."

"Or multiple someones," Digger concurred with a rumble.

Shadow's confident voice came through the intercom speaker once more. "Owens and I are both on the same page, as well. In fact, our insightful boss has already been in contact with his peeps at the DOJ, and from what I've been told, Rahal's entire staff is being rounded up as we speak."

"My money's on either a solo job or a partnership," Beckett added with a shrug.

"Afraid too many cooks would ruin the sauce?" Shadow, who was still very much listening, took a stab at his reasoning.

"Exactly," Digger grumbled. "Either way, the timing's too fucking perfect for it to be anything else."

Continuing along the same subject line, Shadow further shared her thoughts on the matter.

"The synchronicity of the events is what convinced Owens in the first place. I mean, I get that being in the constant spotlight has to get old, and I'm sure people in Rahal's same kind of massively elevated financial position probably get sick and tired of never having a moment of true peace and quiet. But this guy's the tenth richest man in the world. A brilliant businessman, by all accounts. And y'all know I am *totally* against victim shaming, but seriously…what the heck was Rahal thinking?"

"You're not wrong." Apollo was quick to back her up. "The guy purposely put himself into a situation where he's completely alone on four hundred thirty acres of rolling woodland and white, sandy beaches…in the middle of the fucking ocean, no less. And every single one of his sixty-eight-person staff became aware of the man's vulnerability the second he announced their impromptu time off, giving any one of them the perfect opportunity to waltz right onto Rahal's estate and squeeze every penny they can from the guy."

"Some people think money makes you bulletproof." Beckett shrugged. "The more they have, the more invincible they become."

He and his teammates had seen the same sort of unaware, presumptuous entitlement far too many times to count.

"And in reality"—Falcon piggybacked off Beckett's point—"every additional dollar they gain only makes them that much more of a target for greedy, heartless dickheads like the ones holding Rahal hostage."

"Someone will talk." Beckett circled the conversation back to their suspicions as to how the hell these guys pulled off such a big job so quickly. "People who work as closely together as they do…someone either knows who's behind it, or they'll be quick to suspect."

"Well, let's just hope these jerks haven't taken things beyond using scare tactics to get what they want," Shadow hoped aloud. "My equipment is as good as it gets. I should know; I'm the one who built it. But a heat signature only guarantees a pulse, you know? There's no telling what kind of condition you'll find Rahal in once he's located. And one of the signatures I'm picking up inside the residence has been stationary since I first tapped in, which means—"

"Bastards probably have Rahal secured," Falcon presumed.

Not that they expected otherwise.

"The most important thing is the guy's still alive when we get to him," Beckett reminded everyone. "I'll deal with whatever else needs done when our guy's safe and the targets have been neutralized."

As a Marine Raider, he'd been given the opportunity to study up on field medical procedures on the off chance the corpsman accompanying the mission got injured...or worse. Now he used that same training and experience to serve as the field medic for Tac-Ops.

"Copy that," Shadow acknowledged from...wherever in the world the secretive woman called home.

Bucket list item added: Figure out Shadow's true identity and meet her face-to-face.

"Okay, gentlemen." She began wrapping things up. "It's about that time, so I'm going to sign off for now. We'll reconnect once you make it to the target's location, but don't worry. I'll be with you the whole time."

"Thanks, Shadow," Falcon offered on behalf of the entire team.

"Good luck. We'll talk again soon."

The line went dead, and Beckett and the others immediately began preparing for their approach. With their seatbelts fastened and their focus shifted to the job, the team members grew silent as they mentally readied themselves for what they were about to face.

He understood fully the willingness to risk one's life in order to save another's. It was what he and his teammates did on a regular basis.

But for a person to be so infested with greed they're driven to not only risk their own lives, but also hold a man hostage—doing God only knows what to the poor man while they're at it —for the sole purpose of stealing whatever they could...

That was something Beckett would never understand.

What's to understand? Some people are just flat-out dicks.

His inner thought nearly had him smiling as the wheels of the jet touched down. The sudden jolt sending all four men slightly forward in their seats, and as the jet slowed to a stop, the team stood and began gathering their gear.

Minutes later, they were walking across the pavement toward two matching SUVs. Blacked out and tinted to the max, the unmarked vehicles looked more like those of the US Secret Service than one of their boss's wealthy friends.

The doors to one of the SUVs opened, and six tall, fit, and deadly looking men began pouring out. Like Beckett and his team, these guys were dressed in civilian clothes since their usual combat clothing was unnecessary for this particular op.

"Guess that's them." Beckett shifted the strap of his backpack as it hung from one of his shoulders. The straps of his MP5 kept the weapon secured loosely against his back.

Falcon smirked as he stepped up to Beckett's left. "If not, I have a feeling this little meet-up is about to get really interesting."

"You the SEALs from Hawaii?" Digger asked the men point-blank.

"Depends." One of the guys on the other team gave a non-answer. "You Tac-Ops from North Carolina?"

Tall. Bearded. Dark hair and eyes.

The man appeared to be in his mid-thirties, and even beneath the night sky with him fully clothed all in black, it was clear he was fitter than most. But what impressed Beckett even more was the guy's lip-curving response to Digger's not-so-friendly greeting.

Any man—or woman, for that matter—who wasn't afraid to go tit-for-tat with Dig couldn't be all that bad. Right?

"Mustang," the gruff-looking man introduced himself to Dig.

"Digger.

The two men shook hands.

"Ah, one of the two fellow frogmen on your team." Mustang grinned. "And, unless I'm mistaken, you're the one in charge of your team?"

"I am." Digger nodded.

"Good. Now, I hear we have a billionaire to save."

"That's what we've been told."

"Well, then…" Mustang gave Beckett and the others a cursory glance. "What do you say we get through the rest of the intros so we can get down to business."

"Sounds good to me."

"All right, well…like I said, I'm Mustang. And this tall bastard"—he playfully smacked his fist against the shoulder of the man to his left—"is Midas."

Standing several inches above Mustang's six-foot frame, the blond haired, blue-eyed SEAL gave them all a half-wave and a nod. In Beckett's opinion, the guy looked more like he belonged on the big screen, rather than slumming it with the likes of them.

"That's Pid," Mustang continued with the next man on his team. "He's our resident electronics expert."

"And this surly bastard here is Slate." Pid nudged the tall guy standing beside him.

"Surly bastard?" Beckett's brows rose with his smile as he turned his attention to the leader of Tac-Ops. "Damn, Dig. Did we just find your long-lost brother?"

Digger's dark stare intensified as he sent Beckett a look that screamed *fuck off.* So of course, being the immature asshole that he was, Beckett simply blew off the silent warning and landed a friendly slap against the man's broad back.

"Nice to meet you." He offered Mustang his hand.

"Likewise." The other man acknowledged with a smirk. "You're the medic, right?"

"Nah, I just play one on T.V."

A small huff of a chuckle lifted Pid's shoulders, and the man's crooked nose appeared to curve with his smile.

Mustang continued, tilting his head toward the quiet man on his right, "This is Jag. Don't let his quiet nature fool you. What he lacks in conversation the man more than makes up for in the field. And this is—"

"Aleck." The final SEAL didn't bother shaking hands, but instead gave a lift of his smooth-shaven chin. "Guess he saved the best for last."

A few of the other men on Aleck's team rolled their eyes. A couple others released a round of deep snorts.

Beckett remained quiet with a slight tilt of his head as he tried narrowing down his thoughts on the young frogman. Then he realized the smartass seemed familiar because...

He reminds me of me.

"I'm Falcon." Beckett's teammate introduced himself before adding, "And this is Apollo."

Mustang dipped his chin at them both. "Good to meet you, gentlemen. Now, no offense, but if it's all the same to you, we'd love nothing more than to take care of these pirate assholes quickly so we can all get back home to our wives."

"Couldn't agree with you more." Falcon nodded with a grin.

Apollo—the only other member of Tac-Ops who was married—remained quiet, but Beckett knew the hard-hitting former SEAL concurred. With a wife as sweet and talented as Nicki, it was easy to understand why.

Hell, he and Evie weren't even engaged, and he was already itching like mad to see her again. See her. Kiss her. Touch her.

Make her mine.

"This is us," Mustang spoke up again, motioning toward the SUV they'd previously exited. "You guys can follow in that one." He pointed to the one parked behind it. "I'm assuming you've been briefed on the plan for our approach?"

"SCUBA gear's right in here." Apollo patted a hand against one of the bulky bags jostling against his side.

"Good." Mustang reached for the driver's door of his team's

appointed ride. "We can give you a brief rundown on how it's gonna go once we get to the beach."

With a grumbled "See you there", Digger led Beckett and the others to their awaiting vehicle. Once their gear was stashed in the back cargo area, the team climbed inside and waited for the fun to begin.

THIRTY MINUTES LATER, Beckett found himself swimming beneath the water's surface, soaking in the peaceful serenity the ocean granted to all those who entered. His hooded wetsuit was like a second skin, the neoprene holding an insulated layer of water between his body and the suit's black, thick material.

Hence the moniker "wetsuit" versus dry.

The tranquility of the Atlantic surrounded him on all sides as the gentle sway of his fins pushed him closer to the man he and his team were hired to save. Like those around him, Beckett held his dive light securely in his fist, the circular beams from both teams shining through the otherwise impenetrable abyss.

God, I love the water.

He loved everything about it. Being on it. Swimming through it. Diving deep to explore what he'd always considered to be the great unknown.

But tonight was different. This wasn't a mission to explore, and Beckett and the others knew exactly what they were about to face. Even so, they had about twenty more minutes until they reached their target location, making it damn near impossible to keep from getting lost in his thoughts.

As he often was while diving with his team, he was reminded of a childhood spent swimming at the public pool. Those days were some of the best memories, and time had changed very little about the things he enjoyed the most.

Even now, while being swallowed by the monstrous, rolling sea in the dead of night, he felt a sort of peace only the water could bring. Like a dream he used to have over and over again as a child.

The recurrence of the scene always the same...

I'm in the water. I have the pool all to myself. I'm swimming underwater, and I never have to come up for air.

The memory spurred him into action, and Beckett reached a hand over to the man swimming close to his right. Because Digger was his permanent dive buddy during any dive-required op, it was Beckett's responsibility to let the other man know anytime he needed to go up for air.

With his light in his left hand, he used his dominant fist to give Dig's bicep a tap beneath the water. Almost immediately, the other man turned his focus to his partner. The two men made eye contact through the clear shield of their airtight masks.

Beckett pointed toward the surface, indicating his need to take a breath. With a nod, Digger began his ascent as he motioned to the others to do the same.

One by one, each member of both teams became alerted to the necessary change in their positions. Following their deeply engrained training, they kicked themselves closer to the surface, ensuring they remained present and accounted for by all.

As he approached the impending break in the water, Beckett slowly began rolling over onto his back. His mouth cleared the surface, and just as he and the others had a few times during their current swim, he immediately began sucking in as much air as his lungs would hold.

In a seamless move, he slipped back under the water. Beckett kicked his way deeper, not stopping until his dive watch indicated he'd reached the same depth as before.

The others resumed their previous positions, as well, and for the next several minutes, the two teams continued along the invisible path leading them directly to Isak Rahal's freedom.

With his well-trained lungs holding steady and his legs moving at a rhythmic pace, Beckett's mind did what it always seemed to do...

It wandered back to thoughts of Evie.

His pulse spiked as memories of the past few days—and nights—began seeping their way through. Perfect curves. Supple breasts. Her perfect, naked body writhing beneath his as he slid in and out of her welcoming heat.

But while making love to her was hands-down the greatest experience of his entire life, it wasn't the promise of more mind-blowing sex making his legs kick a bit harder. It was his innate need to reconnect with Evie's sweet, sweet soul.

He'd never met anyone like her before, and as he swam against the current, Beckett innately knew he never would again. Which was perfectly fine with him, because as far as he was concerned, his search for the elusive happily ever after had come to an unexpected end.

Evie was it for him. She was The One. And though they hadn't said the words, Beckett knew what he felt was real.

It was also new, however. And though he wasn't ashamed of his feelings in the least, Evie was still dealing with the emotional fallout from her father's earthshattering revelation. Not to mention the aftermath of being kidnapped and held hostage by terrorists who would have had no qualms about executing her and those girls.

The very last thing he wanted was to scare the sweet woman away, so Beckett decided to keep his true feelings to himself. For now. But the second he felt she was ready for more—

A fist nudged against Beckett's shoulder, and he turned his head in Digger's direction. Using familiar hand gestures to communicate, the other man let him know their mile swim was coming to an end.

Since the team's exfil plan included a short chopper ride from Rahal's private island back to their jet—as opposed to swimming back the same way from which they'd come—Beckett and his teammates quickly began shedding the gear they no longer required.

Fins, lights, and masks became offerings to the sea as the ocean's rippling tide carried the evidence of their presence away. He hated to do it, but wasting perfectly good equipment was an unfortunate part of the job.

Private or active duty, it didn't matter. The fact was, sometimes the need to cover their tracks trumped being frugal, and no amount of guilt would ever change that.

A few additional strokes later, Beckett felt his feet touch sand. Water poured from his body as he stood upright, and he used the opportunity to stretch his spine and give his leg muscles a break.

"Well, that was fun." His tactical dive boots made mirrored impressions in the soaking wet sand.

The SCUBA footwear slipped right inside his fins, offering enough protection to Beckett's soles to make maneuvering through certain terrains possible.

"Was it, though?" Aleck stood near the other five SEALs as they efficiently began stripping themselves of the equipment they had no choice but to stash. "Maybe it's just me but swimming a mile in the freezing cold ocean...in the middle of the night, no less...isn't exactly my idea of fun."

Beckett chuckled as the other team began shoving their own fins and dive lights into backpacks they'd worn for that exact purpose. A necessary step since the group of SEALs would be returning to the other island via water once the mission was complete.

When their stuff was secured, each man then slid his bag beneath a dense group of lush green bushes waving in the breeze a few yards away. Once the op was over and the hostage was safe and secure, Mustang's men would return to this exact same spot to retrieve their gear. They'd then swim back to the other island, get the chopper, and return for Beckett, his team, and Rahal.

Sounds easy enough.

Beckett watched and waited while the SEALS finished concealing their gear beneath the thick foliage. Having done that a time or two himself, he was suddenly damn glad his only concerns now were the MP5 slung across his back, the pistol strapped to his right thigh, and the MK 3 MOD 0 Combat/Diving Knife secured to his left ankle.

Don't forget the seventeen assholes and the hostage.

"You know, I actually didn't mind the swim." He continued

the current conversation by sharing his unsolicited opinion once again. "It calms me."

"That's only because you're like a fucking fish when it comes to the water," Apollo challenged almost immediately.

Beckett couldn't even argue the man's point.

"I don't know what Aleck was bitchin' about." Pid grinned as he came over to where they stood. "I mean, we're SEALS, for crying out loud. You ask me—"

"Good thing no one asked you," Slate grumbled the interruption from a few feet away.

Agreeing with the prickly man, Apollo chimed back in with, "Sorry, Aleck, but I'm with Slate on this one. I love the water as much as the next guy, but I'd much rather take the jet than have to slosh around an op in these damn things."

Apollo waggled a foot as water dripped from his own dive boot to emphasize his point.

"Bitch all you want, brother," Pid kept on. "At least you're not tied down by Uncle Sam's wallet." He motioned toward Beckett's state-of-the-art dive watch.

"No shit," Midas agreed. "Sure would be nice if Command would authorize *us* to use civi gear in the field."

Beckett shifted his rifle back around to his front, the weapon hanging securely from its wide, drenched strap. "Don't get me wrong, active duty was definitely a helluva ride." He referenced his own time as a military man. "But I can't deny, there are definite perks to working on the other side."

The conversation died down as the two groups finished their preparations. A moment later, both teams were ready to roll.

"Everyone commed up?" Dig asked, referring to the earbud communication system they'd gone with for this op.

"We're good to go on our end," Mustang announced after checking with his men. His dark beard made the government-trained killer look even more dangerous as they stood in the shadows of the night. "Since this guy's your client, Command gave the green light for your team to run point. But as far as we're concerned, for tonight, we're all one team."

"So what you're saying is you've got our backs?"

Falcon's question had Beckett and the rest of Tac-Ops watching Mustang closely as they waited for his response. The leader of the decorated group of SEALs turned his dark gaze in Falcon's direction as he rumbled a low, "As much as you have ours."

"Then we're agreed," Digger spoke up again. "Stick to the plan, and we all make it back home."

As far as inspirational speeches went, Dig's was a bit lackluster. But the fact that the man had even attempted to rally the troops made Beckett think there may still be hope for the surly bastard yet.

Maybe.

"Well, then..." Beckett shifted his hold on his MP5 while giving the other nine men a sweeping glance. "What do you gentlemen say we quit standin' around and get our asses to work?"

Because the sooner they rescued Rahal, the sooner he'd be back with Evie.

He and the other nine highly trained men began to move up the beach. *Damn.* He'd been doing *such* a good job not thinking about her since reaching the shore. But now...

Now all I think about is the way her dimples deepen with her smile and the soft, silky feel of her hair against my palms. Or the way my body fit perfectly with hers as I pumped my greedy cock in and out of her hot, wet—

"Bones!" Digger's deep voice pulled Beckett from his recent, erotic memories as the former SEAL walked beside him as they left the soft, open sand for the thick cover of trees. "Did you hear what I said?"

"Sorry, what?"

The other man's dark eyes bore into his. "Thought you said you were ready."

"I *am* ready," he challenged back.

"Are you?"

"The hell is that supposed to mean?" Beckett frowned, confused by Dig's concern.

"It means I need you focused and on-point. Christ, Bones.

We talked about this shit that day at the range." His team leader shook his head with frustration. "I *thought* you and Evie getting together would take care of the issue, but—"

"I'm good, Dig." Beckett fixed his gaze on the other man's as they walked side-by-side. "Really. Just ready to kick some pirate ass so we can all get the hell back home."

To say the other man was a hard man to read would be a massive understatement. Hell, most days, it was damn near impossible. But while it wasn't clear whether Digger believed Beckett's claim, the man didn't continue pressing the issue.

"So that's it." Dig sounded more annoyed than pissed.

"What's what?"

"I finally figured out what's pulling you away this time."

"There's nothin' pulling me awa—"

"Bullshit," Digger growled. "Your head's filled with thoughts of getting back home to your woman, just like Falcon's and Apollo's were the first mission they took after getting with theirs."

"You say that like it's a bad thing." Beckett smirked.

"It is if it becomes a distraction that gets your ass killed. Or mine, or any one of us out here standing by your side."

"Look, I get what you're saying, Dig. Really, I do. But just because I'm anxious to get back home doesn't mean I'm not in this thing one hundred percent."

"You'd better be." He slid his dark gaze Beckett's way. "I'd hate to have to kick your ass."

Beckett threw his head back with a low, hushed laugh. "You could try, brother." His lips curved into a sideways smirk. "You could try."

CHAPTER FIFTEEN

"All right, gentlemen." Dig kept his deep voice low as he came to a stop a stretch later. He waited for the others to gather in closer, ensuring their attention was locked onto him before speaking up again. "Just as we discussed, we'll move west for approximately one and a half clicks to the island's main property. From there, we'll split into groups and initiate our plan of attack. Any questions?"

"What about Shadow?"

"Don't you go worrying your pretty little head there, Bones." The woman's voice filled Beckett's ear right on cue. "I'd never let my favorite boys play in the sandbox without me."

"Sandbox is right," Falcon scoffed. The former Ranger kicked one of his feet to the side as if he were trying to shake some imaginary sand particles free. "I swear, no matter how tight my dive suit is, I still end up with the shit all over me."

"Tell me about it." Aleck made a show of picking at the seat of his wetsuit.

Beckett grinned as he and the others started to move. The thick bed of dried-up needles gathered beneath the tall pines swallowed their footfalls, making their approach virtually silent.

Minutes passed, and yards were covered as they kept their eyes peeled and their weapons held tightly in their fists. When they reached the end of the tree line, Digger lifted a fist, giving both teams an order to stop.

"SITREP," the man in charge asked Shadow for an updated report on their current situation.

"Satellite feed is still showing eighteen warm bodies. Same locations as before. Once you exit those trees, you'll see the property's concrete privacy wall positioned about ten yards directly in front of you."

"Damn." Aleck smirked, having heard the interaction through his team's linked comms. "Sounds like she's as good as they say."

"Shadow?" Beckett glanced over at the other man and smiled. "Oh, yeah. She's awesome. Best tech support I've ever worked with."

"I'm sorry, did you just call me your *tech support?*" Shadow sounded immensely offended. "You do realize I can hunt you down anytime...anywhere. Right?"

"Ah, come on, now,'" he drawled slowly. "You know what I meant."

"For your sake, you'd better *hope* I do."

Aleck's shoulders shook with the man's deep chuckle. "You know, if I wasn't already head over boots for my gorgeous wife, I'd think I'd be downright smitten."

"Why thank you, Aleck." The woman's response was sugary sweet. "It's nice to know at least *some* people appreciate my many talents. Apparently there are those who don't share your wise insight into—"

"Let's cut the chit-chat and focus, yeah?" Digger grumbled from Beckett's right.

"Focus," Shadow repeated after a slight pause. "Right. Sorry, big guy. Anyway, as I was saying...the main property's concrete barrier is a few yards from where you are now. You'll climb over the wall and then make your final approach through the lawn. There won't be much cover, if any, as it's mostly cut grass with a few adult trees strategically placed throughout. There *is* a decent-sized pool house, however. You know, just in case you need someplace to hunker down in a hurry."

"And the water?" Digger asked next.

"Quiet on all fronts. From what I'm seeing, it's just the baddies and their hostage. All that's missing is a group of badass heroes to swoop in there and save the day."

"Missin', hell." Beckett shot the others a grin. "Better take another look at that crystal ball of yours, darlin'. 'Cuz we're standin' right here."

The sound of hushed laughter was cut short by the sight of Digger's raised hand. "All right, boys. Playtime's over." His assessing gaze fell over the entire group. "You heard the lady, and you know the plan. Stick to it, stay alert, and whatever you do"—he turned his intense stare Beckett's way—"make damn sure you stay alive."

With the man's final reminder to keep his focus solely on the mission at hand, Beckett filled his lungs, gripped his rifle tight, and gave his teammate a nod.

Digger looked away, leading them through the nearby clearance. As promised, the massive wall instantly came into view.

Seven feet tall, the massive structure stretched on for as far as the night sky allowed him to see. To the average person, the wall screamed no way in. But for guys like Beckett...

He looked to Dig, waiting for the signal to climb. The moment his leader motioned for them to move, Beckett readied himself for the ride.

His right hand slid down toward the end of his rifle's barrel, grabbing the thick shoulder strap at the spot where it connected to the weapon's rail. There were about five yards separating him and the wall, which allowed for plenty of space to gather speed.

Beckett took a broad step forward, using the grip on his rifle's strap to swing it up and over his left shoulder with ease. With it hanging behind his back and out of his way, he picked up his pace and jumped.

Arms stretched high above his head, Beckett's upper body slammed against the concrete with an audible *oof*. He curled his fingers around the wall's upper ledge, grunting as he immediately began pulling himself up.

The rubber soles of his boots kept his feet from slipping free as he worked his body up the wall. Biceps burned, and the muscles in his thighs screamed from their efforts, but thanks to countless hours spent training, Beckett and the others cleared the crest of the wall with relative ease.

A quick glance at the ground below confirmed he was cleared to land. Not wasting any time, he pushed himself off the ledge, and for a full second and a half, he was completely airborne.

His feet hit the manicured lawn as the others dropped to the ground around him. Before they could take another step, Shadow made herself known once again.

"Excellent job, boys. Now comes the fun part." The sound of Shadow typing resonated throughout the comms. "Everything's still showing a go from my end." A few more clicks. "Just watch your backs and stay alert. This thing will be over before you know it."

Easy for you to say, sweetheart.

Using nothing but hand signals, Digger put the next stage of the mission into motion. The two teams moved together as one, like a well-oiled machine designed to kill...and protect.

With their focus on point and their rifles at the ready, the highly trained group of men spread out wide. Moving side-by-side in a long, horizontal line, they crossed the first part of the estate's expansive backyard with ease.

Beckett scanned the area where they were headed. The home's outdoor lighting was more than sufficient, making it easy as hell to spot their first two marks.

Two men. Both early thirties, if he had to take a guess. Dark skin, closely shaved heads, and baggy clothes that looked more than a little worn. In their hands were matching automatic rifles, but their focus was on each other and the conversation they were having, rather than where they should have been looking.

They have no idea what's about to go down.

Their suits and weapons were black as night, helping to conceal their presence as they covered more ground. Water squished around Beckett's toes as he walked, but as he'd done numerous times before, he ignored the uncomfortable sensation and kept on.

Digger caught their attention with a sharp wave of his left arm. With all eyes on him, he gave further instructions without ever uttering a single word.

In a methodically smooth transition, Mustang, Midas, and Pid broke away from the rest of the group. They flanked out to Beckett's left.

Their goal was to neutralize the targets standing guard at the massive structure's southwest corner before making their way to the assholes watching over the front door. From what Beckett had read about the badass group of sailors, he had no doubt in their ability to get the job done.

Next to cut loose from the pack were Jag, Slate, and Aleck. Taking the opposite approach, the three SEALs kept their rifles up and their steps purposeful as they moved to cover the north.

With the other team initiating coverage for those areas of the estate, Beckett, Digger, Apollo, and Falcon headed due west. Twenty yards in, Digger pointed to the left of the pool they were quickly approaching.

He gave Falcon a silent order to head that way as Digger and Beckett continued straight. As they moved, their team leader used the same sort of hand signals to send Apollo to their right.

Knowing his teammates were covering both him and Dig, Beckett's focus lasered in on the man standing to the left of the patio door. He kept the man in his sights while moving across the freshly cut grass. Using a tree as cover, he came to a stop while Digger did the same behind a different tree several yards away.

Digger looked over to where Beckett stood, checking to make sure he was ready. A curt nod was all it took for the former SEAL to initiate their final approach.

Here goes nothin'.

On Digger's mark, he took aim, readjusting his sights to ensure a fast, clean kill. His target came into perfect focus, the man's attention still honed in on whatever his buddy was saying.

Beckett's finger slid down into position, slowly curling around his rifle's trigger as he watched and waited for Digger to make the final call. When he did, both men took their shots, and the two targets standing guard by the mansion's back door dropped to the concrete below.

Neither Beckett nor Digger wasted time thinking about what they'd just done. Instead, the two hostage rescue specialists each rounded the trunks of their respective trees before moving swiftly toward the edge of the impressive in-ground pool.

As they did, Falcon and Apollo took care of the four targets they'd been authorized to kill, which gave their entire team a clear path to the home's rear entrance.

"East side clear," Digger spoke through the comms, giving everyone—including Shadow—an update on their status.

"Copy that," Shadow came through first. "It looks like Mustang and his men are almost finished—"

"North side clear," Slate announced gruffly.

Mustang followed that with a quick, "South and West are, too."

"That's twelve down with only five more to go. Stand by…"

The woman's voice faded as Beckett and the others waited for her to pass along to them whatever it is she was seeing. Luckily, they didn't have to wait long.

"Okay, so three of the five targets inside just moved from their previous positions. From what I'm seeing, it appears as if one went into a bathroom upstairs, and the other two are heading straight for the kitchen."

"That leaves two with the hostage?" Beckett checked, just in case.

"Affirmative," Shadow confirmed. "The unmoving signature is still in the Great Room, still in the exact same spot as before."

The guy's definitely restrained.

"Mustang, you and your men still holding steady at the front entrance?" Digger asked the man in charge of the other team.

"Affirmative. Just waiting for the signal to breach."

Digger looked down the line, his sharp gaze finding Falcon and Beckett before turning to check with Apollo. Seeing his men were ready to roll, the moment they'd all been waiting for finally arrived.

"Remember…" He spoke to every man there. "Shock and awe

is the best chance we have at keeping Rahal alive. They hear us coming, they might cut their losses and kill him to keep him from talking. So move fast but stay quiet for as long as you can."

"Copy that, Dig," Mustang acknowledged on behalf of his team.

"You ready?" Beckett looked to Digger and waited.

In total mission mode, the other man gave a slight dip of his chin and repositioned his gun before rumbling a low, "Let's do this."

Beckett's damp feet hit the smooth pavement surrounding the pool clearly built to entertain. Complete with a diving board, fancy slide, and a waterfall feature that probably cost more than his car, the outdoor area was just one of many signs that whoever lived here had money to burn.

Maybe if the guy toned things down a bit, he wouldn't have made himself a prime target for dickhead pirates lurking in the waters, waiting to stumble upon their next big payday.

But Isak Rahal did make himself a target, and now those dickhead pirates were holding him captive in his own home. And it was up to Beckett and the others to see to it the billionaire made it out of this alive.

Just a few more minutes to go...

Beckett and his team stepped past the two dead guys on the way to the home's French doors. The lights were on inside, making it easy to clear the immediate area, and when Digger saw the coast was clear, he reached for the door.

Trip wires weren't a concern, given the men at their feet would've gone in and out the same way, so Dig simply turned the shiny knob and pushed open the door before crossing the threshold while using his weapon to do an automatic sweep from side to side.

Beckett followed his teammate, the other two men zippering into a single-file line, and within seconds, the entire team was inside Rahal's house.

Chill bumps raced down his spine as he was met with a blast of cold air. As if the AC had been left running on full blast.

The glassed-in sunroom the team had just entered was a

spotless display of white marble. Chic lounge furniture and several lush, green plants gave the space a comfortable and relaxing feel.

Beckett didn't feel comfortable, and he sure as shit wasn't relaxed. But he was ready to do his job and help put an end to Rahal's terror.

"Okay, boys, listen up," Shadow returned with some helpful intel. "Dig, if you'll go out that door directly in front of you and take a left, there's a hallway that will lead to the Great Room. At the moment, your path is clear. Mustang, yours, too. The targets in the kitchen are still there, but I don't know for how long. Your fastest route is through the front door and to the right. If you get to the library, you'll know you've gone too far."

"Copy that, Shadow," Mustang responded for his team.

Beckett and his other two teammates followed Digger the remaining distance to the door. It was already half-open, making slipping through it damn near effortless, and in no time, the men of Tac-Ops were on their way down the hall.

The sound of whispering gunshots filled their ears, and Digger's fist flew into the air. Beckett's entire team stopped on a dime, standing one in front of the other while they held their breaths and waited.

"Kitchen clear."

Mustang's hushed voice was music to Beckett's ears.

"Copy that, Mustang." Shadow's response was immediate. "I'm still showing a target in one of the second-floor bathrooms. Sixth door on your right once you reach the top of the stairs."

"We passed the staircase on our way to the kitchen," Mustang let her know. "Midas, Pid, and I will head that direction. Jag, Slate, and Aleck will meet your men in the Great Room to provide additional backup."

"Copy that, Mustang," Shadow let the man know she'd heard his plan. "You're clear to head to the second floor now." To Digger, she said, "Tac-Ops, your pathway is also clear, so you're good to go whenever you're ready."

"Copy," Dig confirmed the final stage of their plan.

Ten down, two to go.

It was like taking candy from a baby, really. Especially with the other team's added support. So much so, Beckett almost felt bad about outnumbering the remaining two targets.

Almost.

He and the others followed Digger's lead as they made their way down the home's spacious and elaborate hallway. Beckett's gun remained steady as he kept its barrel pointed out in front, his fists holding it tight, and his trigger finger ready for the call.

"Uh...Dig? We may have a slight problem."

Another fist brought the team to a halt before Shadow continued.

"One of the two target signatures is moving. And I think... damn. I *know* they're headed straight for you. You'll have to cut him off at the pass without alerting the remaining HT."

Because alerting the remaining hostage taker would put Rahal's life in even more danger than it already was.

"Copy that," Digger whispered as he resumed his previous steps.

Beckett's heartbeat filled his ears with a sizeable rush of renewed adrenaline. Any minute now, they'd come face-to-face with the man, and it would only end one way.

Taking a life—even a piece of shit thief like the one they were about to encounter—was never something to be taken lightly. And while he knew he'd someday have to answer for each and every black mark on his soul, Beckett's peace of mind came from also knowing the world was a better...much *safer* place without them.

The sound of booted footfalls echoed down the curved hall. He drew in a long, cleansing breath, his gut clenching with anticipation as his feet carried him closer and closer to the source.

The man was still out of their view, thanks to the pathway's sharp curve several feet from where they were. But any second now, the man they were after would come into view, and when he did...

Their target rounded the corner, his eyes growing wide as saucers when he saw that they were there. He lifted his hand, revealing a pistol as the man shouted something in a language Beckett didn't understand.

All four Tac-Ops men opened fire at the same time their target pulled his own trigger. The man's shot went wild, but Beckett's hit with perfected precision.

His. Apollo's. Falcon's. Dig's.

They'd each fired their weapons with no other choice but to kill.

It was either him or us, brother. It was either him or us.

With their cover having been blown, there was no longer a need for discretion. They moved quickly, their one and only goal in that moment to get to Rahal…before it was too late.

"Upstairs clear," Mustang announced after another single gunshot sounded through the comms.

At the same time, Digger pointed to an arched entryway about five yards up ahead.

"You're almost there," Shadow let them know. "You should see a big opening coming up on your right."

They continued forward, reaching the entry to the Great Room without any further incident. Inside the massive space, they found exactly what Beckett had imagined.

Billionaire software mogul Isak Rahal was strapped to a chair in the middle of the room. His wrists and ankles had been secured with plastic ties, and the guy looked like he was about to piss his pants.

The remaining threat stood directly behind him. Eyes wide, sweat beading on his shiny forehead. And the pistol in his hand was pointed straight at Rahal's head.

"Drop your guns, or I shoot!" the HT warned.

Like his counterparts, the man's Hispanic accent was thick. Also similar to the newly deceased, this man's clothes hung loosely on his thin, lanky body. The worn t-shirt and pants covered in small rips and noticeable stains.

Desperate men with nothing to lose and everything to gain. Which is probably what they tell themselves to justify their criminal actions.

It was also what made the situation that much more volatile.

"Come on, man." Beckett worked to control his breathing as he and his teammates stood frozen in place. "Look around you. The only way out of this is to surrender your weapon and let Mr. Rahal go."

"I said…" The HT spoke through a set of clenched teeth. "Drop your guns or this man dies."

There was no way in hell he and his teammates were giving up their guns. Not for him or anyone else.

"You either toss your weapon and stand down, and or you'll be full of holes before you ever hit the ground," Digger warned.

The man's eyes were wild with the urge to fight or flight. Rahal winced as the gun's barrel was pressed even harder against his skull.

"Sitrep!" Mustang spoke through their comms.

"We're all good and in the Great Room," Aleck informed the other man. "Final tango has a gun on the hostage, and we have ours pointed at him."

"On our way."

"Copy that."

Beckett half-listened to the interaction between teammates, his focus more on watching the HT closely. He studied him with an operator's eye, looking for even the slightest sign he was about to shoot.

"Seriously, dude." Beckett tried his hand at negotiating a second time. "If you shoot, then we gotta shoot. And if we shoot, there's gonna be a huge, bloody mess to clean up. And that shit won't be easy on this fancy white tile."

"You won't shoot me." The man denied Beckett's claim. "You won't risk killing the man you came all this way to save."

"Oh, but we will." Digger took a slow step forward. "And trust me when I say, we hit what we aim for."

Doubling down on their promise, Apollo flashed the man a sinister grin, doubling down on Digger's claim. "If you don't believe us, just ask your buddies."

"Probably won't work, though," Beckett chimed back in. "Seeing as how they're all already dead."

Fury raged behind the man's dark stare as his focus bounced

back and forth between all five men. The gun trembled in the man's hand, giving away the bastard's heightened level of desperation. Fury raged behind his dark stare as his crazed focus bounced around the room as he attempted to keep an eye on the multiple threats he faced.

Which meant their plan was working.

If they pissed the guy off enough, he might be pushed to the point of doing something stupid. And when criminals get stupid, they start to make mistakes.

Come on, asshole. Take the fuckin' bait.

"You can still walk away from this right now if you'll just lower your weapon and take a step back." Falcon tried next.

"Bullshit!" Spittle flew from the angry man's mouth. "I drop my gun, and I'm dead."

"Well, if you shoot the man you're holding, we're *definitely* going to shoot you," Slate's deep voice sounded from somewhere close behind.

Beckett's lips twitched with the urge to smile even as Digger gave the man in their sights his final warning.

"Last chance, asshole." The former SEAL was as serious as Beckett had ever heard him. "Drop the fucking gun and let the man go!"

Their target's frantic stare swept the room once more in what appeared to be a last-ditch search for a means of escape. But there were no such means, and like any cornered animal whose very existence was being threatened, the asshole followed his instinct to do whatever it took to survive.

Beckett forced his pulse to remain steady as their target shifted his hold on his pistol. The slight move was almost indiscernible to the untrained eye. But Beckett's eyes were those of a former SF operative, and he wasn't about to risk missing a single fucking beat.

Pulling the pistol away from Rahal's head, their target appeared ready to surrender. The dumbass must have had a sudden change of heart, however, because with Beckett's very next breath he heard himself shouting—

"Don't!"

The echoed warning filled the expansive space as the man in their sights lifted the gun in Beckett's direction. The target pulled his trigger at the same time Beckett and the others fired their weapons, the barrage of booming shots ending with their target dead on the floor.

Several seconds passed by before anyone said a word. When they did, it was Shadow who broke the silence first.

"Tac-Ops, what's your status?"

"Target down, hostage is safe, and both teams are present and accounted for."

"Holy shit!" Isak Rahal exclaimed as he remained tethered to his chair. He was looking down, his eyes glued to the guy bleeding all over his expensive marble tile. "W-who are you guys?"

"We're with Tac-Ops." Digger reached down to his thigh and pulled his tactical knife free.

"Tac-Ops?" The wealthy man frowned.

"It's a...subsidiary to Travel Assurance." Beckett carefully explained while his team leader cut through the plastic ties holding the other man in place. "I believe you hold a policy with our company."

"Travel Assurance..." Rahal let the company's name linger on his tongue. But then recognition flashed behind the man's weary eyes, and he gave a jerky nod. "Ah, yes. You're Rafe Owens' men."

"The four of us are." Falcon motioned to Beckett, Apollo, and Digger.

"Does the hostage have any injuries we need to be made aware of?" Shadow cut back in.

"You hurt?" Beckett asked the billionaire while giving a cursory assessment of Rahal's physical condition.

"Nothing a long, hot shower and a few stiff drinks won't cure." The man didn't sound as if he was joking.

He had to admit the guy was holding himself together damn well after being terrorized in his own home for the past several hours.

"You catch that, Shadow?"

"I did, and that's wonderful news. What about you guys? Anything that needs to be reported?"

"Negative on all counts," he answered for the others after getting a thumbs up from each of the other men.

"Excellent. I'll let Owens know you have yet another mission success under your belts."

"Correction, darlin'…" Beckett slid his knife back into its protective sheath. "*We* have another mission success. You know we couldn't do this job without you."

"Yeah, you could," Shadow disagreed. Her tone became laced with humor as she added a quipped, "But wouldn't be nearly as much fun."

"Truer words were never spoken." He chuckled.

"I guess the only thing left to do now is to bring you boys back home."

Hell, yes!

A few tantalizing thoughts—all featuring a particular brunette he couldn't wait to see—ignited a spark of excitement Beckett barely managed to keep hidden. He couldn't wait to get back to Evie, but the last thing he needed was another lecture from Digger about staying focused in the fucking field.

"And you?" Rahal's gaze landed on the group of men standing behind the men of Tac-Ops as he pushed himself into a trembling stance. "You are—"

"Their backup," Mustang responded truthfully. He didn't elaborate. To Digger, he asked, "You guys still good with the previous plan for exfil?"

Digger gave the other man a curt nod. "We'll wait for you here."

"There's enough of a clearing east of the pool it shouldn't be a problem putting the chopper down there."

"We'll listen for your approach."

With that, Mustang and the others disappeared down the hall as they began their trek back to the beach. For the next several minutes, Beckett spent some quality time with Rahal, giving him a more thorough field triage before escorting him into the kitchen to get something to eat.

Once their hostage finished his sandwich and chips...along with two large glasses of crystal-clear water, the billionaire excused himself to shower and change before the flight back to the mainland.

Beckett was standing in front of the sink finishing off his own offered glass of water when Falcon's concerned voice pulled his attention away.

"Holy shit, dude!" His teammate rushed over to his side. "Were you hit?"

"What?" He frowned. "No, I'm not—"

"Your suit." Falcon reached up and began messing with the material at the side of Beckett's neck. "Sure as shit looks like a bullet hole to me."

What the...

Beckett set the glass back down onto the counter before lifting his hand to the exact same spot. Beneath his fingertips, he could feel the area Falcon had referenced.

Holy shit.

A small, almost perfectly round hole had been torn clear through the section of his wetsuit covering the left side of his neck. His pulse spiked as he spun on his heels, immediately scanned the immediate area in search of the nearest mirror.

He remembered seeing several throughout the areas of the mansion he and his teammates had covered. Surely there was one around here somepla—

There!

He took off, his dive boots smacking loudly against the tile with every purposeful step.

From behind, Falcon hollered after him with a confused, "Hey! Where the hell are you going?"

But Beckett didn't hear his teammate. Or maybe he did, and he was simply blocking him out. Either way, it didn't matter. Right now, his entire focus was on getting a look at the damage to his suit.

He came to a casual seating area located a few yards from the kitchen's open exit. Beckett's movements were swift as he passed between a pair of twin couches, both pieces of furniture facing one another from their position in front of an impressive brick fireplace.

Centered high above the structure's heavily polished mantle was one of the biggest mirrors Beckett had ever seen. His image appeared as he came to a stop directly in front of it, as did Falcon's, who stood a few feet behind.

He sucked in a quick breath when he got his first real look at where the bullet had struck. His hand went back to that spot as his feet slowly carried him forward, inching him closer and closer until he had no other choice but to stop.

"Damn, brother." Falcon's tone was somber as he kept a respectable distance. "I'd say that was about as close as it can get."

Beckett used the reflection for a closer inspection, moving the slightly gaped material between his forefinger and thumb. The projectile had gone clean through both sides of the suit, searing the neoprene mere centimeters from the base of his neck.

It was one of the very few places where the wetsuit wasn't flush with his skin. And if that bullet had hit just a few centimeters the other direction...

I'd have already bled out all over the fancy tiled floor.

He'd be dead. Fucking dead. As in no longer walking the face of this earth. His parents would be utterly gutted; the team would mourn his loss, and Evie...

She never would have even known I loved her.

That realization, above all others, left his head spinning damn near beyond comprehensible thought. He'd been so sure holding back his true feelings was the right call. Damn it, he hadn't wanted to scare her away when he'd finally found the person he knew deep down—he *knew*—he was meant to be with for the rest of his life.

Evie was smart. Funny. Sexy as hell with curves that drove him mad with need. But even more than that, she was sweet, selfless, and had the biggest heart he'd ever known.

Yet, despite the massive blows life had recently thrown her way, the woman hadn't let them break her. It wasn't as if her abduction and captivity hadn't happened, nor was the bullshit with the man who'd pretended to be her father something anyone should ever have to face.

But she had. Evie had faced both him *and* those Taliban assholes with courage, strength, and an unwillingness to surrender. She was, in essence, the absolute perfect woman for him.

A partner he could count on and trust. A future he wasn't wasting another minute waiting to begin.

"Bones, you good?" Falcon appeared beside him.

Beckett blinked, realizing only then that he'd just been standing there, staring at that damn hole in his suit that whole time.

"Yeah." He dropped his hand to his side and turned to face his friend. "I'm good. In fact"—a goofy-assed grin spread wide across his face—"I'm fuckin' great."

He was alive and in love, and that's exactly what he planned to tell Evie the second she opened the door. Because her friend Lo was scheduled to return home in a few more days, and after that...

I can't let her go back to Portsmouth without telling her how I really feel.

So yeah. That was the first step in his rapidly evolving plan. As for the second...

Beckett put a hand to his earpiece, activating the one-on-one option on his mic. "Hey, Shadow, you still around?"

Silence filled the tiny speaker a few seconds before he heard—

"Are you back home, snuggled safe and sound in the comfort of your own bed?"

With any luck, my bed won't be the one I'm crawling into. "Not yet," he told the smartass woman what she already knew.

"Then of course, I'm still here." Shadow's tone held a slight hint of admonishment. But by her next question, the brilliant woman had already returned to her naturally chipper tone. "What can I do for you, Bones?"

"I have a favor."

"Ooh...so like...you'd owe me one?"

"Yes, but it's not actually for me."

"Color me intrigued. Who's it for?"

"A...friend."

"Friend, huh?" A soft chuckle filled his ear. "Would this friend happen to be of the female species, and would her name happen to be—"

"It's for Evie," he offered up what the woman already knew. "The favor's for Evie, and...it's kind of a big one."

Apart from giving Evie a ring—which he'd damn well be doing as soon as he could find the time to visit a jeweler's—this was the biggest, most personal gesture he could think of to show her just how much she meant to him.

"Oooh, a challenge. Okay, then..." Shadow sounded almost as excited as he felt. "Lay it on me, big guy, and I'll see what I can do."

CHAPTER SIXTEEN

I can't wait to see you, either!

Evie smiled wide as she sent the message she'd just finished typing on her phone. She'd woken to find a text waiting from Beckett letting her know his team had completed their most recent mission, and he'd be back home before dinner.

A dinner he was planning to make for them both...at his place.

I'll finally get to see where Beckett lives.

Evie yawned as she sat the phone down onto the kitchen counter, grabbing the coffee pot and pouring herself another cup. Her first had been consumed earlier, when she'd come downstairs after her shower, but she hadn't slept well since Beckett had been away, and the lack of a good night's rest was starting to hit.

Just a few more hours, and he'll be back where he belongs.

It was crazy to think someone who was such a recent addition in her life could have this much of a stark impact on her day-to-day living. But he did. Every day. And from what Evie could tell, there were no signs that was about to change.

Memories of the two of them laughing hysterically over leftover pizza would strike at the most unexpected of times. Visions of the two of them talking into the wee hours of the night about nothing and everything created hidden smiles from stories only she would understand.

And then there were the other times. Times when Evie would be taking a shower—or hell, just doing the dang dishes— and she'd almost *feel* the warmth of his hands caressing her body to new, exciting heights.

Logically, it didn't make much sense, but in her heart, Evie felt as though she'd known the man her entire life. He'd somehow gone from being a stranger who'd helped rescue her and the girls to someone who owned a piece of her. The very *best* piece, in her opinion.

Because Beckett Stone owned every beating inch of her heart. Even if he didn't know it.

You should tell him.

A shot of fear raced through Evie's system at the thought of putting herself out there in such a vulnerable way. Could she do it? Was she ready to risk what she and Beckett had only just found by dropping a massive bomb like that at his feet?

Her nerve endings began to fire, and there was a slight tingling at the tips of her fingers. It wasn't as if rejection was a new concept to her. She'd dealt with that her entire childhood.

Kids made fun of her unruly curls. Her deep dimples and upturned nose. The curves Beckett couldn't seem to get enough of garnered countless unkind nicknames and whispers behind her back.

And though Evie knew inside her heart Beckett cared for her deeply, to lay it all out like that, and admit she was falling for him—that she had *already* fallen for him—was another level she wasn't quite sure he was ready to face.

Soon, though. She'd tell him soon. Because life had already proven its unpredictability to her too many times recently to take too much of it for granted.

As for today, Evie was going to focus on what she already had planned. Lo was coming home tomorrow, and there were some last-minute things she wanted to do before then. And since she was presumably staying over at Beckett's…

Laundry. Dishes. Dust. Floors.

Her goal was to have the place so spotless Lo wouldn't have to lift a finger for at least a few days. It was the least she could do after the woman let Evie use the place as her own personal hideout.

She took a sip of her coffee relishing the extra dose of caffeine as she made her way out of the kitchen. Since laundry was first on the list, she'd get a load going and then set to work emptying the dishwasher.

Evie was walking through the living room on her way to the stairs when the sound of a car door being shut caught her attention from outside. She went to the large picture window overlooking the street, reaching up to push aside the curtains hanging low.

There was a car parked on the street in front of Lo's condo. A man was climbing back behind the wheel of his yellow taxi, and there was a woman walking up the drive.

Her head was down, and a hoodie covered her downturned face as she pulled two suitcases behind her, and—

Suitcases? Why would someone be here with... Ohmygosh!

"Lo!" Evie hollered her friend's name as she excitedly ran the rest of the way to the front door.

Moving quickly, she nearly spilled her coffee as she set it on the small accent table positioned between the window's edge and the door. Evie rushed to type in the security code she'd memorized weeks before, and as soon as the tiny light turned green, she opened the front door and ran outside.

"You're home!" She hurried to the woman she considered a sister.

"Surprise!"

Lo released the handles attached to her bags and threw her arms around an incoming Evie. Squealing like a couple teenagers, they greeted each other with a mutual bear hug.

After a moment of tight squeezes and a few back-and-forth sways, Evie released her sneaky friend. "I thought you weren't coming home until tomorrow."

"I wasn't, but I changed my mind."

ANNA BLAKELY

"How come?" Evie asked as she went for one of the wheeled bags.

"For one, I'm pretty sure my sister was ready to kick me out," Lo teased, grabbing the other suitcase. "And two...to be perfectly honest..." Lo's pretty blue eyes lifted to the condo as they walked side-by-side the remaining stretch of the way. "I was just ready to be back home."

"What about blind date guy?" Evie propped open the door with her hip, holding the door open for her friend. "What was his name? Shane?"

"Shawn? Yeah...no." Lo lifted her suitcase over the slightly raised threshold before entering her home for the first time in weeks. "That's gonna be a hard pass for me."

"Really?" Evie fumbled with the suitcase a tad as she followed the other woman inside. With the door falling shut behind her, she rolled the bag out of the way, butting it up against the nearest wall. "I thought you said he was cool."

"He was...at first. At least, I thought he was. But then things got...I don't know. Weird, I guess."

"Weird how?"

Lo smiled wide, her shoulders falling with a friendly sigh. "I promise to tell you all about it, but I took an insanely early flight to get here, and their in-flight coffee tasted like ass."

"I've got you covered." Evie chuckled as she retrieved her own forgotten mug. "I made a fresh pot an hour ago, and it's still steaming hot. I'll fix you a cup."

"See?" Lo started to follow. "This is why you're my best friend."

"I'm pretty sure I'm your *only* friend."

"Fair enough. But hey, listen. I'll tell you all about Shawn if you promise to share more about your trip to Afghanistan. You haven't said a whole lot, and I *know* there had to be at least *one* exciting thing happen while you were there...I mean, it's the Middle East, woman! I'd die for the chance to go someplace like that. Can you imagine the pictures I could capture? What am I saying, of course you can. You were *there*."

Evie's footfalls nearly stuttered, and she was thankful her

back was to Lo so the other woman couldn't see her face. Giving vague answers and hiding the truth over the phone was one thing. Even during their few video calls they'd made, Evie had been able to hide the truth.

All she'd had to do was either turn the camera away or pretend to become distracted by something on T.V. But now...

"Evie?"

"S-sorry, what?" She cleared her throat as she stopped in front of the coffee pot and began pouring her friend a cup.

Lo turned and pushed herself up onto the countertop, letting her legs dangle over the edge. "I was saying I want to hear all about your trip."

"Oh. Um...there's not much to tell, really." Heat crawled into her cheeks from the lie.

This is so much harder than I thought it would be.

"Come on, there has to be something interesting. The food... the clothes...the *men*." Lo waggled her light brown brows up and down with a suggestive expression.

A man's face did flash within Evie's mind, but unfortunately it wasn't Beckett's. Instead, it was the guard. The one who'd hit and kicked her when he learned her so-called father wouldn't pay.

Don't think about that now. Quick! Change the subject. Talk about something else. Anything, as long as it has nothing to do with—

"Oh, before I forget, I think you only have maybe one more load of laundry detergent left in the bottle." She turned slowly, carefully handing her friend the steaming white mug. "I was planning on getting more when I go to the store later, but if you want to throw a load in now, I can—"

Lo's doorbell rang, the sound taking both women by surprise. Nearly spilling the coffee she'd been preparing to sip, a startled Evie sat it back down and headed for the door.

"Wait." Lo slid from the counter, effectively blocking her path. "I'm back, remember?"

"So?"

"So relax and enjoy your coffee while I answer *my* door."

Evie smiled as she watched her friend turn and walk away.

She understood what the other woman was saying. Her door, her responsibility.

Which was perfectly fine with her because whoever was at Lo's door obviously hadn't come to see—

"Um...Evie?"

The uncertainty in her friend's tone caused Evie's brow to furrow deep. "Yeah?" She began making her way to the door where Lo stood.

"This woman says she's here to see you. She said she has a package for you that's really important."

An important package? For her?

Frowning, Evie picked up her pace and covered the remaining distance between her, Lo, and a woman she could barely see. When she got to the door, she found a young, attractive woman standing on the other side of the threshold, and in her hand was a large manila envelope.

"Evelynn Mitchell?"

Evie nodded slowly. "Yes, that's me."

"Hi. I'm, Ashley, and I was asked to hand this directly to you."

"Okaaay..." She let the word dangle in the cool morning air as she took the offered envelope. "What is it?"

The young woman's smile grew a bit more. "I think you should open it up and see for yourself."

"Wait, you can't just tell her what it is?" Lo interjected with a slight bite to her tone.

Evie fought the urge to chuckle at her overprotective friend. Lo always was the first to come to her defense.

As it turned out, however, the unsolicited protection wasn't actually needed.

"Mr. Stone's instructions to me were to deliver that envelope to you ASAP," Ashley explained to Evie, rather than Lo. "He didn't give me permission to share what's inside, but he did say he'd like for you to read them over at your earliest convenience, and that you'd understand."

Mr. Stone?

"Beckett sent this?"

"He did." The woman smiled. "But since that has yet to be

signed, I didn't want to reveal anything you weren't ready to share."

Ready to—

"Beckett?" Lo turned to her with a frown. "Who's Beckett?"

Evie turned to her friend, only then realizing what Ashley had been trying to say.

Oh, shit!

She'd been so thrown off kilter by the unexpected visit—and subsequent mysterious envelope—and then to learn Beckett was the one who sent it, despite him not having said a word about it in any of his earlier texts…

And now you've said his name in front of Lo, and she's staring back at you expectantly, waiting for an answer.

"Beckett's, um…" Evie felt like a deer caught in a car's headlights. "He's…this guy I know."

"A guy who sent a hand-delivered envelope to you at my house with instructions to read its contents at your 'earliest convenience.'" Lo used air quotes on that last part for emphasis.

More focused on what she should say vs whatever it was she was holding in her hands, Evie opened her mouth but closed it again. Twice more, she'd start to say something—she had no idea what—before clamping her lips shut for fear of inadvertently breaking the law.

When she began the fish-out-of-water impression a third time, the woman still standing at the door became a sudden and surprising ally…

"Miss Mitchell, if I may." She flashed Evie a genuine smile. "I believe this whole situation will be much easier for you to understand and to"—her blue stare slid from Evie's, to Lo's, and back to Evie's—"*explain* once you've seen what's inside the envelope."

The contents. Right.

Blinking quickly, Evie gave herself a mental slap so she could look over whatever Beckett had sent with a clear head. With hurried moves, she released the small metal clasp holding the envelope closed before lifting the flap and reaching her hand inside.

She pulled out a set of stapled papers, and for a moment, she felt even more confused than before. But after a quick scan of the very front page, she realized...

He didn't.

"Evie" Lo's voice became protective as she tried seeing the paperwork from over Evie's shoulder. "Why did this Beckett guy send you something from...holy shit! Does that say Homeland Security?" The other woman slid more to the side to reveal the shocked look all over her face. "You have an NDA from Homeland Security?"

Ohmygod. He did.

Tears welled in her eyes, and it took several emotional swallows before Evie finally found her voice again.

"I-I do," she answered Lo with a jerky nod. "But this one isn't mine." She held out the papers for the other woman to take. "It's for you."

"Me?" Lo snatched the documents from Evie's hand, her eyes frantically scanning the top page once more. "Holy hell. This has my name on it." She looked back up at Evie. "Wanna tell me why 'some guy you know' sent you a Non-Disclosure Agreement with Homeland Security for *me* to sign?

Because he's the most amazing man I've ever known.

"You want to know all about my trip to Afghanistan?" She stared back at her best friend in the whole entire world. "Sign that and I'll be able to tell you everything."

Another rush of emotion blew past, and it was all Evie could do not to break down and cry. Beckett knew how badly it hurt not to be able to share what happened with Lo, so he'd somehow managed to make it possible for her to do so.

The man was on a mission to who knows where to do only God knows what, and he'd still managed to pull something like this off. And he'd done it, not for himself...but for her.

He did this for me.

"You're serious." Lo looked to the woman still standing before them and asked, "Do you have a—" She cut herself off when a shiny gold pen appeared twisted and ready for use. "Oh. Um...thanks." Bending down, she popped one knee forward and used the top of her thigh for support as she scribbled her name on all the lines flagged for her signature. "There." Lo handed the stranger the papers when she was finished.

"You can keep the pen." The other woman smiled. "I have loads more." To Evie, she added, "I'll take care of the notarizing and filing."

"Hang on." Lo frowned. "Aren't I required to be present with the notary? Or at least show someone my ID…"

"Typically, yes." Ashley's rosy lips curved into a sly grin. "Lucky for you, the man I work for is anything but typical."

"So, that's it?" Evie needed to be absolutely certain moving forward. "As far as our end is concerned, it's done?"

She needed to be absolutely certain.

"It's done." The other woman nodded.

She wasn't sure what to say except, "Thank you."

"My pleasure." Ashley waved as she spun on her heels to leave. "Have a great rest of your day, ladies."

"You, too!" Lo hollered after her as she shut the door and turned around. With her arms set in a tight crisscross across her hoodie-covered chest, she arched a brow and gave Evie a demanding gaze. "Okay, woman. Let's talk."

AN HOUR AND A HALF LATER—AFTER Evie sent Beckett a thank-you text that included the promise of more at his place later on —Lo knew everything there was to know about Afghanistan. The girls. The kidnapping. The men who'd held them hostage. Being rescued by Beckett's team.

Evie also shared the part about her father's response to her desperate call for help…and everything she learned about him after the fact.

"Holy shit." Lo sat back against the couch, the look of utter shock still plastered all over her beautiful face. "I can't even…I mean…" Her wide eyes blinked several times. "God, Evie. I don't know what to say."

"Not much to say, really. But at least now you know everything."

"Wow." Her friend sounded as stunned as she appeared. "I mean, that's...so fucked up in so many ways."

"Pretty much." She gave a watery laugh. With a sniffle, Evie wiped her eyes with the wad of tissue still crumpled up in her fist.

"So now what? I mean...what are you going to do? Will you still go back to the Hamptons, or do you think you'll move someplace totally different? Not to sound harsh, but it's not like there's really anything left there for you."

Ouch.

The sting from her friend's words was as real as the truth behind them.

"I don't know what I'm going to do." She gave Lo the most honest answer she could. "I mean, I'll have to go back to my apartment at some point. The school year will be over soon, and I'll have to figure out things with the district."

Until she and Beckett had a chance to sit down and really talk out things as far as they were concerned, it was impossible for Evie to even *try* to plan for the future. All she knew was that she wanted him to be a part of it.

"And Beckett? How does he fit into all this?"

She looked over at her friend and smiled. "I think this part of the conversation calls for something a bit stronger than coffee. I bought some orange juice the other day. And I'm pretty sure that bottle of champagne on the top shelf is the same one what's-their-names gave you last Christmas when you did their family pictures."

Lo burst out laughing. "It is. But I mean...who just randomly opens a bottle of champagne and starts drinking it?"

"Uh...we do." Evie pushed herself up from the couch. "Sit tight. I'll fix us a couple of glasses and bring them in here where it's more comfortable."

"Good idea. But you may as well save some time and bring the bottle in here, too."

"On it!" She gave her friend a thumbs up before disappearing into the kitchen.

She moved around Lo's kitchen with familiarity and ease.

"Hey, Beckett's team is coming home today, and we're supposed to have dinner at his place." Evie spoke loud enough her friend could hear her in the other room. "But I can reschedule for tomorrow since you got home today instead of—"

"Don't you dare reschedule!" Lo cut her off sharply. "Any guy who can make you smile like that at the mere mention of his name is not a man you should keep waiting."

Her shoulders shook with soft laughter as she reached high in one of the cabinets for a set of crystal flutes. "You don't even know what I'm going to say about him."

"Don't have to. I saw the look in your eyes when that Ashley gal told you he was the one who sent those papers."

Evie grinned even as a rush of heat crept up the back of her neck. She'd had a look? She never realized that before. Of course, she'd never had anyone in her life like Beckett before, so there was that.

God, I can't wait to see him again.

"Okay, but if you're sure." She walked over to the refrigerator, pulling open the stainless-steel door before reaching in and grabbing the bottle of champagne. "Hey, what if I have dinner with Beckett tonight, but you and I do something tomorrow?" She smiled wide as she used her hip to seal the appliance up tight. "We could go out to dinner, or stay here and relax with a PJ, popcorn, and movie night…whatever you want."

Evie started for the living room but stopped when a soft thud reached her ears. The sound was odd enough to give her pause, so she set the two flutes and the bottle of wine down onto the kitchen's generous island before starting her search.

She looked toward the wide archway that led from the kitchen to the living room. "Lo?" Evie started back to where her friend was waiting. "What happened? You already crash and burn from the red-eye?"

With a smile on her face—and a far lighter step than normal —she bounced into the living room expecting to find Lo crashed out on the couch. But her friend was no longer on the couch. She was lying face-down in the middle of the floor.

And she wasn't moving.

"Lo!" Evie called for her as she ran over to where she lay.

Dropping to her knees, she ignored the sharp pain rolling through her joints from the impact and began moving Lo's hair away from her face to see if she could figure out what the hell happened.

"Are you okay? Lo, can you hear me?" Evie's heart dropped when Lo's face came into view.

The other woman's eyes were closed, and she still hadn't moved. So no, she didn't think Lo could hear anything anymore.

No!

Evie pressed the pads of her index and middle fingers against the side of Lo's neck. Relief flooded her eyes with tears when she found a steady pulse and saw the shallow rise and fall of the other woman's chest.

Thank you, God!

Reaching behind her back, she attempted to grab her phone. But when her hand met nothing but denim, Evie remembered setting it down onto the counter earlier, right before Lo's unexpected arrival.

Dammit!

"You're going to be okay," she promised her unconscious friend. "I'm calling for help!"

Evie pushed herself back up to her feet and sprinted for the kitchen. The phone was exactly where she remembered, and she grabbed it so quickly, the damn thing nearly fell from her hands.

She dialed nine-one-one as she ran back to where Lo still lay. Crouching down beside her sweet friend, she did another check to make sure the woman was still breathing.

"Open your eyes, Lo." Evie shook Lo's shoulder in an attempt to wake her. "Come on, damn you. Open your freaking—"

"Nine-one-one, what's the address of your emergency?"

"Hello?" She spoke to the man on the phone. "Is this—"

"This is nine-one-one, ma'am. Are you experiencing an emergency situation?"

"Yes!" Evie blurted loudly. "Um, I-I mean, not me, but my friend. We were just sitting and talking and laughing and I left the room for like two minutes, and when I came back she was lying unconscious on the floor."

"Okay, ma'am, I understand, and I'll send first responders your way as soon as I have the address where you and your friend are located."

Evie rambled off the address to Lo's condo as quickly as she could. "Please. You have to hurry! I have no idea what happened. She just got home from an early flight, so maybe she's just exhausted? I don't know. She seemed fine just a second ag—"

A gloved hand filled Evie's vision half-a-second before it pressed painfully over her lips. Her heart leaped into her throat, and she instinctively dropped the phone and began clawing at the meaty arm holding her against her will.

No!

She tried to scream, but the muffled cries for help became lost behind a wall of black leather. Her attacker was big and strong, and she was no match for his bulging muscles. But still, she continued to fight.

Flashbacks consumed her, painful memories from the day the Taliban had stormed into her classroom, filling her every thought. It was still so heart wrenching, still so very real, but Evie managed to separate the past from the present.

If she let the memories of what happened in Afghanistan take over completely, the bastard pulling her away from Lo would succeed in his plan to do whatever he came to do.

Whatever it is, it sure as hell isn't good. So fight back, Evie! Fight back as if your life depends on it!

Another memory filtered through with the encouraging thought. Another time when she *had* fought back.

Evie had been no match for Beckett that very first day inside the cave. And she was probably no match for the man attacking her now. But at least she'd know she tried.

For Lo. For Beckett. And dammit, for herself.

I love you, Beckett! I love you, and I'm not ever giving up!

Evie flung her right elbow back as hard and fast as she could. Pain shot down her forearm, her fingers on that hand tingling on impact. The deep, male grunt she heard was more than a little satisfying, but she was too busy trying to get free to celebrate the minor victory.

Let me go!

She screamed the words nobody could hear thanks to the hand still covering her mouth. Evie's sneakered feet scrambled to find purchase, her feet and legs kicking and flailing about as she was forcefully dragged through the room.

Away from Lo, who was still lying helpless on the living room floor. Away from her phone—and the emergency operator who had hopefully put the call in to send somebody here. Away from…

Beckett.

Tears poured from the corners of Evie's eyes, but her fight against the hand at her mouth and the arm squeezing painfully around her waist prevented her from wiping them away. She twisted her body this way and that, but nothing she did was enough.

A sharp sting burned at the exposed side of her neck. Evie cried out in pain, but any sound she attempted to make was in vain.

Just like her efforts to fight off a man twice her size and triple her strength. No, make that quadruple…

Evie's legs kicked with a little less force, her muscles feeling heavier and heavier by the second. Her arms fell limply to her sides after having rapidly lost all her strength.

Whatever they'd given her was acting damn fast. So fast, Evie barely had time to panic.

A cloud of black began filling her vision, and before she knew what was happening, her entire world turned upside down. Her face became chilled by a sudden breeze, and just before she lost the battle completely, Evie realized…

I'm outside.

She was also upside down, hanging over the man's broad shoulders. Though her vision was fading more with each second that passed, she could make out just enough to know he was carrying her to an SUV parked in the alley behind Lo's condo.

Big. Black. Tinted.

This was it. He was going to stuff her into the back and drive away. Why, she had no idea. It wasn't as if Phillip was going to have a change of heart where she was concerned and decide this time he'd pay the ransom. He sure as heck wouldn't pay to have someone risk their own life to find her.

I'll find you, darlin'.

Her racing heart kicked hard against her ribs. That was Beckett's voice. She was certain of it. He was...here, and he... promised to...

Please...find...me...Beck...ett.   There's   something...I   need...to tell...you.

There was something she wanted to tell the mouthwatering former Marine. But as the world began to spin and Evie was unceremoniously dumped into the back of the SUV, for the life of her, she couldn't remember what it was.

Oh yeah...I...member. I wanted...to say...l-love...

She didn't finish the last of the fading thought because she couldn't. Evie had already fallen unconscious.

CHAPTER SEVENTEEN

Beckett turned onto the street that would take him to Evie. He was crawling out of his skin with anticipation of seeing the tantalizing brunette once again. Lucky for him, he only had a little ways left to go, and then she would be...

Mine.

Music blared from the car's speakers, the off-key lyrics blasting from Beckett's overworked lungs. The song was a ballad sung by his favorite eighties big-hair band, its lyrics telling the story of an unbreakable bond shared by two people in love.

That's right. I'm a softy at heart. And I'm man enough to fuckin' admit it.

A break in the chorus gave way to the same wide, toothy grin he'd worn on the entire flight home from Rahal's private island. All he could think about was getting back home to Evie.

The flight home, the ride from the airport back to the office, and any downtime during the team's video conference debriefing with the heads of Homeland Security and the DOJ. His thoughts were consumed by the image of her welcoming him back with open arms.

Just a few more blocks...

Beckett's smile grew impossibly bigger as he imagined Evie's face when she'd received the NDA. The text she'd sent him shortly after Ashley—Tac-Ops' young but impressively efficient manager—had delivered his surprise told him his plan had gone off without a hitch...

I can't believe you did that for me. I'll never, ever forget it.

He pressed down on his brake as he approached the next stop sign before flipping his turn signal and taking a right. Beckett's chest filled with joy, knowing his gift had brought *her* so much happiness, something he realized was now his new life goal...

To make Evie happy.

That, more than anything else in the world, had become his number one priority. To make her smile and laugh. To be the one—the *only* one—to bring her so much pleasure she cries out his name.

To keep her safe.

Okay, so he had two new goals. Making her happy and making sure no one ever fucking hurt her again. And the second she opened that door, Beckett was going to rush inside, pick her up, kiss her senseless, and then...

And then I'm going to tell her exactly how I feel.

Nerves sparked to life throughout his system, but he ignored them and kept on driving. He'd come within centimeters of dying just a few hours before, so his nerves could fuck the hell off.

This was right. *They* were right. Beckett believed that with every fiber of his being. And as the palm of his hand smacked the steering wheel in time with the beat of the band's drums, he belted the song loud and proud, as if he were singing every precious word to Evie.

Beckett was so lost in his thoughts of love and happily ever after it took him far longer than it should have to notice the drove of flashing blue and red lights up ahead.

What the...

His spine stiffened as his foot automatically lifted from the accelerator. Reaching up, he turned off the radio completely, transitioning seamlessly from a man in love to an operator assessing a scene.

Four cop cars, three news vans, and an ambulance were all

parked half-a-block away. Neighbors on both sides of the street were outside standing around, staring at the comings and goings of the law enforcement and first responders.

Crime scene tape had been stretched across the road several yards from where the unmanned police cruisers remained in place. And when Beckett got closer to the makeshift barrier, he realized the condo the police officers were walking in and out of this very minute was the one that belonged to Evie's friend, Lo.

Oh, god! Evie!

Fear and panic enveloped him as he did put the accelerator to the floor. A few seconds later, Beckett slammed on the brakes, jumping out of the car while the damn thing was still rocking.

"Sir, this is an active crime scene." A uniformed officer hurried toward him. Palm up out in front of him, the young man looked as green as a Leprechaun at a St. Patty's Day parade. "You'll have to turn back around and go—"

"I'm not going anywhere until you tell me what's going on." Beckett scanned the entire scene, his heart racing with his desperate search for Evie.

"Sir, I'm not going to ask you again."

"Fine." Beckett started to reach back for his wallet but froze when the cop's eyes grew as wide as saucers. "Easy," he crooned to keep the other man from drawing his service weapon. "Just getting my wallet so I can show you my I.D."

"No sudden movements." The young but well-trained officer rested his hand on the butt of his holstered gun.

It wasn't lost on Beckett that the guy had just unsnapped the small leather strap holding the weapon in place. Not that he blamed him. If the roles were reversed, and Beckett was the cop, he would've drawn his weapon the second the kid put his hand behind his back.

"Here." He pulled his official Tac-Ops ID from his wallet and held it out for the officer to see.

The kid's eyes widened a second time as he went from being suspicious to being in awe. "You're with Tac-Ops?" The young officer's blue gaze locked with Beckett's. "Dude, I've heard all about you guys."

"Then you know what I'm capable of." He took the ID back from the kid's outstretched hand, not feeling the least bit bad about the look of fear in the kid's eyes. "The woman I love has been housesitting in that condo, so I'm going to go in there so I can make sure she's okay."

"There was a home invasion," the officer shared. "Two victims, both female. One was knocked unconscious, and she's being treated in the ambulance now. And the other—"

"Victims?" Beckett stumbled back a step, his lungs suddenly struggling to pull in a full breath. "W-what are you...?"

He sidestepped the officer, ignoring the other man's hollered requests for him to wait as he ducked under the thin yellow tape. The ambulance was parked in the middle of the street with its back doors sitting wide open.

Due to its slightly cockeyed position, he couldn't see fully inside. But as his booted feet carried him mere feet from the emergency vehicle's back bumper, the patient being treated finally came into full view.

Tall. Thin. Disheveled blonde hair. Pretty blue eyes that were red and swollen from her tears.

An oxygen mask had been placed over the woman's nose and mouth, but Beckett recognized her instantly.

"Lauren!" He hollered loud enough for her to hear him over the paramedic administering care.

Evie's best friend turned and looked at him, surprise widening her eyes, their recognition taking *him* a bit off guard.

"Beckett?"

Gut tight, he stopped just shy of climbing inside. "You know who I am?"

"Evie showed me your picture."

"Where is she?" The breath in his lungs froze as he waited for her response.

"He took her." Tears poured down Lo's flushed and splotchy cheeks as she grew more and more agitated with each new word she spoke. "One m-minute, w-we were sitting on the couch t-talking..." Lo's tortured gaze met his. "I-I signed the p-papers so she could t-tell me about A-Afghanistan. I can't believe...after everything she's already b-been through. Overseas...and her dickhead f-father...n-now this..."

He took her.

Evie's friend continued on with her shock-ridden rambling, but Beckett had lost her the second he'd heard those three terrifying words...

He took her.

He took her.

He took her.

The silent taunt played over and over again in his head as he fought the losing battle to understand. Someone had broken into Lo's home in the middle of the day and taken Evie? But they left Lo alive and seemingly unharmed?

Who the fuck would do that...and why?

"Beckett?"

"Who took her?" he demanded.

I want a fucking name.

"I don't know." Lo began to cry again.

Motherf—

"Okay, let's start from the beginning. Tell me everything that happened."

With a jerky nod, Evie's best friend shared all she knew...

"I came home a day early to surprise her, and we were talking about...everything. I was in the living room, and she'd just gone into the kitchen to get stuff for mimosas." Her watery blue gaze softened as it became fixed with his. "We were going to sip on them while she told me all about you."

Ah, Christ.

"I got up to get something out of one of my bags," Lo continued. "That's when the man grabbed me from behind. I tried fighting him off, but he injected something in my neck that knocked me completely out. The next thing I knew, I was waking up on my living room floor, surrounded by EMS and police, and Evie was...gone."

"I love her," Beckett blurted it right out there for the world to hear.

He hated telling Lo how he felt before getting the chance to tell Evie first. But he needed her friend to know. Lo had to understand.

"You...what?"

"I'm in love with Evie," he repeated the clarification. "I'd planned to tell her when I saw her today, but now...." His voice cracked, forcing him to clear the emotion from his throat. "I'm only telling you this, so you'll know."

"Know what?"

Beckett met Lo's beseeching gaze, praying she could see the truth in his eyes when he promised her, "I'll go to the ends of the fucking earth if that's what it takes, but I *will* find her. And I will goddamn bring her home."

A slow smile lifted the corners of the woman's weary lips as she carefully lowered herself back down onto the cot. "You really are the badass she said you were."

No, he wasn't. He was just a man willing to do whatever it took to save the woman he loved.

"I'm sorry, sir, but we need to get her to the hospital to get checked out." A second paramedic appeared at Beckett's left.

He took a step back to make room for the man to work, but before the medic could close the doors completely, they heard Lo's elevated voice call out—

"Wait!" Evie's friend shot up from the cot, her moves desperate to the point of near panic. "She told me all about you and your team. The kinds of things you guys do. Please, Beckett. You have to find her. You *have* to!"

The doors slammed shut before Beckett could even respond.

"Sorry, man." The other medic rounded the bumper on his way to the driver's side door. "But we've gotta roll." Climbing behind the wheel, the man drove off, leaving Beckett standing alone in the middle of the street.

He turned and looked at the condo, struck by an onslaught of memories he and Evie had already made. The terror building up from deep inside grew larger and larger with every stuttered breath of his lungs.

Evie was gone. She'd been taken against her will again, and she was fucking *gone*.

Ah, Christ.

Beckett bent at the waist, gripping his knees with the palms of his hands to keep from falling. Jesus, he felt sick to his very soul. What the hell was he going to do?

You're going to get your shit together and call up the team. That's what the fuck you're going to do, because that's what Evie needs.

The voice in his head was right. Evie needed him to be at his very best now, more than ever before. And standing in the middle of the street, fighting the urge to vomit, wasn't it.

Beckett pushed himself back up and drew in a long, deep, cleansing breath. Exhaling slowly, he repeated the move twice more. After that, he gave the condo one last glimpse before turning away and walking back the same way he'd come.

He could lose his shit later, if the need arose. But until such time, he needed to be one hundred percent focused on the mission at hand. It was, after all, the most important mission of his life.

Beckett pulled his phone from his back pocket and made a call. Digger answered on the second ring.

"Yeah?"

"Get the team to the office, ASAP. I'm already on my way."

He ended the call, not wanting to waste time explaining what he'd end up going back over in a few minutes, anyway. The planning would start the second he and his team were together, but right now...

Right now, I need a minute to think.

But the longer he drove, the harder it was to keep himself in check. But he had to. For Evie. Whether she knew it or not, the woman was his life. No, she was his *everything*.

And he wouldn't stop until she was safe, and the son of a bitch who took her was dead.

* * *

EVIE WAS AWAKENED to near consciousness by a strange sensation. One that was familiar yet somehow out of place.

It was as if she were floating on top of the water, yet her skin and clothes felt perfectly dry.

Wait, that's not right. There's no water next to Lo's place.

She tried opening her eyes, but her lids felt weighted down. Why did they feel so heavy? Why did *everything* feel so incredibly heavy?

Have I been sick?

The only time she ever woke up feeling this way was after she'd downed a full dose of that nasty cherry-flavored nighttime cold medicine she always kept in her closet. But she didn't recall being sick.

In fact, the last thing Evie remembered was...

Crap. What is *the last thing I remember?*

Eyes closed, she lay still, trying hard to pull up her most recent memory. As she did, Evie could hear what sounded like the water's edge slapping against her bed.

Though it had to be a dream, she could almost *feel* her body swaying back and forth to the soft waves' gentle rhythm. The imagined scene gave way to an idea. A wonderful, glorious idea.

Beckett and I should go away together.

She smiled to herself at the oh-so-tempting thought. A whole weekend—or heck, maybe even an entire *week* away with nothing to worry about but sipping Mai Tais on the beach during the day and making mad, passionate love at night.

Actually, Mimosas sounded better than Mai Tais. She should totally switch it to—

Mimosas.

Evie frowned as another memory filtered in. She was in Lo's kitchen getting all the supplies to make mimosas. But not just for her.

I was making them for me and Lo. She got home early, and I told her all about what happened overseas. We were going to drink mimosas while I told her all about Beckett, but Lo...

No!

Lo was on the ground. She wasn't moving. The man on the phone said help was on its way, but then...

Evie's eyes flew open as memories of her attack came back

with a terrifying vengeance. On reflex, she shot straight up from where she'd been lying, but something wrapped around her wrists brought her forward motion to a sudden and painful stop.

"Ah!" She winced as she turned her head to see what held her back. Her heart dropped into her stomach when she realized why she was unable to move.

She was lying on a bed with her arms stretched high above her head. Both wrists were being held in place by a pair of white plastic ties. The bindings had been secured to two shiny, stainless steel screw eyes that had been purposely inserted into the wooden wall serving as the bed's pseudo headboard.

Ohmygod!

Real panic set in, sparking a primal, desperate need to escape. Tears fell freely from Evie's eyes as she pulled and tugged and yanked with all her might in a failing effort to break free.

Trickles of bright red blood marred the stark white plastic as it cut into her delicate skin, but she continued to fight against the unforgiving restraints. She couldn't go through this again. Not. Freaking. *Again!*

Yet, here she was, having been taken against her will a second time. And she had no idea by whom…or why.

What happened to her and the girls in Afghanistan was horrific. But despite the terror those men had instilled in her and her young students, their heinous acts were, in a strange sense of the word, understandable.

Kidnapping for ransom wasn't a new concept to the Taliban. Especially when it came to Americans helping those affected by the terrorist organization's violent ways. But to come into a nice American neighborhood in broad daylight, and kidnap her a second time…

That doesn't seem like the Taliban's style.

Nor did holding her captive on a boat. Which, as Evie had finally figured out, was exactly where she was.

She was being held against her will in the cabin of a boat she didn't recognize. Correction, not *just* a boat…

King-sized bed. Pristine white walls with dark, varnished wood trim. Twin nightstands with matching lamps.

Looking up, Evie could barely make out the bottoms of several small, rectangular windows lining the top section of the wall behind her. Sunlight filtered through them from the outside, its deep amber glow hinting the fiery orb was quickly approaching the horizon.

Her eyes fell closed, and she breathed slowly through her nose. Doing her best to ignore the nausea threatening to make itself known, she repeated the move a few more times before lifting her lids and looking around the room.

Evie decided to do what she'd done when she and the girls had first been taken, and focus on learning as much as she could about her present situation...

She looked down toward her feet to the wall facing the bed. A massive flatscreen TV stared back at her from its powerless screen, and though her current vantage point prevented her from seeing it fully, Evie was certain the frosted door to her left led to the cabin's en suite bathroom.

Yeah, her earlier assessment was in definite need of a slight adjustment. Because this wasn't just any plain Jane boat. This was a freaking yacht.

Who the hell would kidnap me and bring me to a yacht? And why?

The door to the cabin flew open, and Evie thought for a moment she was about to get her answer. But when she got her first look at the man who'd just entered the room, Evie realized...

I have no idea who this man is.

The guy was tall and incredibly muscular, like one of those professional wrestlers, she'd seen on TV. Evie's pulse raced, her stomach clenching with fear as he walked toward her with a plate of food and glass of something that looked like water in his hands.

"Who are you?" she demanded.

The man said nothing as he set the food and drink down on the nightstand to her left.

"Please," she shamelessly begged. "There's been some sort of mistake. I-I'm not supposed to be here."

The obvious statement nearly had Evie's own eyes rolling. Of *course*, she wasn't supposed to be here.

She watched and waited, and still, the man said nothing. Instead, he picked up one-half of what appeared to be a ham sandwich with all the fixings and brought it closer, as if he intended to personally feed her.

Evie's stomach growled with a hunger she hadn't noticed until now. But as much as her tastebuds begged for even the tiniest morsel, she couldn't help but wonder what else the bastard had included in the offered food...and what it would do once it hit her system.

"You really think I'm going to eat anything you bring in here after you've already drugged me once?" She stared up at the unattractive beast.

Because something else Evie had concluded over the last few seconds...this was definitely the man who'd attacked her and Lo.

She hadn't gotten a good look at him back at Lo's condo, but the nauseating scent of his musky cologne was instantly recognizable. And somewhere in the back of her mind, Evie had the passing thought that at least this kidnapper cared about personal hygiene.

Focus, dammit! You're in serious trouble here!

The man pushed the sandwich back in her face, but she turned her head to avoid the unwanted food.

"Eat," the man ordered. His voice was baritone deep and without so much as a hint of patience.

Though it was risky to say the least, Evie stood her ground and kept her mouth clamped shut. A low, inaudible curse was her only warning before the man grabbed her jaw hard with his free hand and forced her to look back at him.

Tears formed in her eyes, and her vision blurred as he increased the pressure in his already painful grip. Evie couldn't hold back the whimper when his meaty fingers dug into her skin, and she was almost certain her jawbone would shatter when he forced her mouth open and shoved one corner of the sandwich inside.

Evie struggled to get free of his excruciating grasp. But the man was far too strong, and without the use of her hands...

He pulled the food away, leaving a chunk of the meat, bread, and cheese still in her mouth in the process. Then the son of a bitch stared down at her and waited, the smug look on his face pissing her off almost as much as his attempt to forcefully shove food down her throat.

"Chew."

Following the command, she chewed slowly as her eyes remained locked with his. But rather than swallow it down, like a dutiful hostage, Evie waited until he came closer as if to prepare to offer another bite and then—

She spit it all right into his face.

Probably not the most brilliant move, pissing off a man who could snap her like a twig. But she'd already lost her freedom, and unless another miracle happened and she somehow managed to escape, the only thing Evie had left was her dignity.

I'll be damned if this man—or anyone else, for that matter—takes that away from me, too.

Fury filled the muscled bastard's deadly gaze as he slowly wiped a palm across his soiled face. Less than a second later, that same hand flew toward her so fast that Evie didn't have time to even try to avoid the blow.

The back of his hand slammed against her left cheek. She cried out, a blast of pain radiating from the point of impact as dozens of tiny black dots filled her watery vision.

Tears fell from the corners of Evie's eyes as she lay helpless at the mercy of a man she didn't even know, and all she could think about was how badly she wished Beckett were here.

If he were, this man would already be dead.

Everything around her became blurred with a fresh onslaught of self-pitying tears. Beckett had to know she was missing by now. And poor Lo...

God, please let Lo be okay!

The man reached down and grabbed her jaw again. His immovable grip hurt even more this time around, and his hot breath struck with a rancid wave as he leaned in with an ominous warning.

"Eat. Don't eat. I don't give a fuck what you do. But you spit in my face again, I'll fucking kill you myself."

He released her with a rough, angry shove before turning around and walking away. Evie's throbbing face crumbled as she realized whatever this was…it wasn't like the last time.

The terrorists who'd kidnapped her made their cause clear from nearly the moment she and the girls were taken. But this man…Evie had no idea what he planned to do with her.

One thing was certain, however. If she didn't find a way out of this room and off this yacht soon, she was as good as dead. And for the first time in her seemingly privileged life, she had something she wasn't willing to lose.

Beckett.

They'd only just found each other, but she loved him with all her heart. So, as hard as it was, Evie forced the rest of her tears away and began devising a plan.

Because the next time that muscle-bound asshole returned…

I'm damn well going to be ready.

CHAPTER EIGHTEEN

Tac-Ops Headquarters
Downtown Charlotte

"Breathe."

Beckett turned to see that Digger had joined him at the back of the team's private conference room.

"I don't need to fuckin' breathe." Beckett ran a frustrated hand over the short beard covering his tightened jaw. "I just need to find her."

"We will," the other man promised. "And we're doing everything we can to make sure we do."

The entire team was there, ready to act the minute they received even a hint of trustworthy intel. But they were still waiting on their boss to arrive, and until he did—

"It's not enough!" He slammed a palm viciously against the wall behind him. "We're all just standing around with our thumbs up our asses while Evie's out there somewhere, at the mercy of who the fuck knows? Ah, Jesus…"

Beckett raked his fingers through his short, dark hair, and he had to physically fight the urge to rip every strand from its roots. What the hell was he going to do? If they didn't find her in time…

"I can't lose her, Dig." The bite in his tone all but vanished with a sense of impending defeat. "She's—"

"Your everything." The other man put a supportive hand to one of Beckett's shoulders. "Yeah, brother. I know."

"We all do." Falcon and the others made their way over to where he and Dig stood. "Back when Avery was taken from me…" He gave a slow shake of his head. "Trust me, Beck. I felt just as pissed…just as *helpless* as you do right now."

"I thought I'd go out of my mind with fear and worry when I faced the possibility of losing Nicki forever." Apollo's dark gaze met Beckett's as he backed up Falcon's point. "But we did whatever it took to get our women back, and we'll damn sure do the same for you and yours."

"He's right."

Rafe Owens entered the room with purpose. At six-four, the beefy forty-eight-year-old was one of the most brilliant, level-headed, and calculating men Beckett had ever worked with. Add in the fact that he was former British Intelligence—accent included—and the handsome, silver-haired operative was like James Bond come to life.

"Tell me you got ahold of Shadow." Beckett hurried toward the imposing man while the others took to their usual seats.

"Unfortunately, no." An uncharacteristic look of concern flashed behind Owens' steel gray eyes, but it was gone as quickly as it had appeared. "I've asked Ashley to continue her efforts to contact Shadow, and in the meanti—"

"Continue her efforts?" Beckett cut his boss short. "All due respect, but Evie doesn't have time to wait for Shadow to decide to pick up the fucking phone."

In typical Owens fashion, the man kept his expression steady and his temperament calm and in control.

"Everyone here understands what's at stake, Bones." The man's intelligent stare met Beckett's. "And I assure you, we're doing everything in our power to find Evelynn Mitchell."

"We have nowhere to start, Boss." Beckett's harsh tone softened with a desperate fear. "I called a contact I have within the CPD on the drive over here. Whoever drugged Lo and took Evie likely left no prints, and their techs are so backed up, he couldn't even tell me for sure when they'd even be able to start going through the area's CCTV footage. And every minute that goes by without someone out there, actively trying to find her, the less Evie's chances are of making it out of this thing alive."

"Then it's a good thing we aren't waiting on the Charlotte Police Department to actively try to find her," Owens stated matter-of-factly.

"You got someone else?" Digger asked the man in charge.

Their boss picked up the small remote from the conference room table and activated the giant screen mounted on the wall behind him. Seconds later, a man Beckett didn't recognize appeared.

Guessing him to be in his early fifties, the guy's black hair was generously streaked with gray. The thick strands on top longer than those on the sides, and the matching beard covering the man's strong jaw was kept well-trimmed.

Beneath a burgundy t-shirt, a set of broad shoulders gave way to a pair of tatted, equally muscular biceps. But it was the look in the man's eyes that grabbed Beckett's attention.

One that left him feeling glad this guy was on their side.

"Gentlemen, I'd like you to meet Baker Rawlins," Owens' accent was thick as he introduced their surprise guest. "Former SEAL turned jack-of-all-trades." Pointing to each member of the team, their boss told the other man, "This is Digger, our team lead, Falcon, Apollo, and Bones."

"Bones." Baker looked him dead in the eyes. "You're Evelynn Mitchell's—"

"Can you help us find her or not?" Beckett didn't waste time beating around the bush.

"Yes." The guy's deep voice resonated through the system's speakers. "In fact, I'm pretty sure I know who took your girl."

A sliver of hope began to seep in for the first time since learning of Evie's abduction. "Who?"

"Her father."

And just like that, all remnants of hope Beckett had been feeling vanished. "You're referring to Phillip Mitchell."

"I am."

"Then I'm sorry we wasted your time because Mitchell isn't Evie's father." When all eyes in the room turned his way, Beckett shared the part of Evie's story he hadn't let them in on before now.

"So as you can see, the man clearly wants nothing to do with Evie. And I don't see how Mitchell would benefit from her abduction, either."

"Abduction, no. But he's still listed as the sole beneficiary on her ten million-dollar life insurance policy."

Ten million dollars?

Beckett looked at Digger before bringing his focus back to his boss. "That's the same amount the terrorists demanded when they made the ransom call to Mitchell."

"Wait!" Falcon interjected. "Are you saying Evie's dad, or whoever the hell he is, is the one behind all of this?"

"I'm saying, the evidence I've gathered up to this point sure makes it seem that way," Baker answered from the screen.

"What evidence?" Beckett frowned.

"I accessed the CCTV footage from the cameras in the area of the condo where your girl was taken. A blacked-out Chevy Tahoe is seen entering the alley behind the condo approximately ten minutes before a nine-one-one call was made from a woman identifying herself as Evelynn Mitchell."

Beckett's gut clenched as Baker began typing on his keyboard. A beat later, the conference room was filled with the panicked sound of Evie's sweet voice...

"Nine-one-one, what's the address of your emergency?"

"Hello? Is this—"

"This is nine-one-one, ma'am. Are you experiencing an emergency situation?"

"Yes! Um, I-I mean, not me, but my friend. We were just sitting and talking and laughing and I left the room for like two minutes, and when I came back she was lying unconscious on the floor."

"Okay, ma'am, I understand, and I'll send first responders your way as soon as I have the address where you and your friend are located."

Beckett's heart broke into a million pieces as he listened to Evie recite Lo's address for the man on the other end of the line. The fear in her voice tore at his insides, but then his own fear grew to an almost unbearable level when he heard the last part of the call…

"Please. You have to hurry! I have no idea what happened. She just got home from an early flight, so maybe she's just exhausted? I don't know. She seemed fine just a second ag—"

His hands curled into painfully tight fists as they rested atop the conference table's smooth wooden surface. The nausea he'd felt earlier returned with a destructive force, but thankfully Baker began talking again, and Beckett's focus was pulled away from his body's desire to puke.

"The SUV pulls back out of the alley less than two minutes after the call ended. I was able to track it to a marina there in Charlotte, down on Lockwood Drive."

"Someone came into her friend's condo in the middle of the day, drugged her friend, kidnapped Evie, and then drove her to a fucking boat?" Beckett stared back at the man as if he'd lost his damn mind. "That doesn't make any sense."

"It will in a minute," Baker stated with confidence. "When I saw where the SUV was headed, I hacked into the marina's security system. From there, I could see the asshole carry the missing woman—"

"Evie," Beckett corrected sharply. "Her name is Evie. And she's not just some missing woman, she's…"

"I get it." Baker's hardened gaze softened just a touch as the man gave a slight dip of his bearded chin. "As I was saying, the cameras show the asshole carrying Evie like a sack of fucking potatoes to one of the yachts docked at the marina."

"You get the name of the boat?" Owens asked before Beckett got the chance.

"Even better." Baker grinned. "I'm sending you a digital copy of the yacht's title, along with a bank statement from an offshore account, and information on the shell company attached to both the account and the yacht."

The laptop Owens always kept inside the conference room

dinged with an incoming email. A few clicks of the keys later, and Baker's image shrank to make room for the three windows that popped up on the screen.

Beckett stood up and walked to the front of the room to get a closer look. He scanned the electronic documents, his pulse spiking when he saw what Baker was referring to.

"Jesus Christ." He stared at the name scribbled on the dotted lines. "It really was him, wasn't it?"

Phillip Mitchell was listed as the CEO of a shell company with an address far away from his East Hampton estate. That same company was listed as the yacht's purchaser and current owner, and the individual who signed the bill of sale on behalf of that company...

Phillip. Fucking. Mitchell.

"I'm going to kill him," Beckett stated calmly and with conviction.

The threat was far from empty, and he was as serious as he'd ever been.

Rather than try to talk him out of cold-blooded murder, Digger responded to the deadly vow with a rumbled, "Might want to hold off on that until after you make him tell you where he has Evie."

"Problem's going to be finding the son of a bitch," Beckett groused. "If he's with her on that boat—"

"He's not," Baker cut through again.

Falcon stared up at the former SEAL's enlarged image and frowned. "How can you be so sure?"

But Baker simply looked back at Falcon and straight-faced said, "Because I'm damn good at what I do." And then he shared the rest of what he knew. "Phillip Mitchell isn't on that boat, because he's hosting a fundraising gala later tonight at his East Hampton Estate."

"The man orchestrates a kidnapping the same day he's hosting some hoity toity event?" Apollo's brows dipped low. "That doesn't make any sense."

"It does if he's using the event as his alibi." Beckett started for the door.

"Where the hell are you going?" Digger asked from behind.

"I'm going to see Phillip Mitchell. I'm going to make him tell me where Evie is, and then I'm going to get her the fuck back."

"You'll need to be on the list to get in," Baker spoke from wherever the hell the man was. When Beckett stopped and looked back at him, he added, "The event is invitation only, and evidence from the past shows he overindulges when it comes to security."

But Beckett was already shaking his head. "I'll break down the fucking gate if I have to."

"You say that now, but you go in there causing a scene, how close do you think you're going to get to talking with Phillip Mitchell?"

"Baker's right." Owens supported the other man's point. "The only way you're getting into that mansion is looking as if you belong. Which means—"

"Which means, it's a good thing I just hacked into Mitchell's electronic invite list and added your name in the mix."

"Put mine down, too," Digger stood and joined Beckett by the door.

Before Beckett could ask Dig why he'd offered to go with, Owens said, "Good idea. Might look suspicious if you show up by yourself."

"Okaaaay..." Baker's fingers danced over his keys. "There." He hit 'return'. "Anyone checking the list at the gate will see Beckett Stone and Slade Garrison as confirmed attendees. While you two are up north, I'll keep working on trying to figure out where the hell that boat went after it left the marina. With any luck, Mitchell will fold like a house of cards, and this whole thing will be over by morning."

No one bothered asking how the guy knew their given names. The guy had already proven himself to be as useful and technically talented as Shadow. As for morning...

I'd love nothing more than to wake up to find Evie wrapped up safe in my arms.

"Oh, and there is one more thing." The intelligent man's

steely eyes fell over Beckett and Digger. "Do either of you own a tux?"

FOUR HOURS LATER, Beckett and Digger stood in a sea of black and white as they did their best to blend into the upscale crowd.

"You see Mitchell yet?"

"Not yet," Digger spoke as he pretended to take a sip of his complimentary champagne.

Both men continued scanning the guests, the air of wealth and entitlement swirling about doing little to settle Beckett's already churning stomach.

Come on, you evil son of a bitch. Where the fuck are you?

The question had no more rolled through his mind when Dig nudged his shoulder and jutted his chin. Beckett followed the other man's line of sight, and there he was.

Phillip Fucking Mitchell.

The arrogant asshole stood front and center with a small group of formally dressed men. Some were in their sixties, like Mitchell, while others—if the absence of silver strands and wrinkles were any indication—were several years younger.

No matter what their age, the men were all smiling and laughing like a bunch of dumbass puppets with more money than sense. Each one of the idiots more than happy to let a rich asshole like Mitchell pull on their strings.

"You got this?" Digger asked while keeping an eye on their target.

Beckett placed his glass of untouched champagne on the tray of a passing by server. "Oh yeah." He started walking toward the man he'd flown two hours to see. "I've got this."

Both men walked with purpose across the shiny tile floor. It reminded him of the flooring in Isak Rahal's island mansion... the place where he'd almost died.

His steps threatened to falter as his brush with death shot to the forefront of his mind. If that bullet *had* hit him...if his ass had bled out on Rahal's floor...he and Dig wouldn't be here now, fighting for Evie's life.

Rather than slowing down, Beckett picked up the pace. He'd survived that close call for a reason. And to the depths of his soul, he'd forever believe it was so he could find the woman he loved and bring her back home.

To him...where she belonged.

"So I told the chef exactly what I thought of his overcooked lobster."

Phillip Mitchell's pretentious voice came within earshot as Beckett and Digger closed the distance between themselves and the small group of men.

"Good for you," another man commented his support. "I swear, good service is so hard to find these days."

"Do you think you'll give him a second chance to prove his worth?" someone else asked.

"Oh, no." Mitchell huffed. "I assured him under no uncertain terms that I would *never* step foot in his restaurant again."

"Damn, that's a bit harsh, don't you think?" Beckett boisterously inserted himself into the conversation. "Of course, it's not nearly as heartless as, say kidnapping your only daughter. Oh, wait." He snapped dramatically. "I forgot, she's not really—"

"Excuse me?" Mitchell looked even more appalled than his rich bitch friends. "How dare you—"

Beckett leaned in close, keeping his voice low so only Mitchell could hear as he said, "Oh, you really don't want to start the whole how-dare-you bullshit with me. Not after what you've done to Evie."

The small hitch of the man's breath revealed the asshole's guilt.

"I don't know who you are or how you got in here," Mitchell started his own low-spoken warning. "But—"

"I'm the man who's about two seconds away from telling everyone in this room all about how you left Evie to rot in a fucking Afghanistan cave after lying to her, them, and everyone you fucking know about the fact that Evie is another man's child. Or, you can put a smile on your face, we can laugh as if what I just said was an inside joke between you, me, and my friend, and you can excuse yourself so we can go somewhere more private to finish this conversation. Your choice."

Mitchell pulled back to meet Beckett's cold hard stare. His swallow was audible but then—

"You sly dog!" The man threw his head back with a chest-heaving laugh. "I thought you said you and your friend couldn't make tonight's festivities."

"Trust me, Phil." Beckett's lips curled as he slapped the man hard on the shoulder. "I wouldn't have missed this for the world."

Another hard swallow preceded Mitchell turning to his so-called friends with a smile still plastered on his piece-of-shit face. "If you gentlemen would excuse me, I promised my friend if he attended tonight...and was generous with his wallet...I'd give him a glimpse at the first-edition collection I keep in my den."

The other men nodded, a few offering words of understanding. Mitchell turned and faced Beckett and Digger, the man's smile vanishing in an instant.

"Follow me." He led Beckett and Digger out of the ball room, and into the impressive foyer they saw when they first arrived.

The three men made their way beneath the home's massive main staircase and down the hall to Mitchell's private home office. He shut the door behind them with far more force than necessary before spinning on the balls of his black paten shoes.

With a glare that would have killed if the ability existed, Phillip Mitchell attempted to take control of the conversation.

"I don't know what you think you're going to accomplish by coming here and accosting me in front of my guests, but—"

Beckett filled his fists with the lapels of the man's designer labeled tux. With his next breath, he shoved Mitchell's back up against the nearest wall, leaving little space between them for anything other than air and rage.

"You son of a bitch!" he growled, his teeth clenching painfully together as he spoke. "I know you're the one who had Evie kidnapped, and I swear to all that's holy, if you don't tell me where she is right this fucking—"

"Kidnapped?" Mitchell's silver brows dipped low above the man's nose. "Th-That wasn't me. It was those...those terrorists. The Taliban. At least, that's who they said they were when they—"

"I'm talking about what happened today, in Charlotte, asshole," Beckett seethed. "Not Afghanistan."

Confusion mixed with the alarm that had filled the guy's eyes. "Today?" He shook his silver head. "What are you—"

"The yacht, asshole!" Spittle flew from his mouth as he yelled in the guy's face. "Where's the fucking yacht?"

"What...f-fucking...y-yacht?" Mitchell struggled to speak past the added pressure Beckett was currently putting on the man's chest.

From his peripheral, Beckett saw Digger's hand holding up the printed proof of the yacht's title with Mitchell's name scribbled on the dotted line. He also had the paperwork Baker had shared providing the shell company's information, including the fact that Mitchell was its currently listed CEO.

"That's...n-not...mine."

"I swear to God, if you lie one more time—"

"I'm...t-telling you...the *truth!*" Mitchell cut off Beckett's deadly warning with a stuttered shout. "Not my...company. Or...yacht. I own...different...yacht ...two sailboats...a p-pontoon...and four j-jet...skis. T-Titles are locked up in my... safe. I can assure...y-you, th-that...isn't one of th-them. Just like...*that*"—the privileged asshole pointed to the papers still clutched in Digger's hand—"isn't my...s-signature."

"You just expect me to take you at your word?" Beckett shook his head slowly, despite letting up on the guy a smidge. "Because from what Evie's said, your word doesn't mean jack shit. Now we know she was last seen being forced onto this yacht, and I will move heaven and earth if that's what it takes, but I *am* going to find her."

"You don't have to take me at my word." Mitchell spoke with a little more ease. "There's a contract sitting on my desk waiting to be put in the mail first thing Monday morning. My signature is at the bottom of the very last page. Go ahead..." he challenged.

"Compare the two. Then tell me you still think *I'm* the one behind Evie's disappearance."

Beckett let the man go with a rough shove before marching across the room to the polished mahogany desk. Just as Mitchell claimed, there was a crisp new contract sitting to the side.

He picked it up, immediately flipping to the last page in the stapled stack as he carried it over to where Digger stood waiting. They compared the signatures in silence, Beckett's gut tightening when he saw the striking differences between the two.

The scripted name on the yacht's title was Mitchell's. But the formation of the letters, the style of cursive used...even the direction of the slant was noticeably different from the one Beckett had just picked up from the desk.

In fact, minus the first and last names being spelled the same, nothing about the two signatures looked similar in the least. Which could only mean...

He's telling the truth. But still...

"If the person who signed the yacht's title wasn't you, and therefore, the purchase of the vessel is technically null and void, then you wouldn't *technically* be lying when you say it isn't yours."

"All true," Mitchell agreed. "But I'm not lying."

"Why should I believe you?"

"Why the hell would I kidnap Evie?"

"A ten-million-dollar life insurance policy sure seems like motive to me," Beckett rumbled. "Same amount the Taliban demanded for the release of her and those four girls. Remember that?"

A look of resolve fell over the older man, and Beckett wasn't expecting the volunteered confession that followed.

"In case you didn't notice, I'm doing just fine without Evie's ten million in life insurance. Yes, I was willing to let Evie die at the hands of those terrorists when they called here demanding I pay her ransom. But it wasn't because I wanted her money."

"It was because you wanted to wipe your hands clean of her."

Mitchell's aged gaze met Beckett's without hesitation. Though there was the slightest hint of shame there, he held his stare steady as he gave a muted, "Yes. I'm not proud of it, but you wanted the truth. There it is. So, now that you know what kind of man I am, do you really think I would go through the trouble of paying someone else to set up a dummy corporation, purchase a luxury yacht in that company's name, and then make arrangements for Evie to be kidnapped again? What would I possibly have to gain from that? You think I'm going to pay a ransom to myself? For what purpose?"

"Oh, I don't know," Beckett drawled. "A hefty tax deduction, perhaps?"

"You're out of your fucking mind."

"You're right!" Beckett yelled, slamming the guy back up against the wall. "I *am* out of my fucking mind because the woman I love has been taken from me, and I'm trying to get her the *fuck back!*"

"I don't know where Evie is."

"But you know who took her."

Beckett's eyes flew to Digger, who was too busy staring Mitchell down to notice.

"I know nothing of the—"

"Bullshit." Digger inched closer to the man they were questioning. "You may fool those rich bastards you play poker with, but not me."

"I have no idea what you're going on abou—"

"Your tell." Digger held the man's nervous gaze. "You see, while you were busy looking at the papers in my teammate's hand, I stayed busy watching *you*. It's small, really. An almost indiscernible twitch of your left eye. It's well-hidden; I'll give you that. But not well enough. Which is how I know you recognized the handwriting on the deed to the yacht. All we need is a name."

"You're wrong. I-I don't—"

"Stop. Fucking. *Lying!*" Beckett's angry words echoed off the room's wooden walls. "Don't you get it? Evelynn is going to die if we don't find her. Now, she may not share your blood, but for thirty-one *fucking* years, you led her to believe she did." He got right in the man's weaselly face. "You say you had nothing to do with her kidnapping, prove it. For once, in your pathetic, miserable excuse for a life, be the father you should have been, and tell us who signed that *goddamn deed!*"

Mitchell's shrinking form trembled as the bastard cowered beneath Beckett's wrath. His voice shook as he finally gave up the name of the man likely behind Evie's kidnapping.

"L-Landy Granger." His shoulders fell with defeat. "That's Landy's handwriting, but...he's been my partner for nearly thirty years. He loves Evie like a—"

"Like a what?" Digger asked. "A daughter?"

Beckett's stomach churned with dread as he processed what his teammate was actually saying. If Landy Granger loved Evie the same way Mitchell did, her life was very much in danger.

"He'd never hurt her, and he certainly has no reason to kidnap her!"

"There's always a reason." Digger stared back at the sorry excuse for a man. "Nine times out of ten, it's money."

"Then this is the one out of ten because he doesn't need the money. That guy has plenty of his own. And even if I'm wrong on that front, the Landy I know would *never* resort to kidnapping for personal gain. Financial or otherwise. And he especially wouldn't hurt a woman he considers to be his family."

"Family, huh?" Beckett shook his head in disgust. "See, that word actually means something to me." His gaze slid to his teammate's. "To us. But hearing it being spouted off by a lying piece of shit like you lends zero credibility to pretty much anything you have to say."

"I'm telling you the truth. Landy would never hurt Evie."

"You'd better pray to God you're right," he warned the man quivering before them. "Because if anything happens to her...if I find out you knew what your snake of a partner was planning..." Beckett brought his face almost nose-to-nose with Mitchell's. "The last thing you'll have to worry about is being embarrassed in front of your snobby-ass friends."

He didn't wait for a response before turning his back on the pathetic excuse for a man and walking away. Nothing else Mitchell could say was worth the time it would take to listen.

And every second wasted here was time Evie didn't have to spare.

They'd just stepped outside and were about to make their way down the massive exterior staircase when a woman's voice called for them to stop.

"Wait!"

Beckett and Digger halted their steps, turning their attention to the silver-haired woman rushing toward them. Short, mid-sixties, a bit round in the middle. Add in the high-collared blouse, flowered skirt, and frilly white apron, and the woman looked like the quintessential grandma ready to bake cookies with the grandkids.

Only he and Dig weren't her grandsons, and the look on her face said she had something more on her mind than baking.

"I apologize for chasing you down, but I had to speak to you before you left."

She spoke quickly, making her Irish accent come out even stronger than he guessed was the norm.

"Can we help you with something?" Beckett forced a polite tone.

They needed to get the hell out of here and find that fucknut, Landy Granger.

"I've worked for the Mitchell family for decades," she shared willingly. "I was walking by his office a moment ago, and I couldn't help but overhear some of what was said. Was it true, what you told my boss about Evelynn?" Her worried eyes pleaded for him to say otherwise. "Has my sweet girl really been kidnapped?"

Her sweet girl.

"You're Helen," Beckett guessed. When she blinked up at him with surprise, he explained to her, "Evie told me about you."

"Then you know I care very deeply for her."

"I do." He nodded. "And to answer your question, yes. Evie's really been taken."

"Oh, sweet Jesus!" Tears instantly welled in the poor woman's eyes. "But you're going to find her, right?" Helen's gaze slid from his, to Digger's, and back again. "I heard you tell Mr. Mitchell you would."

"I won't stop until I do."

They shared a look of two people who cared greatly for a woman they were both terrified to lose.

"Thank you," Helen offered softly. "Please. Evie is such a sweet, precious soul. Please, do whatever you have to in order to save her."

Beckett looked down at the kind woman who'd been one of the only bright spots in Evie's childhood, and with every fiber of his being he vowed, "I'll fucking die for her, if that's what it takes."

CHAPTER NINETEEN

Evie lay in the center of the bed and stared up at the low-lying ceiling. The entire left side of her face throbbed to the beat of her heart, and the corners of her eyes felt uncomfortably tight from the dried-up tears her earlier pity party had created.

But she was done with that now. Done with the tears and cursing her spectacularly crappy luck. Feeling sorry for herself hadn't helped her when she'd been holed up in that Godforsaken cave, and it sure as hell wasn't going to help her escape this freaking boat.

Actually, she'd put an end to her self-wallowing sob session several hours before. Since then, Evie had spent the passing of time trying her best to think of a way out.

There was no way for her to know what dangers lay waiting behind that closed door. But just as she had before, Evie knew she had to at least try. Step one was to convince the next person who came into this room to cut the ties holding her captive.

Several minutes passed by, and for a moment, Evie started to think no one would come. But then she heard a shuffling noise from just outside the room. A beat later, the door opened, and the man who'd brought her food earlier appeared.

In one hand was a plate holding a slice of pepperoni pizza. And in the other was a glass with ice and what appeared to be some sort of clear soda.

"You spit in my face again, and you and I are going to have a problem," the man warned.

"I won't," Evie promised. "I promise."

His suspicious black gaze met hers. With a quick nod of his big head, he set the plate and glass down onto the nightstand, but Evie spoke up just as he started to reach for the pizza.

"But first!" She caught his attention, giving him the best puppy-dog eyes she could muster. "Please, I really need to use the restroom."

Thanks to her achingly full bladder, she didn't have to pretend to be ready to burst.

"I don't have permission to—"

"I'm not kidding," Evie spoke the truth. "I'm seriously about to pee all over this bed." When he continued to hesitate, she let her tears of desperation break through. "Please," she whispered, not bothering to fight the genuine quivering in her chin. "I promise I'll be good. I just need to use the bathroom."

While grumbling something under his breath, the man reached for a small knife sheathed at one side of his waist. Evie felt a hopeful spike in her rising pulse because...

It worked! He's really going to cut me loose!

Keeping her excitement under wraps was much harder than she'd have ever imagined, but she managed to school her expression so he wouldn't suspect her of having ulterior motives.

He held her left wrist steady with one hand and the knife with the other. The man's upper body hovered directly over her face, his cologne unable to fully mask the scent of sweat as he slid the blade of the knife between her skin and the plastic tie.

Evie held her breath and waited, the anticipation enough to drive her certifiably mad. She was so busy trying to think three steps ahead that she hadn't expected the sudden rush of pain that immediately filled both arms the second she was freed.

A small whimper escaped before she could stop it, and she cursed the show of weakness. Then she remembered guys like him probably viewed every woman as inferior, and she pushed the useless thought out of her head.

It didn't matter what this man thought about her. The only

thing she needed to focus on was getting the hell out of here and back home.

To Beckett.

Please, God. Please, help me find a way back to the man I love.

"Come on." The man grabbed hold of Evie's arm and pulled her to her feet. "Make it quick."

"Okay, okay." She stumbled the first few steps. "Please. I haven't walked for several hours, and my legs need a moment to adjust."

A deep, frustrated sigh filled the room, but he granted her request and stopped moving long enough for her to regain her footing.

"Thank you," Evie offered sincerely, even going as far as to look up at the man and smile.

The only response she got was a deep grunt and another tug on her arm, but at least he didn't get angry or strike out at her, so that was progress…right?

"Stay here," he ordered when they got to the bathroom door. "You move, I tie you back up, and you can lay in your own filth."

"I won't move." She shook her head. "Promise."

Evie kept that promise, staying stalk still as the man gave the bathroom a cursory glance. Checking for anything she could use as a weapon, she assumed. Unfortunately for her, there didn't seem to be any.

"Go." The man returned. "I'll be right outside this door."

In other words, even if she thought about trying to run, she'd have to get past him to escape.

Good thing my plan doesn't include trying to sneak past you at the door.

No, she had another plan. One that was simplistically desperate and probably the worst Hail Mary she'd ever seen. But Evie was desperate, and after hours of wracking her brain to come up with something better, in the end…it came down to this.

Here goes nothing.

"I'll try to hurry," she promised as she stepped past him on her way into the other room.

Elegant in its design, the spacious restroom was one more bit of proof that this yacht was definitely high end. A full-size garden tub faced her from the wall opposite the door. To Evie's left were his and hers sinks fitted with expensive fixtures and elaborate mirrors.

A stand-up shower filled the space between the end of the long vanity and the edge of the curved tub. And snuggled all the way back behind a small, partial wall was—

The toilet!

As if her body somehow knew relief was mere feet from where she stood, Evie's need to pee grew exponentially urgent, and she raced across the room. Once she was finished taking care of business, muscle memory had her automatically reaching for the toilet's knob.

Thankfully she stopped herself just in time, otherwise her entire plan would have been blown clear out of the water.

Water? Really?

Evie mentally slapped her inner voice for pointing out the poorly executed pun. But yeah, if she'd flushed the toilet like a normal human being, the one idea she had to get herself out of this mess would have been ruined.

She stood, returning her panties and jeans to their rightful place as quietly as she could. Moving with what she prayed was the same kind of stealth Beckett and his team used in the field, Evie carefully lifted the tank's porcelain lid.

Her eyes immediately looked to the locked door before gently setting the lid down onto the top of the bowl. After making sure it wasn't going to fall, she then raced to unhook the tiny chain connecting the refill tube to the round, rubber flapper.

Evie watched as the string of metal links sank to the bottom of the tank. She smiled to herself, but then shook the celebratory moment away. She wasn't out of the woods yet.

Not even freaking close.

Using the same slow, quiet movements as before, she returned the heavy lid to its rightful place atop the shiny white tank. When she was finished, Evie went to the sink and washed her hands with the small bar of soap next to the faucet before taking a moment to soak in her alarming appearance.

Curls sprang from every direction, and her shirt was full of wrinkles. The skin beneath her eyes had grown puffy and shadowed, and there was a sizeable bruise forming on her tender, swollen cheek.

Tears threatened to form, but this time, Evie forced every one of them away. She had a plan, and by God, she was going to stick to it. Even if it meant dying while trying to escape.

I love you, Beckett. With every single beat of my heart, I love you. Please know, I did this for us.

She didn't let herself think about the fact that he couldn't hear her. Because in Evie's mind...in that moment...she needed to believe that he could.

Her feet carried her back to the frosted bathroom door. Evie unlocked it and turned the knob but stole just a second to draw in a deep, steeling breath. She opened the door, and as promised, her bulldog of a guard was standing in the very same spot as before.

"We have a problem," she announced with a very serious tone.

"If you're on your period, use some fucking toilet paper."

Asshole.

"It's not that. It's the toilet." She glanced behind her. "It won't flush."

"And?"

"How long is your boss planning on keeping me here? Another hour? Two? Twelve? A few days?" She did her best to get through to him.

"What's your point?"

"My *point* is, if we don't get it to flush, it won't take long for this entire room to start smelling really bad. I'm assuming you probably don't want to have to face that every time you come in here...do you?"

The twisting of his upper lip was the first sign Evie had that her plan might actually work.

"Fine. But you're going to come into the bathroom with me and stand right the fuck next to me while I take a look."

That's the only way my plan will work, big guy.

"Of course." Evie gave a dutiful nod.

She followed the angry man back into the bathroom and over to the awaiting toilet. Unlike her, he was rough and loud, pulling the tank's lid off with a grumble, letting it clang loudly against the bowl's closed lid.

"It's just the fucking chain." He reached into the reserved water to reattach what she'd recently undone.

Now!

With his dominant hand submerged, Evie took full advantage of the moment and reached for the asshole's gun. She yanked as hard as she could, nearly stumbling back in the process, but even as the man's startled form swung around to stop her—

"Freeze!" Evie shouted, taking several steps backward to widen the space between them. The gun was much heavier than she'd imagined, and it was impossible to conceal the trembling in her hands.

She'd only shot a gun a few times, and that was back when Preston and his so-called friends had fancied themselves future marksmen. She'd accompanied them to the range, and that's where she'd learned the basics of firing a pistol.

"That was very, very stupid." The man's deep voice sounded as he held out a hand. "Give me back the gun before you hurt yourself."

"I don't plan on hurting myself," Evie warned. "I only plan on hurting you."

She didn't. Not really. She only wanted to be free.

"You have no idea what you're doing, little girl."

"Maybe not, but I am the one with the gun."

Anger flourished behind his deadly gaze, and she could tell he wanted nothing more than to kill her. But unless he somehow managed to get the gun from her, that wasn't going to happen.

"What do you want?" he asked, as if he actually cared.

"I want you to stay right where you are and don't even think about following me."

"You know I can't do that."

"If you don't, I will shoot you."

Please, don't make me shoot you.

"You're not going to shoot." He scoffed. "Look at how shaky you are. In fact…" He started walking her way. "I bet I could walk right up to you, and take that gun from your poor little han—"

A deafening blast filled the small room as he reached for the gun with the intent of taking it away. Evie didn't even remember pulling the trigger, but she must have, because with her very next breath, the man stumbled back and fell to the floor.

Bright red blood began to seep onto the tiled floor beneath him as he lay still with his eyes closed. There was a growing stain in his shirt surrounding a singed hole in the man's upper right shoulder, and…

Holy shit!

She'd just shot him. Actually freaking *shot* him! His chest still moved with slow, shallow breaths, so he wasn't dead. Yet. Still, Evie hadn't planned on shooting *anyone* in her attempts to escape.

What did I just do?

Another thought forced its way through the massive shock of what she'd done. The gunshot had to have alerted others, which meant Evie needed to get as far away from this room as she could.

Or a bleeding man was going to be the least of her worries.

She spun on her heels and ran out the door. She closed the bathroom door behind her, hoping to deter the discovery of the carnage being left behind.

Her footfalls were silent as she made her way to the cabin door. The gun in her right hand shook as she opened the door with her left. Evie's knees nearly buckled with relief when she found the hallway empty, and after a quick back and forth about which direction to go, she decided to go right.

She moved quickly along the narrow corridor leading to a set of stairs several yards away. As she jogged closer and closer to what she hoped was her freedom, Evie passed by a handful of other cabins on the way.

A noise sounded from somewhere behind, and she turned her head to check over her shoulder. Evie's heart leaped into her throat when she spotted the man she'd shot, the wound in his shoulder still bleeding as he ran toward her with a murderous expression.

"You fucking bitch!" He sprinted as fast as his heavy muscles would take him.

No!

Evie turned back around and sprinted toward the stairs. The gun in her hand felt even heavier than before, but she didn't dare drop it. It was her only means of defense, and if she lost it—

A wall of muscle slammed into her from behind less than three feet from the bottom of the stairs. Evie hit the floor with a bone-jarring thud, pain radiating throughout her entire body.

The gun she'd been so determined never to let go flew from her hand and skidded across the floor.

"No!" she cried out, reaching for it with every ounce of strength she possessed.

She twisted and turned beneath the man's massive form, scrambling with all her might to get free. But the sheer weight of his body kept her from moving even a single inch, and before Evie knew what was happening, he was sliding himself up her back, moving himself closer to...

The gun!

If he got to it before she did, Evie knew she'd end up dead. So the second his body cleared hers enough to reposition, she took off in a fitful rage.

The base of her throat burned with an animalistic growl as she jumped onto the man's broad back. They both went for the fallen gun, his meaty fingers reached the pistol at the exact same time as hers.

A fight to the death ensued, and Evie knew deep down this was it. There could only be one winner in this deadly game, and unless she was the one who got the gun first—

The pistol was ripped from her hand, and she was spun roughly onto her back. The man she'd been fighting stood at her feet, the gun's barrel pointed straight at her head.

"Please, don't!" She raised a useless palm in front of her face, as if flesh and bone could stop a bullet's penetration.

Truth was, there wasn't *anything* she could do now that would prevent her impending death. All she could do was lay there and wait.

The man stared down at her, looking her square in the eyes. And without so much as a hint of humanity or remorse, he started to pull the trigger.

"No!"

Evie turned her head away and squeezed her eyes shut. A loud blast filled the entire hallway. The sound eerily similar to the one she herself had created mere moments before.

She waited for the pain to strike. To feel the white hot fire she'd read about in stories where victims had been shot.

But there was no fire. There was no pain. There was only—

The man who'd been a hair's breadth away from ending her life fell dead to the floor beside her. Evie gasped when she saw the gaping exit wound that had decimated the front of the man's throat.

And as she remained where she was, still frozen with fear, she realized the eyes that had once been filled with anger and hate were now completely void of sight. Because the man they belonged to was dead, killed not by Evie's hand, but by—

"Landy?" Her eyes grew wide with shock as she turned to see the person responsible for saving her life.

"Evelynn, I—"

"Oh, thank God!" She rolled to her side to push herself to her feet.

The dead man's knife came into view.

Evie thought about the size of the boat they were on, and others who may be on board. So as she moved into a standing position, she grabbed the sharp weapon at the last minute, carefully slipping it between her waistband and her lower belly. With the hem of her shirt concealing it from plain sight, Evie got herself back onto her feet and started running straight for her family's friend.

She didn't bother asking Landy how he'd found her. All Evie cared about was that he was here, and he'd just saved her when she'd been seconds away from—

"I'm going to need you to stop right there." Landy lifted the gun still clutched in his hand, a look of resignation falling over the man's face.

She stumbled to a stop in the middle of the narrow hallway, nearly tripping over herself in the process. "Landy, what are you...It's me, Landy! It's Evie! Now, put down the gun, and let's get the hell out of here!"

"I'm sorry." He shook his head with a nervous lick of his lips. "It wasn't...it wasn't supposed to end up this way. You were never supposed to get hurt."

She was never supposed to get...

"Landy, what are you talking about? You know what? It doesn't even matter. Just put the gun away, and you and I can just walk away from whatever all this is."

"We can't." He stared back at her, his voice wooden and free of emotion. "It's too late for that now."

"No, it's not! Whatever this is...whatever you're involved with...I can help you! My dad and I can—"

"You and I both know Phillip's not your father," he revealed surprising knowledge of her secret. "I just wish I'd known sooner."

There were so many thoughts swirling through her over-whelmed mind, Evie was having a hard time trying to remain focused on her top priority, which was getting the hell off this yacht.

"You're right," she acknowledged what the man had just said. "Phillip's not my real dad, but he is your best friend. So whatever trouble you're in, I know he'll do whatever he can to help you."

"He can't help me!" Landy shouted, becoming more agitated than Evie had ever seen him.

With the gun held tightly in his hand, the man she'd known nearly her entire life began pacing the short distance between the hallway's long, narrow walls. She watched, trying to follow his ramblings as he began muttering about owed money and deals with what she gathered were some very unsavory characters.

"No one can help." He gave several jerky shakes of his head. "Not anymore."

"Landy—"

"You weren't supposed to get hurt. You were never supposed to get hurt! And those guys in that cave...they weren't really going to kill you and those girls. They were just trying to scare you, so you'd get Phillip to—"

"What did you just say?"

Evie's question was little more than a whisper, because she was too stunned in that moment to muster anything more. She had to have heard the man wrong. Landy was like an uncle to her.

No way was he involved in what happened to her and her students in Afghanistan. After all, he was her father's oldest and most trusted friend.

Surely, he wasn't saying what it sounded like he was...

"I'm sorry." He stared back at her, a broken reflection of the man she used to know and finally confessed his full truth. "I got into trouble. Financial trouble. So I did what everyone in my circle does."

"You borrowed the money you needed."

Landy nodded. "Eight million dollars."

"Landy..."

"I don't need your pity, Evelynn," he spat. "I didn't want *anyone's* fucking pity. That's why I went to the men I did to get what I needed. I couldn't let anyone in our world know I'd messed up the way I had."

"Did my..." She cleared the near-miss from her throat. "Did Phillip know?"

"No." He shook his head. "I made sure to keep him out of it."

"Except the part where you tried extorting ten million dollars by way of terrorists demanding a ransom, though...right?"

Because those horrifying pieces were finally falling into place.

"The men I owe money to have connections all over the world."

"Including within the Taliban." Evie surmised.

Her stomach retched, and if there'd been even an ounce of food in her system, she would've vomited right where she stood. Not only was the man she considered family behind the first abduction, but he was also the reason she was here?

"When I found out about your trip, I saw a way out. The people I owe said they'd take care of things on their end…but then I got a call that Phillip had refused to pay the ransom. The next phone call after that was to tell me the men they'd hired to take you had been killed, and you and the girls had been rescued."

"Sorry to disappoint you, Landy." Anger quickly replaced Evie's shock from the man's betrayal. "Let me guess…the guys you owe money to told you to try again. But here's the thing…if Phillip didn't pay the first time, what makes you think he'll give a shit about saving me now?"

"That's just it." Landy shrugged one of his shoulders. "He won't be paying me to save you. He's going to pay me, so I don't tell the world the truth about the kind of man he is."

"You'd do that?" She shifted her stance slightly. "You'd expose the fact that I'm not really his daughter?"

"That, and the fact that he was ready to willingly let you die, rather than lose a penny of his precious fucking money."

Evie huffed out a humorless laugh. "Look at where you are, Landy. You act as if you're not just as bad as him."

"I'm not!" The man yelled his denial. "I'm only doing this because I *have* to! If he'd paid the ransom from the get-go, if he hadn't refused to pay those terrorist assholes, we wouldn't even *be* here!"

"We're only here because *you* borrowed money from a bunch of well-connected *criminals!*"

The hallway grew silent as the two continued standing off

with one another. But it wasn't much of a standoff, really. Not when he was the one holding the gun.

Only a fool brings a knife to a gunfight.

"It doesn't matter," Landy spoke up again. "What's done is done."

"What do you mean?"

"I mean, I have no choice but to see this through. And since the team that rescued you killed the men working for those I owe money to, they're asking for the full ten million for themselves."

"And if you don't find a way to get them their money—"

"I'm dead."

Tears fell from the corners of Evie's eyes as she realized she'd been nothing more than a pawn in everyone else's games…

The man she'd once thought was her father had taken the resentment he felt toward her mother's affair out on Evie. As a child. As an adult.

Landy had used her in his first attempt to extort money from Phillip to pay off his ill-gotten debts. And when that didn't work, he arranged for her to be kidnapped a second time with the intent of blackmailing his partner and friend into paying for Landy's silence.

But there was part of what she'd learned that didn't make sense. And with nothing left to lose, Evie went for broke and asked the man holding the gun—

"Why am I really here?"

"I just told you why you are here. I need you to get Phillip to pay—"

"Actually, you don't." Evie stared back at him. "You said you were going to force him to buy your silence, and then use the money he pays you to pay off the debt you owe. So I'll ask you again…" She took a daring step closer. "Why am I here?"

Guilt clouded the man's weary gaze as he uttered the final part of his plan. "Paying off the people I owe still leaves me with nothing. I need…" He cleared what sounded like real emotion from his throat before telling her, "I'll still need money to live on after that."

ANNA BLAKELY

Money to live on...money to live on...money to...

"Oh, my god."

"Evie, I'm so sorry. I told you, I have no—"

"You had a fucking choice, Landy!" she screamed the uncharacteristic profanity. "You always have a choice! And you've already made yours, haven't you?"

"Evelynn, please—"

"Haven't you?"

Landy's silver head moved in a slow, shameful nod. "Yes," he whispered, still meeting her furious gaze. "A man has already agreed to buy you. He's scheduled to arrive tomorrow night."

CHAPTER TWENTY

The next evening...

"DAMN. THAT'S ONE HELLUVA BOAT."

Beckett followed Apollo's dark brown gaze to the high-powered vessel their boss offered up for the mission to rescue Evie. Even in the midst of worrying himself sick for the woman he loved, he had to agree with his teammate's assessment.

Rafe Owens was a man of taste in all of life's finer things. Including his Outerlimits SL-36 high-performance speed boat.

"I'll say," Falcon agreed as the team began boarding their boss's boat from the man's members-only covered slip. "Staggered Mercury Racing five-twenties? This bad boy will get up to eighty, ninety miles per hour, easy."

"I don't care how fast you have to go." Beckett dropped his dive bag onto one of the boat's leather cushions and turned to Digger, who'd already taken his place behind the wheel. "As long as you get us to Evie."

Thanks to Baker's genius, they knew exactly where they needed to go. In Shadow's worrisome absence, the impressive man had worked his computer magic yet again.

Last night, while Beckett and Digger had been chatting it up with Phillip Mitchell, Baker had spent the evening trying to locate Landy Granger's yacht. Using a program Baker had personally designed, the system was able to estimate the yacht's projected trajectory after it left the marina.

Once he had the estimated location, the computer genius accessed satellite imagery to confirm the yacht's precise coordinates. And after that…

He put in a call to Owens.

That was hours ago, and they were just now heading out. But everyone on the team had agreed a nighttime approach was their best chance at mission success.

Including Beckett.

Despite being out of his mind with worry for Evie, the others were right in their decision to wait. Just as it had with Isak Rahal, the coastal night sky would offer the best chance for concealment as they made their approach.

And since this was Evie they were talking about, Beckett would suffer in silence for as long as it took. He'd *do* whatever it fucking took. As long as this thing ended with her still being alive.

"The man has a point." Someone commented on the conversation he and Apollo had been having about the boat. "Although personally, I would have gone with the five-sixty-fives."

Every man on the boat turned to see who it was. When Beckett spotted the two men headed in their direction, he blinked a few times, untrusting of what he was seeing.

"Aleck?"

Both Aleck and Mustang—two of the SEALs they'd recently worked with—were making their way down the wooden dock. Slung over their shoulders were what appeared to be dive bags similar to the ones Beckett and his team brought.

Between their unexpected presence, the bags, and both men's purposeful steps, Beckett couldn't help but assume they were planning on tagging along.

"Hey, Bones." Aleck jutted his chin in Beckett's direction. "Heard your girl ran into some trouble and thought you might need some extra hands on deck." The corner of his lips curved as he looked at the group. "Get it...'cause it's a boat, and boats have decks..."

Mustang muttered a deep curse as he and his teammate stopped just shy of boarding the boat. "What Aleck is *trying* to say is we're here to help."

"Let me guess..." Apollo spoke up next. "Owens called your commander, gave him a rundown of the situation, and your guy gave you two the green light to assist."

"Something like that." Mustang grinned. "Lucky for you, as soon as we landed after rescuing Isak Rahal, the two of us were voluntold to help with some training a few miles down the coast."

"We landed with you all, then picked right back up and went south," Aleck further explained. "Our initial orders were to be there for the next ten days, but when Command agreed to loan us to you, he made arrangements for us to be choppered in."

A rush of emotion Beckett hadn't been expecting left him uncharacteristically silent. Owens had called in yet another favor. For Evie.

Not just for Evie. For you, too.

"Thank you." He finally found his voice as he and the others made room for Mustang and Aleck to board.

As he passed by Beckett, Aleck reached up and gave one of his shoulders a friendly squeeze. "No problem, brother. We've been where you are, so trust me when I say we get it."

"He's right." Mustang adjusted the wide strap of his bag. "And just so you know, we'll treat this mission as if your girl were our own. Whatever it takes." He offered Beckett his fist.

Beckett blinked against the sudden stinging in his eyes. "Whatever it takes." He bumped knuckles with the other man.

A beat later, Digger fired up the vessel's engines.

Beckett and the others settled in, getting to work changing into their wetsuits and gear. A small cloud of white smoke billowed up from beneath the boat's low stern, and the scent of fuel filled the cool evening air.

The deck was a bit crowded with the unexpected addition of

their new friends, but he wasn't about to complain. He'd gladly take all the help he could get on this mission.

After all, it was the most important one of his life.

"Here." Beckett handed Aleck the two extra ear buds he kept in his bag, just in case.

"Thanks." The other man took the small communication devices, placing one in his left ear as he handed the other to Mustang.

As soon as the rest of the team had theirs in place, Beckett reached up and activated the wireless comms. "Baker, this is Bones. You there?"

The system allowed the men to communicate with each other, as well as their borrowed eyes in the sky, over the engine's loud roar.

"Said I would be, didn't I?"

"Baker?" Mustang tilted his head with a grin. "Rawlins, is that you?"

"The one and only."

"Well, damn. Guess I should've known you had a hand in this one, as fast as it was thrown together."

Beckett's gaze swung across the boat's open cockpit to where Mustang and Aleck were sitting. "Wait, you know Baker Rawlins?"

"Duh." Aleck shot him an incredulous look. "Everyone who's anyone in this biz knows Baker."

After one last check to make sure the final ropes had been freed from the dock's metal cleats, Digger gave them the signal he was ready to roll.

"Hang on boys." Digger slowly reversed the expensive boat from its covered slip. "Water's a little rough tonight, so we're in for a bumpy ride."

And a bumpy ride, it was.

For seven miles, they were bounced and jostled as they cut through the water's choppy waves. It wasn't storming, thank fuck, but the wind had picked up. Making the ride to their destination anything but smooth.

With nothing else to do as they traversed across the wide-open sea, a few of the men carried on side conversations. Not Beckett, though. No, his mind was on Evie. His thoughts consumed with worry that they may already be too late.

He looked out into the low-lit abyss the night sky and dark waters created. A shimmering streak of silver danced on the ocean's surface, the moon's reflection offering sailors whatever light it could.

His focus lifted to the million stars shining high from up above. The brilliant, cloudless scene visible as far as the eye could see, and all Beckett could think was—

Is Evie looking at these same stars, too?

The memory of finding her in that cave shot to the forefront of his mind. She may not be in an Afghani desert, but that didn't mean she wasn't suffering.

Please, let her be okay. She has to be okay.

"Okay, boys." Baker's voice pulled Beckett's attention back into focus. "Lights from the yacht should become visible due east of your current location right about...now."

Every man on the boat looked up ahead, their trained eyes spotting their target almost instantly.

"Got it," Digger confirmed, bringing the boat to a slow-rolling stop.

With the engine cut, the scene grew quiet. The ocean's current created a soft, steady beat as its waters splashed against the boat's sleek hull. Baker continued giving them helpful intel while Beckett and the others listened closely.

"Current sig count is six," he referred to the heat signatures his program was picking up. "We've got two on deck, two at the helm, and two more down below. Best bet, your girl's being kept in one of the cabins, but that's only a guess."

It also made the most sense.

"All right, gentlemen, listen up!" Digger took charge. "We use the same, non-regulated approach through the water, using the buddy system to stay safe. You know the drill. You have an issue or need to come up for air, alert your dive buddy, they'll get the next guy's attention, and so on."

"We board the yacht, the first thing will be to clear the deck,"

Apollo reminded them all. "Once that area is secured, Dig, Bones, and I will take the first level down. Falcon, you, Mustang, and Aleck will handle any sigs still at the helm."

Picking things back up, Digger added, "From there, we'll all make our way through the rest of the yacht until every target is accounted for, and the hostage is safe."

"Evie's top priority," Beckett reminded the entire group. "She's the whole reason we're here. If we can bring Granger in alive to face charges for what he's done, great. But finding Evie and ensuring her safety is our number one goal."

"Understood, Bones." Aleck dipped his neoprene hooded head. "Like I said, we get it."

"There's something else," Baker spoke up again.

"Can it wait?" Beckett's tone did little to hide his growing frustration. "Evie's two miles away, which means we still have about an eighty-minute swim to get to her."

A lot could happen in eighty minutes, and he wasn't about to waste a minute more standing around shootin' the shit.

"This is important, Bones. I figured out Granger's motive for kidnapping Evie."

While he could appreciate the other man's tenacity and willingness to help, right now, motive was the last thing on Beckett's mind.

"No offense, Baker, but I really don't give a shit about why Granger did what he did. All I care about is getting our asses on that fucking yacht."

"Normally, I would agree with you. But I think you're going to want to know what else I uncovered before you put even one of your ten little piggies on that boat."

Beckett filled his lungs with air before releasing it out into the passing ocean breeze. "Fine. But make it quick."

Less than a handful of minutes later, Beckett had to admit, the man was right. One of the first rules of war was to learn everything you could about your enemy.

And if Landy Granger hadn't already put himself in the center of Beckett's sights, the crooked son of a bitch would most definitely be there now.

I'll fucking kill him.

The deadly mantra pushed him through the frigid waters as he and the team made their way to their floating target. As if playing on a silent loop, Beckett used the unspoken words as his own personal battle cry. Each push of his fins matched with a piece of the ominous vow…

I'll. Kick. *Fucking.* Kick. *Kill.* Kick. *Him.* Kick.

In his mind, he saw the scene play out like the most satisfying ending to a harrowing action movie. His team would board the yacht. Neutralize those stupid enough to get in bed with a man like Granger. And then…

I'll. Fucking. Kill. Him.

So that was the plan. They'd locate the asshole, take him down, and Evie would be safe. Then, once they were back on shore, the two of them could live out the rest of their days lost in their own happily ever after.

It was the only ending he would accept. The only one he would allow. Because a world without Evie lighting it up was a world in which Beckett had no desire to live.

Time stretched on as the team plus two made their way through the ocean seemingly undetected. Finally, after what felt like the longest dive of his life, Digger indicated that they'd reached their long-awaited destination.

"Just like we planned," Digger spoke low enough only they could hear. "We'll clear the deck together, and then you three"—he looked to Falcon, Mustang, and Aleck—"will head to the helm while the three of us take the next level down. At that time, we'll do an all call for a quick SITREP and decide where to go from there. Questions?"

When no one spoke up, he gave a curt nod and told Baker, "Going silent upon approach. Boarding vessel now."

Beckett and the others followed the former SEAL's lead as they began making their way onto the yacht. Thanks to the training they'd all received on Uncle Sam's dime—and the night sky and black wetsuits offering the perfect cover—their climb up the side of the hull and onto the impressive deck was completed with relative ease.

"Nice job, boys." Baker's voice filled his left ear. "I know you're running silent, but I figured you could use a couple eyes in the sky. First on the list are two sigs standing guard on deck. One at the stern, the other at the bow."

Using hand motions, Digger split the six operators into two separate groups. Using the same set-up as planned for the second stage of the mission, Falcon, Mustang, and Aleck went left, while Beckett and Apollo followed Digger to the right.

The wind started to pick up, but Beckett ignored the cold shivers racing down his spine. He'd walk through a fucking blizzard if it meant finding his way back to Evie.

I'm here, sweetheart. I'm here, and I am not leaving this boat without you.

Digger raised a fist, and all three men came to a sudden stop. With their guns at the ready, he and Apollo watched Dig's hand as their team leader motioned to something up ahead.

No, not something. Someone.

Their first target stood several yards away. His back was to them, and he was looking out over the water. A long, automatic rifle was slung across his muscular chest, and from his stand, the guy looked ready to use it.

Too bad for him, he had no idea they were coming. Because by the time he heard their approaching steps and turned with the intent to shoot, he was already lying dead on the deck. Beckett's bullet to the head having effectively eliminated the threat.

"Stern clear," Digger quietly relayed through the comms in their ears.

"Copy that, Tac-Ops," Baker confirmed he'd received the update. "Mustang?"

The low zip of a suppressed shot being taken filled the mics a beat before the SEAL responded with, "Bow's clear, too."

A deadly satisfaction began seeping into Beckett's veins. Two down, three to go, and this whole thing would finally be over.

"Heading to the helm, now," Falcon whispered his group's update.

"Copy that, Falcon," Digger acknowledged. "There's a door back here that leads inside. Making our way in, now."

He opened the aforementioned door, holding it wide for Beckett and Apollo to make their way through. Moving in a single-file line, the three teammates stayed within a step of each other. Keeping their guns up and their eyes ready for any threat that may come their way.

"Digger, I'm picking up a sig heading toward the interior door six feet up and to your right," Baker gave them a heads-up.

Since Beckett was still first in line, he held up a fist, stopping to center the door in his crosshairs…

The door opened. A man carrying a rifle crossed the threshold and entered the hall. He looked their way, his eyes growing wide as saucers. But like the man up on deck, this one never stood a chance.

Beckett pulled his trigger, the zip of his bullet leaving the chamber simultaneous to his target's body jerking. The man was dead before his body ever hit the floor.

"Got 'em," he confirmed as he and the other two resumed their steps.

"Nice job, but don't celebrate too soon," Baker warned. "Remember the two heat sigs I told you about that were down below? Well, they're moving directly below you right now. It looks like they're headed to a staircase not far from where you are now."

"Take us there," Digger ordered.

The man in their ears did just that. Following Baker's directions, Beckett and his teammates used hurried steps to get to the other end of the hall before their two targets reached the top of the stairs.

"Go north," Baker instructed as the wall to their right came to an end.

As Beckett entered to the floor's main entertainment area, he did what their temporary overwatch suggested and swung his body—and the barrel of his MP5—around the corner toward the opening to the stairs.

He stopped a safe distance away as Digger and Apollo flanked each of his sides. All three men held their weapons at the ready.

Beckett watched and waited, his right index finger precariously close to his trigger. He could hear his own heartbeat as it pounded through his ears. But he pushed his nerves back and remained focused on his one and only goal.

Save Evie.

It was the only reason he was here. *She* was the only reason. And as he and his teammates waited for whoever was about to come up those stairs, Beckett prepared himself to kill again.

CHAPTER TWENTY-ONE

Evie carefully made her way closer to the stairs. Walking behind her, Landy kept his gun pointed straight at her spine. The weapon meant to, as he'd put it, "keep her in line".

This can't be happening.

This couldn't be the way her story was supposed to end. Not after everything she'd already managed to survive.

And yet…

She tripped, nearly tumbling up the first step when the toe of her silver stiletto caught the hem of her gown. In another life, she'd think the white sequined dress was stunning. But in this one…

It's what Landy forced me to wear for the man on his way to buy me.

After the horrific scene with him and his guard the day before, Landy had forced her back into the same cabin she'd escaped from, tied her up once again, and then he'd left her there alone for the rest of the night.

This morning he'd come in with a cup of coffee, some eggs, and a smile. But Evie was still too sickened by the man he turned out to be, she couldn't even think about putting a drop of anything into her stomach.

Her sense of nausea had only grown worse when he'd forced her to shower at gunpoint. Thankfully, Landy had at least had the courtesy to stand just outside the bathroom, rather than watching her like a disgusting perv. But he'd threatened her with death if she tried anything on him like she had the man he'd killed.

And for some reason, despite their history, Evie believed the threat to be very, very real.

So, she'd showered, done her makeup and hair with the items Landy had so generously provided, and then she'd gotten dressed in the gown he'd had boated in for the special occasion.

This must be what it feels like to take that final long walk as a prisoner leaving death row.

It was a macabre thought, and one that would no doubt be offensive to some. But as far as Evie was concerned, if this happened—if she didn't find a way to escape her most recent nightmare—then her life may as well be coming to an end.

There was a monster on his way here this very moment. One who fully believed women like her existed solely for his sick and twisted pleasure.

So yeah, if Landy handed her over to someone like that, Evie may not be killed. But she'd be as good as dead inside.

Please, don't let this happen.

She silently pleaded with God as she slowly made her way up the stairs. This couldn't be her future. Not when she had another one all planned out.

A future filled with love and laughter and joy. One she'd dreamed about every night since Beckett came into her life.

But now that future was about to disappear. Stolen from her by a man she'd considered part of her family. But that family was nothing more than a farce. A smokescreen of wealth and prosperity built on a foundation of lies.

The man behind her had been a part of it all along. Unfortunately, Evie had been too blinded by the need for some semblance of familial love to notice. Now Landy was leading her to a life worse than death, and unless she found the perfect moment to act on a plan she wasn't sure would even work...

It's the only way, Evie. You have to at least try. Otherwise, you'll never see the man you love again.

Tears sprang to her eyes, spilling over her bottom lids. Her mascara was probably streaking down her cheeks, but she didn't care.

The only thing Evie cared about was the fear of never getting to see Beckett again. And that, more than anything this man—or any other—could ever do, was the one thing she didn't think she'd survive.

"Watch your step," Landy offered as they approached the top of the stairs. "Wouldn't want you to fall."

As if you give a shit what happens to me.

But Evie did watch her footing, because there was something Landy didn't know. A secret she'd been keeping hidden since the day before.

She reached down, gathering the gown's thick, shimmering material to keep from tripping a second time. As she did, Evie inconspicuously ensured the knife she'd stolen from Muscle Man the day before was still secured to her inner thigh.

The night before, after she'd been caught trying to escape, Evie had managed to talk Landy in to letting her use the restroom before being retied to the bed like before. While in there, she'd hidden the weapon for safe keeping.

When he'd forced her to shower a couple hours before, Evie had taken advantage of the opportunity and retrieved the knife from its hiding place under the sink. With the shower concealing her movements, she'd then used the silk thong Landy had so generously provided. Using it as a makeshift thigh strap to secure the knife to her inner thigh.

A jolt of adrenaline rushed through her as the heel of her hand brushed over the hidden hilt on her way up the last of the steps. But she'd checked herself in the mirror countless times before leaving the room, and as long as she moved or stood just-so, there'd be no reason for Landy to suspect she was armed.

Yes, he had a gun, but at least with the knife, Evie wasn't completely helpless. And the first chance she got to use it—

"Stop right there, Granger!" A man yelled as she and Landy cleared the top step. "Put the gun down, and let the woman go!"

Evie's eyes flew to her left. It took her a full two seconds to realize who'd just given Landy the order, but once she did...

"Beckett?" She instinctively took a step toward him.

But Landy grabbed her upper arm and yanked her back. The cool barrel of his gun pressed against her temple as he kept the back of her body flush with his front.

He's using me as a human shield.

One more bit of proof the man only cared about himself.

"Drop your guns, or she's dead!" he shouted next to her ear.

Evie winced when the gun's cold metal began cutting into her skin.

"P-Please, Landy," she tried begging. "If they're here, that means there's no way out."

"She's right," Beckett spoke directly to Landy. "It's over, Granger. So put down the gun, and let Evie go."

He's really here! Beckett's here, which means everything is going to be okay!

But even as the wistful thought drove through her frantic mind, Evie knew his team's presence alone wasn't enough to secure a positive outcome. And until Landy agreed to lower his weapon...

"Please, Landy. Do what he says, and no one else has to get hurt."

"It's too late for that," her father's partner growled.

"No, it's not."

"Enough with the bullshit, Granger," Digger chimed in. "Drop the gun and step away from the woman, or you'll be as dead as the rest of your crew."

"Wait!" Evie heard herself coming to Landy's defense. Not because she forgave him for what he was doing, but because she didn't want to see him or anyone else get killed. "Y-You need money, right?" She spoke directly to Landy. "You said you made some bad investments, so you used your clients' money to cover it. And when that didn't work, you came up with the plan to use me to get money from Phillip. And because that fell through, we're here, right? But we don't have to be."

From her peripheral, she could tell Landy was already shaking his head.

"You don't know what you're talking about," he dismissed her completely.

"Yes, I do!" she pleaded with Landy as the man held her in place with a gun to her head and an arm around her neck. "And I think I have a way we can all get out of this thing without anyone else getting hurt."

Beckett and his teammates remained quiet as Landy considered what Evie had just said.

"How?" he finally asked after a long, tortuous few seconds of silence.

"My trust," Evie announced. "My grandparents on my mom's side set it up for me shortly after I was born. It's a living trust, and one my father can't legally access. But I'll be able to as soon as I turn thirty-two, which is in just a few—"

"Months?" Landy's laugh held no genuine humor. "I can't wait months, Evie. The men I owe will kill me long before that time comes."

"Yeah?" Apollo shot daggers from his deadly stare. "What do you think we're going to do to you if you don't drop that fucking gun and let Evie the fuck go?"

"It will work, Landy!" Evie kept fighting a losing battle. "You can live out here in the middle of nowhere until after my birthday. I'll wire the money to whatever account you want, and—"

"Shut up!" He pushed the barrel even harder against her temple. "Everyone just shut the fuck up!"

"P-Please, Landy. I'm b-begging you."

"He doesn't care, do you, Granger?" Beckett taunted the man with the gun to her head. "Then again, I know the real reason we're all here."

Real reason?

"Wha…what do you mean?" Evie asked.

"You wanna tell her, or should I?" Beckett asked. The question must've been rhetorical, because with his next breath, the man she loved said, "Never mind. I'll give it a go. But feel free to stop me if I mess up."

He brought his gorgeous brown eyes her way, and for just a moment, Evie almost forgot she was facing imminent death.

"I don't know what you're—"

"It's pretty easy to follow, really," her hero continued. "Basically, you pulled an impressive Madoff impression, right? Although, from what we were told, your Ponzi scheme would've put his to shame. You know, if you'd actually gotten away with it."

Evie frowned. "Ponzi scheme?"

"That's right, darlin'. Turns out, Granger's spent the last several years bilking his clients out of hundreds of millions of dollars."

"You don't understand—"

"You're right!" Beckett shouted. "I don't understand how someone as smart as you could be stupid enough to think you'd get away with stealing other people's life savings. Not to mention the additional crimes of colluding with known terrorists for the purpose of kidnapping young children and an American woman. A woman you practically helped raise, for Christ's sake! But none of that matters to you, does it? *She* doesn't matter to you. That's evident by the fact that you made a deal with the fucking devil himself and tried selling her to a goddamn *sex trafficker!*"

Evie had never seen anyone as angry as Beckett was in that moment.

His face was beet red, and there was a bulging vein running vertically down his entire forehead. He was on the edge of no return, and though she wanted this to be over more than her next breath, she also didn't want to be the cause of another death on Beckett's shoulders.

"Please, Landy," she whispered softly, trying to reach the man she'd once thought of as blood. "Please, listen to what he's telling you. You can still get out of this. There has to be a way. There has to be *something* we can—"

"Shut up!" Landy turned into someone she didn't recognize. "Jesus Christ, Evie. Don't you see? No matter how hard you try to put your Pollyanna spin on it, the only way you're getting out of this alive is if your boyfriend and his buddies drop their fucking guns!"

Tears flooded her vision, but Evie blinked them away as best she could. The time to act had come. She could feel it deep inside her bones. If she didn't do something now, it was going to be too late.

If she did make it out of this alive, she'd look back at this moment and mourn the man she'd once looked up to. A man she'd loved as much as if he'd actually been related.

There was a time she would have trusted Landy Granger with her life. But now, he was trying to take that same life. Threatening to put a bullet in her head if Beckett and his teammates didn't let him go free.

Well, she knew one surefire way to guarantee that didn't happen. And despite the risk to her own safety, Evie knew exactly what she needed to do.

Landy's movements became more and more erratic. He yelled at Beckett and his friends to put down their guns. The men of Tac-Ops shouted back for him to do the same.

The confrontation was the perfect distraction.

With her left hand still holding onto the meaty arm wrapped tightly around her neck, she slowly lowered her right hand down until it hung loosely in front of her thigh. As the men continued yelling back and forth at one another, she used just her fingers to inch the sequined material further up her leg.

Evie kept a close eye on the men standing in front of her, which is how she'd noticed the way Digger's gaze caught the slight movement of her hand. Apollo, too, though neither man reacted.

Instead, they brought their focus back up to Landy. Acting as if nothing about the situation had changed, even though Beckett saw the knife secured at her trembling thigh.

His gaze immediately became fixed with hers. Evie thought for sure he'd give her some sort of negative signal. A way to let her know he was *not* on board with what she had planned.

However, in true Beckett form, the incredible man took her

by complete surprise when he gave an almost indiscernible dip of his chin.

He knows what I'm going to do. He knows...and he's ready.

The sound of her racing heartbeat filled her ears. With her time dwindling faster by the minute, she pushed past her fear, envisioned what she was about to do, and put the plan in motion.

Three more men entered the room, and Evie recognized Falcon immediately. She had no idea who the other two were, but she didn't care. They were clearly working with Tac-Ops, which meant the two strangers were on her side.

"Who the fuck are you?" Landy shouted as he took two jerky steps back, away from Beckett and the others. "You know what? It doesn't matter. You can all go straight to hell, as far as I'm concerned."

"Tell it to the jury, brother." One of the men she didn't recognize held the big gun in his hand steady.

"Jury?" Landy snorted. "You think I can get a fair shake after everything I've done? No." The gun at her head began to shake. "I've worked too fucking hard to just give up and quit now."

As the crazed man continued ranting about what he was owed and how he planned to get what he was due, Evie repositioned the knife in her fist, so she had a better, tighter grip on its handle.

With the blade pointed backward, toward the man using her to keep himself alive, she waited for the perfect moment to strike. Landy's voice grew more turbulent, and the gun pressed against her head pulled away just a touch, and Evie knew it was now...or never.

I choose now.

Moving lightning fast, she swung her fist backward, bringing the blade toward the meatiest part of Landy's right thigh.

"Ah!" The man cried out as the tip of the knife pierced his skin and beyond.

On reflex, Landy dropped the gun. His hand going straight to the knife still sticking out of his leg. In a quick, swooping motion, Evie swung her left foot out toward the fallen weapon.

She kicked the gun away. The sound of metal scraping against wood tore through the chaotic scene as the pistol skidded across the floor to where Beckett and his teammates stood.

Landy started to pull the knife free. "Fucking...bitch!"

"Evie, run!" Beckett shouted for her to get herself to safety.

But she was already reaching for the knife. If given the chance, there was no doubt in her mind, Landy would use it to kill her long before she ever got away.

They each had a desperate hand on the knife's leather handle. Evie struggled against his tight grip as the two fought for control of the weapon.

A sickening, wet sound reached her ears as the blade slid free from Landy's bleeding, wounded flesh. He howled again, but his hold on the knife never wavered.

As their fight to the death continued, Evie found herself in a twisted dance of deadly survival. Her arms were stretched out as far as they would reach, both hands coated with Landy's blood. And for the next several, terrifying minutes, the pair swung themselves back and forth with their battling efforts to gain control.

She could hear Beckett screaming her name from some-where close behind her. But she was too busy focused on the slick blood that had dripped from blade to hilt.

Her immovable grip she'd vowed never to lose began to slip as her palm became coated in Landy's blood.

"Beckett!" Evie shouted his name as if there was something he could do.

The knife slid against her palm, partially giving way to the man's forceful pull.

No, no, no, no, no!

"Evie!" Beckett shouted for her again. His desperation clear from the heightened tone of his panicked voice.

Everything that happened next did so as if time and space began moving in super slow motion.

The knife slipped from her hand. Landy pulled his elbow

back, positioning the weapon so the bloody blade pointed straight at her gut.

"Landy, please!" Evie's shouted plea came as she started to lift a hand to block the attack.

But his deadly decision had already been made.

She looked up into the eyes of a man she'd once loved and respected as he started to swing the knife toward her. The deafening sound of gunfire drowned out everything else around her, and Evie thought she may have screamed when Landy's body jerked beneath the force of the bullets.

What felt like minutes later but was actually less than a handful of seconds, she found herself standing over the man's dead body.

"Evelynn!"

Evie blinked, and Beckett was there, pulling her into his arms the same way she'd prayed he would.

She wanted to hold him close. To wrap her arms around him and never let go. But her hands were trapped between their bodies, pressing against the fire that had been ignited from somewhere deep inside.

"God, baby!" Beckett pulled away long enough to give her a kiss. "Are you okay? I was so fucking scared."

"B-Beckett?" Evie glanced down, confused by the growing inferno in her belly.

"Evie? What is it? What's…" His sharp intake of air sounded as he saw what she was seeing.

Thick, bright red blood had begun seeping out from between her fingers. She pushed harder against the wound, hoping to stop the hemorrhaging. But the move caused even more blood to escape, and soon her entire hand was covered.

"Ah, Christ." Beckett sounded sick to his soul as he cried out to the others, "She's hurt!"

"I can't…" Evie's legs gave out from beneath her, but he was there to break her fall.

Just like he was always there, having put his life on the line for hers…again. Only problem was, this time, he may have been too late.

"Open your eyes, Evie!" he yelled from somewhere far way. "Come on, darlin'. Let me see that gorgeous stare of yours."

They're closed? When did I close my eyes?

Evie's lids fluttered open to find Beckett's wild gaze hovering directly overhead.

"There you are." He smiled, placing his hands over hers to apply more pressure to the still-bleeding wound. "That's it, Evie. Just keep lookin' right at me."

There's nothing else I'd rather see.

Tears fell from the corners of her eyes. "I-I'm...sorry."

"No, darlin'," he soothed. "Nothin' about any of this is your fault."

"Need to...t-tell you...something."

"I'm right here." The corners of his lips curved even as his eyes shimmered with what appeared to be a sudden well of unshed tears. "And I'm not going anywhere."

"Good." Evie forced a weak smile of her own. "'Cause I l-love you."

The moisture she'd suspected were tears fell over his rugged cheeks. "Ah, Evie." He leaned down and pressed his lips to hers. "I love you, too. So fucking much."

"Y-You do?"

"More than I've ever loved anything or anyone." His watery smile filled her overworked heart. "And I gotta say, it's a damn good thing you love me back, because I have all sorts of plans."

"P-plans?"

"Oh, yeah. But you just relax for now, because we have the rest of our lives to talk about all that."

The rest of their...

The world around her began to fade, but Evie was determined to keep the darkness pulling her under at bay.

"I want to...hear the...p-plan."

His worried stare closed in on hers, but he kept his voice calm and light as he spoke of her dream come true.

"Basically, you're stuck with me," he told her flat-out as his hands worked to keep her stable. "And I want it all, too. We're going to get married, have lots and lots of wild, crazy monkey sex…and babies."

"B-babies?" Her heart swelled at the idea of the two of them creating a family.

"Oh, yeah." Beckett nodded. "As many as you'll agree to have. I'm serious, Evie." He brought his loving gaze back up to hers. "I want it all. With you. From now until forever."

Until forever…

Evie felt her eyes falling shut, and this time, there wasn't a damn thing she could do to stop it. But as she gave herself over to the darkness, she sent up another silent prayer, begging God to let her live. To give her a chance at the future that had just been described.

Because spending forever with Beckett Stone…

I can't imagine anything better than that.

EPILOGUE

Two weeks later...

"I sure hope that smile has something to do with me."

Evie's smile grew even more as she looked up from the note she'd been reading to see her fiancé standing by the door.

Fiancé

Two weeks, and the title still felt exciting and new. And yet, in some ways—in the very *best* of ways—it was as if he'd been there her entire life.

Protecting her.

Supporting her.

Loving me.

Life with the former Marine-turned-super soldier was like an amazing dream come true. Though he tended to be a bit overprotective, her fiancé was also incredibly attentive and sweet.

The days following her rescue had passed by in a whirlwind of doctors and official reports. Statements were made; evidence was shared, and in the end, Landy had paid the ultimate punishment for his crimes.

With so many high-level clients, it wasn't long before news

broke of the shocking story. Every secret Landy had hoped to carry with him to the grave was being exposed.

The lying. Stealing. His massive Ponzi scheme cost families millions. Even the truth about Phillip Mitchell not being Evie's father—as well as his refusal to pay the Taliban's ransom demands—was out there for the world to see.

By the time it was all said and done, both Phillip's and Landy's reputations had been destroyed. Both known only as a pair of greedy, selfless, untrustworthy, miserable men. And, despite Landy having once been like family to Evie, she couldn't help but feel a sense of vindication, knowing he was already burning in hell.

She also refused to spend her days obsessing over what had happened. Refused to waste a second of her precious time lost in memories of the past.

Instead, Evie chose to focus on the future. One where she got to live out her dream with the man she loved.

Though he'd officially been given the last two weeks off from work, there had been a couple of days like today, when Beckett had run into the office for a quick meeting or to fill out a report for this or that. At Evie's request, they had yet to share the news of their engagement with the team or anyone else.

Not even Lo.

Despite being over-the-moon ecstatic about marrying Beckett, she wanted to relish in their shared joy in private. Just the two of them.

Just for a little while.

As she'd explained to Beckett that day in her hospital room, so much of her life had been spent under a microscope. Every decision she'd made had been scrutinized by others. Every movement overshadowed by Phillip Mitchell's smug, resentful eyes.

So as excited as she was knowing they'd soon be tied to one another in every way humanly possible, Evie had wanted to enjoy the moment as a couple in private before sharing the news with their friends.

"You know you always make me smile." She went to Beckett, holding out the handwritten note for him to see.

He took the offered paper from her hand. But rather than read it, he pulled her body flush with his before giving her a proper—and *very* thorough—kiss.

"Hi."

Evie's heart swelled to the point of near bursting as she stared up into his heated gaze. "Hello, yourself."

He stepped back to allow for enough room to read the note still held in his hand. "What do we have here?"

"It's from the girls." She pointed to the written words on the page. "Each of them wrote a little note to us both, but they used the same piece of paper. Armineh and Sadia took up most of the front, and Malalai's and Benesh's messages are on the back."

She waited, giving him a quiet moment to read over the sweet words.

Armineh had shared that she and her family had moved to a safer area. Benesh's family had moved in with her grandparents, and Sadia and Malalai were still at their original homes.

All four girls reported the area they all lived in was becoming safer and less volatile than it had been in recent months. The girls were back in the same school as before and reportedly doing very well in each of their subjects.

Warmth spread throughout Evie's chest as she waited, knowing the girls were able to thrive once again. She just prayed those in charge of that part of Afghanistan heeded the recent warning that had been handed down by the U.S.

If there is another American captured on Afghan soil, it will be considered an act of war, and you and your people will feel the weight of my entire military.

It was a direct quote from the leader of the most powerful country in the world. One Evie, herself, had heard fall from the president's lips as she and the members of Tac-Ops—along with the SEAL team from Hawaii—stood in the Oval Office exactly one week after the incident on the yacht.

"Sounds like the girls are doing well." Beckett handed her back the treasured note with a grin.

"Yeah." Evie nodded as she carefully refolded the paper and set it on the decorative table to her right. "I just hope they can finally live their lives in peace."

"Come here." Her fiancé wrapped his arms around her waist and pulled her close once more.

Looking up, Evie teased him with a slow, sly grin. "What's the matter? You didn't get enough of me this morning?"

Tantalizing flares of their early morning lovemaking still tingled through her lower belly. He'd been so sweet, so careful, moving torturously slow. Evie knew he still worried about hurting her healing wound but planned to prove to him later she could handle a whole lot more.

"Not even close." He leaned in for another deep, consuming kiss. When he was finished, he moved back just enough to allow his darkened gaze to become fixed with hers. "And just so you know..." Beckett rumbled low. "When it comes to you, it will never be enough."

"That's good, because I'm pretty sure the ring I'm still waiting to get back from the jeweler includes a lifetime membership to your bed."

"You mean this ring?" He held up the shiny diamond wedding set he'd surprised her with the day she'd left the hospital. "The jeweler called on my way home from the office and said it was ready."

Evie squealed as she held out her left hand—palm-down, fingers splayed. The gorgeous set had been a tad too big when he'd surprised her with the impromptu hospital proposal, so Beckett had taken it back in to get it resized.

He slid it onto its designated finger on her left hand, his thumb caressing her gently as he kept his gentle hold.

"It's perfect." She admired the diamond's sparkling shimmer.

Beckett pulled her back into his arms with a rumbled, "Just like you."

No, baby. You're the one who's perfect.

"I love you so much." Evie lifted onto her tiptoes and pressed her lips to his.

"Yeah?" He smirked, though the man knew full well that she did.

"Need me to prove it?" The tip of her nose brushed his in a purposefully teasing move. "Because I was thinking maybe we tell the guys about my new bling when we see them all this weekend."

Beckett's fingertips dug into her hips as a flash of excitement darkened his heated gaze. "You mean it?"

Evie nodded, her belly fluttering like mad from the sight of his giddy grin. "It's time." She looked at her ring from over his shoulder. "The perfect time, really. Everyone will be at Falcon and Avery's cookout on Saturday, including Mustang and Aleck and their team. And since I have my ring back, I can show them all just how much I love you."

"You know you don't have to prove anything, right?" His tone —and expression—grew serious. "Not to them or me."

"I know." She placed a palm over his beating heart.

Strong.

Steady.

Resilient.

Just like him.

"Told you before, I'm not going anywhere." He pressed a sweet kiss to the center of her forehead. "So take as long as you need."

Love unlike any she'd ever known filled her heart to the point she thought it may burst. Snuggling in close, Evie ignored the slight pull at the place where the knife had entered her body as she rested her cheek against his chest.

"They're your family, Beckett," she whispered softly. "I want them to share in the joy of the love we've found."

"Wrong, darlin'." He put a hand beneath her chin, gently forcing her eyes back up to his. "They aren't just my family. They're yours, now, too. And trust me when I say, they're going to be fucking thrilled for us both when we tell them the news."

Beckett leaned in, his mouth devouring hers until her knees were weak and her thoughts filled with nothing but him. And

ANNA BLAKELY

when he picked her up and took her to bed, she showed him just how thrilled *she* was knowing he was going to be hers.

Today.

Tomorrow.

Forever.

What started as a fight to the death in the middle of a dark, desert cave had miraculously ended in a glorious mess of tangled sheets and unbreakable love. Only Evie and Beckett's story hadn't reached its end at all.

In fact…

It's only just beginning.

* * *

SLADE GARRISON STEPPED into his boss's home office. Located in the plantation's newly renovated wing, the impressive room exuded classic masculine power.

Deep woods met earthy tones. Windows that stretched from floor to ceiling. Bookcases covering the walls to Slade's left and right. Their shelves showcasing hundreds of hardcover titles his boss couldn't possibly find the time to read.

Speaking of his boss…

"Thank you for coming." Rafe Owens stood at one of the massive windows, his back to Slade as he stared through the glass.

His deep voice sounded rougher than normal. His British accent thick. Dressed in jeans and a button-down shirt, the man's strange tone and stiff demeanor instantly put Slade on edge.

"Got here as soon as I could." He stepped further into the room. "Now, you gonna tell me why you sent a cryptic as fuck message to get me here?"

Owens slowly turned around to face him, the uncharacteristic concern in his intense blue stare raising all sorts of giant red flags.

Slade's heart kicked against his ribs as he worked to keep his breathing steady, and his unmoving expression schooled. "This is about her, isn't it?"

Owens nodded, the man's thick hair noticeably mussed on top. He looked disheveled, as if he'd been raking his fingers through the silver strands, and dark shadows marred the skin beneath his weary eyes.

More alarm bells began to ring deep inside Slade's head.

Please don't say she's been hurt. Not her. Please, just...don't fucking say it.

"She's in trouble, Digger." The former MI6 operative took a sip of whatever liquor he currently had in his glass. "Real trouble."

"What did she do?" Slade demanded, his pulse spiking from the man's ominous words.

"I'm afraid it's more about who she's planning to do it to."

"Goddamn it, Rafe!" He marched angrily around his boss's desk. "Quit with the ambiguous bullshit and tell me what the hell is going on with Shadow."

Yes, the guy was technically his boss. And yes, Slade owed him more than he'd ever be able to repay. But they'd also known each other a long damn time, and he'd never seen the other man as nervous as he seemed just then.

And if Rafe Owens was nervous...whatever this was, it sure as shit wasn't good.

He also couldn't stop thinking about the mysterious woman who'd saved his and the team's asses more times than he could count. It had been two weeks since Shadow had vanished from the face of the earth.

It had been radio silence ever since.

No calls. No texts. No messages to him or anyone on the team letting them know she was still alive and that she was okay.

Shadow had simply up and vanished without a single fucking word. And though he'd never admit it to this man—or anyone else—Slade had been so damn worried he hadn't had a full night's sleep since.

"I don't have all the details." Owens handed him a file from the top of his desk. "But I'm fairly certain she's going after this man."

Slade opened the folder and scanned the glossy photo, along with the first of what appeared to be several pages of personal intel. He didn't recognize the man's face or name, nor any of the multiple aliases listed at the top of the page.

"Am I supposed to know who this is?"

"No, but I know him very well. And unfortunately...so does Shadow."

"Why is she going after him?" Slade needed the man to get to the damn point. "What the hell did he do?"

"He killed Shadow's mother." Real pain flashed behind Owens' worried stare. "He murdered her in cold blood, and if we don't find Shadow before it's too late..."

Owens let his worried voice trail, but Slade's lungs froze at the thought of what had been left unsaid.

Shadow dead? That wasn't an option.

No fucking way I'm going to let that happen.

As far as he and the others were concerned, Shadow was one of them. There was no way any of them would leave her hanging out to dry. Especially when she'd come through for them time and time again.

"What do you need?" Slade asked, willing to do whatever the man said if it meant ensuring the mysterious woman's safety.

"I need you to find the man in that folder before Shadow does. But you'll have to be careful, and...you'll have to be discreet."

"Discreet?"

Shadow's missing and in potentially mortal danger, and this man's worried about being discreet?

"It's not what you're thinking, Digger." Owens seemed to read Slade's mind. "I only mean this is a very delicate operation. As such, you'll be going in alone."

"You want me to work this thing solo?" He frowned. "Boss, this is Shadow, we're talking about. Why the hell wouldn't you want every man on the team on this?"

"Because if she's doing what I think she's doing, there's only one way this works…and that's you going in after her, alone."

Slade spun on his heels and stormed back around to the other side of the desk. Reaching behind his head, he dug his fingertips into the tensing muscles at the back of his neck.

They didn't do solo jobs. That wasn't how Tac-Ops operated. But now Owens was not only asking him to go after Shadow, secure her safety, and bring her back home…he was asking Slade to do all that without the help and support of his team.

It's Shadow, dumbass. You know you're going to say yes. Besides… what's the worst that could happen?

"Why me?" Slade turned back to his boss

"Because if anyone on the team can get through to her, it's you."

A deep, humorless chuckle rumbled through his chest. "And what makes you think I'll be able to convince her of anythi—"

"You were ten when your mother was killed by that coked out kid, correct?"

Digger's spine stiffened and his heart kicked hard at the familiar pain that never seemed to completely go away. "Fuck you, Rafe."

"No, fuck the asshole who stole your childhood!" The other man slammed his glass down onto the desk so hard Slade was surprised the damn thing didn't shatter. "And fuck the man who did the same thing to Shadow when she was only six." He shoved a pointed finger toward the folder. "Only *that* son of a bitch didn't just steal Shadow's childhood. He murdered her beautiful, innocent mother when that little girl was standing less than five feet away."

Jesus.

"So that's all this is about?" He stared back at his boss. "She's gone after this man for revenge?"

"Yes."

"I'll do it." Slade stared back at his boss, ready to do what was needed to keep Shadow from diving headfirst into danger. "I'll find her, and I'll bring her ass home. But there's something I want in return."

"And what is that?"

"Tell me who she is to you."

One thing that was crystal clear to Slade from his very first days with Tac-Ops—Owens and Shadow had a special bond that stemmed far deeper than employee to boss.

The forty-eight-year-old former British spy blinked away his widened gaze, clearly taken aback by the unexpected demand.

"Shadow is part of the team." Owens cleared his throat before adding a deep, "I thought that was obvious."

"It is. Just like it's obvious there's something more between you two. Something personal."

"My relationship with Shadow is none of your concern."

"Like hell, it's not." Slade didn't back down. "Look, you can tell me yourself now or wait for me to find out. But if I'm in this thing, then I'm going to be in it all the fucking way. Which means, I will use every resource I have to dig up everything I can about those involved…starting with the woman we're both clearly desperate to find."

And Slade *was* desperate. More than he had any right to be.

He may not know the woman's real name…or anything personal about her at all. But he knew enough. Shadow was one of them, and he needed to find her and stop her before she did something stupid.

Like get herself killed.

I won't let that happen.

Owens picked up his glass, shooting back the remainder of his drink. This time, when he set it back down onto his desk, he did so with the control and reserve Slade had come to expect from the guy who signed his paychecks.

"The man in that file…" Owens' steely blue gaze shimmered with a layer of moisture. "He's the same man who killed my wife."

Holy shit.

Slade frowned, glancing back down at the folder. "Your wife? You saying this man killed both her and Shadow's mother?"

"No, Slade." His boss stared back at him from across his desk.

"What I'm saying is Shadow's mother and my wife...were one and the same."

* * *

Want to find out if Slade "Digger" Garrison can find the elusive Shadow in time to save her? Be on the lookout for **SLADE'S VOW (Tac-Ops #4)**
Coming 2025!

ALSO BY ANNA BLAKELY

Check it out! Anna Blakely has three new series:

TAC-OPS Series

Garrett's Destiny

Ethan's Obsession

Beckett's Desire

Creed's Future (TBA)

Marked Series

Marked For Death

Marked for Revenge

Marked for Deception

Marked for Obsession

Marked for Danger

Marked for Disaster

Marked for Vengeance

Charlie Team

(R.I.S.C. Spinoff Series)

Kellan

Asher

Greyson

Rhys

Other Books by Anna

Eagle's Nest Securities Series

Keeping His Promise

Playing With Fire

Flirting With Danger

R.I.S.C. Series (Alpha Team)
Taking a Risk, Part One
Taking a Risk, Part Two
Beautiful Risk
Intentional Risk
Unpredictable Risk
Ultimate Risk
Targeted Risk
Savage Risk
Undeniable Risk
His Greatest Risk

Bravo Team Series
Rescuing Gracelynn (Nate & Gracie)
Rescuing Katherine (Matt & Katherine)
Rescuing Gabriella (Zade & Gabby)
Rescuing Ellena (Gabe & Elle)
Rescuing Jenna (Adrian & Jenna)

R.I.S.C. Charlie Team Series
Kellan
Greyson
Asher
Rhys
Parker

R.I.S.C. Delta Team Series
Christian
Brody
John

ABOUT THE AUTHOR

Author Anna Blakely brings you stories of love, action, and edge-of-your-seat suspense. As an avid reader of romantic suspense herself, Anna's dream is to create stories her readers will enjoy and characters they'll fall in love with as much as she has. She believes in true love and happily-ever-after, and that's what she will always bring to you.

Anna lives in rural Missouri with her husband, children, and several rescued animals. When she's not writing, Anna enjoys reading, watching action and horror movies (the scarier the better), and spending time with her amazing husband, four wonderful children, and her adorable granddaughter.

FB Author Page: facebook.com/annablakely.author.7
Blakely's Bunch (reader group): https://www.facebook.com/groups/354218335396441/
Instagram: https://instagram.com/annablakely
BookBub: https//www.bookbub.com/authors/anna-blakely
Amazon: amazon.com/author/annablakely
Twitter: @ablakelyauthor
Goodreads: https://www.goodreads.com/author/show/18650841.Anna_Blakely

[f] facebook.com/annablakely.author.7

[X] x.com/ablakelyauthor

[instagram] instagram.com/annablakely

[a] amazon.com/author/annablakely

WANT TO CONNECT WITH ANNA?

Become one of *Anna's Angels* by joining her Facebook reader group: www.facebook.com/groups/blakelysbunch/

Newsletter signup (with FREE Bravo Team prequel novella!) BookHip.com/ZLMKFT

Instagram: https://instagram.com/annablakely

BookBub: https://www.bookbub.com/authors/anna-blakely

Follow Anna on her FB Author Page: https://www.facebook.com/annablakelyromance

Goodreads: https://www.goodreads.com/author/show/18650841.Anna_Blakely

There are many more books in this fan fiction world than listed here, for an up-to-date list go to www.AcesPress.com

You can also visit our Amazon page at:
http://www.amazon.com/author/operationalpha

Special Forces: Operation Alpha World

Christie Adams: Charity's Heart
Elizabella Baker: Challenging Luke
Linzi Baxter: Dangerous Rescue
Misha Blake: Flash
Anna Blakely: Rescuing Gracelynn
Julia Bright: Saving Lorelei
Cara Carnes: Protecting Mari
Kendra Mei Chailyn: Beast
Melissa Kay Clarke: Rescuing Annabeth
Gia Cobie: Saved from Revenge
Samantha Cole: Handling Haven
Cassie Colton: Rescuing Ryder
KaLyn Cooper: Spring Unveiled
Jordan Dane: Redemption for Avery
D.M. Earl: Claire's Guardian
Riley Edwards: Protecting Olivia
Dorothy Ewels: Knight's Queen
Lila Ferrari: Protecting Joy
Nicole Flockton: Protecting Maria
Amy Gamet: Guarded by the SEAL
Lea Griffith: Finding Ava
Desiree Holt: Protecting Maddie
Danielle M. Haas: Crossroads of Betrayal
Bree Hera: Trusting the Team
Jesse Jacobson: Protecting Honor
Rayne Lewis: Justice for Mary
Ireland Lorelei: The Detective
Kristin Lynn: Worth the Risk
JM Madden: Rescuing Olivia

A.M. Mahler: Griffin
Ellie Masters: Sybil's Protector
Trish McCallan: Hero Under Fire
Naomi McKay: Twist
KD Michaels: Saving Laura
Olivia Michaels: Protecting Harper
Annie Miller: Securing Willow
MJ Nightingale: Protecting Beauty
C.K. O'Connor: Delaney's Bodyguard
Melinda Owens: Betraying Katie
Victoria Paige: Reclaiming Izabel
Danielle Pays: Defending Sarina
Lainey Reese: Protecting New York
KeKe Renée: Protecting Bria
Taryn Rivers: Savage Cove
TL Reeve and Michele Ryan: Extracting Mateo
Ariana Rose: Chasing Paige
Angela Rush: Charlotte
E.M. Shue: Discovering Tyler
Rose Smith: Saving Satin
Tyler Anne Snell: Cowboy Heat
Dee Stewart: Fighting for Brielle
Lynne St. James: SEAL's Spitfire
Bella Stone: Rexar
Jen Talty: Protecting Ainsley
Reina Torres, Rescuing Hi'ilani
LJ Vickery: Circus Comes to Town
R. C. Wynne: Shadows Renewed

Delta Team Three Series
Lori Ryan: Nori's Delta
Becca Jameson: Destiny's Delta
Lynne St James, Gwen's Delta
Elle James: Ivy's Delta
Riley Edwards: Hope's Delta

Police and Fire: Operation Alpha World

Freya Barker: Burning for Autumn
B.P. Beth: Scott
Jane Blythe: Salvaging Marigold
Julia Bright: Justice for Amber
Gia Cobie: Saved from Revenge
Hadley Finn: Exton
Danielle M. Haas: Crossroads of Betrayal
Deanndra Hall: Shelter for Sharla
Jenna Harte: Dead But Not Forgotten
India Kells: Game Master
Amber Kuhlman: Protecting Paisley
Reina Torres: Justice for Sloane
Aubree Valentine, Justice for Danielle

Tarpley VFD Series
Silver James, Fighting for Elena
Deanndra Hall, Fighting for Carly
Haven Rose, Fighting for Calliope
MJ Nightingale, Fighting for Jemma
TL Reeve, Fighting for Brittney
Nicole Flockton, Fighting for Nadia

As you know, this book included at least one character from Susan Stoker's books. To check out more, see below.

SEAL of Protection: Alliance Series

Protecting Remi
Protecting Wren
Protecting Josie (Mar 4, 2025)
Protecting Maggie (Apr 1, 2025)
Protecting Addison (May 6, 2025)
Protecting Kelli (TBA)
Protecting Bree (TBA)

The Refuge Series

Deserving Alaska
Deserving Henley
Deserving Reese
Deserving Cora
Deserving Lara
Deserving Maisy
Deserving Ryleigh (Jan 7, 2025)

SEAL Team Hawaii Series

Finding Elodie
Finding Lexie
Finding Kenna
Finding Monica
Finding Carly
Finding Ashlyn
Finding Jodelle

Eagle Point Search & Rescue

Searching for Lilly
Searching for Elsie
Searching for Bristol
Searching for Caryn

Searching for Finley
Searching for Heather
Searching for Khloe

Delta Team Two Series

Shielding Gillian
Shielding Kinley
Shielding Aspen
Shielding Jayme (novella)
Shielding Riley
Shielding Devyn
Shielding Ember
Shielding Sierra

SEAL of Protection: Legacy Series

Securing Caite (FREE!)
Securing Brenae (novella)
Securing Sidney
Securing Piper
Securing Zoey
Securing Avery
Securing Kalee
Securing Jane

Delta Force Heroes Series

Rescuing Rayne (FREE!)
Rescuing Aimee (novella)
Rescuing Emily
Rescuing Harley
Marrying Emily (novella)
Rescuing Kassie
Rescuing Bryn
Rescuing Casey
Rescuing Sadie (novella)
Rescuing Wendy
Rescuing Mary
Rescuing Macie (novella)

Rescuing Annie

Badge of Honor: Texas Heroes Series
Justice for Mackenzie (FREE!)
Justice for Mickie
Justice for Corrie
Justice for Laine (novella)
Shelter for Elizabeth
Justice for Boone
Shelter for Adeline
Shelter for Sophie
Justice for Erin
Justice for Milena
Shelter for Blythe
Justice for Hope
Shelter for Quinn
Shelter for Koren
Shelter for Penelope

SEAL of Protection Series
Protecting Caroline (FREE!)
Protecting Alabama
Protecting Fiona
Marrying Caroline (novella)
Protecting Summer
Protecting Cheyenne
Protecting Jessyka
Protecting Julie (novella)
Protecting Melody
Protecting the Future
Protecting Kiera (novella)
Protecting Alabama's Kids (novella)
Protecting Dakota

New York Times, USA Today and *Wall Street Journal* Bestselling
Author Susan Stoker has a heart as big as the state of Tennessee
where she lives, but this all American girl has also spent the last

fourteen years living in Missouri, California, Colorado, Indiana, and Texas. She's married to a retired Army man who now gets to follow *her* around the country.

www.stokeraces.com
www.AcesPress.com
susan@stokeraces.com

Made in the USA
Columbia, SC
06 June 2025

59019652R00187